RACHEL L. SCHADE

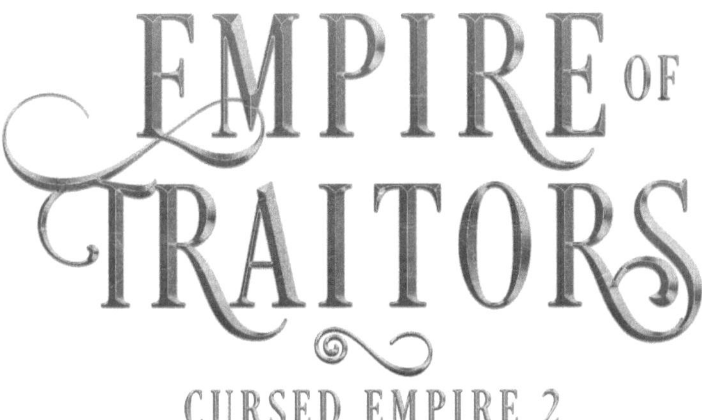

CURSED EMPIRE 2

RACHEL L. SCHADE

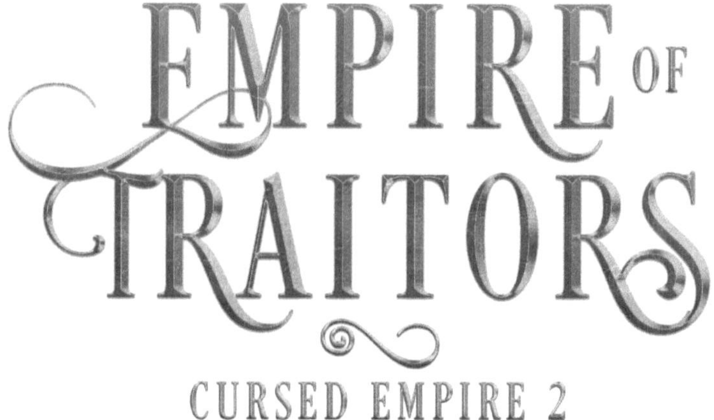

EMPIRE OF TRAITORS

CURSED EMPIRE 2

DRAGON SHADOW
PUBLISHING

OTHER BOOKS BY RACHEL L. SCHADE

Silent Kingdom Series

Silent Kingdom (Book 1)

Forsaken Kingdom (Book 2)

Broken Kingdom (Book 3)

Cursed Empire Series

Empire of Dragons (Book 1)

For those who keep dreaming despite the odds.

PRONUNCIATION GUIDE

People

Lo'laeni (LO-lane-ee)
Nolanhou (No-LAWN-hu)
Jaliana (JAY-lee-ahn-uh)
Kovi (KOH-vee)
Ettonou (ETT-uh-new)
Caesiem (KAY-see-um)
Xalenos (Zuh-LEE-nos)
Revaed (Ruh-VAYD)
Pauni'a (PAWN-ee-uh)
O'emia (OH-em-ee-uh)
Wilvhe (WILL-vay)
Mio'e (MEE-oh-ay)
Naina (NAYN-uh)
Karye (KAR-yay)
Yaelti (YAYL-tee)
Leanai (Lee-AN-i)
Marukio (Muh-ROO-kee-oh)

Locations

Alrenor (Al-REN-or),
Alrenian (Al-REN-ee-uhn)
Forwyth (For-WITH),
Forwyn (For-WIN)
Teramyl (TARE-uh-mill),
Teramese (TARE-uh-meez)
Inalgoth (I-NEEL-goth)

Other

Ryke (RY-kee)
Karos (Kair-OHS)
Elhani (Ell-HAN-ee)
Nesrelle (NEZ-rell)
Vylae (Vill-AY)
Kowra (KOW-ruh)
Hilvoku (Hill-VOH-ku)

The Great Kingdoms
N
W
E
S
TIRALOHN
Jaedrah River
Meravin Wood
ME
MISROTH
VORVINIA
Evren Forest
Emr
Lai
MISROTH CITY
Vorvinian Mountains
Kelwed
EMLEK
VER
Irevek Swamp
TORYN
MAUROK
Alrenian
Sea
Elhalin River
CALIDAR
HAEMIL
Haemil Mountains
Wastelands
INA
Terebrys Oc

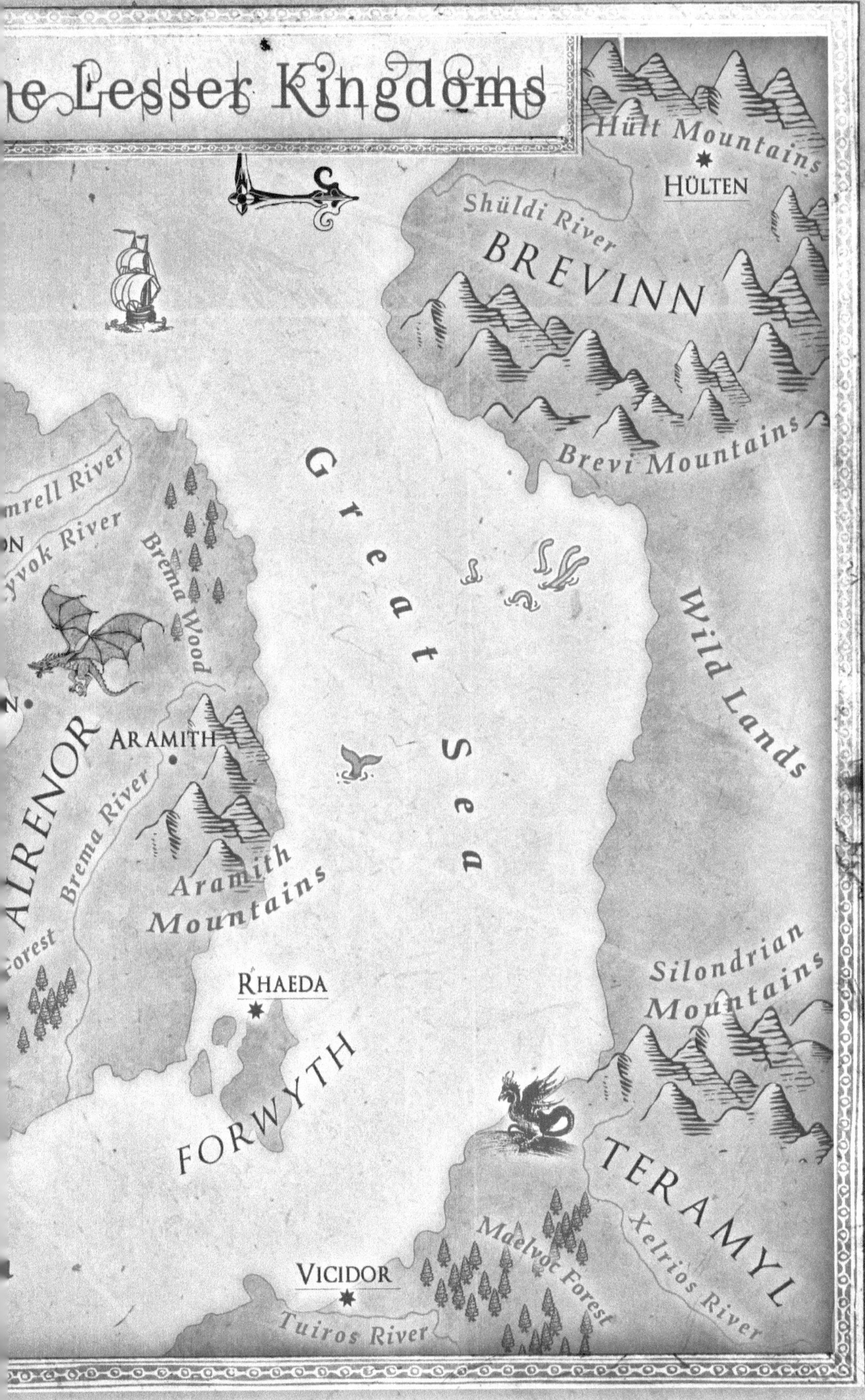

The Lesser Kingdoms
Hült Mountains
HÜLTEN
Shüldi River
BREVINN
Brevi Mountains
Wild Lands
Amrell River
Ryvok River
Brema Wood
Great Sea
ALRENOR
ARAMITH
Brema River
Forest
Aramith Mountains
Silondrian Mountains
RHAEDA
FORWYTH
TERAMYL
Maelvor Forest
Xelrios River
VICIDOR
Tuiros River

CHAPTER ONE

Lo'laeni Nolanhou

THE SUN ROSE LARGE AND bloody that morning, like a garish reminder of all I'd done and all I'd lost. In my cramped room at the Imperial Dragon, I lay curled on the hard mattress and scratchy blanket the innkeeper called a bed and watched the red light cast enormous shadows along the walls. My head pounded and my eyes ached from lack of sleep, but otherwise, I was numb. Hollow. Shocked.

It was difficult to grapple with what had happened the previous night, even as the images played on an endless loop through my head. Less than twenty-four hours ago, I'd been sorrowful yet resigned, prepared to give up my peaceful life as part of the Circle of Serenity so I could protect my people from brutal murders and prevent—or at least weaken—a war. I'd been certain that helping Caesiem, Renni, and the other vigilantes in their mission to assassinate Empress Jaliana at the Autumn Ball was the only option to help my people.

But I'd been wrong. I'd lost everything in the worst way possible. Caesiem had betrayed me—had betrayed all of us—by helping Teramese warriors infiltrate the ball and attack the Forwyn Court of Elders. I'd finally heard Elhani's voice, and rather than assassinate Empress Jaliana, I'd saved her life. Instead, I'd killed Wilvhe.

Wilvhe.

My heart stuttered at the thought of his name, of his gloved hands—coated in vylae, a lethal poison that had no known antidote—extending toward me. Of the knife I'd hurled at his throat. Of the blood that had splattered across my face.

Bile crawled along my tongue, and I curled in on myself, as if I could force myself to become smaller and smaller until I disappeared.

Elhani, forgive me, I thought, even as my aching heart was certain he'd never listen to me again.

Even if it had been in self-defense, even if I'd been trying to follow Elhani's command to save the empress, I'd shed blood. In one night, I'd broken two of the vows I'd made when I'd committed to becoming a nun. I'd kissed Caesiem, the worthless traitor, and I'd killed a Forwyn man. One of my own people. An ally.

I'd damned my soul and relinquished my life, and what did I have to show for it? The searing memory of that passionate, forbidden kiss, stolen from a thief and a spy, a liar and a traitor. The gruesome images of Wilvhe's bloody death at my hands. The picture of a bewildered Jaliana, frozen in that shadowed garden, looking so much like her mother as she stared back at me.

Now, I was on my own, with little money. I'd calculated I had enough to spend a week at this inn, cheap and dingy as it was despite its grandiose name. Beyond that, I had no idea what to do next.

The enraged part of me, the part that wanted this bloody empire to crumble to dust, thought longingly of Forwyth. What would it be like to finally bid goodbye to Alrenor and the nightmarish memories I had of this place, and explore my ancestors' kingdom? Would I find peace and a new life there?

What would I be, if not a nun? It was difficult to fathom my life without the abbey and Naina's gentle words, without my training sessions in Elhani's magic with my sisters, and without my rounds to serve impoverished Forwyn families in Inalgoth.

I'd failed everyone.

I'd lost everything.

At last, I yanked myself from bed, raw anger propelling me. I stood before the cracked mirror hanging from the dirt-stained wall and stared at the ribbons wound through my braids. My jaw was a hard line; my midnight eyes seethed with a hidden flame. I looked the part of the name the Alrenians had bestowed upon me years ago, a whispered title given to an anonymous girl: *Amara'rekni*, Empress-Slayer.

Strange to think that—though I'd gladly slit Karye's throat to save my life, to avenge my brother, and to grant my people freedom—I'd been the one to spare her daughter's life.

Although it had been Elhani's voice that had guided me to do so, I felt a hard knot in my chest every time I remembered what I'd done. Could sparing Jaliana's life do anything but harm to my people? It seemed blasphemous to doubt the wisdom of Elhani's guidance, and yet… I'd already been irreverent in my actions. I wasn't even a nun anymore. I wasn't sure what I was, except a killer.

With vicious fingers, I unwound the braid woven with an orange ribbon. A ribbon that reminded me of Naina's gentle hands and steady voice as she'd explained the meaning of the color. It represented loyalty, after years of faithful service to Elhani and his people within the Circle of Serenity. But it was a lie. Now I was nothing but a traitor to Elhani and his cause. A promise-breaker. A blood-spiller.

Angry tears flooded my eyes as I tossed the ribbon into the empty hearth. As autumn turned chillier, someone would eventually light a fire and my ribbon, forgotten and buried within the ashes, would burn away. If only I could burn my guilt just as easily.

The longer I looked within the cracked mirror, the more I hated my reflection. Each ribbon represented something I no longer was, or a memory I could no longer cling to with anything but pain and remorse. I was about due to take out my braids and let my hair rest anyway—now was as good a time as any to make the change.

Hands shaking, I unwound another braid, tossing one more ribbon into the hearth. Then another. Another. I let my dark curls free until I was completely unadorned and every beautiful, colorful ribbon I'd earned over the years lay in a pile of ashes. Each one told a story. The good deeds I'd done. The memories I'd made. The losses and pain I'd overcome.

The only ribbons I kept were the braided golden ones I wore like a necklace, the ones a Misrothian had given to me the night I'd slain Empress Karye. They concealed the scar that sliced across my throat, the mark the woman had left on me when she'd tried to take my life. They helped keep curious eyes from guessing about my past, about my identity as the *amara'rekni* the Alrenians hated and the Forwyn revered.

Now when I stared into the mirror, I found a Forwyn woman without her traditional ribbons—ribbons we'd fought hard to wear again after the Alrenians had enslaved us, taken our ribbons, and shorn our hair. My curls were as untamed as my anger, my eyes as dark as the churning emotions in my heart.

It seemed fitting, this new look.

This, I thought, *is who I am now.*

It was early afternoon when I'd finished bathing in the tiny washtub crammed into the corner of my room. My wet hair made me feel chilly as wind whispered through the cracks between the walls. Outside, the sky had grown grey and cloudy, a restless breeze swaying the palm trees and sending the birds for cover. From my glimpse of sea out my window, I could see a gathering darkness over churning water that spoke of a swiftly approaching storm.

After dressing in the same outfit I'd worn last night—the only clothes I owned that weren't grey, I slipped downstairs, where guests clustered about tables. Some were already at the bar. The stale scent of tobacco smoke and toast greeted me as I sank into a seat at a table in a shadowy corner. A Forwyn girl shuffled over, her grin appearing far too cheerful as she took my order.

"Coffee. Lots of it," I said, and she laughed softly to herself as if I'd made a joke.

"I'll be out with the largest pot I can find," she said with a wink.

She trotted away, and I was left alone, thinking miserably of Pauni'a and all the other friends I'd left behind. Mother and my younger brother Edi were dead, and I was as good as dead to every member of the Circle of Serenity. If any of Renni's vigilantes found me, they'd doubtless ensure I truly *was* dead.

And Caesiem… I winced inwardly as I thought of how I'd foolishly kissed him, all because I thought he cared, and I was losing my life as a nun anyway. I thought if I was going to break one vow, he'd be worth breaking another.

I was wrong.

When the girl plopped the coffeepot and a mug in front of me, I started.

"Any food?" she asked.

My stomach felt squeamish at the mere mention of food, so I shook my head. She left me to my dreary thoughts as I poured the steaming beverage into my mug and drank it black, while it was still too hot and burned my tongue. I was so lost in my own thoughts, I almost didn't notice the pain.

"Ale," came a sharp, familiar voice near the bar.

My eyes snagged on the figure, whose back was to me as she leaned against the counter. Her form was slight but strong, as unyielding as she was. With her shorn hair, she still looked the part of a Forwyn slave—because, until recently, she still had been. Mio'e.

Scowling, I shrank further back into the shadows, praying I could disappear.

Fool, I thought. *Of course you can't hear Elhani's voice now. Why would he let you use his magic after what you've done?*

It didn't matter, because Mio'e already knew I was there. As soon as the barkeep slid her a drink, she spun on her heel and strode directly toward my table. My stomach writhed like the choppy, angry waves outside. I sat up straighter and set my jaw.

Mio'e couldn't know I'd killed Wilvhe—but I was sure she'd suspect it after I'd fled without bothering to seek her and the other vigilantes out after our failed mission. She probably wanted her revenge. But she wouldn't try to kill me in a public place...would she?

As much as Mio'e had always made her dislike of me clear, I really didn't want to have to kill her.

"Lo'laeni Nolanhou," she said, almost chanting my name, like it was a prayer. Probably her way of mocking my status as a nun. *Former* nun. Her dark eyes darted over my face, taking in my wild, damp curls and clothes—still shabby and plain, but no longer in nun grey. Normally, her expression was hard. Today, she was inscrutable.

"Mio'e," I muttered, my frustration audibly scratching up my throat.

Slamming down her ale, she plopped into the chair across from me. Her taunting manner vanished as her eyes again flicked over me. "You disappeared quickly last night, but I'd expected to find you hiding away in your precious abbey. No one seemed to know what had happened to you, except your friend Pauni'a, who said you'd packed and left in a hurry. Running away from something, nun?"

"*Former* nun." I glared, deliberately taking my time responding. I took another sip of coffee, letting the bitter flavor and invigorating caffeine lend me extra courage. "Considering how everything failed, do you blame me? What do you expect to do against a Teramese army?"

Mio'e merely blinked. Lifting her own drink, she took a large gulp. "We didn't run from the Alrenians, so I don't see why foreign invaders should change anything. This is your *home,* Lo."

I glanced away, studying the Forwyn chatting and drinking at the bar. "Not anymore," I mumbled. "Maybe Alrenor is past saving."

Mio'e narrowed her eyes, as if I'd made a confession. "We found two bodies," she said quietly, but there was a steel edge to her words. "One was Eloreth, almost unrecognizable but for her red hair and the ribbon she always wore on her wrist, her gift from that man of hers who was killed."

I swallowed, my throat painfully dry. The only Alrenian ally we'd had in our group of vigilantes, determined to help the Forwyn after she'd fallen in love with a Forwyn man who'd been murdered, Eloreth had never shown last night. Apparently, she'd been killed within the palace grounds.

"She's dead?"

"From the empress's unnatural power, it looked like," Mio'e said. "And then we found Wilvhe, a blade in his throat." She cocked her head, eyes darkening with malice. "I suppose I underestimated you after all, and you aren't the meek nun I thought you were. Tell me what happened, Lo. Tell me why I saw you chase after him and the empress last night, and today I find you cowering in this dingy rat's nest."

My blood hammered in my ears. "Wilvhe tried to kill me," I said gruffly. "I defended myself."

Mio'e's words shook with barely repressed anger. "And why would he have tried to kill you?"

Fear prickled along my scalp. Ugly images shot through my head: Mio'e returning that night to slit my throat, dumping my body in an alley to rot. All the remaining vigilantes cornering me in a dark section of the city. Someone paying off the barkeep to slip some of the vylae meant for the empress into a drink. My eyes landed on the coffee in front of me.

Mio'e wouldn't believe me, but I lowered my voice, determined to explain anyway. "I heard Elhani speak to me last night. He told me to protect the empress—I don't know why. I tried to stop Wilvhe from assassinating Jaliana. I didn't *want* to kill him, but when he tried to attack me…" My words drifted away as my throat tightened with renewed grief. I'd thought he was my friend, but he'd turned on me first.

Mio'e's face was so still it could have been chiseled from stone. Her eyes, however, were endless, glistening pools, so dark in the dim room that they looked inky black. They spoke a thousand words that her expression did not, and I knew in my bones she would never believe or forgive me. "Liar! You betrayed us, just as we feared," she snapped. *"Avili'o ye mui hoku."*

The words were an ancient vow quoted in the sacred Ihlu'i Text itself. *I have become a blood avenger.* It meant that she declared Wilvhe's death as murder, and that she invoked the deeply held Forwyn belief that anyone close to the victim could rightfully, without punishment from Elhani, the guidespirits, or any mortal, claim my life to avenge his. Once the promise was spoken, a blood avenger would not rest, would let nothing sway them from their purpose, until their target was dead.

My muscles coiled to fight as I fisted my hands, half-expecting Mio'e to launch herself across the table right then. A blood avenger could, in theory, kill me right here in the open without punishment from the law. But even a blood avenger needed proof they were in the right, and Mio'e was no fool.

Instead, she calmly slipped a knife out from where she'd tucked it in her leggings and sliced it across her palm, letting drops of blood stain the table between us. "I vow to avenge him," she whispered, continuing the sacred Forwyn tradition, "by the shedding of my very own blood."

Her eyes bored into mine as she hesitated—maybe considering taking the risk and stabbing me right then anyway—before she wiped the weapon on her sleeve and hid it away again.

"I'll see you again," she vowed.

She moved as if to stand, leaving her promise echoing in my mind, when a steady pounding reached our ears.

Everyone in the inn turned as one toward the windows, caked with a layer of dirt thick enough that it skewed our view of the street. It made the world outside seem even darker than it already was, and with the swirling grey clouds above, it looked more like evening than late morning. The wind kicked up tiny whirlwinds of dust and debris, swirling it across the cobblestones. In the distance, between city buildings, I could make out glimpses of the churning waves of the

Great Sea, but we were too far away to see the port.

I'd thought at first that the rumbling was distant thunder, that in a moment the sky would alight with a flash of lightning and a torrent of rain would follow. But frantic voices of citizens in the streets—Forwyn and Alrenian alike—told me that it was something else. It only took another moment for me to realize what it was as the first soldiers came into view.

It was the beat of hundreds of boots pounding along the street, of an army marching into Inalogth under a Teramese banner. The flag snapped wildly in the wind, making it difficult for me to study the dragon sigil on its red background. But I remembered what I'd learned about Teramyl, a land afflicted by wild dragons. They'd adopted a fire-breathing dragon as their symbol, a sign that they refused to be overcome by the very thing that plagued them the most.

Rows of uniformed men and women with bronzed skin, bright eyes, and painted faces flashed by the window in a seemingly endless succession. All were clothed in midnight black, as if their intention was to blot out this dazzling white city. The war paint along their brows, cheeks, and noses, however, was not identical: each man or woman wore different colors in distinct patterns.

These weren't the only soldiers I'd heard marching through the city since last night, but they were the first who'd come close enough for me to see.

I stood abruptly, making my chair legs scrape gratingly along the floor. The rage that had ignited within me the night before, the rage I'd buried in the face of my guilt, flared back to life. *Caesiem.*

Alrenor was being invaded because of him. Because the Teramese, whom we'd considered allies, whom Alrenor had traded with, had decided our empire was fractured and weak, and they'd taken advantage of that fact. Because, apparently, the Teramese had sent at least one spy to lie his way into Renni's group of vigilantes and try to charm his way into my heart.

Alrenor deserves to fall, I thought darkly, thinking of the Alrenians murdering my people and the Elders who'd not bothered to stop them. All our leaders had failed us. Maybe this empire was meant to crumble, and the only thing left was to abandon it.

Still, though I couldn't ignore the horror crawling up my throat as Forwyn guards shouted at the advancing army. From inside the inn, the guards' voices sounded muffled beneath the thundering footsteps of Teramese soldiers, but it didn't matter what they had said. The soldiers didn't pause, didn't respond, didn't react at all, except for a few in front who drew wicked, circular-looking blades from their belts and hurled them at the guards blocking their path. A few hapless citizens—Forwyn and Alrenian alike—were struck as well, blood spurting into the air and bodies dropping like puppets severed from their strings.

Neither the growing pools of blood slicking the cobblestones nor the corpses themselves slowed the Teramese, who trod over them without missing a beat in the hideous rhythm they pounded through the city.

I'd seen so much death over my lifetime that perhaps it should have felt commonplace, but it never lost its nauseating grip on me. My mind whirled from the sight of deaths occurring now and memories of deaths in the past. Karye's cruel murders. My brother Edi's body, looking so much smaller in death than he had in life. The clean slice of the dagger as I'd slit Karye's throat, and the glint of the blade as I'd hurled it toward Wilvhe's neck.

Only one voice cut through the commotion around me as guests erupted into horrified murmurs, most stepping back from the windows so as to conceal themselves within the shadows. I didn't expect the soldiers to storm into the inn and slaughter us, but I couldn't blame them for their terror.

"I have work to do," Mio'e snarled, tossing me a sideways glance, her eyes as sharp as the Teramese blades. "But wherever you flee, wherever you cower, *hilvoku*, I'll find you."

She shoved through the guests toward the kitchen, meeting no resistance as she rushed for the rear exit.

I turned back to the window, where the Teramese were still marching past, stretching on and on. It made me wonder how many had arrived on additional ships this morning, how long they'd hovered off our coast until it was safe for them to land and overwhelm us. These soldiers were just one of endless lines of others marching through other streets, all throughout Inalgoth, tracing a slow, ascending path toward the palace overlooking the city.

"Why haven't the Elders sent the Dragon Keepers?" one of the guests asked, as if he expected one of the Elders to step into the inn and explain what was happening.

Thoughts of finding steady work and earning passage to Forwyth were dissipating, disappearing as swiftly as the debris tugged away by the wind. With Teramyl occupying the capital, I didn't expect any ships would be permitted to leave the docks for a while. And unless I wanted to fend off and kill every single one of the vigilantes I'd once worked with, I would have to keep my head down in this city.

I needed a new way out.

With their control of the palace—and, I assumed, the dragons, Teramyl would control all of Alrenor.

Dragons.

I closed my eyes and imagined what I could do with a dragon.

CHAPTER TWO

Caesiem Xalenos

IT TOOK A FULL BATH and three vigorous hand scrubbings to remove all the blood. The guilt, though, would not wash away so easily.

In the absurd luxury of the vast rooms I'd claimed within the palace, I was more uncomfortable than I'd ever been in Alrenor. I preferred the smoky interior of The Broken Crown, a drink close at hand while I plucked the strings of my *luta* and sang to the Forwyn crowd. There, I'd almost been able to forget why I was there in the first place. There, I'd almost believed the lies I'd woven about my life, until I ached with the desire for them to be true.

Life would have been a lot simpler if they were.

Every time I closed my eyes, I could see Lo's face, her deep brown eyes narrowed and simmering with fury. The line of her jaw taut as she spun on me. She'd regretted saving my life. Regretted everything.

The lingering memory of her kiss stung as much as the one of her punching me in the face. She hadn't broken my nose, but it was swollen and discolored. I deserved so much worse than that.

Life would have been a lot simpler if I hadn't met her, either.

It was strange to think that those fleeting final moments alone with Lo had occurred only yesterday, when she hadn't hated me. By now, after an endless, sleepless night and a long, restless morning, that period before the Forwyn Elders' Autumn Ball could have happened in another lifetime. To another person. To the man I wished I was.

I couldn't help but imagine the possibilities if yesterday had gone differently, and Lo had agreed to run away with me. But that was ridiculous, because I knew, deep down, that I'd never actually had the freedom to run away. To run away would have been to betray everything I was, to be an even worse man than the one who'd broken Lo's heart.

This had always been my destiny.

Moving stiffly because of my aching muscles, I slipped into the fresh Teramese uniform someone had left for me. Without even sparing it a glance, I knew it would be an exact fit. Revaed was always a careful planner. Those little details meant everything to him.

The knock on my door came right when I expected it. For a moment, I lingered by one of the windows, staring at the expansive Alrenian garden, with its palm trees bending in the stormy breeze and endless rows of bright, exotic-looking flowers. The brewing clouds overhead were as dark as my mood as I mindlessly tapped a rhythm against my leg, the beat to a jaunty tune I'd often played at the pub.

Another knock, more insistent this time.

Forcing my fingers to still, I braced myself. "Come in," I called, my voice sounding as drained as I felt.

The door opened and footsteps crossed the small sitting room to stand within my new bedroom. Vander Arros cleared his throat.

"Prince Revaed has requested your presence, Lord Xalenos," he announced, not waiting for me to turn around.

I inhaled a slow breath, both hating and loving the sound of my own title. Xalenos was almost always spoken in fear, in awe, in subservience. It was time to shove aside the life of a nobody—a thief and spy, a musician and singer, an outsider and orphan—and replace it once again with the life of a lord.

At last, I turned. "Why are you using my formal title?" I said, too loudly. Too harshly. Guilt immediately washed over me—Vander had always been among the few mages I considered a friend. He'd been my only companion when we'd both been sent as spies to Alrenor, ahead of Revaed and the rest of the Teramese army.

But last night's memories had made me irritable.

Vander narrowed his silver eyes. Though he was a few years older than me, my greater status and power made him behave deferentially toward me more often than I'd like. Though it was refreshing to be respected by someone, I deeply longed for a friend.

"Forgive me, Caesiem," he said after a moment's hesitation. "With the guards outside and everything that's happened…it seemed like the moment for formality."

"It's fine," I replied with a sigh. "Tell Revaed I'll be right there."

Vander retreated with a swift nod.

I fidgeted with my uniform collar, my eyes snagging on the mirror hung over a vanity table. With my bruised nose, I looked anything but impressive, but there was nothing I could do about that detail. I could only hope Revaed would assume I'd received it in the fighting, not from chasing and pleading with a Forwyn woman like a lovestruck idiot.

Summoning every ounce of energy I had, I slipped out of my rooms and through the grand Alrenian halls I'd used to sneak through.

Now I walked with my head held high, and Teramese guards posted throughout the palace stood to attention and saluted as soon as they saw me. Everyone looked battle-weary, wearing bandages and dark circles beneath their eyes, but they were proud. Victorious.

As expected, I found Revaed lounging in the meeting room off the throne room, his perfectly polished boots propped on the table. His hair was cut short like he preferred, without a single dark curl out of place. His bronze skin was a shade darker than I remembered it, likely from the days at sea. It'd been hard to notice details like this last night, when he'd embraced me.

Last night, when I'd experienced joy and horror, relief and guilt, all at once.

Hovering in the entrance and waiting for him to acknowledge me, I scanned the room. No one else was present. I found the tight knot in my chest loosening, just a little. There was less pressure if I didn't have to perform for an entire crowd. Though Revaed expected much from me, he was informal when it was only the two of us. And I didn't have the energy to be a well-mannered lord as easily as I'd been before, not after months of living someone else's role.

Revaed glanced up with a warm smile. In the dim greyness seeping through the single window, his violet eyes were especially vibrant. It was understandable that, despite the fear surrounding the Xalenos name, the nobles' daughters didn't protest when their fathers tried to marry them off to the young prince.

"You're a sight, Caes," he said, his lips twitching in a smirk. "I hope you gutted the man who dared to tarnish your pretty-boy face."

My response stuck in my throat when images of Lo flipped through my mind. Her flawless complexion and those warm, full lips of hers I'd wanted to kiss almost as soon as I'd met her. Her dark eyes, glimmering with intelligence and spunk. She was strong and brave and full of passion in ways I'd never seen in anyone else before.

Immediately, my stomach sank. As soon as I remembered the way she'd looked at me before the ball, I had to remember how she'd looked at me after Revaed and I had wrested control from the Forwyn Court of Elders. That same passion with which she lived her whole life had been directed toward me, but not in the way I'd longed for it to be. Her anger had been intense—and understandably so.

She'd somehow, miraculously, once accepted me as a thief. But now, even if I saw her again, she would never forgive me for who I truly was.

This is what you get for flirting with a nun, I thought wryly. *Of course it was doomed from the start.*

Instead of responding, I sank into a chair opposite Revaed at the table, shoving aside scattered maps and papers the Elders had probably scoured only hours before. Quietly, I tapped out a beat with the toe of my boot on the tile floor, softly enough that Revaed might not notice and grow annoyed. Even though I was exhausted, it was difficult to be still.

I nodded at Revaed's scrubbed face, immaculate uniform, and polished boots. "You cleaned up well."

Revaed smiled almost lazily. "A ruler must look his best." He paused, considering. "Do you think good old Father would be annoyed if I assumed the title of Emperor upon my coronation?" He smirked. "You know he will insist upon being the High Imperator until he dies, no matter what land *we* conquer for him." He gestured about, as if imagining the whole of Alrenor spread before us in his mind's eye.

"I'm sure it would drive him mad," I said, fidgeting with the buttons of my jacket. Honestly, the Teramese Imperator terrified me, even if he'd accepted me when Revaed had adopted me, declaring me his heir. I was convinced Revaed alone in the entire kingdom dared to annoy his father.

The High Imperator had honored Revaed's request to make me a future prince, and someday the heir to Teramyl itself, but I couldn't shake the feeling that he was dissatisfied that Revaed hadn't married and sired his own son.

Probably the only reason the High Imperator had ever given me any measure of power or honor in the palace was because I possessed skills and powers that were valuable to him. Valuable to Teramyl. I held no illusions that the great Imperator cared about me, not the way Revaed did.

Revaed quirked an annoyed eyebrow at me as I continued to fidget in my seat. "Would you hold still?"

I bit back my grin. "Emperor or prince, it's good to know I can still drive you mad, Revaed."

Rolling his eyes, my guardian repressed his own smile in response. After a moment, he tilted his head, considering. "It does have a nice ring to it, doesn't it? Emperor Revaed." His lips twitched. "And when Father passes, High Imperator."

I held in a snort, though I wasn't surprised. "Only you would speak so casually of your father's death."

Revaed shrugged. "No one loves him, and he knows it. He's only ever wanted everyone's fear and obedience." He leaned further back in his seat, his eyes alight with passion. "I, on the other hand? I'll be a High Imperator our people will love."

I nodded, my insides warming with the possibilities. Revaed and I could ensure true changes occurred. Good ones for our people. But I couldn't resist landing another playful jab at my guardian. "That title makes you sound wiser and more formidable than you truly are."

This time, Revaed laughed outright. "It certainly does. As much as I would be loved, it couldn't hurt to make my name sound a bit more fearsome too." He shook his head and sighed dramatically. "No one speaks my name with quite the same hushed awe they speak Father's."

I laughed along with him, warm memories burbling up, almost assuaging the pain and doubt and darkness in my heart. "You've hosted a few too many raucous parties at the palace for that."

Revaed's brow furrowed. "I thought you liked my raucous parties."

"I do, but they don't exactly inspire fear."

As our laughter settled, Revaed's expression turned more serious. "And think about your new title: Prince Xalenos." He smiled. "Or we can take on the Alrenian tradition and use our first names, to avoid confusion. If I'm Emperor Revaed, you can be Prince Caesiem." Amusement twinkled in his eyes. "We're finally free of my father. We lead our own lives, Caes, just like we'd hoped."

The knowledge settled over me, both reassuring and heavy. It was relieving to be away from the High Imperator and the fear he instilled, but the new responsibilities of leading Alrenor—and the guilt that came with the hard decisions leaders must make—were pressing.

With a half-hearted grin and a shake of my head, I changed the subject. "Don't call me prince until the actual coronation ceremony. Anyway, shouldn't you be resting instead of dreaming of being High Imperator? Everything is…well, settled for now, isn't it?" I waved a hand through the air, as if it could signify the quiet that had drifted over the palace after a night of fighting.

"The last of the troops will arrive any minute to finish securing the rest of the capital." Dragging his boots off the desk, Revaed leaned forward, steepling his fingers together and settling his chin atop them. "There's far too much to do for sleep just yet. For both of us," he added pointedly. "For one, it's come to my attention that despite a careful search, the Alrenian empress is nowhere to be found. That's concerning."

I frowned thoughtfully. I'd been sure Wilvhe and the others would have managed to poison Jaliana, despite Revaed's and my invasion. But maybe all the vigilantes had fled in the chaos, not feeling it worth the risk to stay and finish their assassination attempt.

"She was supposed to be poisoned with vylae," I explained, lifting my hands as if I wore the gloves Wilvhe had coated in the lethal stuff. "Renni and the others had it all under control." I hesitated. "Or, I thought they did. Maybe Jaliana fled the palace grounds and died from the poison elsewhere?"

Revaed scowled. "I can't live with maybes, only certainty. Facts." He sighed, leaning back in his chair again. "Besides, Vander reported that they discovered the body of a male Dragon Keeper within the garden. Vander and the others suspected his gloves were coated in vylae, though they haven't tested it. The man was dead, a blade in his throat."

Wilvhe. Despite myself, I cringed. Thankfully, Revaed didn't comment.

"If that was one of your vigilantes, then it's possible he never managed to poison the empress. I can't have loose ends like that. I need her to be dead—and I need her death to be confirmed." Revaed shifted his gaze from the papers scattered between us to my face. "That's why I want you to interrogate the Forwyn we have in the dungeons. One of them might know something."

I tensed at the thought, my restless hands stilling. At the word *interrogate,* all I could think of was more violence, more bloody images to join the ones from last night.

Revaed smiled pleasantly, waving away my unspoken concerns with an airy hand. "Just ask them a few questions," he said. "No reason to make it a big ordeal. It's not likely any of those Forwyn will want to protect an Alrenian anyway. She might have been their pawn before, but they have bigger problems now." His grin stretched wider, as if we were sharing a private joke.

I returned it uneasily. It was difficult to be light-hearted and carefree when all I could see was Lo's disappointed, hate-filled eyes. But all I said was "Of course," because disappointing Revaed, the guardian who was more like an older brother to me, was unthinkable.

Revaed winked. "I knew I could count on you. Now, with you putting my mind at ease, maybe I can catch a few moments of rest before the army arrives."

Though Revaed never insisted upon formality between us, it seemed right to stand and salute my new emperor. He nodded, a silent dismissal, and I slipped from the room, my heart pounding in spite of Revaed's reassurances.

Pushing the uncomfortable emotions to the back of my mind, where they'd likely haunt my nightmares later, I focused on the task at hand. Find Vander. Enter the Alrenian dungeons. Speak with the Forwyn Elders.

No, I thought, suddenly remembering the young Forwyn man who'd danced with Empress Jaliana at the start of the Autumn Ball. I'd learned from my days spying in the palace that he was Elder Ettonou's son, and had been appointed by the Elders as a bodyguard to protect others from Jaliana. Kovi Ettonou had also appeared to be closer to her than anyone else, close in a way I'd never expected to see a Forwyn and an Alrenian to be. As if there had been an unspoken understanding between them. I'd start by questioning him.

If anyone knew where Jaliana was, if anyone could find her, it would be him.

CHAPTER THREE

Kovi Ettonou

DESPITE MY EXHAUSTION, I COULDN'T stop pacing the cell I'd been tossed within mere hours earlier. It was impossible to tell the time of day in the unending darkness, because the Teramese hadn't even bothered to light the torches along the dungeon walls. It was almost as if, after a night of blood and death, they'd grown weary of fighting and killing, and simply decided to toss the Forwyn left alive in these cells to slowly starve to death. Or perhaps the Teramese soldiers would recuperate before executing us publicly, using it as a brutal way to announce their takeover to all the empire.

I sank to the floor, too sweat- and blood-stained to care that the stone beneath me was slick and reeked of foulness. Absentmindedly, I toyed with the ribbons I wore around my left wrist—black, red, orange, and gold. Symbols of my status as a soldier, of my loss and grief, and of my loyalty to my people.

My mind wouldn't stop reeling, trying to go back and process what had led my father and the other Elders to such an abrupt downfall. One moment, there had been covert meetings and whispered talk of growing Alrenian uprisings, of a burgeoning new army that threatened us with the possibility of civil war. As long as we had our Dragon Keepers in control of the dragons, the Elders had been confident in our ability to quell any threats.

Somehow, we'd been infiltrated by Teramese while the Alrenians had distracted us. An ally kingdom had seen our weakness, sniffed it out like a predatory animal, and capitalized on it. With the two races of Alrenor torn by years-old animosity, it must have been all too easy to strategize the coup.

Now, my father was one of the few Elders left alive, shoved into another dank cell. The Teramese had separated us Forwyn enough to make it seem, in the hours that had passed, like I was the only person left. Like I was buried alive in darkness, in a living death.

In my weariness, I started to wonder. Maybe I *was* dead.

No, I told myself firmly. *Elhani would be welcoming me into the Golden After by now if so. Mother would be embracing me.*

My heart ached at the thought. It wasn't as if I had a wish to die. I had too much left to do on earth, most important of which was protecting my people from this newest threat. But I wasn't afraid of death, not when I knew what waited for me.

There were other thoughts crowding my head and making my chest ache, but I refused to linger on them. To recall *her*—her expression, her words, her final threats—was too painful and confusing. I didn't want to remember the contradictory emotions she'd made me experience, or the way I'd stood by and let her escape. I didn't want to wonder if that mercy had been a mistake that my people would later pay for in bloodshed.

Footsteps interrupted my thoughts. Other than the sounds of my own scuffling boots on the floor and the occasional rat skittering through the darkness, I'd heard nothing for long hours, until my ears had begun to ring. Perhaps the Teramese had arrived to drag me to my execution.

Elhani, I prayed, my head jumbled. A headache pounded at my temples. It took more focus than usual to shut out the thoughts and feelings and listen instead to Elhani's voice, like a constant song wrapping itself around me. It coursed through my veins, invigorating and warming, a comforting presence despite the uncertainty gripping me. It would be easy to use Elhani's magic to control one Teramese soldier's actions, maybe even two. But I was too weak to keep that up for long.

Still, I had to try. I had to do something. Resigning myself to my own death, if necessary, would be simple. Resigning myself to others' deaths...that was far more difficult.

I shoved against the wall, listening to the footsteps pause outside my cell door. Impenetrable stone with only a small slot near the bottom that could open to insert food trays, the door allowed me to see nothing of the person waiting on the other side. When the lock clicked and the door swung inward, the flickering torchlight stabbed at my eyes, blinding me after the endless blackness.

"This is the one," came a voice with a musical Teramese accent. "Leave us."

"Are you sure, Lord Xalenos?" came a hesitant response.

"Stand in the corridor," the first voice responded impatiently. "If he tries anything, you'll be near to help."

Shuffling steps retreated into the corridor as I let my eyes adjust to the light. In the doorway stood a Teramese man about my age, the sleeves of his black uniform rumpled. His piercing blue eyes were like two pinpricks of light in the dark, as intense as all Teramese eyes tended to be. He was the young man who'd stepped forward during the ball, immediately before the coup. Disguised as a guest.

Lord Xalenos, the other man had called him. In the three years Alrenor had once again been open to trade with other kingdoms, including Teramyl, I'd learned that the current king was a Xalenos. This man was a member of the imperial family.

But he wasn't the one in charge, the one who'd overthrown the Court of Elders. If he had been, he would have sent someone else to do the dirty work of questioning or torturing the prisoners.

I let the magic flowing through my veins dissipate a little as I relaxed my hold. Curiosity piqued, I decided to wait and see what the imperial family wanted to speak with me about before attempting anything. Besides, I could sense from the breaths outside and shifting shadows that there was more than one soldier waiting outside. I couldn't lash out without a calculated plan, or I'd be restrained—perhaps killed—before I could even truly begin.

"Kovi Ettonou," Lord Xalenos said, studying me intently. The torchlight from the corridor flooded my cell, highlighting the man. He didn't appear nervous, but he kept shifting on his feet, as if he couldn't hold still. "Son of Elder Ettonou, graduate of Aerekni Academy, and personal guard to Her Imperial Highness, Jaliana, daughter of the former Empress Karye."

I didn't move a muscle, staring blankly at him as he rattled off this information about me, information I had no idea how he'd uncovered. Had he already questioned the remaining Elders? Were they still alive? Was Father all right?

Thoughts of my father conjured unbidden images of Jalie, of the bruises he'd left along her skin, of the way he'd dragged her by her hair or snapped her finger out of place without a hint of hesitation. Disgust churned through me. I'd never imagined my own father would have given into hatred and bitterness so wholly, to become like our enemies.

To forsake the mercy Elhani called us to and give into the violent ways the Alrenians prized so much.

It made me burn with shame to think, years ago when he'd found me at the academy, I'd so proudly claimed my father's last name as my own. Back then, it had felt like receiving a prize, finally having the chance to share an identity with the one parent I still had left living.

Now I felt trapped with it, the name Ettonou as branded into me as the color of my eyes or the sound of my voice. Every one of my fellow soldiers knew me by that name, a name I wished I'd never chosen to carry.

"You must be aware that Jaliana disappeared last night, since you were tasked with never leaving her side," the young lord went on.

I stared at him, setting my face like stone. I was a soldier. Impassive, immoveable. I'd been trained to withstand interrogation and torture, to always conceal my thoughts and emotions behind a mask. The only one who'd seemed able to see through the cracks in my armor, even a little, had been Jalie.

Lord Xalenos cast his eyes toward the stone ceiling, concealed by shadows, and sighed. "I understand and respect your strategy, soldier. But I hope you realize this is…a *friendly* conversation." His face slipped into a charming smile, and I had a strong urge to seize him by his collar and hurl him into the wall. Though he appeared fit, he was smaller than me. It wouldn't be that difficult.

But what next? Attack the men waiting in the corridor? Overpower countless guards throughout the dungeons? Use my magic to control them and be tied to them the way I was still tied to Jalie?

The thought stung. Even now, I could feel hints of her emotions if I let myself concentrate on them—which I refused to do.

Fidgeting with a teardrop-shaped pendant hanging from a leather cord about his neck, the man went on. "As a soldier, you're trained to be loyal to your people and to always put their needs first, right? You can't tolerate what the Alrenians have done to them…"

"How dare you speak of what the Alrenians have done to us," I said, my voice a guttural whisper. "Not when your people betrayed us, and are equally guilty of shedding our blood."

"I won't deny that." He lifted his hands as if in mock surrender, waving away my concerns. As if my unspoken threat didn't concern him. Surely he knew of Forwyn magic, just as I knew that Teramese mages were few and far between. A magic-wielding soldier against a spoiled lord wouldn't even be a contest. And yet, something about the way he assessed me, about the way his charming, carefree aura seemed like an act, made me think Lord Xalenos was no fool. Did he have a hidden weapon? Something that made him think he had an advantage?

The silence stretched, until my curiosity seized me and wouldn't let go. I realized I was probably playing into the man's hands, but I didn't think asking a question of my own would be all that dangerous.

I shifted on my feet. "What do you want?"

The Teramese lord released his pendant to gesture between the two of us. "It's in both of our people's interests to find the empress before she can harm anyone else with that strange…power…of hers." He halted over the word, as if unsure whether to name it a gift, as the Alrenians called their magic, or something else. Her ability to make a person's flesh seemingly rot and burn away at a mere touch was unheard of in any land. It seemed like something a *hilvoku,* one of the heartless demons who served the Dark Immortal, would possess.

But Jalie hadn't been without a heart…

I waited patiently as Lord Xalenos studied my face, perhaps hoping for a reaction I wouldn't give him.

When I said nothing, Lord Xalenos began tapping a rhythm with his fingertips, drumming them against his leg, before continuing. "If you can help my people find the empress and…dispose of her…we'd consider you to be quite a valuable citizen in this new leadership of ours. Someone too useful to put to death, surely."

Before I could sneer at him, Lord Xalenos raised a hand to stop me. "I know—you're a soldier. You'd proudly die rather than serve your enemy. But can you serve your own people if you're dead? You would be rescuing Forwyn lives from an amassing Alrenian army. You would have influence with Emperor Revaed. He would remember what you'd done for him and reward you well. Perhaps with sparing your father, Elder Ettonou, and maybe some of the other Elders. Perhaps with finding ways to end your people's suffering, the continued enslavement and murders the Alrenians have committed against the Forwyn." He rocked back on his heels, his fingers at last stilling. "A dead soldier can do nothing for his people. But a living one…the possibilities are endless."

It was true—I hadn't underestimated this man and his intelligence. He knew more than he should, and he'd read me despite my impassive expression. Whether he'd guessed because he knew I was a soldier, or he had some other source of information, or he was just extremely perceptive, he'd known exactly how to bait me.

It made anger coil within me like a snake, desperate to strike.

Worse still, there was another motivation, one I was loath to admit to myself. If I were the one to find Jalie, perhaps I could find a way to spare her life. Perhaps I could ensure she wasn't callously *disposed of,* as Lord Xalenos had said, like he'd been speaking of a pest.

No matter the danger she posed toward my people—to *me*—I couldn't deny the ache in my chest when I imagined something terrible befalling her. I could still smell the cinnamon and vanilla scent of her soap on her skin, could still feel the warmth of her body curled beside me in her bed when she'd been too afraid to lay there alone, or when she'd been poisoned and I'd feared she'd slip away into the afterlife. I could see her eyes, sparkling with life and anger and cunning, but also with the softer side she tried to conceal, the side that gentled at my small kindnesses. That recognized my own pain and grief. That balked at the horrors her mother's advisor, Vionn, had said Karye had committed. That ached to keep her people safe with the same passion I had to serve my own.

And then, there'd been our kiss. Though I'd mainly used it as a distraction to slip the poison off her person, I couldn't deny my desire. She'd leaned into my kiss readily, her mouth warm and soft and somehow gentle and demanding all at once. It had been…everything I'd imagined it would be, and more.

Even if she'd used it to drug me into unconsciousness, it had been the single most confusing and electrifying moment of my life. Which, perhaps, didn't say much about the other girls I'd kissed in the past.

I didn't want to think about it. I couldn't stop thinking about it.

Maybe Father was right, and I had softened all because of a pretty face, but I knew it went deeper than that, deeper than my longing to be merciful when my enemies were ruthless, deeper even than the connection I felt because of the magic I'd used on her. The two of us understood one another; we faced similar anger and grief. Jalie was fierce and cunning, stronger than anyone else I'd ever known in ways I hadn't expected. She was determined and brave and resilient.

Despite her arrogance and her harsh exterior, she was not the monster her mother had been.

She'd insisted mercy couldn't exist in war, and that if she and I crossed paths on a battlefield, we'd once again be enemies on opposing sides. She wasn't exactly wrong—I couldn't see a world in which we weren't enemies.

And yet, I couldn't see a world without her in it, either.

Did that make me disloyal to my people?

I'd been quiet for too long, perhaps letting too many of my feelings slip across my face.

"What do you say?" Lord Xalenos asked, his blue eyes studying me thoughtfully. Confidently. It was clear he already knew my answer.

Unease prickled through me.

I relaxed my stance, just a little. "I can find her."

CHAPTER FOUR

Empress Jaliana, daughter of Karye

MY DREAMS WERE BLOODY AND violent, filled with haunting images of the Court of Elders lining up my people to be executed. From my seat on my throne, I chose the victims' fates—death by blade or death by dragon fire—and the Elders carried them out instantly. They commanded Kovi to slay the people, and he obeyed without protest, plunging an already bloody dagger into their chests, or shoving them before Ryke, my own brilliant green dragon.

Horror clogged my throat as the dream shifted, showing me a throne room that was empty save for the kills I'd made: Lady Leanai, Keeper Yaelti, and the traitorous Alrenian woman who'd met with me in the palace gardens just yesterday. Their skin was blackened, in places peeling so badly it revealed muscle and tendon and bone, so bloody and rotting and gruesome they were almost unrecognizable. The air filled with the stench of death until I was certain I'd be sick. I choked down a gag and spun around to face Nesrelle, where she lounged on my throne.

Clothed in a stunning violet gown with a train that spilled across the marble floor, her piercing blue eyes locked on mine. They were as chilling and empty as the eyes of the corpses surrounding me. She swept one of her fiery red curls behind her ear and grinned, her teeth startlingly white against bloody lips. *"Don't be afraid of the curse, little Jalie…"* she whispered.

I jerked awake. Overhead, the sky churned with steel-grey clouds. I could almost taste the electricity building in the air from the gathering storm. Choppy waves roared and crashed against the rocky beach, lying far below the cliff I rested upon.

His warm, smooth scales coiled around me, Ryke snorted and shifted in his sleep. I heaved a sigh at his comforting presence. I had a dragon to protect and transport me. I was no longer trapped in the palace, at the mercy of Elder Ettonou's violent outbursts and unseen assassins' threats. There were still fading bruises on my arm from where the Elder had seized me, and my index finger still ached from him snapping it out of place.

But being out of the palace didn't erase all of my problems.

Alrenor had been invaded—by our Teramese allies, no less. Had the warriors who'd interrupted the Forwyn ball last night slain all of the Elders? Would that make my work to reclaim my throne any easier?

An ache settled in my chest at the memory of Kovi's face as he'd let me escape. There'd been hurt in his eyes as I'd threatened him. I'd reminded him that we were both loyal to our people, and would kill one another if we had to, in order to help our own sides. And I hadn't been wrong...had I? Even if he'd let me go in the end, he hadn't denied the fact that he'd killed Alrenians as part of his duties as a Forwyn soldier.

Had the Teramese soldiers killed him?

I tried to shake away my worry and longing, despising both feelings for making me weak and uncertain in my purpose. I couldn't hesitate. I couldn't doubt. My people, the Chosen Ones of the Life-Giver, had to come before my insipid feelings for a handsome face and a kind heart.

I can't make room for kindness in my heart, I thought.

As if she'd materialized from my dreams, Nesrelle herself strode into view, clothed in a white linen dress that fluttered in the wind. She stared out at the horizon, where the clouds were thickest and darkest, her gaze distant. She stopped right at the edge of the cliff, her bare toes curling over rocks that looked like they could tumble off into the sea at any moment. Poised and unafraid, she appeared unaffected as the wind tugged her hair across her face.

"You're right," she said, her gentle smile contradicting her taunting words. "There is no room for kindness in war."

My heart pulsed uncomfortably against my throat. Had she heard my thoughts?

Nesrelle turned toward me, still standing precariously on the cliffside with her back to the tumultuous waves below. With a careless wave of her hand and a lilting laugh, she rolled her eyes. "I'm an Immortal. Of course I hear your thoughts. I *made* you, little empress."

I narrowed my eyes. I knew she didn't mean her statement literally, because it was only the Life-Giver who could create life, or so I'd been taught at the palace sanctuary. He was also the one who gifted the Alrenians with abilities like my mother's wisdom or her advisor Vionn's power to see and share visions revealing the truth. But he had failed to save my mother, and so, ever since her death, I'd ceased attending sanctuary services. I rarely tried to pray anymore. It all felt empty.

Now, the only immortal being who visited me was Nesrelle,

Queen of Death.

As much as Nesrelle's presence still chilled me, it was also becoming strangely comforting. *She* had given me answers. *She* had condemned the Forwyn's bloody actions. *She* had granted me enough power to fight back, had finally made me feel like I wasn't alone.

But I still couldn't quite keep the tremor out of my voice as I spoke. "Why are you here?"

Nesrelle smiled at me like she was a benevolent queen granting me my greatest desires. "To remind you of your purpose, my little Jalie." She strode toward me, her steps so graceful she could have been gliding above the ground. Her dress was long enough it trailed after her, rustling along the rocks. "It seemed at the Autumn Ball last night that you were allowing one of your enemies to distract you." She inclined her head, cold eyes assessing me, but when she spoke, her voice was gentle. "Are you so lonely that the first handsome face you find can sway you?"

I swallowed back my rising shame and anger. Anger at Kovi or myself, I couldn't even tell.

"I drugged him and threatened him to escape," I bit out, standing and shooting her with a glare. "I'm *here*, prepared to fight for my throne, prepared to kill or even die for it. How have I swayed from my purpose?"

Nesrelle's grin didn't slip. "I can hear your thoughts, remember? I can feel the way you've softened toward him." She sneered. "Don't forget what he told you. He's killed *your people*. He's not innocent. Don't think that his kindness toward you wasn't part of his game. A way to weaken you, trick you to become less of a threat to his people."

Despite myself, tears burned my eyes. Perhaps she wasn't entirely wrong: I *had* been aching with loneliness. Had I really fallen so low as to seek connection with one of my enemies? Was that all it had been?

I longed to believe Kovi's gentleness hadn't been an act. The soft brush of his fingertips as he'd wound them through my hair and pressed his lips to mine. His low, soothing voice chanting Forwyn words over me as I'd fought for my life against poison running through my veins. His steady gaze as he'd talked me through the panic I'd felt after witnessing the brutal execution of one of my people. The anger that had darkened his expression when he'd seen the bruises his father had left on my skin.

And his words: *I'm sorry, Jalie.*

"I know it hurts," Nesrelle murmured, grasping my chin with her cold fingers to tilt my face up to hers. A tear slipped down my cheek, and she wiped it away with her other hand. "I once fell for a human and lost everything. That's why I'm telling you that it's essential you stay strong. Don't let him trick you. It's *not* real."

She grasped my hands in hers, lifting them until we both stared down at my palms.

"The curse you carry, the one that will allow you to avenge your mother, your people, your empire…*that* is real. You felt its power flow through you when that traitorous Alrenian tried to murder you, didn't you?"

I nodded, my eyes still burning. Horror and guilt clawed at my stomach with the memory of the young woman's agonized screams and mangled face.

"Let this power fuel you," Nesrelle whispered. "You are strong, my little empress. Make your enemies pay. Make your mother proud. Save your people from Teramese *and* Forwyn tyranny. Resurrect the glory of the Alrenian Empire."

Her words flowed over me like a healing balm. Like my mother herself was speaking to me from the afterlife, urging me on with her strength and courage.

Nesrelle smiled softly. "Your mother's strength and courage lives on in you, Jalie."

I set my jaw, meeting Nesrelle's gaze with renewed determination.

Her eyes were like blue flames, sparking the embers of my heart.

"Rise, *Amara* Jaliana. Claim your throne."

I looked at Ryke, who was stirring at last, one of his large eyes blinking open to land on me lazily. He'd flown through most of the night, leaving him exhausted, but I was certain he'd want to hunt soon. Hunger pangs were already making me feel faint. I'd never had the chance to eat at the ball last night, which meant my last meal had been yesterday's lunch.

Turning back to Nesrelle, I squared my shoulders to hide my exhaustion and hunger. Even if she could read my thoughts. "Where do I go next?" I asked.

Nesrelle glanced inland, where I could just make out a cluster of smudges that could be a town. "You already passed Aramtih. So enter the town of Wynlaen. Let your presence be known to the people," she said with a daring smile. "Empresses do not cower. Make them bow. Make them tell you where your army waits."

The Aramith Mountains were to the north, appearing like jagged teeth pointing toward the sky as Ryke soared over the open stretch of grassland leading west, toward the town. Even after last night's long flight, even with uncertainty and pain clouding my thoughts and hunger hollowing my stomach, I still felt the familiar thrill that encompassed me whenever I was astride a dragon. Despite the rushing wind, the dragon scale armor I wore and the warmth of Ryke's body kept me comfortable. My eyes stung and watered, but I relished it, leaning into the wind as the town loomed closer.

Below, the buildings that had been only a series of distant forms moments ago were now laid out before us. Constructed of stone or thick beams of hardwood from the forest to the north, the shops and residences seemed like child's toys compared to the elegant, towering structures in the capital. A swift scan of the dirt streets revealed that most of the citizens were Alrenian. If the Forwyn government had ever made its presence known here, it wasn't evident now. They'd probably focused all their efforts on larger cities.

Hope made my heart soar all the way into my throat, but I forced the feeling back down. The memory of the Alrenian woman who'd tried to murder me was fresh in my mind. I knew I was just as likely to receive a hostile welcome from my own people—who might believe the Elders' lies and think I was working with those old, power-hungry Forwyn—as I was from the Forwyn themselves.

The Forwyn would want to murder me because they saw me as a threat. The Alrenians would want to kill me because they saw me as weak.

Somehow, I had to prove the Forwyn were right to fear me, and that the Alrenians should all unite behind me. I wondered if my own people would have to see my power to believe I was worthy of them. To see that I was determined to fight back, to never bow to the unworthy Forwyn again.

I shouted over the roaring wind to command Ryke to land, and he descended directly into the dirt-covered town square. An old, worn-looking statue of Emperor Vilrev stood in the center, glaring at the citizens, who stopped dead in their tracks. I scanned the crowd, my gaze lingering on the plainly clothed Forwyn with their shorn hair and downcast eyes—here, the Alrenians kept slaves openly and without fear of repercussions. This town definitely had been ignored by the Elders.

At booths around the perimeter of the square, vendors froze in the middle of calling out their sales and waving goods before potential customers. It looked like most of the wares were from larger cities like Aramith, and that perhaps the vendors traveled here on special days, for their carts were dirty, their clothes travel-stained, and it appeared most of the town was present, shopping.

The scent of roasted meat and spiced nuts hit me with such force I grew light-headed. I swallowed the saliva pooling in my mouth, forcing myself to focus not on my hunger but on the Alrenians.

"My people," I shouted, my voice carrying over the crowd. "I am your empress, Jaliana, daughter of Karye. I come seeking assistance in a matter of vital importance."

The Alrenians stared, expressions blank. And they were not kneeling.

I injected steel into my tone. "Who is your leader?" I demanded.

Do these worthless wretches think they are better than their Chosen Empress? It was Nesrelle's voice in my head, the sneer evident in her tone. *Make them bow, like you will make the Forwyn bow.*

Kowra, the treacherous Alrenian woman had called me, before I'd killed her with the curse I bore.

Plague. Monster. Abomination. Maybe it was time to show these Alrenians the horrifying, abominable power that flowed through my veins.

I set my jaw and leapt from my saddle.

"*Empress?*" came a taunting voice. A young man with sharp grey and gold eyes stepped forward. His smile was arrogant and lazy, but the rest of his face was set in hardened lines. I could almost smell the anger and bloodlust pouring off him. "You're a mockery to your

Alrenian heritage, little girl. You think because you flew in on a dragon you can impress or intimidate us?"

Before I could speak the words that would command Ryke to attack, two pairs of hands seized me, dragging me away from my dragon. A hand slapped over my mouth to stifle my cries. Despite my struggles, the two men who'd grabbed hold of me effortlessly shoved me to my knees in front of the grey-eyed man.

Hot fury sparked in my heart, building into a raging fire. My fingers tingled with the anticipation of using the curse inside me. If I could just get one hand free…

Behind me, Ryke snorted, plumes of smoke streaming from his nostrils. Despite his growing anger and the clear threat he posed, the townspeople seemed unfazed. Instead, two more men approached Ryke calmly, as if they would force him to submit to *them*.

The grey-eyed man, clearly some sort of leader in the town, drew a dagger from his belt and pointed it toward my face.

"You forfeited your throne when you chose to ally yourself with our enemies. When you lowered yourself, one of the Chosen People, by bowing down to those infidels." His lip curled in disgust. "I'm tempted to execute you for your crimes against your people right here, you worthless traitor."

I sucked in a breath, my chest heaving with my anger. Between the emotions churning through me and my lack of food, I was so light-headed I worried I'd pass out right there, collapsing prostrate in front of this disgusting man.

Focus, I chided myself.

Lifting my chin and glaring into the man's eyes, I spat at him. "You know *nothing* about me."

He barked out a harsh laugh. "Give me one reason to spare your life, little girl."

I forced more confidence into my tone than I felt. "My dragon and I can raze this town to the ground."

"Your dragon will be put in chains." The man smiled lazily. "So what threat do *you* pose alone? What value do you have?"

"You may have the loyalty of these townspeople," I said slowly, forcefully, "but you don't have the loyalty of all Alrenians. You know the throne is *my* birthright. Most will gladly rally behind me and fight with me to take back the empire. Most realize I can slay my enemies with a single touch, and that is enough to earn their respect."

The man's lips twitched, like he'd stopped himself from bursting into laughter again. "Are you sure about all that? Maybe you think the capital represents the rest of the empire. You haven't ventured outside Inalgoth to see how the rest of Alrenor truly feels." He leaned forward, lowering his voice almost conspiratorially. "Do *you* have an army, little girl?

I blinked at him, almost rolling my eyes at his implication. "*You*, hiding in this town, have an army?" I glanced around at the gathered townspeople, scoffing. "Is this your army?"

The man bit back another smile, shaking his head. "Let me show you what a real leader looks like."

CHAPTER FIVE

Lo

B Y THE TIME THE STORM had passed that afternoon, leaving palm fronds and branches littering the streets, I was standing outside The Imperial Dragon. The sweet, clean scent of rain lingered in the air, though it was already growing hot and humid again. Despite the fact that autumn had arrived and the days were relatively cooler than they'd been earlier in the year, Inalgoth was known for its perpetual heat. The dampness in the air made my curls frizz around my face and stick to the back of my sweaty neck. They weren't as comfortable as my braids had been, but they were freeing in their own way.

Sister Lo of the Circle of Serenity is dead, I thought bitterly. *It's best the ribbons Naina gave her and all the memories die with her.*

Thankfully, I'd been able to take the back exit away from the bodies out front, so I wasn't forced to pick my way around corpses and relive the horror of the Teramese army's march through the street.

Between the storm and the army's invasion, the streets were deserted. At every corner I turned, my heart thudded against my chest, but I found no sign of the Teramese soldiers. They must have settled in during the storm or gone on to report to the palace, to whoever was in charge now.

My limbs were heavy and my thoughts crowded as I swept down an alleyway, clinging to the walls of buildings the way I used to cling to shadows during a nightly run. It was strange, how I had never felt safe in this city, had always walked its streets alert and wary, but now I feared an entirely new enemy. It was a bit more terrifying to anticipate strangers in uniforms ready to slit my throat than Alrenians prepared to corner me—because at least I knew what to expect from Alrenians. I knew the sorts of gifts they possessed and their habits and their language. Everything about Teramyl was shrouded in mystery to me. Their motives, their language, their magic, their fighting methods. I couldn't rely on anything Caesiem had told me, since it was clear he'd been lying to everyone from the start.

Elhani, what do I do? I prayed out of habit before stopping myself. Elhani wouldn't listen to me. Mio'e and the others had every right to declare themselves blood avengers, hunt me down, and take my life. I had killed one of our own.

I knew to survive I had to keep moving, that my best chance was to leave Inalgoth behind forever and travel to Forwyth, but that seemed impossible.

Unless, I thought, *I have a dragon to fly me there.*

The very idea of approaching the palace again made my stomach churn. It was anyone's guess what I'd find there. I didn't have a weapon to defend myself, and I didn't like the idea of potentially having to kill once more. I couldn't stop seeing Wilvhe's wide eyes as the life seeped out of them.

Traitor. Vow-breaker.

I cringed and swiped the memories away. Slipping inside the Dragon Keep wouldn't be easy if the Teramese soldiers were monitoring it, but I was familiar with its layout and the dragons inside. Having fed and cared for them for long years as a palace slave, I was confident I could tame one.

I halted in the street to crane my neck, studying the palace that loomed over the city. It was a series of immaculate white buildings, sprawled across the highest point of the capital and surrounded by lush gardens. The Dragon Keep was nearby, a series of tunnels cutting downward into the earth. Outside, the arena where both the Alrenian and Forwyn governments had held public executions extended toward a cliff overlooking the city streets. There were no dragons clustered there now, no riders launching their mounts into the air to soar across Alrenor on patrol. Likely, all the Forwyn Dragon Keepers were dead, and the Teramese either hadn't yet tamed any dragons or didn't know how to get the great creatures to submit to them.

My heart pulsed wildly in my ears as I adjusted the pack on my shoulders.

I could do it, I thought. Even without Elhani's magic to make me vanish and conceal me from enemy eyes, I knew how to make myself invisible and silent. That was one skill all of Karye's slaves had possessed—if they hadn't, they usually hadn't survived for long. Slipping into a dragon's den would be simple. Once I had tamed a dragon, escaping would be even easier.

I hunkered down in an alley and turned my thoughts toward planning. All I had to do was stay invisible for a few more hours, and I could leave the waking nightmare that was Alrenor behind. Leave everything behind.

An ache tugged at my chest as memories of Mother and Edi

threatened to rise up in my mind, but I forced them away. I could take those images of my loved ones with me. I would carry them forever, no matter where I lived.

Just like I would always carry the guilt weighing on me.

Your people need you…

No, I told myself sharply. There was nothing I could do in Inalgoth now but linger and die.

It was time to let go.

Though the cool night air kissed my cheeks, sweat still trickled from my temple and slithered down my spine as I hefted myself up the wall. Each crevice between the stones served as perfect hand and footholds, but I had to move painstakingly slowly, my ears constantly listening for the guards' footsteps.

The Court of Elders may have angered me with their apathy toward my people's suffering, but the thought of strangers overthrowing them and seizing the empire made my stomach roil.

Not your problem, I thought furiously, despite the guilt squirming in my belly.

Sucking in a deep breath, I heaved myself cautiously over the edge of the wall to peer into the palace grounds. Dappled moonlight played along the grass, giving the garden a silver, ethereal glow. Palm fronds whispered in the breeze, carrying the scents of brine and citrus and flowers to my nose. A fountain burbled nearby, its peaceful sound contrasting sharply with the anxiety throbbing in my chest.

The even rhythm of footsteps pounded down one of the dirt paths, out of sight but approaching swiftly. With my heart in my throat, I swung first one leg and then another over the wall and shimmied hurriedly down. My work was far sloppier this time as my sandals scraped against the wall and I slipped more than once, sending pebbles skittering toward the ground. I cringed at each noise, hoping the guard wouldn't hear anything over the fountain and his or her own footsteps.

Breathing raggedly, I dropped to the bottom and hurled myself into a cluster of shrubs just before the guard rounded the path and came into sight. I crouched low, willing myself to become part of the shadows as I stared between the leaves at the Teramese man pacing toward the wall. Dressed in an all-black uniform just like the ones the soldiers in the streets had worn, he stood straight and tall. His bright gold eyes scanned the area sharply, and I couldn't tell if he was always that diligent on his rounds or if his search meant he'd heard me. I lowered my head, sinking even lower toward the ground. After another long, breathless moment, the guard stalked on, disappearing further down the path.

I gave myself a moment to let my pulse steady before I launched forward, darting from shadow to shadow as soundlessly as I could. Diving for cover whenever I heard footsteps. Praying to Elhani to protect me, even if I believed, deep in my bones, I was cast out and forgotten, a damned, traitorous soul he'd never listen to again.

At last, I reached the edge of the garden, where a narrow path led toward the arena and the Dragon Keep. Here I trod especially carefully, unable until the last moment to see if the Teramese had posted any guards at the mouth of the Keep's tunnel. I held my breath until I could peer across the flat expanse of the arena, but there was no one waiting for me. Just like the Forwyn and the Alrenians before them, the Teramese had clearly deemed posting guards at the Dragon Keep pointless. The dragons themselves were intimidating enough, and they probably didn't expect anyone to cross the grounds without being caught by the guards.

I couldn't help smirking to myself.

The flickering red torchlight made the rough cavern walls look bloody as I slipped into the Keep. Within, the air smelled of stale smoke and earth. It was heavy and hot and still, with only the distant echo of things stirring below. Likely the restless dragons, longing for someone to take them out to fly.

Expecting Teramese soldiers, I crept forward slowly until I reached the armory, where an assortment of Alrenian weapons and suits of dragon scale armor in all imaginable sizes hung from the walls. There was no one within, though another lit torch told me it couldn't have gone unoccupied for long. It was tempting to step inside and select some armor, but it seemed foolish to linger.

I pressed further into the tunnel, past more openings leading to dragon dens and the training arena, until the murmur of voices froze me in my tracks.

"I expected more dragons, to be honest," came a man's voice.

"They only breed once in their lifetimes, and the females usually only lay one egg at a time." This voice echoed off the tunnel walls and made my lungs seize. Anger rippled through my entire body, along with something else I quickly shoved aside, refusing to analyze.

Caesiem.

"The only reason the Alrenians have the number they do is because of the trades they made with Teramese dragon egg hunters, long before the barrier," Caesiem went on.

The other man snorted. "You know your history. I'm impressed."

"The Alrenians and Forwyn alike love to go on and on about the dragons." Caesiem paused. "Although, I can't blame them. As you saw, they're stunning creatures. What do you think?"

"Of the one you showed me? Definitely an impressive beast, Caes. Though I wonder, if both the Alrenians and Forwyn failed to tame it all this time, if it's worth the bother. I'm surprised they didn't slay the creature." The man chuckled darkly. "Or did they feed their enemies to it?"

My head buzzed. I remembered the dragon they were speaking of. Karos. He'd been wild and untamable, unpredictable and fierce. Beautiful and terrifying. A king among dragons. Though he'd slain plenty of the slaves who'd cared for him in my time at the palace, I'd always had a healthy respect for him. Perhaps he'd sensed that, because he hadn't ever harmed me when it was my turn to feed him.

Footsteps. Caesiem and his companion were walking up the tunnel, coming right toward me.

Run, I thought. *Return another time.* But my legs wouldn't move.

"Both races revere the dragons," Caesiem explained, his voice soft, full of his own awe. "And both were too proud to admit none of their Keepers could tame it. Neither Karye nor the Elders wanted to give up." He hesitated. "And yes, I think sometimes Karos was used in…executions."

Their voices were close, just around a bend. Heart pounding, I glanced around and discovered a natural alcove, concealed in shadows. I stepped into it and ducked, praying if I was still and quiet enough I would be hidden in the darkness. That Caesiem and whoever was with him would never even look my way.

"Do you think with your magic that you could tame him?" the other man asked Caesiem.

I froze. *Magic?*

More information Caesiem had withheld. My throat tightened. Had the way he'd looked at me, the way he'd kissed me, been a lie too? Had he been sincere when he'd tried to convince me to run away with him? And where had he intended to go, when clearly he'd been planning all along to betray everyone he knew in Alrenor? Surely all his charming words had been a lie.

"I think so," Caesiem said, and he and his companion stepped into my line of vision. He paused midstep, in perfect view for me to study him—and also, if he turned and looked carefully, for him to see me. Torchlight made his bronzed skin glow and his bright blue eyes glisten as he turned toward the man at his side. There was clear swelling where I'd punched him last night, and the sight filled me with satisfaction. Both he and the other man were clothed in black Teramese uniforms, with silver symbols embroidered on their shoulders. I couldn't tell what the design was from my position.

The other man appeared to be in his thirties, still young enough to be handsome. His skin was a bit darker than Caesiem's, like he'd recently spent a lot of time out in the sun, and his eyes were a startling shade of violet, intense and beautiful. His black hair was curlier than Caesiem's, but trimmed even shorter and neatly combed back. There was authority in his posture, in the way he studied his surroundings, as if he'd always received everything he ever wanted and expected the world to keep giving to him.

He turned to Caesiem and smirked. "Lord Caesiem Xalenos, Royal Mage extraordinaire. I don't doubt it. Why be so modest?"

My heart pounded. *Lord?*

Caesiem grinned and shook his head. "Not everyone can be as full of themselves as you are, Revaed," he said with a laugh.

The man called Revaed made a show of pretending to scowl at Caesiem and then shoved him. Caesiem was ready, playfully elbowing him back. Dissolving into laughter, Revaed ruffled Caesiem's hair in a way I'd expect a father or older brother to.

For an instant, my chest felt hollow. I'd had my mother for a short time, and Naina had been like a mother figure during my time at the abbey, but I'd never known the love of a father. What Caesiem appeared to have…this familial affection…I couldn't quite help the envy and wistfulness that clawed my heart at the sight. I couldn't help but wonder, as I had countless times over the years, what it would be like to know my father. If only Mother had shared his name. If only I could find out if he was even still alive…

My thoughts were interrupted as, at that moment, Caesiem's gaze shifted over Revaed's shoulder and landed directly on me.

My breath caught in my chest as Caesiem's eyes widened. I curled my fingers into fists, my mind immediately flying through possible methods of escape. But none looked promising. I might be a fast runner, but I doubted I could pull the lever to lift one of the doors to a dragon den and get the creature to submit to me before the men caught me. I couldn't reach out toward Elhani's voice and use his magic, for the song that had always whispered around me had fallen silent. Lost in my loud, tangled thoughts—or, more likely, closed off to me for turning my back on my vows as a nun.

I was cornered.

But rather than charge toward me or say something to Revaed, Caesiem turned away casually and started strolling toward the tunnel opening. "Are you finally going to rest now?" he asked, slipping his hands into his pockets.

"Yes, I'm exhausted," Revaed sighed. "I'd recommend you get some sleep too."

Caesiem halted abruptly, causing pebbles to skitter along the path. "You know, there's something I need to try. You go on ahead. I'll see you in the morning."

Revaed studied Caesiem, concern knotting his brow. "Impressive magic or no, I don't like leaving you alone with that dragon."

Caesiem waved away his concerns. "I'll be fine. I won't do anything ridiculous, but it's better if I try taming Karos myself. It'll be too much to try protecting us both at the same time." His smile must have convinced Revaed, whose stature relaxed visibly.

"All right," Revaed said. "Be careful, Caes."

Caesiem turned back. He tossed a casual "goodnight" over his shoulder, and then Revaed was disappearing up the tunnel as Caesiem halted in front of me.

I set my jaw, straightening my spine and meeting him face-to-face.

"What are you doing here?" Caesiem demanded.

Breathing a curse, I pulled back my arm, gathering my strength for a punch. But either my anger made me slow, or Caesiem knew me too well. He was faster, seizing both my wrists before I could land a strike.

His hands were unexpectedly gentle, as if we were still friends and not bitter enemies. Even worse was the jolt that went through me at his touch, at the sensation of his warm breath on my face. Of the sight of him standing so close to me, bringing to mind the memory of his mouth on mine.

I growled low in my throat, possibly even angrier at myself than I was at him. "None of your business, *Lord Xalenos.*"

"It's not safe," he went on. "If you're found here, looking like you're trying to steal a dragon, you could be killed."

"Oh really?" I crossed my arms. "You're worried about my safety now? I can't believe you're keeping up that act. Aren't the lies a little obvious now that you've betrayed *everyone?*"

A sound must have caught his attention over my voice. He inhaled sharply. "Quiet!" he hissed, tugging me against him and clamping a hand over my mouth.

"Caesiem?" called Revaed, his footsteps echoing toward us. "Did you say something?"

My stomach lurched. I tried to stomp on Caesiem's foot, but he seemed to anticipate my move an instant before I tried it—he had trained alongside the sisters and me for a time, after all. He knew our defensive strategies.

Revaed stepped into view and lifted his eyebrows in mild surprise. "You caught one," he said, like I was an animal they'd been hunting.

"Revaed…" Caesiem sounded almost pleading. "She's no danger. She used to feed the dragons…she missed them…"

I couldn't help it—I blinked in shock. He was going to try to sell Revaed some lie about me just sneaking into the Dragon Keep, risking my life among the Teramese invaders, simply because I *missed* visiting with the dragons?

Why was he even trying to lie for me?

Light dawned in Revaed's eyes. "Oh, I see. She's one of your vigilante friends, isn't she?" His eyes scanned me from head to toe. My blood boiled, taking me back to my helpless years as a palace slave. To all the times I'd been stared at like I was either dirt to be disposed of or a treat to be devoured.

Though Revaed's gaze seemed merely curious, not overtly hostile or lustful, I glowered. There was no compassion in his eyes. I was sure, if I didn't prove useful, he'd kill me without a second thought. The way I was sure he'd slain the Elders last night.

"Guards!" Revaed called, and two sets of footsteps charged down the tunnel. They must have been waiting for him nearby, though it shocked me to think I'd probably passed them earlier, completely unaware. Of course, they hadn't noticed me either. Likely, they'd been chatting and wasting time in one of the rooms off the main tunnel of the Keep, shamefully letting down their guard when they were supposed to be on duty.

Now, unruffled and not even out of breath, both men paused on either side of Revaed for their orders.

Revaed gestured to me. "Take this girl to Caesiem's rooms. Be sure they're secure so she can't escape, but don't harm her. Don't worry about escorting us—I'll have a private talk with Lord Xalenos before we turn in tonight."

Caesiem didn't offer an ounce of resistance as the guards came forward to lead me away.

CHAPTER SIX

Caesiem

"WHY DID YOU LIE TO me?" Revaed's frown was more bewildered than angry, but I knew from his rigid stance that his anger could easily come soon enough.

I scratched the back of my neck, and waved vaguely in the direction the guards had taken Lo. "I knew you'd see her as an enemy infiltrating your territory—and you're not wrong," I added quickly, holding up a hand when Revaed opened his mouth to object. "If I didn't do something, you'd have her killed on the spot, and…" I shifted on my feet.

She only wants to help her people, I thought. Other excuses followed in quick succession: *She is as kind as she is brave and strong and fierce. Her heart is full of goodness. She might hate me, but I can never hate her.* And the most painful admission of all: *If she died, a light would go out in the world and I don't know what I'd do…*

The words swirled through my brain, but I couldn't vocalize them. Didn't know how to put the way I felt into words, to make Revaed understand. I didn't know if he *could* understand. He saw the Forwyn and Alrenians alike as subjects, people who must bow down to him or suffer the consequences. His priority was Teramyl.

He didn't know the Forwyn people like I did.

But before I could finish my sentence, Revaed was chuckling, an affectionate warmth glinting in his eyes. "I was right, wasn't I? She was one of the Forwyn you worked with when pretending to be a rebel? One of your vigilantes?"

Nodding, I rubbed at my bruised face self-consciously, still remembering the sting of Lo's strike. It was only an echo of the pain I felt from her hatred.

"You care about her," Revaed said. "I thought you were just mesmerized by a pretty face, but you have *feelings!*" He chuckled again, not seeming upset at all, merely curious. "All those Teramese girls we hosted at parties and, other than..." His voice drifted off, an uncomfortable memory tugging at us both as he cleared his throat. "Well, other than *her*...you weren't impressed until you found a foreigner."

I couldn't relax the tension in my shoulders, but I smiled, scuffing my boots across the floor and drumming a finger against my leg. Though my guardian sincerely cared about me, I wasn't sure he would make an exception to Teramese law for me. He might hate to punish her, to see me hurt, but he'd also view Lo as a threat to our safety.

"You do realize I can't have citizens creeping through my Dragon Keep at all hours of the night," Revaed went on, making my gut tighten with the words I'd already expected to come. "She *did* commit a crime." He frowned. "And I know she didn't just miss the dragons, Caes."

I cringed as he brought up my ridiculous attempt at a lie. "We don't know her intentions were against us..." I began, which was foolish. She'd been hiding in the Dragon Keep. She'd joined a cause to save her people and then punched me in the face when I'd betrayed that cause.

"You'll be questioning her," Revaed interrupted. "It's why I had the guards take her to your rooms. That's better than the prison. No one else will be allowed near her." He stroked his jaw, thinking. "To be honest, I'm glad you found…a friend, and some measure of happiness here in Alrenor. It wasn't easy sending you ahead to this strange land."

Laughter threatened. A friend? *Happiness?* The woman I cared about hated me, and guilt and doubt wouldn't stop eating me alive. I wasn't sure what I felt.

Oblivious to my thoughts, Revaed continued. "She'll have to remain under constant guard. Maybe she'll agree to be a part of the alliance we want to forge." He grinned benevolently, like he was speaking about a stray dog. "You can keep her."

I swallowed back the burning sensation rising in my throat. I couldn't *keep* her. I couldn't let Lo be trapped in the palace again, a prisoner in the place that haunted her the most. I couldn't keep her from her sisters—if she'd even be permitted to go back to them—or the streets she loved to run through.

I would rather never see Lo again than *keep* her.

But for now, the only way to spare her life was to go along with Revaed, until I could piece together a better plan.

Nodding, I bid Revaed goodnight, striding out of the Keep ahead of him. I could still hear his chuckles echoing along the tunnel as I stepped out into the fresh night air. I wondered how much harder he would have laughed if he knew the woman I had feelings for was a nun.

I'd expected Lo to lash out at me as soon as my door swung inward, but my rooms were silent and still. Not a single candle burned, leaving the shadows to stretch across the floor, extending toward me like greedy claws. I crossed the sitting room and paused in the entrance to the bedchamber, where moonlight pooled across the lush carpet.

Lo stood near the window, her back to me. Her outfit was simple, but in muted shades of brown rather than the grey I'd grown accustomed to seeing her in. The grey that had marked her as a nun. Instead of braids woven with colorful ribbons, she wore her hair loose, her dark curls spiraling around her shoulders. They were a little wild and unkempt after she'd snuck through the palace grounds, and I almost smiled. It suited her.

Lo whirled around as I stepped forward, her eyes flashing with hatred, her chin lifted in defiance. My stomach dropped. It hurt to look at her, to recall what it had felt like to hold her in my arms.

I'd been a fool to hope anything could ever happen between us. *Even if she didn't hate you, she's a nun, you idiot,* I reminded myself.

Instead of shouting or attacking me outright, Lo watched me warily, her stance ready but controlled. For now.

"Why am I not in the dungeons?" she demanded. Her eyes scanned my rooms. "Why…here? What else could you possibly want from me?"

Not the first question I'd expected. I cleared my throat. "Revaed wants me to question you. You're not…exactly a prisoner."

Lo laughed harshly, crossing her arms.

I held up my hands. "All right, you sort of are, but the alternative would have been a swift execution right there in the Keep. The

Teramese don't waste a lot of time when it comes to doling out punishment to criminals."

"Criminals?" she scoffed.

"Well…to Revaed, you are one. He doesn't know any better. I know you wouldn't…" I couldn't meet her gaze. "He would have killed you. That's why I came back when I saw you. There were other guards nearby. I couldn't let anyone else see you."

She narrowed her eyes, eyes that could shine with such kindness and warmth when she served her people, but now glittered with malice. "Maybe I would have preferred death to imprisonment."

Sighing, I crossed over to the settee and sank onto it, unbuttoning my jacket. Having gone as long as I had without sleep, my eyes burned and my entire body ached with exhaustion. All I wanted was to sink into unconsciousness, where I could shove aside the weight of guilt.

"We'll speak about this in the morning," I said gruffly, my eyes darting to the balcony doors, the windows set within them revealing a guard posted right outside. Those Revaed had assigned to patrol duty had certainly taken their tasks to heart. I doubted even Lo could slip past a man directly in her path.

Lo stormed toward me. "No, *Lord* Xalenos." Each time she spoke my title, it was with mockery. It made a mound of bitterness form in my stomach. She didn't know what the Xalenos family had done for me. She couldn't understand…

"You might be used to everyone obeying your orders," she went on, "but not me. If you want to question me, question me in the dungeons. I don't want you pretending I owe you something by keeping me here."

For the first time, my anger flared. Gods, I was too tired for this. "I'm *not* sending you to the dungeons. If you go to the dungeons, any other soldier could take it upon themselves to question you, to torture you." I finished unbuttoning my jacket and tossed it to the floor like a petulant child. With a quick tug, I had my undershirt off as well. I leaned back on the settee and kicked off my boots, letting each hit the floor with a muted thud. "Revaed ordered you here, so here is where you will stay."

Lo's gaze dropped to my bare torso before she quickly averted her eyes, and for a half-second, I was foolishly pleased. As if her finding me attractive meant anything anymore.

She drew a deep breath, likely preparing to voice the thousands of questions that were no doubt buzzing through her mind. But all she asked was: "Why?" Her voice cracked. "Why did you invade Alrenor?"

I swallowed against the sudden dryness in my throat, yet I didn't glance away from her piercing gaze. "Because my people are dying, Lo. And your government would do nothing to help us."

She shook her head, scowling. "You lived among my people. Claimed to sympathize with our plight—and then you let soldiers in to *slaughter* us. You pretended to be an orphan, someone who'd tasted suffering like us, but you're just a pretentious lord who thinks he's entitled to whatever power he wants."

"No," I cut in quietly. "I didn't lie. I was an orphan. I did steal to survive. I…" My words drifted away as I finally dropped my eyes. Even as I stared off into the shadowy corner of this too-large room, I could feel the burn of her accusing stare. "I'm not having this conversation tonight," I said, this time more harshly. "Hate me if you must, but like it or not, I'm not sending you out there to give Revaed a reason to kill you. And stay up all night if you wish, but I'm going to sleep. You can have the bed."

As if she didn't have the energy to argue anymore either, Lo stalked away. Silence settled heavily.

I stretched out on my back, finding the settee about as roomy as the bed I'd left behind at The Broken Crown. Even its pillows were plusher and more comfortable than the ones I'd used there.

Lo sat on the bed across from me, her spine rigid, her eyes searching the shadows.

My stomach twisted with guilt when I remembered the way she had spoken of her memories about the palace. I knew the nightmares haunted her, waking and sleeping, to this day. I'd been so caught up in protecting her from Revaed tonight, I'd nearly forgotten.

"I know you could try to escape as soon as I fall asleep, but… Just stay, please," I whispered into the darkness. "Just for tonight. Tomorrow, I'll explain. Give me time to show Revaed you're no danger, and you can go free without any soldiers to block your path."

Lo said nothing.

"You have every right to hate me," I went on. "But let me do this one thing for you. Please."

Still she did not speak, but I saw her shadowy form lie down, drawing the covers over her.

CHAPTER SEVEN

Kovi

THOUGH ALL THE DOORS WERE heavily guarded, slipping alone into a private palace bedroom—clearly one belonging to a servant in its functional simplicity—was still a relief. For a few brief moments, I was able to draw deep, relaxing breaths and slump against the wall. I could let my weariness and doubt, my anger and pain, flood through me.

Lift your head, Kovi.

I'd been so young when I'd been taken from the palace, sent to serve as a noble family's slave instead, that it was one of the only things I remembered my mother saying to me.

Though Mother's voice had faded over the years, though her face was only a blurred memory slipping through my fingers—I could feel her presence in moments like these. Her simple reminder to lift my head came to me often, her way of telling me to put away the pains of the past and present and to focus on Elhani's promises for the future. Even if, sometimes, I feared most of those promises for goodness and rest wouldn't come until I reached the Golden After and could wrap

Mother in my arms again.

Blinking, I stared at the ribbons braided around my wrist, focusing on the orange one that stood for loyalty. For now, I could only see one path forward, and like a faithful soldier, I would follow it. I hoped Elhani would guide me in a new direction if it was wrong, if it wasn't what would be best for my people.

Straightening, I sought out the tiny adjoining washroom, where the Teramese had already drawn me a bath. I stiffened at the sight of the black uniform laid out for me, even though I'd expected it. Resigned myself to it.

I tore off my grimy clothes, foul with sweat and dirt and blood that wasn't my own. Sinking into the steaming water, I let my aching muscles relax, let myself savor the sensation of scrubbing off the layers of muck and gore. Despite how soothing the water felt, I didn't waste time. As soon as I was sure I'd removed the last of the dirt, I stepped out, dried myself off, and tugged on the Teramese uniform.

It fit perfectly.

Body tense, I cleaned my teeth and stared at the face looking back at me in the mirror. My eyes seemed dim and harsh, as if they belonged to someone else. Though mixed emotions still churned within me, my resolve was solid.

You know what is best for your people. Jalie is raising an army that will just as quickly kill Forwyn as well as Teramese. You know what you have to do.

Those were the words Father would say. Those were the words that rang out loudest in my mind, in his powerful, uncompromising voice.

At the same time, Jalie's words wouldn't stop echoing in my head. I couldn't stop seeing the way she'd looked as she'd threatened me with a dagger and prepared to escape on Ryke. *My people always come first. Just like your people will always come first for you.*

My chest ached as I strapped on my belt and attached the Teramese sword they'd left for me. I knew it wasn't a symbol of trust, as they'd never leave me unmonitored, but it was still reassuring to feel the familiar weight of a blade at my side.

There is no room for mercy in war.

I wondered if she could be wrong. If agreeing to this mission could be my chance to find a way to save both her and my people.

But if I had to make a choice between my people and her…

I'd already failed that test once before, hadn't I?

Drawing a breath, I left the washroom, passing the breakfast that had been set out for me and heading straight toward the door that led out to the hall. When I opened it, Vander, the Teramese officer who had been assigned to accompany me in my search, offered me a tight-lipped smile. He was young, not much older than myself, but he carried himself with self-assurance. A soldier who knew his abilities.

"Ready to find a runaway empress?" he asked.

Find and dispose of her. The clear order from Lord Xalenos weighed on me like a physical burden, stealing my breath.

Sometimes, we have to be monsters, Jalie had said.

I was no stranger to being a monster.

Falling into step beside Vander, I passed a handful of guards, who all looked out of place beside the garish Alrenian paintings and looming statues of emperors and empresses long dead. My boots thudded against polished marble, walking halls Mother and Father and countless other palace slaves had crept through for years.

I couldn't help the questions that pulled at my brain, always wondering about Mother's time here. Once, she'd found love, despite the odds. She and Father had only managed to both remain at the palace by concealing their relationship. I'd spent three years here, never knowing my father. But a mother couldn't bear a child, nurse and raise one, without Empress Karye growing tired of their bond as well. She saw relationships between her slaves as a threat, and, as she did to so many other families, she tore us apart by selling me.

In a way, Mother had been dead to me long before Karye had slit her throat.

Vander stopped outside a thick wooden door, carved with the Alrenian swirling sun insignia and dragons in flight, and rapped on its surface. After a beat, shuffling footsteps approached, and the door swung inward just enough to reveal half of my father's face. Dark eyes narrowed and face set as hard as stone, he assessed first Vander and then me for a long moment.

I noticed the instant his gaze darted to the uniform I wore and then back to my face. There wasn't any judgement there, only a flicker of something that, for a moment, I thought might be shame.

"Come in, Kovi," he said gruffly, opening the door wider.

As soon as I was inside, Father shut the door with an echoing thud and spun toward me, his expression tense. His short, greying curls were damp, and he was dressed in fresh clothes, a pair of plain linen pants and a loose shirt. Alrenian clothes, rather than Teramese. Perhaps they were ones he'd found in these quarters once the soldiers had freed him from his cell. "*What* is happening?" he demanded. "Are they truly accepting our surrender?"

I stood motionless, keeping my face blank. "Our lives have been spared. For now."

His lips thinned. "I'd held onto hopes of negotiating an…alliance with them. But once we were locked up in those dungeons, I didn't think they had anything but a public execution planned for us."

My heart sank, even though I couldn't judge him. After all, I was working with the Teramese too. Our hands were tied—either we conceded to their terms, or we died. "I've made an agreement with them," I explained, my tone formal. "They want me to find Empress Jaliana. She escaped to gather an army, and therefore, poses a threat to the Teramese too. In serving them, I serve the Forwyn, and the Teramese will spare our lives."

My father glanced away, running a hand through his damp hair and sighing. "Find and kill her?" He turned back, searching my eyes for weakness.

Though my throat tightened, I gave him a single sharp nod.

His eyes darted to my sword before returning to my face. "Do you have the strength of will to do what needs to be done, soldier?"

Anger stiffened my body, but otherwise, I didn't react. I knew he was thinking about yesterday morning, when he'd burst into Jalie's room to find me curled in bed beside her. She'd merely wanted the comfort of someone close. And maybe I had been weak, to be so ready to soothe her. To brush back her hair and speak gentle words when she was panicked, to watch and pray over her when she'd been poisoned, to lean in and kiss her when she'd been trying to drug me.

But I couldn't regret mercy. I could still feel the echo of the pain screaming through her heart when she'd watched one of her people consumed in dragon fire. Could sense her fear and rage when she looked at my father. Could see the bruises marking her skin from where my father had hurt her in his outbursts.

There is no room for mercy in war.

Jalie had chosen her people, and I had to choose mine. It was as simple and terrible as that. As simple as taking her life to save countless Forwyn ones…if there was no other way.

But there had to be another way.

Simple. I repeated the word over and over to myself, as if the chant would make it as easy as I wished it could be, as easy as it would have been to slay any other enemy in a fight.

"I will do whatever needs to be done to protect our people," I vowed, returning Father's steady stare.

He frowned. "Even after all your talk of mercy?"

My eye twitched as my anger flared brighter. "There are honorable ways to conduct yourself, even in war. Even against an enemy," I said in a low voice. "I can't believe you loved Mother, yet never learned that from her. She hated needless violence." I drew in a deep breath, trying to keep my body from visibly trembling. "Striking and tormenting Jalie was stooping to Karye's level, Father. She and her lackeys took joy in cruelty, in making those she hated suffer. I thought we were better than them. I thought *you* were better than them."

Something dark flashed in Father's eyes, but I didn't let him interrupt.

"If I *must* slay Jalie to save our people, then so be it. I can still make it quick and merciful." I swallowed the thickness building in my throat, the bitter taste on my tongue that told me my bold statement was probably a lie. I *had* to find another way, one that could spare her. But I pressed on, keeping my voice level. "That is the difference between myself and our enemies. I kill only when I have to, and I don't do it for some sick pleasure. I do it to protect the ones I care about."

Though I'd never succumbed to angry outbursts like Father, my words made me feel sick, like the worst kind of hypocrite. Images flashed through my mind of bloody deaths and the wide, horrified eyes of my victims. Snatches of rage and pain and grief swirled inside my heart, threatening to overwhelm me with the way they constantly made me taste death. Vicious deaths at cruel hands—*my* hands.

But I carefully concealed my inner turmoil, as a true soldier should. Father couldn't see, couldn't know, and he was too furious at the heated words I'd fired at him. A vein pulsed in his forehead and he stepped forward, opening his mouth as if to shout at me.

I raised my hand to silence him. "I'm here for information," I said, stopping his tirade before it could begin. "Since I know you want Jalie dead as much as anyone, I expect you'll be eager to help me."

Grunting, he crossed his arms. "Go on."

"As I said, last night, she stole a dragon and fled northward. I don't believe she has information about where Alrenian insurgents are gathered, but she must have a guess. I need a place to start looking for her. Somewhere in Alrenor that she could have reached by now, where the Forwyn hold is weak or nonexistent. A small town, perhaps, that the Dragon Keepers rarely patrolled and where you didn't dispatch guards or soldiers. A place she would feel safe."

Father turned away, his face thoughtful.

"She didn't have any provisions, so she'd need to seek help and food quickly."

He smirked, just a little. "Yes, I don't expect a haughty little empress would spend much time living off the land. She'd use that dragon to terrorize the first people she found and start making demands." He tapped a finger against his chin. "If she flew all night, there is a town just west of the Aramith Mountains, a little to the north of Aramith itself, called Wynlaen. We had to focus on quelling the uprisings in Hemlaen, Aramith, and Brema, but I imagine some of the surviving insurgents would have fled to that town.

"We'd begun to suspect the Alrenians were hiding soldiers in the mountains, even. We were amassing forces to explore the region..." Father's smile was humorless. "But as you know, we were interrupted."

I nodded. "Thank you," I said stiffly.

Father's expression darkened and his voice turned rough. "Don't let a pretty face sway you again. Kill the whore. And remember, you don't serve the Teramese."

As if I'd ever forget.

Rather than offer him an ounce of deference for his former position as Elder, I spun on my heel and left him standing there speechlessly as I strode from the room, slamming the door behind me.

"Ah, good to hear it's close," Vander said as soon as I told him Wynlaen would be our first destination. "Lord Xalenos doesn't want us to waste time taming a dragon—since none are familiar with us, it would likely take weeks or months. We're to leave immediately, on horseback."

Though my entire body longed to sag with weariness, I'd been trained better than that. I stood straight and proud, nodding silently and following Vander at a swift clip through the palace, into the gardens, and toward the stables.

In no time at all, we were thundering through Inalgoth's streets, where every building sat still and quiet. No citizen, Forwyn or Alrenian, stirred outside their homes. A few peeked warily out of windows as we rode by, but everywhere I looked, Teramese soldiers patrolled. They crawled all over the city like ants, overtaking everything. It made my heart pound painfully against my ribs to see their numbers. How had we been so blind?

Because we were preparing for a different war, I thought grimly.

We'd already been outnumbered by the Alrenians, but at least we'd had the dragons. Now, I wasn't sure that even Elhani's blessings and magic could give us an advantage. I worried this was a fight my people could not win.

CHAPTER EIGHT

ALMOST THERE, EMPRESS," THE ALRENIAN general—a man the others called Zerik—called with a taunting grin.

I wasn't sure I wanted to know what his destination was, or what fate awaited me there. Along with an entire host of men and women, all heavily armed and dressed in leathers and heavy cloaks to warm them in the cold of the Aramith Mountains, we'd spent most of the day riding up a treacherous path.

Shackles bit into my wrists, attached to a chain that was secured to my horse's saddle. Except for an occasional break in which one of the women—whose name I learned was Daedra—had led me away for privacy to relieve myself, I'd been chained to the horse all day. My muscles ached, and the skin along my wrists was chafed and bleeding. The Alrenians had given me a few gulps of water now and then, along with a hunk of crusty bread, but not enough to truly alleviate my hunger or thirst. My head ached and my body felt weak.

I longed for the freedom to fight back, to flee to Ryke and show these wretches what a dragon could do to their forces, but Ryke was as much a prisoner as I was.

He hadn't submitted to the young Alrenian man who'd chained him, which meant neither he nor any of the other Alrenians could ride him, but all day, Ryke didn't resist them either. As we'd trekked toward the mountains, I'd noticed that each man and woman wore a vial filled with clear liquid from a leather cord about their necks. Vylae. Apparently, even without coating their leathers in it, the poisonous substance had a strong enough scent—undetectable to human noses— that my dragon had fallen completely under their spell. He was docile and almost sluggish as he trod alongside their ranks, snuffling smoke and blinking his eyes slowly, as if ready to curl up and sleep at the first sign of stopping.

Rage curled in my belly. Seeing my beautiful dragon chained and used by these traitors was sickening. As sickening as their refusal to respect me.

For a while, I'd shouted and cursed at them, but Zerik and his forces only laughed at me.

"Missing your palace, empress?" Daedra, who rode beside me, jeered.

Later, I'd calmed myself enough to try to reason with them, to explain that I'd been seeking an army to lead against Teramese invaders. None of them believed my words. At last, Zerik wearied of me, and ordered his soldiers to gag me. The man who shoved the strip of cloth into my mouth and secured it behind my head seemed to take particular pleasure in the task.

"That'll shut you up, little bird," he'd sneered.

Now, I was exhausted and despondent. Nesrelle's voice whispered in my mind: *Make them bow.* But I was powerless.

I was as trapped and humiliated as I'd been by the Court of

Elders.

Shivering, I studied my surroundings. Night had fallen, and fog slithered over the mountain peaks like a serpent, wrapping me in its cold embrace. The chill seeped into everything, making my teeth chatter despite the warmth of my dragon scale armor and the cloak one of the Alrenians had thrown over me hours ago. I stared at the point where the snowy tips of the Aramith range disappeared into the mist. Most of the sky was blotted out too, making the world a dim haze with only a bit of silver light to see by.

We weren't high enough to reach the snow yet, but I could smell a cool dampness that I attributed to it. Mingling with that scent was another new one: the crisp odor from the pines lining our path, each one extending high overhead until they vanished into the fog.

Having never seen or smelled snow in my life, I couldn't help my excitement as I wondered if we'd venture high enough for me to experience it.

Childish, I reprimanded myself. I needed to focus on my predicament. On a way I could either garner these people to my side, or free Ryke and myself.

At last, we crested a rise in the narrow dirt path. Numerous imprints of horse hooves proved this way was well-traveled. From his place at the front of the procession, Zerik paused his horse and glanced over his shoulder. I didn't like the way his teeth gleamed in the shadows as his eyes met mine.

"Here we are, empress."

My mount stopped alongside Daedra's, and I caught a view of the region spread out before us. Tucked in a grassy valley between the mountain we were on and the one towering ahead of us, mostly concealed by the wisps of fog drifting through the air, was a huge encampment. Fires pierced the darkness, promising light and warmth, but the rows of tents gave me pause.

This was an army.

"Like I said," Zerik went on. Though I kept my eyes trained on the glimpses of the camp I could see below, I could hear the smile in his voice. "Do *you* have an army?"

I bit down on my gag, trying to conceal the rising anger and panic flowing through me. If Zerik had this army's allegiance, did he intend to usurp my throne? Was he planning to use me, as the Elders had, or was he preparing to murder me in front of his soldiers?

Zerik led us forward, the company winding its way down a steep, graveled path to the valley. Behind me, Ryke's heavy steps dislodged rocks and shook the ground, making the way even more treacherous and difficult for our steeds to navigate. Shreds of mist wound about us like ghosts, leaving droplets on my armor. I repressed another shiver.

After a long while, we drew close enough that the stillness gave way to the sounds of camp, and the view was clearer. Below the fog, the tents seemed to stretch on endlessly, rows of men and women in leathers pacing the rows or sitting about the glowing fires. Maybe they'd been expecting Zerik and his company tonight, because it seemed as if far more were awake than asleep.

This time, a chill that had nothing to do with the cold air swept through me.

My heart pounded as we descended the last stretch of mountain and entered the camp. Everywhere, soldiers stood straight at the sight of Zerik, extending their hands palm upward in a gesture of submission. It was an old, traditional Alrenian salute, meant to show others that the person was unarmed and not a threat. After years among the Forwyn, I'd almost forgotten what it looked like for someone to offer a true salute.

Mother, I've failed, I thought, remembering the proud, fierce way my mother had always commanded the attention and respect of everyone in a room. No one had questioned her strength or power. Allies and enemies alike had feared her. *How can I guide and defend my people if they don't even want or respect me?*

The realization stung. I was as weak and useless as I'd feared. The Forwyn Elders had turned me into the laughingstock of Alrenor, into someone even my own people saw as a weak child. Not the daughter of Karye. Not a fierce dragon tamer or warrior. Not a protector. Not a Chosen Empress.

But the Life-Giver chose me, not Zerik. He isn't meant for this role. He isn't right. I breathed deeply through my nose, trying to calm my racing pulse and swirling emotions. To think clearly. There had to be a way out of this. There had to be a way the Life-Giver would help me to step into my birthright. *Or...if not him, then Nesrelle. Nesrelle chose me. She believes in me.*

Despite my lingering fear and doubt surrounding the Queen of Death, this knowledge bolstered me. As I thought about it, the power from the curse I carried hummed through my veins.

I am not weak or useless. And I never will be again, I vowed.

As our company passed through camp, clods of mud flying up beneath our horses' hooves, I refused to look away from the soldiers' piercing stares. Everyone studied me openly, taking in my ragged appearance and the flashing dragon scale armor I'd put on so proudly only the night before. Some seemed merely curious, but most sneered, their lips curling nastily, their eyes glinting with hatred and bloodlust.

Rather than feeling relieved to be among my own people, to see ranks of soldiers ready for battle to retake our empire, I felt a shock of grief. Though I'd known some of my own people hated me, seeing it written so plainly on countless faces made me ache. Those I'd always dreamt of defending and leading, the ones I'd pledged my heart and loyalty to, had turned their backs on me.

Murmurs rose through the ranks of soldiers as we trekked further, until we reached a patch of empty grass left before a roaring fire and the largest tent I'd seen yet. Clearly, it belonged to Zerik. Soldiers followed us, clustering about until a crowd formed. I searched the camp for a sign of Ryke, but one of the Alrenians had led him to the shadowy outskirts and I couldn't catch sight of him. My stomach sank.

Zerik leapt off his horse and signaled to a man, who came forward to take his steed away. Others in the procession followed suit, until Daedra unshackled me from my own mount. Halting just before the roaring fire to warm his hands, Zerik assessed the remaining soldiers, an arrogant smirk playing on his lips.

"We have an important visitor today, troops!" he called out, his booming voice rolling over the crowd and thundering through my chest. "Please, take a moment to warmly welcome Her Imperial Majesty." The mockery in his tone made my blood sizzle as Daedra shoved me to Zerik's side.

I lifted my chin and stared straight back at the men and women gawking at me, their fingers fiddling with the wickedly curved daggers at their sides, the firelight making their golden skin shine against the night. One man flashed me a smile, but it was all teeth, a silent threat. A woman licked her lips as if she couldn't wait to taste my blood.

Despite the chill enveloping me, I refused to let them see me tremble. I didn't want to emphasize that I might just be everything they hated: weak and cowardly. Everything that would have made my mother ashamed.

"We've waited three long years for you to join our ranks, empress," Zerik went on, his tone low and deadly. He yanked a dagger from the sheath at his side, twirling it between his fingers. In the firelight, it sparkled a deep, fiery orange. "I think I can speak for all

Alrenians when I say I'm disappointed it took this long for you to step out of your luxurious palace and show your face among your people."

Voices rose from the crowd as the soldiers began to stir restlessly, their hatred growing so intense that it was almost palpable, a living beast roiling among my people. Flashing its teeth. Extending its claws. Opening its gaping mouth to devour me.

"Traitor!" a burly man yelled.

"Kill her!" several others cried, turning the words into a chant.

"She is no empress to *us*. She's an insult to her Alrenian blood!" someone near the back of the crowd shouted.

A woman in front pointed her dagger toward me. "How dare she turn her back on us! She doesn't deserve to draw breath!"

My muscles tensed, my fingers curling in anticipation to fight for my life. The chain that had been attached to my horse now clanked on the ground behind me, but my hands were shackled in front of my body. If Zerik stepped closer, close enough for me to touch…

When Zerik opened his mouth, the crowd quieted to listen to his words. They respected him. With every gesture he made, ever word he spoke, he commanded attention.

"I didn't think the daughter of Karye would welcome Forwyn usurpers so readily to her own throne," Zerik went on, his false charm dropping away as he met my eyes. This time, he didn't disguise the disgust burning within. "Since when did an Alrenian empress trade courage and pride in her ancestry for comfort and security? Since when did she sit back and dine with the enemy while her people burned in dragon fire that should have only been controlled by Alrenian hands? Since when did she accept the heresy of Forwyn men and women, who denounce the Life-Giver and despise us, his Chosen People?"

I spoke through clenched teeth. "Never. They used and abused me, and after long years of being a prisoner in my own palace, I am free. I escaped with a dragon so I could build my army and reclaim my throne."

Zerik burst into harsh laughter, and his soldiers were quick to join in. "Used you? I would have defied them and let them burn me in dragon fire before I ever became their pawn!" His fingers tightened around the hilt of his dagger. "Your excuses only prove you're too weak to lead us."

The soldiers burst into their chant once more. "Kill her!"

"*Kowra!*" others screamed.

Kowra. Kowra.

The curse brought back memories of the Alrenian woman I'd slain in the palace gardens, her face blackening into a misshapen, gory nightmare. Her screams anguished and ragged until they'd cut off.

I bit my tongue so sharply I tasted blood.

But stronger than my horror, my doubts, and my fear, was my rage. It towered higher than the flames dancing between the bloodthirsty crowd and me. It burned hotter than dragon fire. It swept through me, fueling the powerful curse that coursed through my veins.

"As a traitor to your empire and your throne, I condemn you to death!" Zerik roared, charging toward me, his blade slashing at me.

It was almost instinctual, the way my hands shot out, clapping against Zerik's arms before he could shove his dagger into my heart.

The effects were instant, my power burning straight through the leather guarding his arms, right into his flesh. Scorching like fire, but devouring in a swift, unnatural decay. The sickly scent of blood and pus mingled with the stench of rot and death.

Zerik screamed in agony as I slammed my hands against his face. He was too shocked, too overcome to fight back. The curse worked quickly. His soldiers gaped in silent horror, open-mouthed in a strange mixture of fascination and terror.

I knew the feeling, but it was nothing compared to the flush of power roaring through me. The intoxicating sensation of seizing control, of saving my life. Of knowing I would never be weak or cowardly again.

As Zerik crumpled at my feet, I lifted my eyes to his soldiers. Blood and bile swam through my mouth. I spat over my enemy's body. The chain attached to my shackle clanked as I glanced at the blood staining my palms.

I was too numb to fully register the horror trying to crawl up my throat. And I would bite off my own tongue before I screamed or vomited before these people.

No, I would demand respect from them. They would no longer taunt and laugh at me, no longer threaten me or cry out for my death. They would see me as the leader I was meant to be, and they would either love me or fear me.

"I am Empress Jaliana, daughter of Karye, bearer of a curse against all who rise up against my throne," I declared. I didn't bother to raise my voice. The world had fallen eerily still. Even the flames seemed to crackle more softly. "I am here to raise an army to take back my empire. Either you are with me, or you can meet your end like this traitor."

No one spoke. For a heartbeat, no one stirred. And then, one by one, the soldiers dropped to their knees, bowing their heads and murmuring, "Empress Jaliana."

Empress Kowra, a voice whispered in my head.

CHAPTER NINE

Lo

IT WAS IMPOSSIBLE TO SLEEP in the Alrenian palace, in a luxurious room I'd once scrubbed and cleaned each day. In a room I'd once snuck through like a shadow, praying an Alrenian noble wouldn't notice me. Wouldn't decide that was the day I died.

Everywhere I looked, I saw memories from my past, glimpsed the ghost of my brother. Edi smiled at me from the shadowy corner. *She can't hurt us, not really. None of them can.*

I rolled over in the bed, biting my cheek to hold back the tears. But Edi was there too, reaching out as if he would take my hand to comfort me. *Family can never be parted.*

Stifling a groan, I threw off the covers and sat up. I was drowsy and disoriented, like perhaps I'd fallen half-asleep and had been lost to nightmares. But I knew I hadn't. It was just the vestiges of grief, a heavy cloak that clung so tightly it made my bones feel leaden.

I glanced toward Caesiem, but he was motionless, sprawled out across the settee. He slept so still, his breathing so light, for a moment I wondered if he was dead. Then I noticed the slight rise of his chest.

Even in the darkness, I could make out his features: his strong jawline and high cheekbones, his black hair that was just long enough to curl around his ears. With his face relaxed, those bright eyes closed to the world, his charming smile not flashing dimples that could easily trick someone, he looked almost innocent. It didn't seem possible he was a Teramese spy who'd helped overtake my kingdom, or a lying traitor who'd turned on his supposed friends. It certainly didn't seem true that he was *Lord Xalenos*. An imperial mage. He seemed more like what he'd claimed to be, an orphan forced to steal to survive in a harsh world.

A strange tangle of emotions squirmed in my stomach. Anger. Hatred. Hurt. Remorse. Desire. I longed to reach out and brush his hair back from his brow, to hear him repeat the words he'd spoken only a day ago. *We don't have to go. We could turn around right now…* Had he truly meant those words? Had he really wanted to escape and leave this life behind? If he hadn't expected me to be useful anymore in his work to overthrow the Elders, had he had a reason to lie to me that night?

I scowled at the thought. *He probably would have dragged you right back here, in the end. Why would he give up his title? Give up the chance to live here in luxury and power with his followers?*

As if sensing my stare, Caesiem stirred in his sleep. My heart jumped into my throat, and I considered slipping back into the bed and closing my eyes. I didn't want him to detect my feelings, aside from my anger. But I also had a thousand questions spinning through my head.

Before I could make up my mind, his blue eyes flickered open and settled on me. Squinting against the darkness, he furrowed his brow. "I suppose you didn't sleep." He almost sounded…guilty.

Rather than respond, I tossed an impatient look over my shoulder, peering out the windowpanes set in the double doors leading to the balcony. Past the guard still standing at his post, I caught glimpses of the lush garden and the paling eastern sky. Already stars were winking out and the horizon was a steely grey. Dawn wasn't all that far off.

Caesiem sat up, his blanket sliding down to reveal his muscled bronze chest. Embarrassment flushed through me, but rather than avert my eyes, I stared harder at his face.

His eyes flicked to the tangled sheets strewn across the bed before turning back to me, calm and assessing. "*Did* you sleep?" he pressed.

I laughed sharply. "We're starting your questioning with some niceties? What a thoughtful captor."

Running a hand through his thick hair, Caesiem heaved a weary sigh. He stared at a distant point outside, as if unable to meet my eyes. "I know the palace isn't somewhere you'd like to be. I'm sure last night was...difficult for you."

"Again, how thoughtful of you to care about my feelings. Maybe you'll consider releasing me now?"

This time, his gaze fastened on mine. "You're not my prisoner, Lo," he murmured. "You could have left last night, if you wanted to."

I gestured toward the soldier posted outside, but he shook his head. "You and I both know that wouldn't have stopped you."

Swallowing, I didn't respond. Caesiem didn't know that I wasn't actually a nun anymore, that despite Jalie's escape, I'd still killed someone. He probably thought I actually had somewhere to go.

"Fine," I relented after a long moment. "I stayed because escape was only temporary, if you can't convince your precious Revaed not to hunt me down. And because…" I hesitated, daring to meet his eyes. "I want *answers.*" *And because I don't even have a home anymore.*

A shadow flitted across Caesiem's face, making his bright eyes dark and haunted.

"Fair enough. But I'm not discussing anything else with you until I'm dressed and have some coffee," he went on. "You're welcome to clean up and eat something, or to stand in the corner and practice shooting daggers at me with your eyes."

As if on cue, likely because someone had heard our raised voices from out in the hall, there was a knock on the door.

"Lord Xalenos. Revaed was hoping you'd be awake," said the officer, stepping in slowly. She saluted and hovered near the bedroom entrance. "He is sending breakfast, and will give you some time to finish your...questioning...before he wants to see you. He didn't give a specific meeting time, but he said not to..." She cleared her throat. "Waste away the morning with your beautiful new company." I could feel her eyes scan me before returning to Caesiem's shirtless form.

The implications in the woman's comment were all too clear. Indignation sizzled through me. I hoped the woman could see the hatred burning in my gaze.

Looking as uncomfortable as I felt, Caesiem scratched the back of his neck, tearing his eyes off me to face the soldier. "Revaed said that, did he? Well, tell *Revaed* he needn't worry," he said, his tone a warning. "I wouldn't dream of *wasting time*."

The soldier stiffened and saluted again, dropping her stare to the floor. "Of course, Your Lordship." She left silently, not quite succeeding in concealing the fear that had frozen her face.

Almost as soon as she'd disappeared, a Forwyn woman knocked and entered, bringing in a breakfast tray loaded with delicacies and a steaming pot of coffee. I wanted to snag her attention, to learn what the Teramese were doing to the Forwyn who had once lived as nobility within the palace, but she stoically refused to look in my direction and exited the chambers as swiftly as she'd arrived.

I rounded on Caesiem, but he'd vanished into the washroom. The sound of running water made me freeze. He was drawing a bath, and I certainly didn't want to walk in on him.

Silently fuming, I stalked to the breakfast tray to pour myself a cup of black coffee. Watching the steam curl upward, inhaling the earthy scent, I tried to clear my muddled thoughts. I settled into an armchair near the empty hearth and sipped the liquid slowly, savoring the way it awakened my senses as the world lightened outside. Apparently, Caesiem had decided to take his time this morning, because I was on my second cup of coffee before he emerged.

Hair slick with beads of water, his fresh uniform jacket only half-buttoned, he looked slightly more like the charming thief I remembered. The man who embodied everything mysterious and forbidden. There was more liveliness to his steps than earlier as he approached the breakfast tray and filled a plate with eggs and a buttered roll. He ate as he poured himself coffee, keeping the roll in his mouth as he slipped into a seat beside me.

Turning away, I cradled my mug with both hands and frowned at the empty fireplace.

"I need to know what you want from me," I said in a low voice. "I know your supposed concern for my life isn't the only reason I'm here. You're loyal to the Teramese imperial family above all else, *clearly*. What are you planning to *question* me about?"

Caesiem swallowed a bite of his roll and sighed. "You were in the Keep to steal a dragon, weren't you?"

I glared. "*Steal?* Those dragons are *not* yours."

He shrugged casually, scooping a bite of eggs onto his fork. "They don't belong to the Forwyn anymore. What is that old Alrenian saying? *Whoever controls the dragons, controls Alrenor?*" He studied me coolly. "Well, we control the palace *and* the dragons. It sounds to me like both Alrenor and the dragons belong to Teramyl."

I slammed my mug on the table beside my chair, sloshing the coffee inside. "And what is Teramyl doing, invading a kingdom and slaughtering its leaders?" I sneered at him. "I take it your Teramese high imperator or whatever it is you call him…he sent you here to do his dirty spying work for him, didn't he? You lied and stole and cheated your way into the palace."

Caesiem swallowed, his throat working. His nostrils flared, almost imperceptibly, as he took a deep breath and drummed a quiet beat against the arm of his chair. "How is what Teramyl did any different from how your people gained control of Alrenor?"

My mouth dropped open. "How is it *different?* My people were taken from our homeland generations ago, forced into slavery by the empire. For those of us alive now, Alrenor is the only home we know. It *is* our home, same as any Alrenian born and raised here. When we overthrew Karye and her loyalists, we were fighting for our freedom— for our very *survival.* We didn't murder innocent people in cold blood."

Caesiem's jaw tightened, his fingers ceasing their tapping. "And like I told you last night, you don't know why we're here," he said, his tone low and furious. "We aren't here for power or greed. We're here for survival. We slew those who threatened us. If we could have peacefully taken the palace, we would have."

"Oh, really?" I rolled my eyes. "Stop lying, *Lord Xalenos.* You betrayed people you claimed were friends, people who fought beside you, who trusted you with their lives." I balled my hands into fists. "Someone who *saved* your worthless life. All to kill and enslave my people all over again. How *dare* you pretend you have any right to this land, to the dragons, to *using* my people…"

I jerked my head away quickly, blinking back the tears that were threatening. Composing myself, I glared at him again, refusing to flinch when he met my gaze with his own equally unyielding expression.

"I would rather die than lose my freedom again," I whispered. "I won't stay here any longer. Let Revaed send his soldiers after me when I escape. Kill me yourself. I don't care."

Caesiem's meal sat forgotten on the low table in front of him as he stared at me, his body unusually still. "You could be our ally," he said. "I understand that what we did—what I did to you..." For an instant, I thought there was remorse flickering in his eyes. I must have been imagining it. "I understand if you never forgive or trust me again."

"Of course not," I spat, interrupting whatever else he'd been about to say. "You killed my *people*."

Caesiem's foot tapped restlessly against the floor. He sighed, shaking his head. "But maybe you can understand what I'm doing now. If you stay…Revaed *wants* to build an alliance with your people. You could help *all* of the Forwyn, like you've always wanted."

I resisted the urge to laugh mirthlessly. "An alliance?"

Caesiem studied my face. "I can talk to Revaed," he said. "He doesn't want war. And he listens to me."

"What a great brother," I muttered sarcastically.

"He's my guardian," Caesiem corrected, and the same envy that had latched onto my heart last night returned. I shoved it down. Why did I care about who or where my father was now? I'd managed my whole life without him; I'd continue to do so now. There wasn't another option.

Caesiem stared at the floor, seeming to muse over something as he fidgeted with his shirtsleeves. "If you stay, I can protect you and ensure you're treated well. No one will touch you or order you around. They fear the Xalenoses, and if Revaed commands it for my sake, they will listen."

"How reassuring," I scoffed. "You know I don't trust anything you say."

His lips were a thin line as he nodded. "I know, but I'm making this promise anyway."

I crossed my arms over my chest and looked away. "I've had enough lies."

Caesiem quieted. I heard him stir, finally returning to his plate of food as he let the topic drop. "Why did you want a dragon?" he asked.

Guilt squirmed through my insides, even though it annoyed me that I could feel ashamed for admitting my intentions to Caesiem. Why should I care what a deceptive, murdering lord thought about me?

"To go to Forwyth," I admitted.

Caesiem blinked, his food once again forgotten. "You would leave Alrenor?"

It was my turn to study the floor. "You know what I gave up when I came to the ball. There's no life for me here, not anymore."

"That's why you removed your ribbons?" he asked quietly, and I nodded. They weren't symbols unique to nuns, but nearly all had been gifted to me at the abbey. They were memories…memories that hurt. "They really don't want you to return to the abbey?" Caesiem went on, but stopped himself rather than press me for details. "Even with that life gone, it was what you'd planned for. I didn't think you would ever…" Cutting himself off, Caesiem shook his head, but I knew exactly what he'd left unspoken. *I didn't think you would ever abandon your people.*

We sat in silence for several more uncomfortable beats. Inwardly, I allowed my anger to cool enough to analyze my situation. If I didn't have the abbey to return to, perhaps staying in the palace wasn't the worst scenario. I would be safe from Mio'e and her revenge.

And maybe…maybe Caesiem was right, and I couldn't leave my people. I felt guilty and Elhani-forsaken and powerless, but surely here, at Lord Xalenos's side, I could learn vital information that could help the Forwyn. Surely I could do *something*. I'd be in the perfect position to spy on my enemies—to turn the tables on the young man who'd flipped my world upside down.

"Fine," I snapped. "I'll stay, for now."

Caesiem nodded.

For several uncomfortable beats, we sat in silence.

"As soon as we're done eating," he said, despite the fact that I hadn't touched any of the food, "I need to meet with Revaed. You'll be coming with me. If you want to bathe or change into fresh clothes before then, you'll need to do it now."

Revaed. Caesiem's guardian and Alrenor's new tyrant. Swallowing my anger, I decided that for now, it was best to cooperate, to be quiet and submissive and unnoticeable. I'd played that role well before, and it had finally led to my chance to rise against Karye. Maybe, if I could trust Elhani—if I could believe he might ever listen to my prayers again—I could bide my time until I could free my people again.

I hadn't lied to Caesiem. Death was preferable to imprisonment or enslavement. I didn't ever want to return to that horrible life. But I could pretend, for a while. Maybe, this way, I could gain not only my life and freedom, but also a new purpose.

CHAPTER TEN

Caesiem

UNSURPRISINGLY, WHEN I SOUGHT REVAED in his chambers, the soldier posted there informed me he'd already left. He directed me to the palace's training rooms.

As we wound our way out of one palace building and along a short garden path that led to another, Lo remained quiet beside me, her earlier anger swept away and replaced with an impassive attitude that was unlike her. Her gait was nearly silent, her face a mask. If I wasn't constantly and acutely aware of her presence, of her every move, I might have forgotten she was at my side.

She'd relented enough earlier to take a bath, change into an Alrenian outfit of leggings and a linen tunic a Forwyn woman had brought upon request, and pull her damp, unruly curls back into a knot. I'd preferred it down, but she must have tired of having her hair in her face when she'd been so used to her braids before.

It was true that many of my actions haunted me, but if she knew what Revaed and even his fearsome father had done for me… If she knew how the Teramese people suffered…

I repressed a sigh and shook the thoughts away. It wouldn't matter. She wouldn't want to listen, wouldn't want to believe. I'd made my choice, and she was forever lost to me.

Two soldiers pushed open the carved double doors when we mounted the stone steps. Inside, the ceiling was adorned in painted scenes of Alrenian history, many violent and gory. Supposedly, Alrenor hadn't always thrived on bloodshed and cruelty and fear, but if that were true, that history was long buried and forgotten. Low windows lined the bright, open hallway leading to the multiple training rooms, the armory, and the Royal Guards' and Dragon Keepers' quarters.

We found Revaed in the first and largest training room, where he was facing off with Officer Pados. Sweaty shirts clinging to their bodies, their faces glistened as they circled one another, each wielding a practice sword—Alrenian blades with their edges dulled. With a deceptively wide smile and casual stance, Revaed sidestepped Pados's strike and lunged. Revaed's movements were graceful and swift, a frenzied blur of strength and skill, as he forced Pados back until he'd knocked him to the ground.

"Another win," he said lazily as he pointed the practice sword at the officer's neck.

Pados grunted, grumbling something unintelligible as he stood and retrieved his own practice weapon, where it lay several feet away.

I stepped through the entryway and Revaed's eyes met mine. His grin was immediate. "Good morning, Caes. You appear a little more rested today." His eyes flicked briefly over my shoulder to Lo before settling on me again. There was a question on his face, but he didn't voice it aloud.

I knew Revaed well enough to guess what he was thinking anyway. He wanted to know if I'd questioned Lo and discovered not only why she'd been in the Dragon Keep, but also how she'd gotten there.

But of course, with Lo present, now wasn't the time to speak about any of that. I greeted Revaed with an equally large smile. "You do too. Up and practicing early. I half-expected you to be buried in meetings and other tasks today."

Revaed's eyes darted to Lo again. Clearly, he was watching his words carefully in her presence, as I'd expected, but I'd known leaving her behind wasn't an option either. Revaed had made it clear that Lo was my responsibility to guard. "There's much to do, yes," he said lightly, striding toward the wall to hang his sword. "But you know a clever ruler finds trustworthy men to execute some of those tasks, so he has plenty of time and energy to attend to the most important matters." He shrugged. "Preparation is the order of the day, more than anything else. Walk with me," he said, approaching the doorway. He tossed a look at Pados. "You're dismissed."

Preparation. He meant dragon-taming. Leading and organizing troops. Dispatching more soldiers throughout Alrenor. Planning out a showy execution for Empress Jaliana for when she was found, as a message for any who would rise against us. Hopefully, it would be a message well-received by the Forwyn, some of whom might be persuaded to side with us. And it would be a warning to the Alrenians, who, in my mind, deserved everything happening to them. Revaed had readily agreed with me. If we were to have any allies in this new land, it would be the Forwyn.

"Where did you want to start?" I asked Revaed as we exited the building and stepped into the fragrant gardens. Early morning sunlight bathed the surrounding palm trees and flowers in a golden haze. "Did Vander and Kovi Ettonou leave this morning on their mission?"

Revaed nodded. "Before sunrise. Which leaves much for us to plan." He sighed. "But there's time, Caes. For a short while, we can breathe in peace, which feels miraculous. Everything fell into place so swiftly and effortlessly, thanks to you." He shot me a warm smile. "The real trials will come later, I know."

From the distant look in his eyes, I knew he was thinking about potential uprisings from both the Alrenians and Forwyn, and of the rumors of a building Alrenian army.

"We'll be ready," I said firmly.

Revaed shot me a confident smile. "Oh, I know we will be." Slowing his steps, he cast a glance over his shoulder, where Lo hovered in our shadows, like a wraith trying to disappear at the approach of dawn. "First, I'd like to speak with your friend."

I repressed a frown. Lo had an uncanny way of making herself all but vanish. Thankfully, the last thing I'd ever be able to do was forget about her.

Though I expected angry words from Lo, she merely halted in the pathway, watching Revaed with an almost meek expression.

She knows how to play this game, I thought. It was a little sickening to recall that she'd spent long years as a slave in this very place, and that she now felt forced to act in the same ways she had before. I longed to take her hands in mine, to hold her and reassure her that I'd never let her face such a horrible life again. But she'd never believe me.

"What's your name?" Revaed asked.

The pride in her voice was unmistakable. "Lo'laeni Nolanhou."

Revaed recognized the name from messages I'd sent to him while he'd sailed toward Alrenor. "Ah, not just any vigilante, then. You are the Empress-Slayer herself. The famed *amara'rekni.*"

Lo tensed almost imperceptibly before nodding.

"Impressive. You served in the palace and tended to the dragons before, correct?"

"I was *enslaved* in the palace and forced to risk my life to tend and feed the dragons," Lo corrected, her tone turning darker.

"Right." Revaed nodded. "And I take it that after years of slavery at the hands of the Alrenians, you found they still oppressed you. You earned your freedom, but there was more you needed. You decided you had enough from your enemies, and chose to find a way to carve out a better life for yourself?" Revaed turned and strolled down the path, compelling Lo and me to follow on either side of him. His pace was leisurely, as if he had all the time in the world to stroll through and admire the gardens. If there was one thing Revaed excelled at above all others, it was his ability to exude composure, no matter how he truly felt.

"I *did* find a better life for myself," Lo said calmly, studying a butterfly's path to avoid meeting our eyes. "But I gave it up in the hope that my people could find one too. Clearly, I was led astray."

She didn't look at me, but guilt slithered through my stomach anyway.

"My sacrifices were in vain," she added, her level tone never betraying the fiery anger I knew burned in her heart.

"How so?" Revaed asked, a smile twitching at his lips.

Lo tore her eyes from her surroundings to stare at Revaed openly. "You don't appear to be a fool, so why ask me a foolish question?" she asked. Again, she didn't let her voice sound furious, but her brazen attitude gave it away this time.

Revaed grinned outright. "Someone who doesn't appreciate the delicate games of politics." He glanced toward me approvingly. "Intelligent. Spirited. You chose well."

Inwardly, I cringed. *Chose?* What would Lo make of that statement? What did Revaed even mean? I could feel her eyes on me, but I refused to return her gaze.

Revaed halted, turning to face Lo directly. In his shadow, she seemed incredibly small, and yet the fire in her eyes made her more imposing than if she'd towered over my guardian. The quiet power that simmered through her was evident. It shone through in the way she set her jaw, in the way her beautiful eyes gleamed. It electrified the air around us. Was it her magic? Or simply her strong, confident presence? I couldn't ever be sure, but it was always there, that magnetism that drew me irresistibly toward her.

"Let me explain circumstances to you in straightforward terms," my guardian said. Though he still poured on the charm, his lazy attitude had melted away. He was all business, his stance proud. "You may hate me and my soldiers, call us power-hungry or merciless or greedy or cruel. It doesn't really matter how you perceive us. The truth is, Teramyl and all its people have been suffering for quite some time, and your broken, divided empire has an abundance of natural resources." For a moment, he allowed himself to indulge in a grin. "And dragons."

Lo simply scowled at him.

"Your Elders were stingy in their trade," Revaed continued, "and to be honest, there was little my kingdom had left of value to trade anyway. But one thing we have always excelled at is war. Without vylae growing naturally in our land, the dragons native to Teramyl have ravaged our cities and countryside since time immemorial." He waved a hand about, gesturing widely. "Alrenor was fortunate—when our dragons came to you, they were immediately subdued with vylae and then raised in captivity. I know you don't drug your dragons now, but why would you need to? They are familiar with humans, and it is far easier to tame creatures that are fed at your hands."

Lo shifted on her feet, her eyes narrowing as she watched him. Impatient. Frustrated. But interested in what he had to say.

"We've never had that advantage," Revaed continued, "but that means we've never grown complacent after long years of peace. Our army was determined and ready to take Alrenor. I'm here to save my people, Miss Nolanhou, just as you chose to sacrifice and save yours. My people might fear my father and me, and perhaps you'd call some of our ways callous or even brutal, but being soft isn't an option when life is about survival. You would understand, I think, *amara'rekni.*"

Revaed hesitated for only a moment. "However," he added softly, "I could be of service to your people. We can oppose the Alrenians together. All I want is to provide food and necessities for my people." He spread his arms out wide. "Is that so wrong?"

Lo pursed her lips, but said nothing.

"If our enemy is the same, if our motives are similar, is it so impossible to find common ground?"

Lo crossed her arms. "You broke your alliance with Alrenor, invaded my land, killed my people, and overthrew my government…and now you think you can convince me you want to be allies again? How stupid do you think I am?"

Revaed watched her solemnly, not even bothering to hide the trace of sadness that darted across his face. "I understand your anger and grief—even your hatred," he said, his tone low. "But I promise you, what I did—what I ordered my people to do—was for our survival, the same as anything you and your people have done is for yours."

Lo sucked in a breath, like she was forcefully restraining herself from making another cutting remark. Or launching herself at him. Despite the solemnity of the situation, I couldn't help the warm rush of admiration and amusement that flooded me. Of course she wouldn't be afraid of Revaed, wouldn't feel too intimidated to fight for what she believed was right.

But…she didn't know he was on her side. Or at least, that he could be, if she let him.

Slowly, Revaed reached into his jacket pocket and drew out a handful of folded papers, covered in scrawling handwriting. I knew immediately what they were. "We reached out to your Council of Elders, pleading for help," he said softly, offering the letters to Lo.

She blinked before hesitantly taking them, immediately opening the crinkled pages. She scanned them, shuffling through each and every paper to consume the entire exchange. Having helped Revaed pen them myself, I was well acquainted with their contents. They were requests for assistance—any kind of assistance. Vylae that could help us overcome the dragons rampaging through our land. Food for our starving people. Skilled healers who could come to the aid of those who still suffered in what we hoped was the final wave of our deadly plague. Sanctuary for some of our citizens to live in Alrenor, if they wished, either temporarily or permanently.

Anything to help save lives.

The return letters from the Elders were scarce and brief. Most of our pleas had gone ignored, and the rest had received curt responses. All variances of the same answer: *No.* Teramyl was alone.

I could tell how tense Revaed was, his body as tightly coiled as mine. We were both burdened with the same need to help our people, no matter the cost.

"And so you see," Revaed murmured, as Lo folded the letters, handing them mutely back to my guardian, "we were left with no other choice."

I wasn't sure what Lo was feeling in that moment. Her eyes were wide, her expression blank. Stunned. Did she believe us, how desperate we were?

"What do you want from me?" she asked slowly, cautiously.

A bit of the weight eased off my shoulders, and I released a ragged breath. At my side, Revaed stood straighter, a hopeful smile spreading across his lips.

"I want you to agree to an alliance, eventually. To be the one to convince the Forwyn that allying with us is in your best interest. I've already spoken with some of your Elders, and they've expressed a desire to cooperate. But I know your voice will hold the most weight among your people."

Lo's brow furrowed at the mention of the Elders.

"I'll let you consider for a while," Revaed added. "No rush. However, in the meantime, since you are our guest, I do want you to do one thing for me while you decide. I want you to help Caesiem train the dragons."

CHAPTER ELEVEN

Kovi

I WOKE WITH THE SUNRISE, the glaring light on my face forcing me up out of habit. Every inch of my body ached, my muscles sore and stiff. After hours of hard riding, Vander and I had stolen a short period of rest, mainly for our mounts' sakes. They were feisty steeds, both mares who constantly seemed in competition to outpace one another, but we'd ridden them until sweat dampened their coats and they'd snorted with exhaustion. Riding our horses to death wouldn't help us find Jalie any faster.

Vander tossed me a cheeky grin, already seated cross-legged in the grass as he chewed a piece of jerky. "Been a while since you've ridden, soldier? You look a little sore."

I sat up stiffly and glared at him. It was difficult to read the man. Perhaps he thought of us as allies on the same mission, and was truly trying to offer jests and smiles in friendship. Or maybe he was simply mocking me.

In my mind, the latter seemed more likely. Whether we had a

common enemy and purpose or not, we were still on different sides in the growing conflict within Alrenor. I fought and bled for my people, and my people alone. Whatever promises the Teramese tossed my way, my loyalties would never be toward them.

Still, discomfort crept over me as I studied Vander's face. He didn't seem like a cruel man, not from the way he gently tended to his steed or grinned with genuine happiness in his eyes.

But he's a Teramese soldier who threatens your people and *wants to kill Jalie. Better just to kill him.*

The plan had crept into my mind early on. If I killed Vander and returned alone with Jalie, I could find a way to let her escape without it looking intentional, and I could claim the Alrenians had slain Vander. That way, Vander couldn't contradict my story, and none of the Teramese could accuse me of breaking my agreement. The Forwyn being held hostage in the palace wouldn't be executed due to my failure.

Vander finished his last bit of jerky and stood to stretch. He studied the countryside with an appreciative grin. "Whatever either of us feel about the Alrenians who live here, Alrenor is beautiful, isn't it?"

Stifling a sigh, I glanced about to take in my surroundings. This far north, the air was already cooler. Outside of the capital, it also smelled fresher, the scents of green grass and sun-baked earth mingling with a sweet odor I could only describe as the smell of the wind itself. The breeze rippled and rustled the long grass as if the blades were wind-tossed waves in the sea, and I couldn't help but inhale a long draught of air, like a man greedily downing a drink. Even in the cleanest streets of Inalgoth, one couldn't quite avoid the stench of horse manure or the reek from trash littering an alley.

This…this I could get used to. We'd skirted around Aramith miles ago, keeping to farmland and pastureland and now this open grassland.

Everywhere I looked, endless grass and sky stretched toward the horizon. At least, everywhere except toward the northeast, where the Aramith Mountains pointed to the clouds. From this distance, they seemed more like dark blotches against the horizon, though I could just make out their snowcapped peaks.

Out in the open countryside, the pain and doubt that constantly consumed me within the capital seemed distant. As if all it would take to find peace would be to leave the city limits and start a new life in the wild places of Alrenor.

I knew that was a happy lie, but for a few blissful moments, I let myself cling to it.

Then I turned, striding toward my mare, her long grey mane sweeping low as she bent to nibble tender blades of grass. We'd tied her and Vander's mount to the only two trees we'd seen for miles since leaving the Lorin trees and Brema River behind, though they'd both been so exhausted I doubted they would have wandered far. Our packs and saddles rested near our steeds.

Plucking a strip of jerky from my pack, I leaned against the tree trunk and watched the sun stain the eastern sky shades of pink and orange.

Vander approached, reaching for a pendant hanging from a leather cord around his neck. For the first time, he was near enough that I caught a glimpse of its shape. It looked like a grey stone, almost perfectly circular and etched with a pattern of whorls.

"I think you were right to head this way," he said, his eyes distant and unfocused, as if he were lost in concentration. "A dragon definitely flew through this area recently."

I frowned and glanced again at his pendant. I'd always assumed the Teramese were simply superstitious, with their endless list of gods and goddesses and their pendants that supposedly protected them or enhanced their magic. Although, I didn't know much about Teramese culture.

"How do you know?" I asked.

Vander gestured as if to the very air around us. "I can sense it." He smiled softly. "I'm a mage. A wind mage, specifically. Did you think His Majesty would send you with just any soldier? We have to ensure you perform your task. This mission is too important to fail."

"If you can detect a dragon's path, why didn't you tell me to begin with?" I muttered.

But inwardly, my mind was whirling. *A mage.* My control of Elahni's magic was powerful—so powerful I'd stood out among an entire academy of soldiers—but that fact didn't make me invincible. I knew little about Teramese magic and what it could do, and if there was one thing I'd learned at Aerekni, it was to know exactly what your enemy was capable of.

Vander continued to study me with his unreadable smile. "We still needed a direction to take, or we could have wasted days searching the air over hundreds of miles. You simply narrowed the options down, and I was able to confirm you were right."

I finished my jerky and then a bit of cheese and a hard roll, all in silence. If I had to tolerate an enemy's presence on a mission I wasn't sure I wanted to undertake, I would do so quietly and with as little interaction as possible. When the time came, it would make killing him a whole lot easier.

As soon as we'd finished eating, we saddled and mounted our horses to press toward Wynlaen. From what I knew of the small town, it was nestled amongst hills a few miles from both the mountains and the coast, a quiet and half-forgotten world. It didn't take long before the flat lands revealed the rolling hills and tiny homes on the outskirts of the town. We'd be there within the hour.

But as we approached town, Vander paused, his brow creased in thought. His hand reached again for his pendant.

I drew my mare up beside him, waiting silently.

"A procession exited the town," he said slowly. "A large beast disturbed the air. I think it was the dragon, but it was walking."

"Which direction?"

Vander shifted in his saddle, glancing at the Aramith Mountains towering to the east. Father had suspected an Alrenian army could be concealed within those mountains, where they would have been able to bide their time in secret, training and growing their ranks until they were strong enough to march against the Forwyn. They were still close enough to the city of Aramith that they could gather necessary provisions, but far enough that the thin Forwyn forces would have easily overlooked them for too long.

"The Elders were beginning to suspect there was an Alrenian army hiding in the mountains," I said, turning my horse to study the towering peaks. Had Jalie already discovered her army? I grasped my reins and hesitated, glancing toward Vander. "We'll need to proceed with caution. If we're approaching an army—an army with a dragon…" I laughed mirthlessly. "We're gravely outnumbered. Even with my magic and your…abilities."

Vander nodded once. "If we must, we'll scout the area and send word back to the emperor for reinforcements. The important thing is to find Jaliana and her army before they march on the capital."

That was one statement I could agree with.

After hours of hard riding along steep mountain paths, pausing now and then so Vander could concentrate on which direction we needed to travel, the air grew frigid. Each snort from my horse elicited a white plume that rose lazily upward, mingling with my own steaming breaths. Vander and I each removed gloves and cloaks from our packs and draped ourselves in the material, pulling our hoods as low as we could, but still I felt the chill creeping into my bones.

Everything was foreign and strange, from the cold air to the scent of pine needles and the towering rocks and trees on either side of our path. The mountains held a rugged beauty, covered in dirt and rock and moss in shades of brown and green I hadn't ever seen growing up in Alrenor's capital. High above, partially obscured by billowing white clouds, the snowy mountain peaks glistened as if with millions of diamonds wherever the sun touched them.

Once again, I drew a fortifying breath and imagined a world in which I could slip away to this wilderness, soaking up the soothing atmosphere around me. Laying down the burden of worrying about and killing for my people.

Then guilt set in. *Forgive me, Elhani,* I thought. I could never abandon my people like that, not when they were suffering. Not when they were in danger from *two* enemy armies.

Be the dutiful soldier, I reminded myself. No matter what it cost me.

As we swept up another steep incline, our mares carefully picking paths around the loose pebbles strewn along the way, I spotted the first curls of smoke ahead. My heart hammered against my chest in anticipation. At the top of the ridge, Vander and I halted. There was enough space for us to draw our horses abreast as we stared into the valley stretching below.

Between two of the Aramith mountains, the grassy valley was a deep slash of green, dotted with the occasional tree extending toward the sky. But it was the encampment that stole my breath away. Countless rows of tents covered the landscape, interspersed with fires, some lit and some diminished to embers. From this distance, it was difficult to make out the moving shapes below, but it was clear they were soldiers from the disciplined way they carried themselves and the weapons hanging from hips or attached to backs. Rather than dragon scale armor, which was too rare and valuable to be distributed to every soldier throughout Alrenor, the soldiers wore leathers. Likely, that was an easier material for a secret army to procure.

My eyes snagged on the banner rippling in the breeze from a pole near one of the largest tents. The ivory background and golden swirling sun proudly proclaimed that the army was Alrenian.

We'd found them.

A hulking shape near the outskirts of the camp pulled my eyes from the soldiers, some of which appeared to be gathering in an open space to train. The flash of green dragon scales almost burned my eyes. I blinked. It was Ryke, the dragon Jalie had stolen from the Keep.

The empress was here.

Something like a chill rushed through me, one that had nothing to do with the cold wind tugging at my cloak. For an instant, I squeezed my eyes shut against the memory of Jalie's face the night she'd escaped. Her golden hair framing her face, her jaw set in a determined line. In those moments, her eyes had burned with both fury and hope.

As the daughter of the cruel and fierce Empress Karye, Jalie had been everything and nothing I'd expected. There was hardness and stubbornness in her, but also something gentle. She carried grief and anger that I understood, and her grief spoke of a softer heart than I'd anticipated. She'd loved her mother, had believed her to be something better than she was. And she loved her people with a ferocity I admired, because I felt the same way for mine.

It was our mutual loyalty to our peoples that, ironically, both drew us together and tore us apart. We understood each other, and in that understanding, we knew that we would forever be opposed.

I shut out the echo of pain I felt at her words. *There is no room for mercy in war.*

Vander steered his mare around, pulling her a short distance back down the path. I followed after him. It wouldn't do us any favors to be spotted and crushed by an entire army before we could even make a plan to retrieve the empress.

"It seems our mission accomplished two objectives," Vander said with an easy smile. "We've found the Alrenian army and the former empress." He paused. "That *is* her stolen dragon, correct?"

Not trusting my voice, I gave him a single sharp nod.

Vander gazed at the wispy clouds overhead. They were gathering thickly, promising snow for the mountaintops and possible rain for us. I repressed a shiver as I imagined how bitter a cold mountain rain would feel, totally different from the warm thunderstorms Inalogth experienced.

"We'll need to find a place we can wait off the trail, out of sight," Vander mused aloud. "Somewhere we can plan. I know I considered sending word back earlier for reinforcements, but…I don't think we can afford to wait. And I'm not returning to the palace empty-handed."

I raised my eyebrows, though I wasn't surprised by Vander's urgency. "So we need a plan to infiltrate the camp and kidnap the empress." It wasn't a question.

Vander's smile widened. "The Aerekni Academy's reputation doesn't disappoint—you're ready for the challenge, I see. I'm sure between the two of us, we have enough skills and magic to be more than capable."

I nodded despite the growing tightness in my chest. Once again, I banished the memory of Jalie's face. I pushed aside the onslaught of emotions, the connection I could still feel between us. If I let myself fall too deeply into that connection, I'd be able to sense her emotions as clearly as if they were my own. And I refused to do that. I had to block them out.

Because even if I didn't *want* to kill her, I would if I was forced to. Wouldn't I?

I couldn't waver in my duty to my people.

Breathing deeply, I thought of Elhani and listened for his song. Even here, where my fear and doubt threatened to shake my resolve, I could hear it coursing through the air around me and buzzing through my veins.

I will always choose my people, I vowed.

In a thick copse of trees off the trail, we huddled near our horses, planned, and waited. From our vantage point, we could easily peer through the tree trunks and study the camp, spread out below like an old woman's patterned quilt, but it would be impossible for the army's lookouts to spy us from our position. Without a fire, the air grew bitterly cold, each gust of wind biting through our cloaks.

"How well *do* you know Jaliana?" Vander asked, after the silence had stretched between us for a long while, in which we'd each been lost in our own thoughts, scheming how we could best infiltrate the camp.

When I glanced up, I found Vander assessing me, watching my

every movement, my every breath, as if expecting me to lie. How much did he suspect? How much had Lord Xalenos seen and reported to this officer?

Or perhaps Vander had sensed the fact that I'd been considering how to best kill him.

"I was only in the palace for a few weeks before your army betrayed the Alrenian-Teramese alliance and slew my people," I told him darkly.

"I was informed," Vander went on as if he hadn't even heard my response, "that you were conscripted because you'd been a personal guard of sorts to the former empress, to ensure she didn't harm your own people with her…powers? She has some sort of black magic, doesn't she?"

I nodded, slowly.

Black magic. It was an apt description of the powers the Dark Immortal Nesrelle and her demon followers, the *hilvoku*, possessed. Discomfort squirmed through my chest at the memory of Jalie's power, the way she could slam her palms against human skin and cause it to rot away before one's eyes. According to her, it was a curse sent to judge the bloodshed occurring within the empire against her people.

Wherever her mysterious power originated, it felt sinister. Wrong. I understood why so many spoke about it in whispers, why it added to the terror that Jalie swept over the Forwyn, all because of her mother's reputation. But I believed I'd seen into Jalie's heart, catching glimpses of what I believed was her true self. Her tender side.

It hurt to think of the darkness also lurking within her.

But I couldn't blame her for that darkness, not when I carried my own terrible power. She might have shed Forwyn blood, but I'd shed my share of Alrenian blood. How could I judge her for doing the exact same thing I'd done, for my own side? For doing what I would have done, if I'd been in her shoes?

Maybe we're all monsters, she'd claimed.

Maybe there was no escaping the darkness that seemed to be tainting all of Alrenor, staining the hands of every inhabitant, Alrenian and Forwyn.

"How does her power work exactly?" Vander demanded, breaking into my thoughts. "I heard all she had to do was touch someone and they died slowly."

"It's true," I said. "Although I'm not sure I'd call the deaths slow. In a matter of days, their skin would rot away, as if they were devoured from the inside out."

Vander pursed his lips, considering my words. "We'll have to be especially careful not to be touched when we take her. Do gloves protect against her?"

"No," I murmured, images of Jalie's attack on the Dragon Keeper Yaelti flashing through my mind. The anger in her eyes as she retaliated against his violence. The way she'd clapped her hands over his dragon scale armor until it'd melted away. The Keeper's anguished screams. The horrible burning, rotting scent. "Nothing seems to protect against it. We'll have to be faster than her."

Vander stepped closer to the ridge, twigs and leaves crunching beneath his boots. He peered out between two pines, studying the camp intently. "You know I'm a wind mage," he said at last. "Tell me about your Forwyn magic. What can you do, and how can it help against whatever she might throw at us?"

The words threatened to stick in my throat. It seemed wise to hold my secrets close.

Does it matter if he knows, if I'm going to kill him?

Vander didn't seem cruel, only like a soldier following orders for his homeland. The merciful side of me balked at the thought of slaying the man in cold blood.

I just wasn't sure if mercy or callousness would better serve my people.

"I could conceal us from their entire army," I told Vander at last. "Using Elhani's power, I could make us both as invisible as ghosts. We could march through those rows of tents and no one would stop us, as long as we were silent."

Vander turned back, a smile dancing across his lips. He brushed back a strand of black, wavy hair that was decidedly shaggier than that of Lord Xalenos or any of the other Teramese soldiers I'd met. Growing past his ears, it was the longest hair I'd ever seen on any soldier. I wondered if expectations for Teramese soldiers were different, or if he was allowed to grow his hair longer because he was a mage and not simply a lowly fighter.

"Slip right past our enemies," he said, his grin growing wider as the idea registered fully in his mind. "Could we steal into every tent and slit all their throats while we're at it?"

I almost smiled back. How much simpler it would be if Vander and I could take out this Alrenian threat that easily. Instead, I shook my head. "No, I couldn't hold my concentration on the magic that long. We'll have to get in, take the empress, and get out."

Vander didn't seem surprised, as his smile didn't lessen. He nodded. "We'll still have the advantage. They'll know they've been discovered once they find Jaliana gone, but if we ride hard, we could return to Inalgoth before their army has a chance to move far. We may even be able to dispatch troops to meet them here before they can lay siege to the capital."

I mulled over his words, standing to approach the ridge and gaze at the camp alongside him. "That might be what they prefer. They know this land better than us, and they could send their troops into positions along these mountains to attack us while our forces are still ascending." I frowned at the valley. The sun was already dipping below the mountain peaks in the west, staining their white caps bloodred. Everywhere shadows stretched and deepened among the trees. The biting chill in the air was growing.

Vander scratched his chin thoughtfully. "Well, Prince—er, Emperor Revaed and his informants will choose our strategy," he said with a shrug of his shoulders. "All we need to concern ourselves with today is kidnapping the former empress." He shot me a look, once again studying me carefully. "Let me ask again, how well do you know her? A few weeks in her company, and…do you have an idea of what she planned to do when she escaped? Do you suspect where she would be within the camp, right now?"

My heart beat a staccato rhythm in my chest, half dread and half anticipation as I at last relaxed my mind and allowed the feelings I'd been pushing aside all this time to flood to the forefront of my brain. Jalie's feelings. Though part of me had hoped the connection I'd created between the empress and myself would have fizzled out by now, another part of me, a part I almost didn't dare admit to, relished the fact that it still existed. That I could still reassure myself she was alive.

When I concentrated, a sense of safety and relief and hope enveloped me. I leaned into the emotions, letting myself experience them as if they were my own. How much I wished they *were* my own. But they were quickly chased by other, darker feelings, ones I was all too familiar with. Guilt. Fear. Horror. Doubt. All the emotions tangled and swirled together, forming a messy whirlwind inside me until I forced it all back again, into the recesses of my mind.

I pointed toward the largest tent in the camp, one bearing a large Alrenian banner and located near the center of the site. Her people must have greeted her as their leader, rushing to honor and serve her as their rightful ruler. That explained the comforting emotions she felt.

Vander seemed mildly surprised. "I was told her people might not welcome her."

"I believe they did," I said. My eyes flicked toward where Ryke was curled up, contentedly napping, his shimmering scales glistening in the dying light. "If they hadn't, the entire army would probably be burnt to a crisp in dragon fire by now."

Vander quirked his lips. "Sounds like we are about to capture a formidable foe."

I blinked, pushing away the memory of Jalie's clear blue eyes and her constellations of freckles. Her screams as terrifying images of how she imagined her mother's death played out before her, looping mercilessly through her brain. Her fear in the night, when she hadn't wanted to sleep in her large bed all alone.

"Something like that," I murmured.

CHAPTER TWELVE

Jalie

MY SLEEP WAS ONCE AGAIN fitful, interrupted by gory dreams in which I relived the deaths of everyone I'd ever killed. *Four. Four lives.* Those words haunted me as I saw Lady Laenai cry out, as I watched Keeper Yaelti's eyes widen with fear, as I heard the red-haired Alrenian woman and Zerik scream in anguish.

Two were accidents, and two were in self-defense, I told myself, but it didn't erase the horror of my nightmares, didn't melt away the guilt churning in my gut.

My own words echoed in my head, words proclaimed so brashly, so haughtily, to Kovi when I'd burned with fury. *If I must be a monster, I'll be a monster in possession of the throne.*

Words I'd snarled at the dead Alrenian woman after she'd betrayed me. *Empress Kowra.*

Sweat slithered down my back as I jerked awake, my eyelids flicking open to inky darkness so thick it felt like it had weight. My cot was a far cry from the luxurious mattress I'd slept on all my life in the palace, but a vast improvement over the hard earth I'd rested on last night. But then, I'd at least had Ryke's warmth and reassuring presence. Now, despite the troops who'd proclaimed fealty to me, despite the guards posted outside my tent, I felt vulnerable and alone.

Almost unconsciously, I stretched my hand out in the darkness, as if expecting to feel Kovi's warm body beside me. An ache erupted in my chest, like the absence of something I hadn't fully realized was there. It was quickly chased by anger.

He doesn't care. He means nothing to you. He is your enemy, I told myself fiercely.

But my mind was tangled with confusion. For three years, I'd thought all Forwyn were my enemies, hateful and cruel like the Elders were, but Kovi had shown me kindness and mercy, and then a Forwyn woman had saved my life the night of the Autumn Ball.

Don't let them play games with your mind and soften you.

"Awake at last, *amara?*" Nesrelle's lilting voice danced out of the shadows, snapping my gaze to the corner of my tent.

Heart hammering, I took in her milky white skin, which seemed to glow from within. It cast enough light that I could make out her gleaming blue eyes and fiery curls. Clothed in a dress of silver dragon scales, its design a perfect blend of Alrenian palace fashion and Dragon Keeper armor, she appeared especially formidable.

I had a feeling if I stared too long she would transform into the image of the Queen of Death I'd been taught about in my childhood: an ugly woman with paper-thin flesh, bloodied fangs, and curving claws. But despite my inability to tear my eyes away, her appearance remained the same. She was simply a beautiful woman, shimmering with immortality and power as she smiled softly, almost proudly, at me.

Despite her welcoming look, my stomach clenched with rage and guilt. *Take away the burden of this curse you threw upon me!* I wanted to scream the words at her, to find the nearest heavy object and hurl it toward her face. *I don't want to be your monster.*

"But don't you desire power?" she murmured, her tone gentle.

My heart jolted sharply against my ribs.

"Don't you long to obtain your throne and rescue your people?" Nesrelle continued. "To never be viewed as weak or be used like a lowly pawn again? To no longer live under constant threat of pain or death?"

I stared back at her, weighing my words. Of course I wanted everything she said, but did I want to become a monster to obtain my desires?

Nesrelle laughed lightly, like a mother amused at the antics of her child. "You're not a monster. You're only doling out justice." She arched an eyebrow.

She's not wrong, I thought, reminding myself of everything I'd declared in my dreams. The accidental deaths. The killings in self-defense. *I deserve the crown. And the Forwyn...so many of them are guilty and deserve to pay for the blood they've shed.*

Nesrelle nodded sagely. "An empress must be prepared to carry the burden of the power over life and death," she reminded me. "You know this. You must have the courage to sentence the guilty to protect not only the lives of the innocent but also your own." She smiled. "Don't fear your power, little Jalie. You have the chance to be a great empress, perhaps even greater than your mother."

A strange mixture of pain and pleasure rushed through me at her words. I swallowed the rising urge to either weep or smile. I didn't know what I felt, or what I even wanted to feel anymore.

Nesrelle shifted her head to the side, listening. I held my breath and strained my own ears for a sound above the soft rustle of my tent and the snap of the Alrenian flag flying above it. The night remained as quiet as it had before, although everywhere my eyes darted, I could have sworn the shadows moved.

"Be ready," Nesrelle hissed, her eyes piercing, almost as if she were challenging me. "An enemy is coming." Before I could ask her anything, she vanished.

Every one of my muscles tensed as I sat up further on my cot and swung my legs over its side. Perhaps I'd been too confident, trusting these troops not to rebel, trusting that I'd either earned their respect or fear to such a degree that none would dare dream of touching me. Expecting that they would faithfully guard my tent and allow me a full night's rest.

Last night there had been little time for anything but work. After the troops had knelt before me, I'd chosen a few to act as my closest advisors and guards. They were men and women who seemed stalwart and trustworthy. Ones I could tell would always be loyal to someone powerful. Those were the ones I'd ordered to drag specific men and women from the crowd, ones I'd noticed had been especially vocal against me, and to execute them in front of the entire army. My faithful soldiers had carried out my orders without emotion, easily accepting my command as their rightful leader. Their Chosen Empress.

Afterward—as the cold night gave way to morning—had come the work of disposing of the bodies. I commanded my circle of soldiers to carry the corpses to the outskirts of camp, where I unchained Ryke and he obliged me by unleashing a burst of white-hot fire. In minutes, the bodies were burnt to ashes.

From there, the soldiers fell into their regular patterns, preparing breakfast and joining their regiments for morning training. I summoned my circle to Zerik's old tent, which I swiftly commandeered, though I had no belongings of my own to change its appearance much. The only thing I did was throw out his trunk of old clothes, declaring they smelled of him and must be burned. Soldiers silently carried it away without complaint.

I'd spent time outlining how the camp would operate differently: the soldiers were no longer to wear vials of vylae around Ryke or to ever put him in chains again. "If anyone fears him, don't approach him," I said. "But he will not be chained or controlled like someone's mindless pet. He is faithful to me, and I will not see him mistreated."

The rest of the day was consumed with explaining the Teramese invasion and poring over maps as we strategized how to seize the throne. Food was brought at regular intervals, and I ate without really tasting anything. I was too consumed with a burning fire that overcame my weariness and even the lingering horror threatening to overtake me. I was among my people. I was being respected as a true empress. I had an army, a way to retake my throne.

But now, clothed in a plain tunic and leggings one of the women had offered me, I regretted not leaving my dragon scale armor on. Anxiety gnawed at my insides as I fidgeted with my ring—my gold one set with a fiery ruby that had once belonged to Mother. My eyes darted toward where I'd stowed my armor beneath my cot, not trusting to let it out of my sight. I'd left Ryke at the outskirts of camp, where he was free to explore the mountains and hunt as he needed. I wondered if I should have brought him to guard my tent entrance. None would have dared approach me then.

Overconfident fool, I chastised myself. *You should never have trusted these soldiers to guard you.*

Drawing my dagger from where I'd left it beneath my pillow, I crept toward my tent entrance, listening for any noises that seemed out of place in the night. There was the distant hoot of an owl. More rustling wind. The sound of leathers creaking—one of my guards shifting on his feet.

Sweat slicked my palm as I clutched my dagger. I tried to reassure myself, to chase away the old fears that had constantly oppressed me in the palace. The constant threat of death. The frequent bruises left along my skin.

You can kill your enemies with a touch. They have more reason to fear you.

As another whisper of cold wind bit through the tent, I wrapped my arms around myself and repressed a shiver. The dagger's weight was reassuring, despite the ominous fact that I still detected nothing amiss. All the shadows seemed to have eyes as Nesrelle's words echoed through my mind.

And then I heard a shout. Footsteps pounded as my guards charged toward the noise. More cries broke out. My breath caught in my throat.

A distraction, I thought. Before I had a chance to slip outside, the flap pulled back as if of its own accord, affording me a glimpse of velvet sky and distant, ice-blue stars. Though I couldn't see the intruder, I could feel the rush of air and the brush of fingertips as someone reached for me. I reacted on instinct, crying out and slashing my blade through the air where I thought the stranger might be.

A muffled curse in a foreign language—was it Teramese?—told me I'd struck my mark. Two figures blinked into view. Before me stood a Teramese officer, scowling and clutching his shoulder, where his uniform was torn and his skin was cut just deeply enough for a trickle of blood to stain the fabric. Behind him…

Kovi.

For a half-moment, I hesitated, my eyes gazing into his dark ones, the golden flecks in his irises burning like soft embers in the night. His expression was inscrutable. I felt a mingling sense of aching longing and furious resentment. Nesrelle had reminded me that this man was my enemy. He would *never* care, and here was the proof.

I sneered. "You'd side with the likes of him?" My eyes flicked toward the Teramese man, who was shooting daggers with his glare. "It seems Aerekni graduates are no longer respectable if they're making deals with their enemies."

Kovi set his jaw, letting me know my words had hurt as much as I'd hoped they would. He appeared as cold and inscrutable as stone, his body as motionless as one of the palace statues.

"Of course you have no honor," I went on, letting my words drip with derision. I wanted him to feel as much pain looking at me as I felt looking at him. "I knew you were nothing but a self-righteous, lying Forwyn."

"You know *nothing* about me," Kovi said.

But that wasn't true. I knew far too much about him. I knew the rhythm of his breathing as he slept; I knew the tense line of his mouth when he tried to conceal the anger and grief seething within; and I knew the taste of his mouth on mine.

The Teramese man took advantage of my distraction, lifting his hands toward me. Before I could lash out and hurl my dagger toward his face, cold wind rushed through my tent once more. It whirled around me, brushing chill fingers through my hair and tugging at my clothes.

Then, with unexpected force, a gust shoved me backward, slamming me to the earth. Sprawled out on my back, my dagger hanging from limp fingers, I gasped for air that would not enter my burning lungs. Kovi sprang into action, straddling my body and seizing the dagger from my grasp. I lifted my arms to fight back, but he was impossibly swift, catching my wrists in one hand while the other held the blade to my throat.

Blood roared through my ears, reminding me with every heartbeat that this was how everything between us was always supposed to end.

With each of us on opposite sides of an unending war. With both of us prepared to kill the other.

Terror shot through me like a lightning bolt, chased with fiery desperation. I couldn't die. Not here. Not like this.

Kovi leaned forward, his breath warm on my face, and something flashed through his eyes. Hesitation? Desire? It was gone before I could study it, but it sparked hope within me.

"Kovi," I murmured, letting my voice turn soft, letting my eyes linger on his mouth. There was something between us, something I knew he couldn't have forgotten in the short time we'd been apart. The last time I'd seen him, only days ago, he'd confessed to it. Maybe Nesrelle was wrong, and if I could remind Kovi of our connection, he wouldn't land a killing strike.

Kovi tensed, but I didn't need to say another word. Pounding footsteps outside interrupted the moment, and made me break into a smile. My guards were returning.

The Teramese man cursed again. "We need to leave," he muttered in the merchant tongue, his voice thick with a musical accent. "Now." His silver eyes flicked toward me, barely disguising his disgust. "Make a sound, even breathe too loudly, and you're dead."

I couldn't ignore the strangeness of the fact that the threat was coming from him, yet would be dealt out at Kovi's hand. I glanced toward Kovi, but his face was a mask, revealing nothing. He moved as if to lift me, prepared to sling me into his arms like a sack of flour. The moment he lowered the dagger and slid his arm beneath my back, I knew it was time.

My years of training were easy for my muscles to remember as adrenaline flowed through my veins, lending me greater strength than usual. My earlier vow rang in my ears. *I'll never be weak again.*

Instead of struggling to get away, as he would expect, I rolled toward him, slamming my hands against his chest. Whether due to his surprise or my momentum, the movement shoved him off me. He fell back with his hand still clutching the blade, but I was already in motion. Before his companion could stop me, I lunged for my dagger. In another breath, I'd pinned Kovi to the ground and shoved the weapon against his neck.

Kovi's eyes widened, perhaps from how close we were, our breaths mingling, the emotions churning between us hot and heady. And then the thought registered: I'd all but attacked him with my hands, pounding my palms against him. In the past, we'd both watched my power sear through dragon scale armor as if it were nothing. But, despite the fact that Kovi wore a simple cloth uniform, my touch hadn't harmed him.

I took this all in within seconds, before I pushed my confusion away. Leaning in closer, I bit back the longing that unexpectedly hit me as my eyes snagged on Kovi's lips. *Look. Up,* I ordered myself.

The Teramese soldier growled behind me. Out of the corner of my eye, I saw him lift his hands. I didn't know much about Teramese magic, but he seemed to be able to control the air.

Any power he—or Kovi—had to rival mine, however, didn't have a chance. At that moment, my guards charged into the tent, their weapons drawn. Daedra was at the front, snarling like a wild animal as she saw the men threatening me.

The barest trace of a frown flashed across Kovi's face. "Well played," I breathed, thinking of the game of wits we'd engaged in at the palace, "but once again, you've lost this round."

I lifted my head. "Bind them both. We'll take them as prisoners so we can question them. For now."

My soldiers were strong, easily subduing the Teramese soldier before he could attack with his magic. As I rolled off Kovi, I was startled to see he didn't even bother fighting against my soldiers. He dropped the dagger and allowed them to bind him, even though I knew he could control them with a single word, using his uncanny Forwyn magic. In fact, he could have commanded me to stop earlier, when I'd set my blade to his throat.

But he hadn't. Why? He could have killed me and escaped already if he wanted. I told myself there would be time to question everything later.

As Daedra and the other two soldiers led Kovi and his companion away, I refused to meet Kovi's eyes. I refused to think about the electricity that continued to dance between us.

We were enemies, and that was all that mattered. That was all that would *ever* matter.

CHAPTER THIRTEEN

Lo

YOU'RE TO DRESS FOR DINNER, which Lord Xalenos will escort you to shortly." The woman's voice pierced the quiet, startling me from my reverie.

I'd been left alone in Caesiem's rooms for hours, my solitude only interrupted twice: now, and hours earlier when a Forwyn boy had brought me lunch.

All through that time, I'd had nothing but my thoughts for company. *I want you to help Caesiem train the dragons,* Revaed had said. I'd wanted to scoff at him, to laugh in his face, but I'd known feigning obedience was the best path to survival—for both myself and my people.

I couldn't help the dark part of me that wanted the Teramese to try to train the dragons on their own. Unfamiliar with the foreigners, the dragons would be unpredictable and dangerous. It seemed only right for the Teramese to suffer the same sorts of casualties I'd seen my own people face, when Karye had forced us slaves to feed and tend to the beasts.

But when I thought of Caesiem training the dragons and getting injured or killed, my heart stuttered. It was maddening, that I could feel…soft…toward a man who'd betrayed me and killed my own people.

Worse still was Revaed's claim that I might help him build an alliance with my people, as if I hadn't seen the way they already treated the Forwyn. *Liar,* I'd wanted to scream.

And when he'd mentioned that the surviving Elders wanted this alliance too? Rage and disgust had simmered inside me. Those men and women were nothing but self-serving traitors.

But I hadn't wanted Revaed to know my true feelings on the matter. Instead, I'd let him think I was considering his alliance proposal as we'd walked through the garden. Even if it was hardly a proposal when he'd all but hinted I was only a welcome guest if I cooperated and helped them tame the dragons. *Our* dragons.

"I'll help Caesiem train with the dragons," I'd agreed, "but that's not enough." I pretended to be thoughtful, not wanting Revaed or Caesiem to notice my eagerness. "The dragons need to be exercised regularly to stay healthy. As you know, we Forwyn used to tend the dragons—we can do so again. I know some would be willing, if you asked for volunteers."

Revaed watched me warily. "To fly them?"

I shrugged, as if the matter wasn't important. "To help tame and exercise them. Your soldiers might feel safer on dragonback with some Forwyn present."

A gleam of interest sparked in Revaed's gaze at my suggestion that Teramese soldiers might be riding the dragons soon. Just as I'd hoped.

"Of course," Revaed had said.

Soon afterward, he'd summoned guards to lead me back to

Caesiem's rooms, where I'd been left to my own devices while Caesiem and Revaed continued to talk. I'd paced and thought, all the while carefully taking note of the guards' shifts.

Now, I stood from the chair in the sitting room and studied the Forwyn woman hovering in the doorway. She was perhaps a few years older than me, but the timid way she hunched in the entrance made her appear more like a girl. Though her brown eyes were a warm, golden shade that reminded me of honey, they had a glazed, dead look about them. She stared through me, refusing to make eye contact, as she tightly clutched the dress she'd brought.

I crept closer, half-afraid I'd startle her away, and gently plucked the dress from her arms. It was Alrenian in style, which meant they'd probably scoured the palace for formal attire, and dyed a rich green. The top tied about the neck while the back was open, bare except for rows of gold chains adorned with dragon scales. Biting back my sigh, I tossed the dress over the nearest armchair. "You're staying in the palace?" I asked.

Eyes widening, she nodded. "In the old slave quarters."

My limbs went numb. For one painful moment, I was frozen to the floor, my body rigid as my mind returned to my dark days of slavery. The hopelessness. The loneliness. And hovering over all, a constant, oppressive companion: the fear.

I searched her eyes, trying to detect if she'd lie out of shame of serving our enemies or terror of punishment from them. "Did you surrender?" I whispered, my voice raspy. "Did you agree to be enslaved in exchange for your life?"

She shook her head, slowly. "I'm not a slave. They're servants' quarters, now. We're paid servants."

Scowling, I tried to say something more, but footsteps just outside the door made her straighten and reach for the knob.

"Wait—" I began, but before I could say any more, she was darting down the hall and Caesiem was hovering in the doorway instead. His dark hair was disheveled, as if he'd been fidgeting with it, but his eyes shone with the first bit of hope I'd seen on his face since the night he'd betrayed me.

His hope couldn't be a good sign.

Stiffening, I stepped back to put distance between us.

"Did you get the message?" Caesiem's eyes darted to the dress I'd tossed onto the chair, and back to me. A half-smile twitched his lips. "I see you did."

My stomach fluttered at the sight of his dimples, a fact that naturally made me feel annoyed and obstinate. I crossed my arms and set my jaw. "I'm not going."

A frown pinched his brow. "Revaed insisted. I have to go, and he wants you to accompany me."

Go, you fool, I prodded myself. *Learn more. Make a good show of being a potential ally.*

I sighed, perhaps a little overdramatically, but Caesiem grinned, clearly taking it as a sign I'd relented.

"You'll need to hurry," he said as he strode toward his bedroom, presumably to find a fresh uniform.

A short while later, I strode arm-in-arm through the halls with Caesiem, the train of my emerald dress whispering along the marble floor behind me. The chains and scales clinked with each step, and I felt overly conscious of the attention they would draw to my bare back. Similarly to the night of the Autumn Ball, I felt like an imposter in the fine attire, and uncomfortable with the stares it drew from every Teramese soldier we passed. I longed for the inconspicuous grey outfit of a nun.

We exited the palace and stepped out into the gardens, the

evening just cool enough to raise gooseflesh along my bare arms. I gazed at the sky, already navy blue and glistening with stars, and picked out constellations I'd once looked to with hope as a nun. Each name came to me with vivid clarity: the Council of Immortals, the Descent of the Traitor, and Elhani's Victory. Each constellation told a story, a message of hope for his Chosen People to find in the sky, even in our darkest moments.

Now? Now they felt empty, even emptier than when I'd studied them as a child, before I knew their stories of hope, before I understood how to listen for Elhani's song and wield his magic. Then I hadn't known the difference, but now I understood this silence to be my damnation. I was forsaken, cast off. I'd made my choice to turn my back on my god, and he'd turned his back on me.

Swallowing back the wave of loneliness and grief threatening to overtake me, I squared my shoulders and braced myself for the dinner ahead. From the path Caesiem and I were taking through the gardens, I could tell the location would be the same pavilion that had hosted the Autumn Ball.

Caesiem must have mistook my look of distress for fear about the dinner. "You're attending as my guest," he murmured in my ear, leaning in close enough that I could feel his warm breath. I resisted my impulse to shiver. "No need to worry. The soldiers can't so much as look at you wrong tonight without repercussions."

I only nodded, sparing him a quick glance. His uniform, black as usual, was made of an especially fine material and trimmed in shimmering gold. My heartrate accelerated when I noticed how well his muscled chest and arms filled out the jacket. Feeling my cheeks warm, I tore my eyes away.

As we approached the pavilion, flickering torchlight cast a warm glow over the assembled guests. All were seated about a long, rectangular table, at the head of which lounged Revaed, dressed in a finely tailored black uniform accented with red and gold. The Teramese dragon insignia was stitched across the breast in the same shimmering colors, red flame spouting from its maw. When Caesiem and I ascended the pavilion steps, Revaed's eyes landed on us and he offered a lazy smile.

I scanned the space swiftly, taking in the sight of the men and women rising from their seats to face Caesiem and offer their respects. They were all clothed in similar formal apparel, the men in uniforms like Caesiem's and Revaed's—though without the trimming—and the women in fine, close-fitting black dresses they must have brought from Teramyl. Even the Elders—four, I noticed—were all wearing Teramese attire. The only tribute to our own heritage were the braids they continued to wear in their hair or around their necks or wrists. I tore my eyes away, too sickened at their presence to want to even look at them.

It was clear I'd been clothed in Alrenian attire to stand out, but I wasn't sure yet if that was a good or bad thing.

Every man and woman there hesitated for the briefest of moments, their mouths pulling into taut lines when they realized I was on Caesiem's arm—and therefore, they'd appear to be offering respects to me as well.

Maybe this won't be so bad, I thought, fighting back a grin. *Maybe it's a good thing to stand out tonight.*

Still, it felt odd, after my years of being nearly invisible as a slave and then a nun, to have so many eyes upon me at once. The women's bored into me intently, silent threats in their gazes. The men looked hostile as well, but they studied me differently, their eyes sweeping my form from head to toe. I bit back my disgust, realizing my dress must have hugged my curves a little too well. Caesiem seemed to notice their wandering eyes as well, because he scowled before nodding, silently releasing his people from their need to stand at attention.

As one, the assembled guests sat, and Caesiem led me toward two empty chairs at Revaed's side. I tucked my hands into my lap and stared at my empty plate, desperately wishing the food would be served soon so I would have a good excuse to ignore the stares the rest of the night.

"Thanks for joining us," Revaed said pleasantly, his gaze darting from Caesiem to me. Turning to the other guests, he raised his voice to be heard over the quiet chatter. All other talk died at the sound of his voice.

"Tonight, Lord Xalenos has brought an important guest, one that I'm sure you've heard about." There was an unspoken threat in the slight edge to his tone, one that somehow managed to invoke fear while still sounding agreeable. It seemed Caesiem was right, and the soldiers had already been ordered not to even touch me. "Her name is Lo'laeni Nolanhou, and she is representing the Forwyn people as we begin forging an alliance with the blessing of the remaining Elders." He smiled amiably at me. "Miss Nolanhou, we are honored." Lifting his wineglass, he called for a toast.

There was reluctance on a few of the guests' faces, but all followed Revaed's example. I reached for my own glass, which I found was full of a deep red wine, and lifted it, studying its contents. It was such a little thing, to take a sip of wine in a toast, all for the good of my people. But as a nun, my vows had included promises not to drink for pleasure. We'd been expected to always be disciplined and to never waste time or money on such frivolous things.

You're not a nun anymore, I thought, pressing the glass to my lips and letting the liquid slide down my throat. It warmed me instantly and conjured memories of days in the infirmary, weak with illness. Of

Naina's gentle, steady hands as she'd pressed a damp cloth to my fevered brow and offered me a few sips of our medicinal alcohol to help me sleep. We'd never had something so fine as wine in the abbey, but the warming feeling this brought was similar.

I shook off the memories to realize that Revaed was mid-speech, introducing the assembled guests, who were all be important advisors or military officers. "Captain Darix," he was saying, nodding toward a large, beefy man, "and Lieutenant Valentra Arros"—a beautiful woman with her dark hair pulled into a braid that hung over one shoulder.

"Did you serve in the palace?" one of the women whose name I'd missed asked me.

Meaningless small talk. "You mean, was I a *slave?*" I corrected her.

Beside me, Caesiem coughed. I didn't bother to look at him. Whether he was annoyed with me or his soldier, I couldn't tell.

And I don't care, I thought fiercely. *What he thinks no longer matters.*

The woman shrugged, untroubled by my sharp tone. "I meant after the Forwyn takeover, if you'd served for your government here."

"No," I said simply, and took a sip of my drink, signaling the conversation was over.

A few other Teramese tried to ask me questions, but I remained equally short with them, and they soon moved on to more interesting chatter amongst themselves. On the opposite end of the table, the four Elders ignored me as studiously as I ignored them.

Over and over, I felt Caesiem's gaze on me, but I refused to turn toward him. I didn't want to notice him again like I had earlier, didn't want to feel the ache in my chest anymore.

Dinner was brought by Forwyn servants—or that was what the Teramese called them. Seeing my people serve their enemies made my stomach churn with unwelcome memories. Several times, I tried to catch their eyes, but none of them would look directly at me. They kept their heads down, moving as silently as ghosts. I barely tasted the food set before me—dishes of buttered shrimp and steamed vegetables and fresh breads. By the time slices of chocolate cake—chocolate that I knew would have come from Teramyl itself—were set before us, I had fully lost my appetite, despite the fact that I'd only picked at my food.

None of the conversations around me seemed particularly useful. It was obvious the Teramese were carefully guarding their discussions in my presence, avoiding any important information regarding their invasion of Alrenor or their future plans.

Caesiem spoke pleasantly with the people around him, but I could sense how aware he was of me. When my cake sat untouched, he brushed my arm lightly. I gritted my teeth, trying to pretend I didn't feel electricity shooting across my bare skin at his warmth.

He's a traitor and your enemy, I thought.

"I know this isn't easy for you," he murmured, his breath tickling my ear. "But thank you for coming."

Somehow, I'd missed a transition in the conversation happening around us, for in that moment, Revaed turned to Caesiem and me, a smile still in place. "Do you truly doubt the solidity of our alliance?" he was asking. With effortless grace, he gestured once more toward me. "I assure you, the Forwyn will cooperate with us. How could they not, when their dear *amara'rekni* is tied so closely to one of our own?" Heart lurching, his words bounced around wildly in my head. I could scarcely comprehend what he was saying. Surely it couldn't mean what I thought it meant…

Revaed raised his voice. "We will announce it tomorrow: that there is to be a marriage union between the famed Forwyn Empress-Slayer and my heir, Caesiem Xalenos, the soon-to-be Prince of

Alrenor." Revaed winked at Caesiem, like this was all a light matter, not a life-changing discussion.

I could feel Caesiem tensing at my side.

Revaed turned toward me. "I believe, if you choose to work with us, a marriage would be the best way for you to convince your people of your sincerity. I've spoken with your Elders"-he nodded across the table, and Elder Iloha nodded back, the act turning my mouth sour-"and they said they would recognize the union and happily work alongside us if you agreed to as well. Your people respect you, and…"

"My people don't know I'm the *amara'rekni*." My voice was quiet, cold. I wanted to scream, but my ears were ringing, and I couldn't seem to form the words. Every eye turned toward me, and I could feel the weight of their stares. "And I don't want them to *ever* know that I am."

Breathe, ahnla. The memory of Naina's soothing voice filled my head. I leaned into it and reminded myself to be cautious, not quick to react. To shout and refuse here in front of Revaed's officers would probably be a death sentence. I had to survive, had to play the game. For now.

Revaed's smile faltered only a little. "Well, your betrothal will still be of great significance to your people." He paused. "Miss Nolanhou, I know you're surprised, but consider the benefits. Your Elders certainly have. One day, you and Caesiem could rule Alrenor side-by-side, with the Teramese and Forwyn living peacefully together in a united empire. I don't give Caesiem away lightly." His lips twitched, as if he thought he was making a joke.

The rest of the dinner, I sat in silence, refusing to look at Caesiem. Refusing to speak. Unable to eat. My ears continued to ring as I stewed, tuning out the idle chatter occurring all around me. I didn't bother to notice if Caesiem ever said anything at all, and I didn't want to. All I could think, over and over, was how I wanted to punch him again.

As soon as we were out of earshot, back within the palace and on our way to his rooms after dinner, I whirled on Caesiem. "You *garash*," I bit out.

"Ah, a curse in Alrenian," Caesiem said, his smile taut as he tried to force false lightness into his tone. "Kind of you to insult me in a language I know."

I glowered at him, pressing closer. I didn't care what kind of power or status he possessed among these people—I was livid.

"You said I wasn't a prisoner, that I was free to do as I pleased and you were only trying to protect me," I sneered, leaning forward until I was practically in his face. "But those were more lies, weren't they? So what *is* this? What do you want from me? Do your people truly need an alliance this badly?"

"*No*—this isn't what I wanted," Caesiem said, his bright eyes sparking with anger.

My laughter bounced harshly off the walls. "First, I'm the fool you played for information, now I'm the political pawn."

"No," he snapped. "I *didn't know*—Revaed didn't tell me."

"Or am I just some conquest for you?" I continued, ignoring his protests. My voice cracked as the words spilled out. "Did you go around bragging that you stole a kiss from a nun? Is that all it meant to you?" As soon as I spoke the words, I realized I'd revealed how much he'd hurt me. But it was too late to take them back, and I was too angry to retreat.

A muscle twitched in Caesiem's jaw. "So that's what you think of me? That I'm some worthless scoundrel who plays with women's hearts?"

"I think you're a lying, traitorous thief—"

Caesiem grabbed my face and kissed me. I couldn't breathe, couldn't think. There was only the heat of his lips, hungry and demanding, and the feel of his hands on my cheeks, somehow both firm and gentle. "It meant more than you know," he murmured against my mouth, his words low and angry.

I pulled back, my mind whirling. "*Garash,*" I cursed again. We stared at each other, the very air between us taut with fury and desire.

In one motion, I stepped forward, seized Caesiem by the collar, and pressed my mouth to his. There was no gentleness in it, only some frenzied, wrathful desire to prove a point—that he couldn't have meant what he said. I was sure that nothing between us could matter to him. *I* couldn't matter to him, not after what he'd done.

But as soon as our lips touched, desire took over. Caesiem seized my waist, pushing me until my back collided with the wall, the chains and dragon scales on my dress clinking. He traced one hand up my spine, every brush of his fingers leaving trails of fire in its wake. I leaned into him, clutching his collar even tighter to draw him nearer.

A man cleared his throat, and Caesiem drew back enough that I could spring away.

Heart pounding, hands shaking, I tried to force a calm mask back onto my face as a Teramese guard stepped forward. His expression was unreadable as he glanced between Caesiem and me. "Excuse me, Lord Xalenos," he said, but he didn't sound particularly sorry. "I didn't realize it was you." He pressed a hand to his chest in a salute.

"Perhaps now that you've recognized me, you can concentrate on watching for a real threat," Caesiem scoffed.

"Forgive me," the guard said, anxiety darting across his face. "I'll do that."

I gritted my teeth as the man turned on his heel and strode away to return to his patrol of the halls. My earlier anger and hurt swept through me again. I couldn't quite meet Caesiem's eyes. How could I have kissed him…*again*? And this time, while *knowing* who he truly was, knowing that I couldn't trust him?

Several long moments passed, wrought with tension and confusion. I could feel the weight of Caesiem's gaze, but I refused to look at him. Neither of us broached the topic of our interrupted kiss.

At last, Caesiem broke the silence. "I didn't know Revaed would do that," he repeated softly, running his hand through his hair and pushing off the wall. I glanced up to find his expression sincere. "I'm sorry. He surprised me too."

"I know," I murmured, staring at the gold slippers I'd been given to wear. I scuffed the toe of one along the floor.

He turned to me, eyes wide. "You do?"

I nodded. "I can tell you're…shocked."

"But I *should* have seen it coming," Caesiem went on, swiping his hand through his hair again and frowning. "Revaed is always thinking of what would be politically beneficial, what will be the most helpful for Teramyl. Of course the next step in solidifying an alliance between our peoples would be for him…to want *that*." He scowled at the ground. "It's not right. I'll talk him out of it."

I hesitated. "Don't…" I paused, studying his face. "Don't say anything to him yet."

Caesiem gaped at me. "You're not *agreeing* to it, are you?"

I shrugged. "No, I just…it's better if Revaed thinks I am." Inhaling deeply, I offered him a thin smile. *Elhani, if you're listening, forgive my deception,* I thought. "There's still a lot to process, but…I want to do right by my people. Marriage is going a bit far...but an alliance...I can consider that. Don't talk to him about it yet. I don't want him to think I'm opposed to...everything."

Caesiem nodded. "All right," he said. "I'll wait, if that's what you want."

My eyes jerked open, a strangled cry scraping against my throat. Gasping for air, I sat up in bed, scanning the shadowy room for a phantom threat. Somehow, despite how tense being within the palace made me, I must have been exhausted enough to fall asleep soon after the dinner. And based on how dark it was, I must have been asleep for an hour or two, at least.

"Lo?" Caesiem leapt from the settee and crept toward the bed, his forehead crinkled in concern. "What's wrong?"

Slowly, my heartbeat returned to normal and my breathing steadied. Only the lingering terror of my nightmares—my memories—hovered over me. Karye was dead, and Edi had been murdered years ago. I blinked, fighting back the threat of tears burning my eyes. When Caesiem took my sweaty hand in his cool one, cradling it gently, I didn't pull back. "Nothing," I whispered.

His gaze was knowing. "Nightmares?"

When I nodded, he sighed. "You don't have to stay here. I'm sure I could talk to Revaed...you could get away and not have to worry..."

"No," I said firmly. "I'm staying." I was certain now that this was where I needed to be, that fleeing would be forsaking my people. If pretending to cooperate with Revaed is what it took to keep the Forwyn safe, I would bear the nightmares and memories that haunted me in the palace. I'd already borne so much worse.

Caesiem released my hand and stepped back, immediately making me miss the comfort of his touch. "Lie back down," he murmured. "I'll play so you have something else to think about, until you can fall asleep again."

He slipped into one of the dim corners of the room, bringing out his lythra and perching on the settee. As he began to strum the instrument, filling the room with a soft, soothing tune, I watched him in rapt fascination. It felt almost magical, the way the song washed over me like the steady beat of waves crashing against the beach, or the rhythmic pulsing of dragon wings.

When he began to sing, I closed my eyes and shut the rest of the world out. I let the melody consume me, let the rich strains of his voice wrap around me like a blanket. My earlier anger was lost as he wove the song like a spell, enthralling and peaceful all at once.

Old nightmares fell away. My mind quieted. My chest lightened. And I drifted into a dreamless sleep.

When I woke again, the room was still. My eyes darted over to where Caesiem lay curled up on the settee, his lythra leaning against it.

It was still dark. Even the power of Caesiem's music apparently hadn't kept the nightmares at bay for long. This time, I'd been awoken from a dream about my sisters. Naina and Pauni'a's kindly faces and friendly eyes had turned hateful and judgmental when they'd looked at me, noting the blood staining the dress I'd worn to the Autumn Ball. Then I'd once again seen the downcast expressions on the newly enslaved Forwyn at the palace. Finally, the nightmare had shifted again, showing me the abbey, my old home with the Circle of Serenity, engulfed in dragon fire as the sisters tried to flee the ruthless Teramese soldiers cutting them down.

Calming my shuddering breath, I was relieved to find that this time Caesiem wasn't disturbed by my waking. I didn't want to leave, that was true, but maybe venturing beyond the palace walls could help. And I didn't particularly want Caesiem to notice my absence.

I rose from the bed, arranged the pillows carefully within it, and crept out through the balcony doors.

Caesiem might have been a spy, but he'd never been a slave. He'd never had to slink through hallways with his head cast down, doing everything in his power to make himself a part of the wall paintings, or just another shadow. A wraith. He'd never had to hold his breath and pray the sound of his heartbeat would blend in with the thudding of an approaching noble's footsteps, hoping he wouldn't be noticed. Hoping he wouldn't be punished, or worse—seen as something beautiful and perhaps desirable.

But I knew how to be invisible, how to be so silent and unobtrusive it was almost as if I didn't exist at all. There was only the briefest instant for me to make my exit via the balcony: the first guard had left and would soon be relieved by a new one. The Teramese were apparently arrogant enough to think I would remain cowering in their lord's bedchamber during the interim. They didn't believe I knew how to move with the speed and skill necessary to dart out onto the balcony, ducking so as to be unseen by the guards patrolling the garden below, and wait for a moment when it was safe to shimmy over the railing and down a nearby trellis.

They didn't realize that for years, this had been my life. The palace was painfully familiar, each corner stained with memories, mostly horrible. A few were good, but those were the ones that hurt the most.

Mother's smile and gentle voice. Edi daring to meet me in the slave rooms for a whispered conversation before we had to once again return to a life of pretending we didn't care about one another. Other than Mother and Edi himself, I'd had no other family and I hadn't dared to make friends. Too many of the other slaves vanished in the blink of an eye, killed or sold off for crimes Empress Karye found unforgivable. Some slaves even turned on one another, reporting to nobility or the empress herself on other' "misbehavior" in hopes of earning favor.

In that harsh world, Edi had been the only one I'd trusted. Until he'd been killed, and I'd been left alone.

For the longest time, the only person I'd relied upon was me.

My heart ached as I darted from building to building throughout the palace grounds, the waning moon staring at me like some odious monster's eye. I became a part of the shadows, a part of the air itself, there one instant and gone the next. A breath the guards might turn toward and miss.

I'd made up my mind not to leave the palace, to play the game and find what information I could learn about the Teramese, but that didn't mean I'd remain hidden away in Caesiem's rooms the whole time. I needed to see the other Forwyns' quarters, and since I couldn't sleep, now seemed as good a time as any.

It didn't take long to arrive at the building that had once been the palace slave quarters. And whatever the Teramese or even the Forwyn themselves claimed, I believed they were being used as slave quarters again. I'd seen the Forwyn with their lowered heads and bent backs shuffling into Caesiem's rooms to deliver food. Though he might have waved them off as servants, I saw the faded looks in their eyes, the desperate, angry set of their mouths.

As I drew closer to the building, the pressure in my chest became nearly unbearable. I swallowed to push back the tears tightening my throat. My breathing turned shallow.

I recalled the way Naina used to speak into my mind using her magic, grounding me when my panic nearly drowned me. I forced myself to focus on my surroundings: the gentle breeze on my face, the chirping of crickets, and the scent of oranges lingering in the air.

Slowly, my breaths steadied. The tightness in my chest unspooled. Resolve hardening my heart, I trod straight through the slaves' entrance.

Fight back. The voice pulsed through my mind, over and over as if matching the beat of my heart. It was infused with confidence and power, and I wasn't sure if it came from my own thoughts or somewhere else. I didn't dare hope that Elhani was deigning to speak to me after I'd betrayed him by breaking my vows.

It was probably just my own voice, and yet, it gave me courage. I clung to it.

Within, the halls were dim and plain, with no torches to light the way and no plush carpets to soften my steps. There were no statues or tapestries lining the walls and no paintings adorning the ceiling. The only light came from grimy windows set high in the walls, permitting small streams of moonlight to bathe patches of the rough stone floor in a silver glow. Everything about the space smelled stale, the scent of too many bodies who received too few baths lingering in the air, as if the building itself could not release the generations of atrocities and suffering that had occurred here. Even stronger was an odor I associated with fear and despair. It was sharp and bitter on my tongue, reminding me of the tang of blood and the sting of tears. This place was filled with too many waking nightmares. Who would want to enter it again?

And yet here I was, following the sound of lowered voices despite the late hour. Sweat gathered along the back of my neck and I brushed wayward curls away from my eyes.

Memories slammed into me with such force it was as if someone had punched the air out of my body.

Be strong, my sweet Lo. That was my mother's voice as she'd ran her calloused fingers across my fevered brow when I'd been young and sick.

Without access to medicine or the palace healers, there were far too many slaves who had wasted away and perished from curable diseases. I'd whimpered from my place curled up on my tiny pallet. Countless other slaves filled the tiny, dark room, all trying to put as much space between themselves and the sick girl as possible. But my mother had nursed me throughout the night, despite the weariness in her eyes.

She'd been the one to encourage me to hold my head high and push through my duties during the day, pretending I was well so the Alrenians wouldn't sneer at my weakness and harm or even kill me. She'd been the one who had stolen medicine from I-knew-not-where, and somehow, Elhani had blessed her path, for she'd never been caught.

Now, I blinked away the threatening tears and rounded a corner, scanning the rows of doorways on either side of the hall. The crowded rooms where all the slaves had slept too close together. Edi's voice rang out in my mind. *Don't ever give up hope, Lo. You're strong and you're smart. You'll find a path to freedom, I know you will. There will be more to life than this. You'll see. We'll live to see our dreams come true.*

My heart ached, and I bit back a scream of rage and loss. Edi had never lived to see any goodness in the world. His entire short life had been marked with misery and pain, and he'd been so kind, so pure. Out of the two of us, he'd deserved a better life more than anything, and somehow, here I was, still breathing. And he was not.

I'm so sorry, Edi. Please forgive me, because I can never forgive myself. I'm so, so sorry.

I wished I could have saved my little brother. I wished that killing Karye would have brought peace to my broken heart. I wished for a thousand impossible things in that moment, as the tears escaped and slipped down my hot cheeks.

The voices came from further down the corridor than the familiar entrance now hovering on my right. Swallowing back the tears and grief, I wiped my face and crept through the doorway. The dim interior was small, even smaller than my room in the abbey, and yet dingy pallets covered in threadbare blankets filled every available space. A layer of dust coated everything, tickling my nose as I breathed slowly, steadily, trying to calm my racing heart. It was clear no one had entered this room in a long time. The slaves who had once occupied it—myself included—had no reason to return. We'd had no possessions. No nostalgic reasons to come back and linger. So why was I here now?

More memories enveloped me, warming as a blanket yet painful as a knife slipping between my ribs. Edi sneaking from his room into mine to whisper to me. The apathetic glances of other slaves. "You can't keep visiting like this," I'd told him, countless times. "You can't let anyone see that we're family. That we care." And yet, despite it all, he'd continued to risk everything to see me. We'd slip into the hallway, where we had space to move and a bit more freedom to whisper, if we were careful. We'd swapped memories about Mother and shared dreams.

"I want to own a dragon," Edi said sometimes, with a mischievous grin. Other times, he was a bit more realistic, telling me he longed to see the Alrenian countryside. To live in a small cottage by the sea and be a fisherman, where he would always have wide open spaces surrounding him, and enough privacy to be and do whatever he wanted. To be *free*.

I'd shared in that dream, adding that I wanted to find a way to save as many slaves as possible. To ensure every Forwyn we knew was as safe and free as we were. And, of course, we'd both longed to find Mother and learn who our father was. All of our dreams included being a family, whole and happy and never threatened with separation again.

Once more, I forced the images away. As my eyes adjusted to the darkness and skimmed over the rough stone walls, I could pick out my pallet with its dingy tan blanket, tangled from the last night I'd slept in this accursed place. I could still remember the feel of waking up with fresh loss pressing on me like a tangible weight, making my limbs heavy and my movements leaden.

And yet, despite all of the horrors this building held, it brought the memories of Edi and Mother closer. It was as if I could see their ghosts come to life in vivid color all around me, their smiles warm and alive. I could almost trick myself into believing that if I just waited here long enough, they would come trudging down the hall, shoulders hunched with weariness after a long day of work, but ready to greet me with love and kindness sparkling in their eyes.

A male voice tore me from my thoughts, and for one wonderful, awful moment, I half-expected to truly see Edi standing behind me in the doorway. "It *is* you."

I spun and instantly froze.

Renni's pale grey eyes stared back at me, gleaming in the dimness with an emotion I couldn't quite identify.

My pulse pounded in my ears. Mio'e hadn't said anything about Renni being captured by the Teramese the night of the Autumn Ball. Had they brought him in recently? The vigilante didn't strike me as the type of man who would surrender his life to enslavement. No, I was certain he would rather die than submit himself to this life.

"How are you… Why are you here?" I choked out. Every instinct within me was screaming to run. I'd hoped to find allies in this place, but if Renni was suspicious about Wilvhe's death, he was the last person who would side with me against the Teramese.

Renni stepped nearer, his expression hardening. "Did you think because we have new enemies that we vigilantes would back down in our efforts?" he snapped. "Nu'or spied on some of the Teramese *hilvoku* in the palace grounds and heard them talking about a Forwyn woman their Lord Caesiem Xalenos had taken to be his mistress."

I swallowed my fury at the false claim, biting back my protest. It would be worthless with Renni, especially when that wasn't my greatest crime.

"You betrayed us," Renni went on, his tone low. I'd never seen such viciousness in his eyes before, such raw fury. It was terrifying. He took another step closer, and I instinctively took one back. "You and Caesiem brought new enemies down upon us, and now you live in luxury while your people are enslaved again? *And* you murdered Wilvhe." He blinked, as if fighting back tears, willing himself to be strong. "So I let them capture me, surrendered to the Teramese to be one of their so-called servants, all so I could learn more about their plans from the inside." He narrowed his eyes. "And find you."

I clenched my jaw until it ached. "I would never side with the Teramese," I ground out. My eyes scanned his body quickly, searching for weapons, trying to take in any weaknesses I could utilize to escape. As a servant, it was likely he'd been stripped of any weapons, but that didn't mean he wasn't hiding something he could use as one on his person. "Mio'e is the one who swore the oath to be an avenger of blood," I went on, hoping to distract him. "Will you take that from her?"

Renni uncurled the fingers of his left hand and lifted it toward me, palm up. It was wrapped in a bandage, where blood had already seeped through and stained it red. He must have cut it recently. "I did too," he said, and then he lunged for me.

I ducked before he could seize my neck. With a cry, I kicked him in the groin as hard as I could. Hunched over, he stifled a grunt and swung for my face.

Renni's pain made him sloppy, and he gave away the movement, offering me plenty of time to sidestep. With every ounce of my weight and strength, I answered with a punch of my own. It struck his nose hard enough to spray blood, hard enough to make my knuckles sting.

Enraged, Renni launched himself at me. He was larger and stronger, and when I failed to duck out of the way, he overpowered me easily. It was a swift, chaotic move—a shove them slammed me back against the wall.

But it was enough to send sparks dancing across my eyes. My ears rang.

The world spun, and I knew I was too disoriented to survive his attack for long.

This was a fight I couldn't win.

Thankfully, Renni was still in pain as well. When he noticed my dazed look, he hesitated, blinking to clear his own head. Swiping at the blood pouring from his nose.

Taking the only chance I had, I threw myself toward the opening he'd made between himself and the door. I smashed against the stone floor, bones jarring as I used my momentum to roll into a crouch. The world spun, but I didn't have time to reorient myself. Renni's footsteps were already pounding toward me as I launched to my feet and tore back down the hall, toward the front entrance.

Everything lurched and my stomach churned, but I could still escape. I *had* to.

Though I could still hear the other slaves' voices somewhere down the corridor, a few raised in surprise or alarm, I knew I couldn't count on them. All Renni would have to do was lift his hand and explain he was a blood avenger, and the other Forwyn would turn away. Through our traditions, he had every right to vengeance. The same way I had possessed the right to avenge my brother's death by slaying Karye, even if I'd found it had only left me emptier than before.

I shoved open the front door and charged down the steps that led from the slaves' quarters back to the garden path. Renni was right behind me, cursing under his breath. I'd hoped running toward where the Teramese were posted within the grounds, reckless as it was, would hinder Renni. But apparently his taste for vengeance was greater than his fear of the Teramese overpowering him. I just had to be faster than him, to find some guards…

A popping sound filled my ears and it was as if I were plunged underwater, all noises dulling around me. The realization struck me at once: Renni was using magic, placing us in an invisible bubble that silenced any sounds we made. No one would hear me if I screamed. I hadn't known Renni could wield Elhani's magic so effortlessly, hadn't known he'd trained in it at all, but then again…how well did I know him or any of the vigilantes?

I charged toward the path that led to the Dragon Keep, praying the threat of being seen by enemies would hold Renni back. Adrenaline sang through my blood and helped clear my vision as I pumped my arms and threw every ounce of strength into lengthening my stride. At least here I was in my element, running as I had for countless nights over the years. I could put space between Renni and me and give myself a chance.

A rock whistled past my ear, chased quickly by another that found its mark. It slammed against the back of my head, sending lights dancing before my eyes while warmth dripped down my face. Dizzy, I stumbled. I crashed to the ground, blinking against the pounding pain threatening to pull me under.

Renni was there before I could stagger to my feet. Pain hardened his gaze as he seized me by the shirt collar and dragged me across the ground. I groaned in protest, but I was too weak. I slipped in and out of consciousness, yanked under by waves of darkness. Each time I opened my eyes, the world blurred and tilted. I caught glimpses of the moon staring coldly, unmoved by my suffering. Palm fronds swayed above. My heartbeat throbbed in my head, exacerbating the sensation that my skull would burst. Blood dribbled down the back of my neck.

I tried to punch Renni's arm, but each time, my fist struck nothing but air. I kicked and cried out, to no avail. Everything seemed submerged, and I remembered that Renni was using magic to block out sounds. No one would care to help me anyway.

Darkness clutched me in its cold fingers again, before I opened my eyes and found myself staring down a cliffside toward a distant beach. Golden sands extended toward turbulent water painted grey and silver in the moonlight. Choppy waves crashed against sharp rocks that would surely dash anyone to pieces if they fell.

Renni shoved me close to the edge, sending pebbles skittering. An unusually chill wind brushed against my cheeks, tasting of citrus and salt and smoke. The fragrance of the gardens mixed with the tang from the nearby Keep and the churning, restless sea. The scents pulled me into a memory from another night when I'd been threatened with death. I could hear the thuds of bodies collapsing around me; I could smell the blood that permeated the air until it seemed to coat my tongue. I could feel the cold blade pressed against my throat as Karye gloated.

Panic shot through my limbs, blessedly clearing my head. When I glanced up, I could see tears trailing down Renni's cheeks, glistening like diamonds in the night. "He was my friend," he murmured. I felt a stab of pity.

Maybe this is what I deserve, I thought. Maybe it was time for me to atone for my sins, for breaking my sacred vows to Elhani and for slaying Wilvhe. I ached with remorse. *Maybe I should just let him throw me off the cliff and meet my eternal damnation.*

And yet, I'd been fighting to survive all my life. It was all I knew, and even now, as guilt and uncertainty plagued me, I had a fierce desire to live. When I considered the Forwyn once again living in the slave quarters, I knew I still had a purpose. I had to help my people, somehow. I couldn't give into the darkness. Not yet.

Renni choked back his tears, a solemn resignation settling over his features. "According to Elhani's righteous law," he declared, raising his free hand—the bandaged one, "as you have taken a life, so now I take yours. As you have spilled blood, I will spill yours." His eyes darted to my face before flicking away. "May your death avenge Wilvhe's."

Biting the inside of my cheek to keep myself conscious, I twisted in Renni's grip and rolled away. Too weak and dizzy to pull myself to my feet, I lay on my side and prepared to defend. He leapt for me, leaning close enough that I landed a punch to his face. With a grunt, he reared back, clutching his eye, already bruised and swelling.

Snarling, he seized me by the shirt again. I kicked and punched, some of my desperate attempts striking their targets. But Renni was stronger. With a cry, he lifted me into the air and hurled me over the cliff's edge. Briny wind whipped through my curls and tore at my clothes, wrapping its arms around me like a living creature welcoming me to my death. It swallowed me whole in its velvety embrace. I screamed, but the wind ripped the sound straight from my mouth. Flipping in the air, I stared at the distant beach growing closer and tensed for the impact that would break my body and shatter my bones.

A rush of water poured over me. Confusion twisted in my mind. Had the sea itself risen to greet me? The water swept over me in gentle waves, enveloping my body until I was submerged, all while the water floated, impossibly, in mid-air. Foaming and rushing and roiling around me, it rose, pressing me firmly yet gently upward, back toward the cliff.

Wind whipped through my hair, misting the water until my curls clung to my cheeks. The power surging through the air made the hairs rise on the back of my neck. It sizzled in my bones like the sensation right before a thunderstorm. Though the water never rose past my mouth, its sheer strength took my breath away.

Lifting my eyes to the cliff's edge, I spotted Renni, slack-jawed and terrified as he stared at an approaching figure. Black hair sea-slick, water droplets shimmering on his face, Caesiem surged forward as smoothly as the rushing water that not only swirled around me, but also encircled him. He held his arms aloft, manipulating the element with the same grace as a musician working an instrument. His usually bright eyes seemed dark, churning with emotions as tumultuous as the seawater he commanded.

Awe swept through me as I remembered that Revaed had called Caesiem a mage. *He's a water mage,* I thought.

Caesiem tugged his arms back and the water obeyed, drawing me toward the cliff and straight over Renni. It deposited me gently beside Caesiem. Head spinning, I sank to the ground and drew my knees to my chest. I glanced dazedly from the strange lord next to me to the vigilante precariously close to the cliff's edge.

Frozen in fear, Renni didn't even have time to flee or retaliate with his own magic before Caesiem made a sweeping gesture. The water swirled around Renni. It soared through the air like a serpent, beautiful and unstoppable, thrusting Renni along its surface until he hung suspended in the air like I had. Screaming and kicking, he spun and somersaulted as the waves heaved him toward the choppy sea far below.

And then…I blinked, sure I was hallucinating. My head pounded and the world was still blurred at the edges. But when I opened my eyes, tentacles the color of the water rose above the tossing waves of the Great Sea. From this distance, it was clear they were huge and only a small portion of the great beast writhing in the depths. Except…I'd thought the sea was too shallow this close to the coast for large water creatures. When I glanced at Caesiem, I saw his brow furrowed in concentration, the dark gleam in his eyes more intense than before.

Somehow, Caesiem had summoned this beast.

I couldn't help the horror rising in my chest. When I flicked my eyes back to Renni, he was already tumbling in a downward arc toward the ascending creature. A strangled cry threatened to erupt from my throat, but at the last moment it died. I held my breath. The thought flashed through my head like lightning: *As long as Renni lives, he will never stop trying to kill you.*

With a heartrending scream, Renni toppled from the rushing waves and plunged toward the water beast. Among the serpentine arms, I caught a glimpse of an opening maw. Water whirled and foamed around its rows of sharp teeth. It reached up, up, meeting Renni in the air and devouring him in an instant. The tentacles vanished beneath the stormy sea, ripples shooting out from where the beast had risen and disturbing the foaming, bubbling water even more.

I stared, open-mouthed and breathless. I'd been so close to death, and the man who'd wanted to kill me had been slain by one of the legendary water creatures I feared. Head aching, I pressed my brow against my knees, hoping the pounding would vanish and the world would settle. Darkness closed in once more, and I slipped into its soothing arms.

In and out I drifted, lulled into a sense of comfort by the strong arms that carried me, by the warmth that enveloped me. Then the world shifted, and I felt sand at my back. Waves crashed on shore, close enough for saltwater to spray against my cheeks.

Opening my eyes, I found Caesiem gazing at me, his face set in hard lines. Before I could demand why he'd brought me down here, before I could even remember to panic at the memory of the beast he'd summoned, he stood and strode out into the sea. Water whirled around him, the very waves seeming to move their course to be closer to him as he waded into it.

I blinked against another wave of pain. The world shifted in and out of focus, and I wondered if I'd again lose consciousness. Maybe I was dreaming everything.

Drawing something gold and glinting from his pocket, Caesiem tossed it into the swirling water. Instantly, the sea stilled, turning unnaturally calm. It lay smooth as glass, gleaming silver in the moonlight. Caesiem stood motionless, an unyielding silhouette in the night.

After a long moment, a shape rose out of the water. My breath caught in my chest when I discerned a woman's face, her long hair gleaming as white as sea foam in the darkness. She lifted a hand that didn't seem to be quite the right shape, holding something small and gleaming. It must have been whatever Caesiem had tossed into the water. When she turned her head, I caught a flash of silver scales and bright yellow eyes. Inhuman.

I repressed a shudder. *I'm dreaming,* I thought again, squeezing my eyes shut against the pulsing in my head.

Without the rhythm of the waves, Caesiem and the strange woman's voices sounded as loud as if they stood right next to me.

"You summoned me?" The woman's words came out in a lilting tune, more like she was singing than speaking.

"Theslynik." Caesiem's voice was gruff, demanding.

"Terse today," the woman whined. "I thought I'd hear a fun riddle of a message. That I could visit more pretty-faced men and see if they'd want to play any games." A deeper note crept into her tone, one that could have been a threat. "You never play any games."

"There's no time to waste," Caesiem replied. "Theslynik, or return the payment and leave."

There was a sound that reminded me of the wind sighing off the water. "All right." A splash sounded and more long moments passed, moments when I couldn't force my eyes to open to see what was happening.

It seemed a great while later that the woman spoke again. "Here you are, pretty one. Are you sure that's all?" This time, I was sure there was something dangerous in her seductive tone.

Caesiem's words didn't waver. "You know that can't work on me, and no, you're not getting her, either. Go, or I'll let the water beast eat you."

I drifted again, stirring only when Caesiem was at my side, shaking me awake. "Don't sleep. Drink this." He pressed a vial to my mouth, and despite all the questions I had, something in his eyes made me trust him.

It was a tasteless liquid, cool at first, but it burned on the way down. He waited until I'd drank every drop before pulling the vial away. I closed my eyes, feeling darkness tug on me again. He took my hand, his skin warm and reassuring against mine, and pressed a kiss to my palm.

"Stay," I rasped, my eyelids fluttering. As hard as I fought to remain awake, it seemed like a losing battle.

"Of course," Caesiem said, his voice the same low and determined one I'd heard commanding the strange woman. "I'll stay as long as you want me to."

I woke to a dim room and a comforting cocoon of warm blankets. Caesiem leaned over me, his brow knotted in concern as he ran a damp cloth over the bump on the side of my head. Though the persistent, dull ache hadn't fully abated, the pain felt more manageable and the world seemed to have righted itself. My vision was clear. It was all too easy to study Caesiem as he hovered close, his breath gentle against my cheeks. He focused solemnly on his task of cleaning the dried blood that I knew clumped my hair. He brought his opposite hand up, almost absent-mindedly, and caressed my cheek.

He froze when his gaze dropped to my face. His eyes locked on mine, holding me in a breathless stare.

Something in me ached at his attentiveness and longed to reach out and touch him in the same soft way he touched me. At the same time, I wanted to recoil from him and mention the new slaves kept in the old quarters. When I noticed the storm swirling in his beautiful eyes, I couldn't shut out the memory of Renni's screams tearing through the night, of the massive water beast devouring him in the space of a breath. Of the skin-tingling power Caesiem had woven around me as he'd commanded the sea and its creature. Or the way even the waves had seemed to beckon to him, how the strange woman had heeded his threats.

My eyes snagged on his waterdrop-shaped pendant, which had fallen loose from where he'd tucked it beneath his shirt. It was a smooth stone, broken only by a small hole at the top that allowed the leather cord tied around his neck to loop through it. I extended a hand and ran my fingertips over its cold surface. It seemed unnaturally cold when I'd expected it to be warm from the contact with Caesiem's skin. When I held it, I felt a jolt of power course over me, a memory of briny wind and sea mist and churning, powerful waves.

"I didn't know Renni was here," Caesiem said. His voice was rough, and with my hand clutching the pendant attached to his necklace, he couldn't pull away. His face was dangerously close to mine. Fury pinched his lips into a firm line. "Why was he trying to kill you?"

I ignored his question. "How did you find me?"

"I woke from…a dream." He hesitated only for a beat, but it was enough for me to see the darkness in his eyes. It was enough for me to recognize that he had nightmares too. "When I found nothing but pillows piled beneath the bed to try to fool me" –he didn't resist the smile tugging at the corners of his mouth– "I knew where you'd go. I reached the old slave quarters just as Renni was dragging you on the path toward that cliff." He scowled. "I'm sorry I didn't arrive sooner."

"You didn't expect me to escape? You didn't look in the Keep first?"

"I know your heart, Lo," he murmured. "I knew you wouldn't

leave when your people are here in Alrenor."

A part of me couldn't tear my eyes away from his piercing gaze, the one that *saw* and knew me uncannily well. The rest of me wanted to spit in his face, to remind him that *he* and his Teramese friends were the reason my people were once again facing life under an oppressive government.

It was infuriating, the ways in which Caesiem contradicted himself. How genuine he seemed rushing to save my life, to tend to my wounds. It didn't match with the traitor lord I knew, the one who had condemned my people and me to more tyranny.

"If you know my heart," I ground out, releasing Caesiem's pendant, "then you know I'll never forgive you. Saving my life tonight doesn't make up for everything you've done to my people."

Caesiem swallowed, pulling back slowly so his face no longer lingered near mine. The distance was simultaneously disappointing and relieving. "I know," he said.

Silence lingered heavily between us as he moved slowly, returning to wiping at the blood crusted on my temple. As much as I wanted to crawl away from him, to pull myself out of this luxurious bed and join my fellow Forwyn in the slave quarters, I lay still. Between the pounding in my head, my exhaustion from my fitful night, and the adrenaline draining out of me, my will to fight was spent.

It had been a long while since someone had tended to me like this, and I found myself tempted to close my eyes and pretend I was back in the abbey, that Caesiem was just an orphan thief and not Lord Xalenos, that he'd never betrayed us and I'd never broken my vows. Or that we'd run away together after all, and he'd remained loyal to the Forwyn cause.

I wanted to lose myself in unrealistic daydreams, where I could lean in to Caesiem's touch, and maybe even reach out to touch him back, tracing my fingers along the stubble lining his jaw or through his still-damp hair.

I swallowed back those thoughts, shame burning through me. *Girlish fantasies.* Whatever tenderness Caesiem felt toward me was dwarfed by his will to serve his disgusting Emperor Revaed and the cruel, conniving Teramese people.

At last, Caesiem broke the silence, his voice a low rumble. "How do you feel?"

I choked back a laugh. *Furious. Defeated. Devastated. Lost.* It felt like there were too many powerful emotions swarming through me for one body to contain, and I would surely burst. Through it all, like the pounding of a battering ram against my skull, my head ached and throbbed fiercely. "Like someone tried to kill me," I said at last.

Even Caesiem couldn't completely hold back his smile, despite the soberness in his eyes.

"You're going to need to rest for a while," he went on. "I'll inform Revaed you're…unwell. I'll make excuses until you've recovered enough to work with the dragons." He hesitated. "You will heal fast, but you'll still need to take it easy for a bit." He shot me a pointed look, as if he expected me to try to launch myself from the bed and charge out into the night again.

I shifted my head on the pillow, turning away from him so I could gaze out one of the windows, into the gardens. The world was bathed in shades of grey and black, all shadows and stillness. Peaceful. The moon must have set, and the stars were beginning to wink out as the eastern sky lightened. Dawn was approaching.

I wondered, if I'd made a different choice tonight, if I would have succeeded in securing a dragon and escaping the Keep. If I would be halfway to Forwyth by now, high above the wild sea and the monstrous creatures swimming in its depths.

The monsters Caesiem could control.

"How does your magic work?" I didn't meet Caesiem's eyes. I didn't want to face that mingling sorrow and tenderness he wore. I didn't want anything to soften my anger toward him, even a little. "You control water…and you can summon its creatures?"

Caesiem scooted back on the bed so he could set his elbows on his legs and lay his head in his hands. He drew a deep breath before lifting his face to study me. For the first time, I noted how exhausted he looked, with his slumped shoulders and his bright eyes shadowed by dark circles.

"Yes," he muttered. "It takes a lot of energy and concentration."

"The pendant helps you, doesn't it?"

"The pendant keeps me connected to the water, even if I'm not close to it," Caesiem agreed softly. "Even when I am, it acts as an amplifier. It was taken from the ocean, and it helps me channel the magic more easily." He paused. "Only the most skilled and promising mages in Teramyl are gifted pendants, all associated with the element they wield. But I don't need the pendant to use my magic."

"But what about the…the water woman? What did she give you?"

"She's a nymph," he said. "They prefer the ocean, but my magic can call to them. They'll run errands or perform favors, for a price, and even then, you can never fully trust them. But the nymphs' medicine is extremely powerful. Theslynik should have you mended within hours rather than weeks or months. Still," he finished wearily, "despite its strength, you should be resting right now."

"I can't," I said, my voice weak. My entire body felt shaky and invigorated from the adrenaline coursing through my veins.

Silence hung over us as the events of the night replayed through my mind. I repressed a groan when waves of nausea rushed through me in time with the pulses of my aching head.

"Why didn't you use your magic before?" I asked at last. "Back when we were helping the vigilantes, and that Alrenian man nearly killed you. You could have stopped him so easily, and instead you almost bled to death."

Caesiem's jaw worked. "I didn't know how much news in Teramyl spread to Alrenor," he explained. "What if it was common knowledge the Xalenos family had taken in a water mage?" He shrugged. "And even if everyone knew next to nothing about Teramyl, as is the case, I still didn't want to draw too much attention to myself, or make anyone ask too many questions. Wouldn't it have seemed a little strange for a mage to be an unknown orphan? Wouldn't you have asked more questions about why I'd come here?"

I swallowed, averting my eyes from his as his betrayal stung me all over again. "Maybe so."

"It wasn't worth taking the risk. I needed to pass as ordinary, to be unremarkable."

Smiling feebly, I shook my head. "You failed," I whispered, daring to glance up into his beautiful eyes again. I could have sworn his cheeks were a little ruddier than usual.

"You should at least rest," he urged. "Lie down."

Sighing, I leaned back against the pillows, tracing shadows with my gaze. "Renni is dead," I breathed in disbelief, stating the obvious.

Caesiem's eyes were intense and dark, his jaw rigid. "He threatened you. I'm not sorry."

"He made an oath to be a blood avenger," I went on. I wasn't completely sure why I was telling Caesiem this, only that I ached for companionship, and everyone I'd had before was lost to me. Naina. Pauni'a. O'emia. "According to Forwyn tradition, it's a sacred vow, one that means the oath-taker will not rest until they've avenged a death."

Caesiem's brow furrowed. "Whose death was Renni avenging? He wanted justice by killing you, the nun who has vowed to never shed blood?"

I fought the threatening grief. "I broke my vows. You know that. The first time when we…" My words trailed off; even now, after our second kiss, I couldn't say it. The memory consumed me: his warm lips moving against mine, his gentle hands cupping my face. The heated desperation and aching desire we'd felt for something that could never, *should* never be.

A flush crept up Caesiem's neck, and he glanced away, staring out the window to avoid looking at me. "You were expelled from the abbey because of that?" he asked, his voice husky. Recovering himself, he shook his head and glanced at me sharply. "That doesn't explain why Renni wanted to kill you."

"No, I wasn't expelled; I ran away from the abbey," I whispered, squeezing my eyes shut. "The night of the ball, I…" I swallowed. "I broke the most sacred vow of all. I killed Wilvhe."

When I opened my eyes, Caesiem was staring at me, wide-eyed. "Why?" he asked at last.

I pursed my lips. "He was about to kill me with the vylae poison when I tried to stop him from attacking the empress. So I…killed him."

Caesiem blinked. "You broke your vows? You…gave up your life? Left your home? All to save the *empress*?"

Impatiently, I drew a deep breath. "You already knew I was prepared to break them."

"To save your people. To *assassinate* Jaliana, not to defend her." He shook his head in confusion, as if still trying to process my words. "Why did you do it? Why save *her*?"

"Who cares now why I did it?" I snapped. "You've all but

enslaved my people again anyway. Who cares if the empress is dead or not? It turns out, the real threat was the man kissing me and throwing around words about running away together."

Caesiem's eyes flicked again toward the window. "I meant what I said. I would have run away."

"You would have left your precious guardian behind to launch his coup alone?" I scoffed. "For good?"

Tensing, Caesiem's expression hardened, and he didn't answer. He gathered the cloth from where he'd laid it in his lap and stood, turning his back to me. "Get some sleep," he said coolly.

He moved as if to walk away.

"I want to stay in the slave quarters," I bit out. "I can sleep and recover just as well there. It's where I belong. With my people."

Caesiem didn't bother to turn around. "Absolutely not."

Afraid I'll start a revolt among them? I thought, a jolt of satisfaction warming my chest. At least Caesiem knew my strength.

"I don't want the other Forwyn thinking I want to be here," I said instead, glaring at his back, or at least, doing my best attempt at a glare with a pummeling headache. "They'll think I chose this. That I *want* to be betrothed to you." It burned me with shame to think my people might imagine I had turned my back so easily on them, all for luxury or a handsome face. That I could be that dishonorable.

Caesiem's hands fisted at his sides, the damp and bloodied cloth enclosed in white-knuckled fingers. "Why do you care what they think?" he breathed, still not turning around. "They were the Forwyn serving in the palace, and they didn't think twice to surrender and serve us to save their own skin. They don't care about you. Like the Elders, they care about no one but themselves."

"Because they're my people," I said, "and if they're going to be treated like slaves again, I want them to know—"

"They're not being treated like slaves," Caesiem interrupted.

I tried to sit up, but realized I was still too weak and dizzy. "Then prove it," I said. "Don't have them live in the *slave* quarters."

Before I could say anything more, he was gone, tossing the cloth to the floor and shoving his way out of his chambers.

I was left in darkness, where at last, even my stormy emotions calmed in the rising tide of exhaustion enfolding me.

CHAPTER FOURTEEN

Caesiem

I DIDN'T EVEN KNOW IF my birth parents were alive or dead, and, truth be told, I didn't want to. Despite this fact, random memories of them occasionally snuck upon me unawares: a certain scent I couldn't quite identify that conjured the vague remembrance of a gentle female voice, or the notes to some of the Teramese songs I played and sang that brought an echo of a feeling, comforting and warm and all but forgotten. Mostly, though, I only felt a deep, lingering anger and betrayal whenever the thought of my mother and father crossed my mind.

The only reason I'd known that they'd abandoned me as a baby was because some of the older children in our ramshackle home had told me so. They'd found me swaddled in rags, filthy and screaming, on their doorstep, with a tattered paper pinned to my front. The message only shared my name, scrawled in spidery script.

That paper was in my pocket now, worn and wrinkled and faded, but always somewhere I could find it. Sometimes I told myself I kept it because I wanted to believe my parents had been dying from the plague, and had wanted me to have a fair chance at life with fellow orphans who could teach me how to survive. Sometimes I told myself it was simply because I needed the reminder of who I'd been and how easily my fate could have been different. And sometimes, I simply clung to it as a way to fuel my anger and drive me to better myself. To keep fighting, keep surviving.

Despite being surrounded by luxury, it had been clear for a long time that even the Teramese nobility and imperial family could fall prey to the plague, the dragons, or starvation. We'd been forced to find resources to survive. To seize a land where we could train dragons in captivity, and perhaps finally overcome the dragon threat in Teramyl.

So now, as I strode past the guards clustered in the hall outside my chambers, I reached for the paper with my name, almost unconsciously. *Remember why you're here*, I told myself, trying to block out the memory of Lo's accusatory stare, her furious words. *Survival above all else.*

"Trouble in paradise?" asked one of the men, perhaps the only soldier present who was high-ranking and foolish enough to dare address me so brazenly. His lips were twisted into an obnoxious smirk, his gold eyes gleaming with a knowing light. "You know, the fights might be troublesome, but making up afterward is always a pleasure." He winked. "Once, I..."

"Don't be crude, Darix," I retorted, pausing mid-step to throw him a scowl. As much as the people feared the Xalenos family, I was always a subject of gossip and jealousy, as the impoverished orphan— the *nobody*—who had been taken in and elevated by royalty. Never mind my magic. "And don't address me unless I speak to you directly," I added, straightening and continuing to march down the hall.

In those early, dim moments before sunrise, the palace remained quiet. The only other occupants stirring were the posted guards. Torches sent eerie shadows dancing along the walls, which were painted in vivid scenes of Alrenian wars and conquest. As I neared Revaed's quarters—the chambers that had once belonged to Empress Karye and had sat vacant for the past three years—plush carpeting lined the center of the floor, softening my steps. Solid wood doors were carved with immaculate imagery of the swirling sun insignia, sea creatures, waves, and plants.

At last, I stood outside Revaed's chambers, where two guards nodded at me as I knocked loudly on the door.

"Enter," Revaed called out, his voice muffled, and the door swung inward to reveal a Forwyn girl. The scent of food made it clear she'd recently arrived to serve breakfast. She blinked, stepping aside to allow me to enter.

For a too-long moment, I stared back at her, Lo's accusations filling my ears. *She's not a slave,* I reminded myself stubbornly. I pushed past the girl.

Since the rooms had been vacant ever since Karye's death, I hadn't seen them when I'd spied at the palace. Therefore, I was unprepared for their sheer size and opulence. I passed through the sitting room and a library filled with floor-to-ceiling shelves of leather volumes, all clearly tended to even after the Forwyn takeover. I couldn't help but feel surprised that none of the Elders had claimed these rooms, but perhaps, as they all ruled equally, they'd agreed it would be unfair for one of them to live here while the others had less luxurious living arrangements.

After the library was a small armory, where a suit of dragon scale armor that must have been sized to fit Karye hung from the wall alongside an assortment of wickedly beautiful Alrenian weapons. There were curved swords with bejeweled hilts, finely crafted bows and quivers, long daggers, and a double-bladed axe. Near the dragon scale armor rested a fine helmet, shimmering with gold and ivory dragon scales and embellished with fiery red rubies that were reminiscent of a crown. Clearly, each piece had been made for an empress.

"You're up early," Revaed greeted me, meeting me in the doorway leading from the armory to the bedroom. The huge space could have fit all of my quarters in it, and the massive four-poster bed looked large enough for half a dozen people to sleep in comfortably.

I listed my head to study my guardian, taking in his combed hair and fresh uniform. His eyes were clear and bright, his smile genuine. The dark circles beneath his eyes were gone, proving that despite the early hour, he must have slept longer and better than I had. I swallowed back a hard pit of envy at how simple this appeared for him.

Really, our takeover was too *easy,* I thought, trying to ignore the chill that swept through me. We might have the palace and the dragons for now, but I, like Revaed, suspected we were careening toward a war. One we had come prepared to fight. Or so I hoped.

"How is…" Revaed began, but I held up an impatient hand and pushed past him into the bedroom.

I sank into the first seat I found, a plush armchair near a window. It offered a stunning view of the gardens, where a small pond lay smooth as glass, surrounded by palm trees and flowers in every color imaginable.

Frustration boiled inside me, and I was half-tempted to blurt out how annoyed I was about him springing the idea of a marriage alliance on Lo and me last night. But Lo's words held me back. It would be better if Revaed thought we were both open to his idea.

"She's hurt," I said abruptly, continuing to stare out the window to avoid his gaze. "I think she will be all right, but she needs time to rest."

I could feel the tension and suspicion rolling off Revaed. Despite how much he hated it when I fidgeted, I couldn't stop myself from tapping out a steady beat with my toe. It took me a moment to realize I was playing the melody to a common Teramese love song. Stiffening, I froze and finally dared to meet Revaed's eyes.

"She tried to escape, didn't she?" he said, sighing softly. "The marriage alliance scared her, and she tried to run."

"No, she actually told me she's…she didn't outright refuse to consider your proposal," I said. "And she didn't try to escape. She went to see the old Forwyn slave quarters."

Revaed paused, frowning at his pristinely polished boots. "Interesting," he murmured.

A smile tugged at my lips as I thought of her, strong-willed and full of a fierce love of her people that made her braver than anyone I'd ever met. "She deeply loves her people. I've never met anyone so dedicated, or so passionate and strong and brave. She'd do anything for them."

I hesitated a beat, hoping I wasn't pushing too fast, too soon. "And because I can tell you with full confidence that she won't try to escape, I need you to stop posting guards out on the balcony. She's not a prisoner, and no one will believe this marriage alliance business, least of all her, if you keep ordering our men and women to treat her as one."

Revaed watched me with a wide-eyed gaze. "You're…in love with her, aren't you?" He blinked, as if he'd never imagined me becoming romantically involved with anyone before. "It's not just…some passing fling?"

I hesitated, my first inclination to protest. But…that would be lying, and what was the point in that? "Yes," I said quietly, my voice sounding low and raw in my ears.

For a long moment, my one-word confession hung heavily in the air, echoing endlessly around us. It changed nothing. And everything.

Revaed studied me intently. "You never seemed interested in committing to someone before. I thought you were more interested in passing romantic encounters." He flashed me a brief smile. "But I'm glad to hear it. I hoped the marriage alliance would please you, if you can persuade Lo of its merits. I'd hoped for the political advantages, but I also want you to be happy. I'm glad this can do both." He leaned back. "And you make a good point. I'll remove the guards posted at the balcony."

I bit back a hundred retorts about how I didn't want to marry Lo to solidify an alliance or *persuade* her into anything, and instead cut to the other topic weighing on me.

"Also…I thought we weren't going to take any slaves." I set my mouth into a thin line. Other than his father, who was miles away and a heartless, cruel wretch, I was the only one who could hold Revaed accountable. "I thought we weren't going to repeat Alrenor's past cruelties and mistakes. This conquest is only about survival. Right?"

Revaed's mouth twitched in a smile. "Of course. The Forwyn staying in the slave quarters are the ones who pledged service to us. For *payment*. The Alrenian coffers are full; the mines they have in the Aramith Mountains have kept the imperial family wealthy for generations." His smile broadened. "We have enough to pay any Forywn or Alrenian who chooses to side with us handsomely."

"So we're paying them off, not forcing them into slavery."

"A much better way to gain loyalty," Revaed said with a nod. "Who will want to rebel against the ones providing them with everything they could ever need? There's no need to stoop to barbaric Alrenian ways. It's much simpler to choose bribery."

I shifted in my seat. "Since they're not slaves, we need to move them into the palace. You trust our soldiers to keep us safe if the Forwyn change their minds, right?"

Revaed cleared his throat. "Of course."

"Then the Forwyn servants and anyone else who chooses to help us—in any way—need to live within the palace like true staff and allies. Otherwise, people will get the wrong impression."

Revaed smiled. "This is about your betrothed."

I worked a muscle in my jaw, meeting Revaed's gaze steadily. "This is about doing the right thing. Anyone who sides with us…there's no reason why they shouldn't be treated like one of us. Anyone against us…" I shrugged. "We serve Teramyl's people first."

"Survival above all else," Revaed said, his and my mantra over the years. And a personal mantra I'd lived by for many years prior to my life as a lord. Survival for our people. Survival for ourselves. Everyone, in the end, put survival—whether for themselves, a loved one, or their people—over every other motivation.

"Survival above all else," I agreed.

Revaed tapped his chin thoughtfully. "I'll send out the order today and have rooms prepared for the Forwyn." He smiled. "Very thoughtful advice of yours."

I murmured my thanks, feeling a heavy weight lift from my shoulders.

"Speaking of survival…" Revaed said, adjusting his sleeves. "I have some tedious tasks ahead of us today. Have you had breakfast? We'll want to be well-prepared."

Unease squirmed within my stomach, threatening to squelch my appetite, but I had a feeling Revaed was right and I'd need the strength later.

I shook my head. "No breakfast, yet."

Revaed's brow furrowed as he studied me again, his eyes piercing. "I know I said you'd be responsible for Miss Nolanhou, but I really think it'd be wiser if she wasn't staying in your quarters. Just to…keep you focused."

Dread slithered through me. Moving Lo would mean that Revaed would assign other guards to watch her, potentially men like Darix. I wouldn't trust that pig of a man within an inch of her.

But I merely laughed Revaed's suggestion off with a shrug. "I don't think that's a good idea. Can you imagine the ideas she'd put in the other servants' heads? Maybe she'd try to persuade them the money isn't worth it." I frowned, hesitating. "She's…she knows how to be quite convincing."

Revaed nodded slowly and turned toward the huge side table placed near the four-poster bed. A veritable feast was spread out upon it already, the scents of coffee, ham and eggs, fresh fruits, and sugared pastries tempting me. My stomach growled, reminding me that no matter how I felt, I needed to eat.

"The Alrenians and Forwyn certainly know how to prepare a meal," Revaed said with a contented sigh as he shoved food onto a plate. "You don't know how wonderful it is to have fresh food after that trip," he added, referring to the long voyage from Teramyl.

"You're wrong," I said with a grin. "I made that voyage first." I followed him, choosing a mug and filling it with coffee before even considering the food. After taking a long sip despite the steam curling from the beverage, I glanced to Revaed. He'd settled himself at a round table and had already begun tucking into the food. When he met my eyes, he gestured toward the seat across from him.

I plopped into it, setting down my mug and clearing my throat. "What tedious tasks do we have to perform today?" I asked.

The slice of a blade through flesh. Blood pooling across a marble floor. Rising waters churning, foaming, consuming their victims until they drowned. Despite the necessity of those executions, and my part in them, the memories still made my skin crawl. Unlike his father, Revaed also took no joy in meting out justice and punishments. It was, as he put it, simply the burden of royalty.

"Securing our empire," Revaed said vaguely, his mouth twitching in a half-smile that didn't reach his eyes. It was all the evidence I needed that he dreaded the work as much as I did. I bit back a grimace and reached for my coffee, suddenly wishing the Forwyn servants could have brought something stronger to drink. Was it too early? Was it ever too early, when such tasks lay before a man?

"I'm sorry," Revaed sighed. "I told you this would be tedious work, and I'm afraid with the possibility of Alrenians amassing troops in the mountains, it's likely to grow much worse before it's better." He met my eyes, his gaze steadfast and reassuring. "But we know what we must do."

I nodded. "Survive."

Once again, descending into the dank Alrenian dungeons was a sharp contrast to the opulence of the palace's upper levels. It was clear from the dim, cramped rooms filled with wicked-looking tools and weaponry and covered in suspicious red stains that Empress Karye and her lackeys had never had any qualms about torturing prisoners. The stale air reeked with blood, sweat, and urine, all comingling into one horrible stench, a lot like the way I imagined abject misery and humiliation would smell like.

Guards led Revaed and I into the bowels of the dungeons,

winding through damp, echoing corridors. Distant shuffling and murmuring echoed from various prisoners further away, along with a skittering noise—rats. I glanced toward Revaed, who looked like he'd bitten into a whole lemon as he avoided the dirt-smudged stone walls surrounding us and brushed imaginary muck off his shoulder.

"Here we are," said Malec, the soldier in front of us, pausing before one of the cells.

"At last," Revaed muttered under his breath.

If it weren't for the weight of what we had to do burdening me, I might have laughed at Revaed's obvious relief, even though I doubted the cell would be any less disgusting than the damp corridor. As Malec unlocked the door with a clink and it creaked inward, scuffling sounds emerged. For a moment, my breath caught painfully in my chest.

Crouched in the corner, blinking against the flickering torchlight from the corridor, knelt a tiny figure that appeared more like a wounded animal than a criminal. Gold-flecked amber eyes gleamed with a stormy mixture of ferocity and fear as the Alrenian boy studied us. He sneered, showing his teeth, as if prepared to claw and bite his way free of his prison.

From his small, overly thin frame, he seemed younger than me, although years of malnourishment might only have made him appear so. Clearly, he'd been scraping out a living for years—not unlike the way I once had, stealing and scrounging and nearly starving. My chest tightened as if my heart would burst.

"Revaed?" I murmured, that single word coming out hoarse and strangled.

At my side, Revaed stiffened, though he did a good job of covering up his reaction with feigned nonchalance.

"How proud you must be, Malec," he drawled. "You and your men have caught a lowly rat."

Malec made a remarkable effort to conceal his indignance, but I caught it flare in his eyes just the same. "He was bearing this, vowing to poison you, Your Highness," he said smoothly, drawing out a tiny vial from his breast pocket. Clear liquid shimmered within, tinged orange only from the dancing firelight. "Vylae."

Revaed sighed. "A shame some murderers start so young," he said, straightening his jacket and glancing at me. "What shall we do?"

My head pounded. I knew this was a test, for one day I would take Revaed's place, and mercy couldn't take precedence over my people's survival. A leader couldn't allow would-be assassins to run free and murder him and everyone he loved.

And yet... My eyes met the boy's, seeing the same burning determination, the same lividness and hatred I had once studied the world with. Like me, all this boy wanted was to survive another day. Perhaps someone had paid him, in coin or food, to carry out this mission. Perhaps he'd undertaken it himself, thinking he'd have a better life if the Alrenians or even Forwyn were again in control. Who could know his reasoning?

I cleared my throat. "If we are to rule the Forwyn and Alrenians as our own people," I began, "then perhaps this boy should receive a trial, as Teramese citizens would."

Revaed studied me shrewdly, his violet eyes glittering in the firelight. Behind him, Malec hovered, his face set like stone but unable to fully douse the curious flicker in his gaze.

"Normally, even the Teramese do not receive a trial for an obvious assassination attempt," Revaed reminded me.

I nodded along with his words. It was well-known that the Xalenos family meted out justice swiftly for such violent crimes, often—under Revaed's father's decree—in the cruelest ways imaginable. Disembowelment. Chained to a rock in the ocean and left for the water creatures to devour. Hung from one's limbs until starvation and predatory birds ended the slow torture.

Unlike his father, Revaed was one to accomplish the business swiftly. It wasn't a game or a joy to him, only a necessary evil.

"Normally," I responded, "the prospective assassin is older and more formidable."

Silently, Revaed mulled over my words.

I went on, trying to keep my voice smooth and unrushed so as not to come across as desperate. "Perhaps showing the Forwyn and Alrenian people that we are willing to offer mercy, even for the most violent of crimes, could prove we really are offering them peace?"

The silence drew on several moments longer, broken only by the distant echoes of shuffling feet or scurrying rats. The flicker of flame. The boy's frantic, ragged breaths.

Finally, Revaed's mouth stretched into a slow smile. "You'll make a wise emperor," he told me, patting my shoulder.

Emperor Caesiem.

I thought of the Forwyn and Alrenians kneeling before me. Of living in Revaed's luxurious quarters someday. It made my skin prickle and my uniform suddenly feel too tight, too constricting.

"Come," Revaed said, already leading me from the cell, one hand still clutching my upper arm. "No time to dawdle, Caes." He tossed a glance over his shoulder at Malec. "The boy will face a trial soon enough." As he continued down the corridor, leaving the officer and the boy behind, he told me, "I'll want you present, of course. My chief advisors and generals, too." He paused a beat. "And we'll let the Forwyn Elders and your Miss Nolanhou attend, if she's well enough. Let's see what they make of this would-be assassin."

The next cell we entered was guarded by two men. It caged three prisoners, all chained in a row to the far wall. They lunged for Revaed and me, eyes blazing with hatred, but their chains wouldn't allow them to go far. The shackles bit into their wrists as they struggled, drawing blood that trickled down their arms and blotted the grimy floor.

Two of the men were Alrenian and one was Forwyn. All were tall and burly, dressed in sleeveless tunics that revealed the corded muscles lining their arms. They cut imposing figures with their sneering faces.

Revaed stood in the doorway assessing the men curiously, as if they were simply a problem on paper he had to solve.

One of the Alrenian men, with shaggy brown hair and green and gold eyes, spat on the floor. "Come closer, you coward," he taunted Revaed, "and show me if you're man enough to face the people you think you can rule."

The other Alrenian laughed haughtily. "Do you skinny men even know how to hold a sword? Worthless *kowra*."

The Forwyn man stood still and silent, his eyes so intense and furious it was as if he could bore holes into our skin with them.

"Shut your trap," one of our guards ordered, shifting away from his post to stand beside Revaed and me. "Your Imperial Majesty, my lord." He dipped his head at both of us in turn. "Two of these men are suspected Alrenian insurgents, and the other a Forwyn guard. All three were brought in from the capital streets, refusing to submit to the Teramese soldiers enforcing your rule. They're worthless scum, to defy you like this. I can show these men the meaning of respecting the imperial family…"

Revaed lifted a hand to silence him, never moving his gaze from the prisoners. "That won't be necessary. The Xalenos family is perfectly capable of doling out our own punishments."

The man dipped his head again. "Of course, Emperor Revaed."

Revaed's eyes flicked to me as the soldier retreated into the corridor. "It seems we need to send a clear message to our new people, Caesiem."

Weariness settled into my bones as I imagined a long string of executions, most ones we would perform ourselves. Quick. Efficient. All business.

This is the price of being Lord Xalenos, I thought, not for the first time. *The price of a roof over your head and food in your belly, of security and survival.*

A fleeting uneasiness coursed through me as I wondered if any of these men possessed Alrenian gifts or Forwyn magic. But, from everything I'd learned, the Alrenians had lost many of their most dangerous gifts, and few Forwyn knew how to listen to Elhani's voice and wield his power. Or at least, that was what Lo and the other sisters at the abbey had told me.

Stepping forward, I settled my gaze on the bucket of water in the corner. Revaed must have made the command to collect it for me hours ago. I couldn't help the chill that slipped down my spine, couldn't help that, though I knew it was necessary, I *hated* this.

As if sensing the tension inside me, Revaed laid a gentle hand on my shoulder. "Make it fast. If we create an example of these violent men, we can dispatch the others in our usual public executions."

Those executions, at least, wouldn't have to be carried out by me.

I knew exactly what needed to be done as I clutched my pendant, its ever-cool surface soothing against my skin. I could execute two of these men swiftly, right here in this cell, leaving only one alive as a witness. He would go free to spread the word about Teramese power.

I drew a deep breath to rally myself. Quieting my mind, I

concentrated on my magic. It buzzed through me, sometimes as unpredictable and violent as the sea—but as beautiful and mesmerizing, too. It was a rising tide in my heart, a swirling whirlpool in my soul. Fueling me as much as it drained me. A wonderful blessing from the gods and a burdensome curse.

Tensing my shoulders, I lifted my hand and gestured toward the first Alrenian man. Water rushed from the bucket, a mere puddle compared to the sea waves I'd commanded last night, and swirled through the air like a living beast. It coursed in serpentine twists, plunging the wide-eyed man into a blast of water.

His shock turned to panic as the water remained suspended in the air, covering his head in a churning torrent. He thrashed against his shackles, the metal clanging off the stone walls. Through the foaming water, I caught glimpses of his desperate expression as he tried to stretch himself out of the water's reach, toward air.

Beside him, the other prisoners cried out in shock and pulled as far away as they could, unable to look away. It was a morbid performance, a gruesome dance with death.

Next to me, Revaed stood still, his face revealing nothing. Neither of us could show disgust or hesitation, not now. Not here.

I swallowed and didn't relent until several long moments had passed and the man's body slumped, hanging awkwardly from the wall. Reclaimed by gravity, the water fell to the ground, splashing into a pool at his sandals. It mingled with the layers of dirt and grime coating the stone floor, turning to a muddy, mostly unusable mixture.

Unwilling to let the other men see my discomfort, I tore my gaze from the dead man's horrified expression—from those staring, accusatory eyes. Instead, I turned to the next Alrenian man.

"Demon," he gasped, his face paling and his bloodshot eyes wild and terrified.

I forced every ounce of anger I had into my actions. It was all I could do to keep myself from weakening my resolve and collapsing to the floor in revulsion. My energy felt depleted, but my work wasn't done.

It would take more strength than I had left to summon the water now mixed with dirt on the floor, which meant this death would be far worse. My stomach churned as I pushed myself to focus, drawing on every ounce of liquid I could find. It settled on the most accessible: the blood coursing through the man's own veins, a river of life that would now turn against him.

I extended my hand, and the water inside his body obeyed: leaping toward me in a rush, bursting through his veins, seeping from his nose and eyes and ears, bubbling from his mouth, and even leaking from his pores. For one ear-splitting, earth-shaking instant, the man let loose a ragged scream that tore from his throat like the cry of a wild beast. And then it was lost in a burble of blood, his strangled cry cut off as he collapsed.

The sight was horrifying, far worse than anything I'd ever done before. Bile soured my mouth as blood dripped to the floor and splattered against my face.

I stared at what was left of the man, a gory mess suspended from chains like a puppet on a string.

Next to him, the Forwyn man was openly weeping, his own skin and clothes coated in a layer of blood. The entire prison stank with it, swam with it. My vision ran red with it.

Whirling on my heel, I stormed from the cell, bursting into a run once I reached the corridor. There was no one left to witness my weakness once I turned the corner, so I slumped against a wall and vomited all over the stone floor. I wiped the blood off my face with my jacket sleeve.

All I could think about was getting out of there. The dungeon walls were closing in, the world was rocking, sinking, crumbling, exploding. Echoing footsteps chased after me, but I couldn't hear over the roaring in my ears. My breathing came in ragged gasps, my chest heaving and lungs aching until I wondered if they'd collapse. Perhaps my gift would rebel and draw *my* blood from my own body as well.

The only thing I could hear clearly was an echo of my own voice, repeating over and over to the rhythm of my pounding heart. *Survival. Survival. Survival.* Afraid to look back, afraid to look at my own bloodied hands, afraid to stop for one more second and *think* about what I was, I ran.

But I couldn't outrun who I was.

CHAPTER FIFTEEN

Kovi

THE TROUBLE WITH BEING THE star student of Aerekni Academy had been the constant demands, the unrelenting weight of duty, and the incessant need to do more, to be better.

Tonight, the memories returned in full force. As soon as General Ilowhe had realized just how talented I was with the unusual ability to control others with Elhani's magic, word had spread. I was needed to serve my people, to do my duty. I was expected to train harder, to spend more time than the rest of my fellow students studying, practicing, and disciplining myself.

Over time, the general had taken me on quiet missions to prisons throughout Inalgoth, for I'd been the Forwyn's best interrogator of Alrenians they suspected were members of a growing uprising. Sometimes, whether due to the fact that I was still learning how to wield the magic, or that over time I grew to fear it and struggle to focus it, the prisoners resisted. Or perhaps those with a strong enough will could fight my commands. All that mattered was that I gathered information from a few, forcing them to talk. I'd never discovered anything about this hidden army here in the mountains, but I'd learned enough to put down rebel groups within Inalgoth.

I wasn't the one to hurt or kill those prisoners, but my connection with them forced me to experience their pain. I bore the weight of what I'd done to them, even if I knew it had been for my people. Always for my people.

Now, I squeezed my eyes shut, trying to block out the echo of agony I'd felt right along with the dead. Though they could no longer feel emotions themselves, the memories of their final feelings lived on in me. It was all part of my gift, my curse.

I stretched out with my mind and sought Jalie's emotions, trying to determine what she was planning to do with Vander and me. Currently, we were bound to trees just outside the Alrenian camp, far enough away from Ryke that he was just a distant shadow in the night. Gentle curls of dragon smoke, swept toward me by the soft breeze, tickled my nose and brought back the memory of flying with Jalie—an experience that had been terrifying and strangely euphoric, all at once. The chill air bit at my face and numbed my gloved fingers. If I shifted my head to the right, I could discern Vander's form in the darkness, but I couldn't make out his expression, and even if I wanted to, we were too far apart to speak.

I found Jalie's emotions to be as tangled as my own, so snarled it was difficult to pull them apart and understand them. Fury, fear, guilt, doubt, pain…it all whirled together in so many ways it was impossible for me to be sure what she wanted to do.

She thinks you were prepared to kill her, I reminded myself darkly. *Of course you know what she plans to do.*

Except…when she'd touched me, her curse should have burned

through my jacket and eaten away at my skin. I should be dying by now, my own shrieks of pain piercing the stillness of the night. Though I wasn't entirely sure how Jalie's curse worked, I assumed that if she willed it, anyone she touched would be harmed. The fact that I hadn't been…did it mean she didn't want me to die?

Footsteps pulled me out of my thoughts, and I turned toward the camp to see the silhouette of a woman approaching. I could tell by the way she walked, her back straight and proud, her every step graceful, that it was Jalie.

My throat tightened as she drew close enough for me to make out her face, to see the piercing blue and gold of her eyes, the brilliant sheen of her gold-toned skin, the hard set of her mouth.

She bore no weapons, but she didn't need to. She was the weapon.

"Jalie," I whispered, voice raspy. I couldn't help it. A part of me ached to rekindle the closeness we'd shared, however briefly, in the Alrenian palace. I was weary of being her enemy, even if the logical side of my brain knew there wasn't anything else we could ever be.

"Command me to release you—use your magic in *any* way against me—and I'll kill you. Understand?"

Normally, I would think there was a flaw in her threat. If I commanded her, she wouldn't be in possession of her body and therefore unable to kill me. But tonight—there was an aura of power around her that seemed stronger than before, and somehow, I had a feeling she could fight against my magic.

After all, other Alrenians had managed to resist it, and I was certain Jalie could too, with her iron will.

"I won't use magic," I promised. "I'm not *actually* here to kill you."

Jalie's eyes narrowed as she stepped nearer, until she was leaning dangerously close. Her breath brushed my face as her eyes searched mine. Her expression was as cold as ice, impenetrable as steel, but all I wanted was to reach out and touch her. Beneath her hard exterior, her emotions were a storm. Pain. Betrayal. Uncertainty.

"You show up with a Teramese soldier and shove a blade to my throat, then tell me you aren't here to kill me?" she demanded. "I don't believe you. Explain to me exactly why you shouldn't die right now."

I didn't flinch. "You already know why I should live, or I'd be dead already."

It was Jalie who blinked first, pulling back to stare at me.

"You know I'm useful to you alive, with my magic." I paused for a beat before lowering my voice. "But my usefulness isn't the only reason I'm alive. Why didn't your curse kill me, Jalie?"

She frowned. Lifting her hands, she glanced at her palms, as if the answers were written there. "I thought the curse was judgment against the Forwyn for the shedding of Alrenian blood." Her eyes darted up, meeting mine and holding my stare. "You've killed Alrenians. I thought all it took was my anger and you'd be dead."

A smile threatened to curve my lips. "Maybe it's not about how you feel in the moment. Maybe it only works if, deep down, you truly *want* the Forwyn you're touching to die." I leaned closer, letting my lips brush against her ear. She stiffened, but didn't pull back as I whispered, "You can't pretend you don't care, Jalie. I can feel exactly what you're feeling, right now."

Drawing a shuddering breath, Jalie turned away. "Is your Teramese friend worth keeping alive?" she bit out, ignoring my comment entirely. "He appears to have their kind of magic. Would he be valuable in a negotiation, perhaps?"

He's not my friend, I thought. *Kill him and save me the trouble.* But something stayed the words from leaving my lips. Maybe it was the fact that Vander hadn't been malicious or cruel to me at all. I didn't truly want him to die.

"He's a wind mage," I murmured. "Not only valuable to them, but potentially useful to you too. Definitely worth keeping alive."

"I'll consider it."

Jalie didn't bother to turn around, didn't even bother to look at me again, before she strode away, melting back into the night.

CHAPTER SIXTEEN

Lo

D RINK THIS," THE HEALER MURMURED, pressing a cup to my lips.

An older Teramese woman, the healer wasn't at all what I'd expected. She bore wrinkles at the corners of her eyes and around her mouth, hinting at frequent laughter. Her thick black hair, streaked with grey, was pulled back in a practical bun, but a few wavy tendrils framed her bronze face. She had a warm aura about her, wildly at odds with the black uniform she wore, identifying her as a member of the Teramese army.

I swallowed the cool liquid, finding it bitter, spicy, and strong. I choked it down and coughed in surprise, my aching head pounding even more as I gasped for breath.

The healer laughed gently. "It's a powerful painkiller, native to Teramyl," she explained. "One of the only great resources we have. But the best is our mages. Lord Xalenos told me he was able to obtain some theslynik for you. You should heal remarkably swiftly."

I bit back a grimace and accepted the proffered cup once again. As soon as I forced the rest of the concoction down, I lay back on my pillow. The woman tucked the covers gently around me and drew the curtains to block the morning sunlight streaming in through the windows. I closed my eyes, already feeling the ache in my head dull and exhaustion wash over me.

"Your body needs rest," the healer was saying, her tone soft, her footsteps light as she crept around me. "And to avoid too much light or noise."

My brain was already turning sluggish, and yet my natural curiosity wouldn't relent. "Why did you end up with the Teramese army?" I blurted, keeping my eyes closed.

"Survival," the woman said, her tone turning somewhat curt. "My family was near to starving, but my healing abilities earned me a position with the imperial family. When Teramyl ran short on resources and Prince—I mean, Emperor Revaed—was sent here with his army…I followed. This is my duty. To my people, and to my family."

"And you don't mind tending to your enemies?" I pressed. I opened my eyes to see the woman purse her lips.

"I go where Emperor Revaed or Lord Xalenos command," she said. "And you are not my enemy. Teramyl doesn't want strife. We're here to provide new leadership, to bind up your broken land and strengthen it as part of the Teramese Empire."

I resisted the urge to snort. "You truly believe that garbage?"

The woman frowned, but another powerful wave of weariness swept through me. I closed my eyes, letting the heaviness consume my body. As blackness closed in, suddenly and irresistibly, I thought I heard her repeat her earlier statement: "You are not my enemy."

The sun was high in the sky when I awoke. Had I been asleep a few hours? Or for days? I was groggy and disoriented enough that it was difficult to be certain.

My mouth was full of sand and my eyes were gritty as I sat up, rubbing at them. The pounding in my skull was gone, reduced to a slight ache that I could ignore. But when I moved, the world seemed to spin. I blinked and it righted itself. I felt refreshed, though parched and confused.

I scanned the bedchamber for any sign of life, but it sat silent and dark. Caesiem was gone, and I didn't notice any posted guards on the balcony outside, either. Were they in the middle of a shift change, or had they decided I wasn't a threat anymore?

On the side table against the far wall, where the Forwyn generally delivered meals, an array of dishes and a huge pitcher of water rested. I inhaled deeply, registering the scents of fresh bread and stew. My stomach grumbled in response. Someone must have just brought the food, which was probably what had awoken me.

Slowly, blearily, I swung my legs over the side of the bed and cautiously settled my weight on my feet. Though a little light-headed, I wasn't too weak or dizzy to walk. I downed two glasses of water before I served myself a slice of bread and a bowl of hearty stew, made with beef from some of the cattle kept in the countryside north of Inalgoth, and fresh vegetables from the palace grounds.

As I ate, memories of Renni's attack ran through my mind, along with my conversation with Caesiem afterward. I couldn't avoid the accompanying ache in my chest when I thought of how I'd once trusted him.

I wondered if the Forwyn woman I'd tried to talk to earlier, the one with honey eyes who'd insisted she was a servant, had been the one to bring my food. Would I have a chance to speak with her again?

I could slip a note to whoever comes to retrieve my dishes.

None of the Teramese knew the Forwyn language, or at least, I was fairly certain they didn't. After all, Caesiem had been, if not the only spy, definitely the most important one that they'd sent ahead, and he didn't know Forwyn.

My hands trembled as I stood, depositing my empty dishes on the waiting tray and then snatching paper, pen, and ink off the desk in the corner of the room. I tore it until it was only a small square, something even the Forwyn themselves might overlook.

I started with the first thing that came into my mind: *I am the amara'rekni, and my alliance with these invaders is a ruse.*

I've convinced their ruler to let you help their soldiers train the dragons. The dragons will know you better and be more likely to submit to you. I can send advice to ensure this. We can let our enemies think the dragons trust them, that they are the ones in control. But it will be us. You will be the new Keepers.

Don't lose hope.

Footsteps sounded outside. I returned the items to the desk and darted across the room to the dishes, where I tucked my note beneath my empty bowl. There was a brief knock on the sitting room door before it swung inward and the healer shuffled through, pausing at the entrance to the bedroom to offer me a gentle smile. "I see you're up." Her eyes scanned the empty dishes before me. "And had an appetite. A good sign."

"What day is it?" I asked, as she guided me back to sit on the bed and began to check me more closely.

"No temperature," she muttered, feeling my forehead. "So no bad side effects. Perfect." She blinked, as if just processing my question. "You only slept a few hours. But it's normal to be disoriented after that—the theslynik puts you into such a deep sleep, and helps your body do work that would normally take much longer. Patients often wake up feeling like they've lost a week of their lives. But you haven't." She grinned.

"I do feel a little drugged still," I said softly, and she laughed.

Before either of us could say more, the door to the chambers burst open, banging against the wall before slamming shut. Caesiem appeared in the bedroom doorway, and I couldn't repress my gasp. His dark uniform was even darker, his face and hands were splattered, and his hair was matted—all with blood. He stumbled like a drunken man, wide eyes looking, for a moment, too dazed to see anything. Then his gaze fell on me, and he stiffened, blinking as if coming to. Something dark flittered through his eyes, and his jaw hardened.

"Are you hurt?" I demanded, at the same moment the healer scurried toward him, grasping his arm gently and trying to scan him for injuries.

Caesiem waved the healer away. "I'm fine," he said, tugging his arm from her grip and stalking toward the washroom. "If you're finished with Lo," he added to the woman over his shoulder, "you're dismissed."

The woman dipped her head and, with a final glance toward me as if to reassure herself I truly was fine, she darted out into the hall.

As Caesiem disappeared into the washroom, I scowled at his retreating form. I didn't want to care, knew I shouldn't care, and yet I couldn't help the tight feeling in my chest when I imagined him hurt.

Sitting up, I found my headache had improved significantly. I stomped after Caesiem and burst into the washroom.

"What happened?" I demanded. "Is that your blood?"

I hesitated only a moment in the doorway when I found that Caesiem had already stripped off his bloody jacket and undershirt, revealing the smooth, bronze skin and toned muscles in his back. He spun around to face me, and I averted my gaze.

Sure, act awkward and practically scream the fact that you've been a nun living with women for years, I berated myself. I'd seen plenty of shirtless men while living in the palace's crowded slave quarters, so I hated that one glance at Caesiem could make me so self-conscious.

He narrowed his eyes. "Shouldn't you be in bed?"

I tore my gaze from the tub he was filling with water and back to him, skimming over his bare chest and stomach for any signs of injury. Blood from his uniform had soaked through to his skin, leaving behind smears. When I lifted my eyes to his, I found they were red-rimmed.

I waved away his concern. "Are you hurt?"

Caesiem turned away, staring at the tub as steaming water poured from the faucet. "No, I'm not hurt," he muttered. He found some bath soaps and started dumping them in haphazardly, as if he needed something, anything, to keep his hands busy. Bubbles frothed in the water and floated through the air, a whimsical contrast to the bloody, defeated-looking man before me.

Finally, he asked, "Why do you care?"

I cursed. "Because I'm a fool."

His back still to me, Caesiem froze. Silence stretched between us. My blood pounded in my ears.

When he turned back toward me, his expression was a mask. "No," he murmured. "You're not a fool for caring. You're one of the only good people in this world *because* you care."

I swallowed against the dryness in my throat. Desire and frustration tangled together in my heart. Whatever he said, I knew I was a fool when everything proved—no matter how many times he saved my life or soothed my nightmares or pressed me against a wall and kissed me—that he was my enemy. He could claim to be forging an alliance with my people all he wanted, but I knew the Teramese would always come first for him.

Caesiem turned back toward the tub and turned off the water. He leaned over it once more, slumped in weariness.

"You watched someone die," I said at last, studying the blood splattered across his skin.

This time, Caesiem didn't turn. "I don't want to talk about it," he said gruffly. "Please leave."

"Caesiem—"

"Leave, or I'll strip naked in front of you so I can wash this filth off." As if to prove his point, he reached to unbutton his trousers. Embarrassed heat flashed through me, but not as fiery as my determination.

"*Wait*," I demanded, striding forward and seizing his arm, turning him to face me.

He didn't resist as I tugged him closer. The darkness of his expression had faded, leaving behind something vulnerable and achingly sorrowful. I stared into his eyes, blue as the sea and just as vast and bottomless. There were mysteries buried within that he might never share with me, and as much as I hated that, as much as I knew he would forever be against me, I couldn't help but hurt for him. In his pained look was a hint of the man I'd seen before: the one I'd thought I'd known before I'd learned he was Lord Xalenos.

"What does Revaed make you do?" I whispered.

Caesiem swallowed hard, his unguarded expression vanishing into hardness once more. "He doesn't *make* me do anything."

I sighed, but I didn't protest. Despite his stormy gaze, Caesiem hadn't pulled away, and I could see something else behind his pain and frustration. It looked like a glimmer of hope. Of wanting.

His eyes dragged up from where I clutched him and studied my lips.

"I think," he said, his voice growing huskier, "that unless you want me to kiss you again, you should let go of me." He nodded to my fingers, wrapped firmly around his wrist.

Heart skipping a beat, I let go, but I didn't step back.

"I've considered Revaed's offer to build peace between the Teramese and Forwyn," I announced. "Like I said I would."

"*Emperor* Revaed," Caesiem cut in.

I ignored him and continued. "And I'm willing to speak with the soldiers at Aerekni Academy as a representative, someone who could explain the advantages of Forwyn-Teramese cooperation to my people."

Caesiem quirked an eyebrow. "How hard did Renni hit you?"

I glowered. "Do you think I'm not capable of setting aside my anger for my people's interests?" I hesitated. "After all, I've already told you to go along with Revaed's schemes of…behaving as if we're engaged."

Caesiem watched me carefully. "I was sure you were going to order me to make Revaed call it off by now. I didn't think you were convinced any association with us would be in…your interests."

He was so close that I could feel his warm breath on my face. So close I couldn't quite think clearly. His gaze dropped to my mouth again, and I inhaled sharply.

It was Caesiem's turn to mutter a curse as he stepped forward, cupping my face and—

His eyes landed on his blood-coated hand, on the stain he'd left on my cheek. Darkness marred his expression again, and he jerked back as if burned.

Turning away, he returned to leaning over the tub. His hands were shaking. "I think you should go."

My chest felt hollow as I crept from the washroom.

You idiot, what were you thinking? I wondered. *When will you learn?*

I didn't want to feel like this about Caesiem. I couldn't *allow* myself to feel this way. Not when he was covered in someone else's blood.

Not when everything he did was in service to Revaed.

CHAPTER SEVENTEEN

Jalie

DRAWING A DEEP, SOOTHING BREATH, I pressed my forehead to Ryke's, inhaling the scent of dragon smoke that always lingered around the beast. It was familiar and comforting, bringing back childhood memories of riding with my mother, and a sense of nostalgia both wonderful and aching. Blinking back tears, I ran my fingertips along my dragon's vivid scales, marveling at the way they captured the light of the early morning sun and glittered a thousand different shades of green. Beneath my armored gloves, I could feel the solid comfort of Mother's ruby ring on my finger, a reminder that I carried her with me, both in my similarities to her and in my memories.

Though the sounds of my rousing camp enveloped me, none of my soldiers intruded on my privacy. Between my commands and their fear of approaching the dragon without vylae, they gave Ryke a wide berth. I listened to my people's chatter and the sounds of campfires being built up, of food hunted and gathered from the mountains being prepared.

My mind whirled as I considered my power and what to do next. Despite Alrenor's reputation as a land of conquerors, it had been many long years since we'd engaged in a real war. And, though I hoped the Teramese hadn't yet learned how to tame the dragons, they'd successfully cut my people off from them. Ryke was a fearsome beast, but he was no dragon army.

From the hordes of Teramese soldiers I'd seen already trekking over the Alrenian countryside on my flight from the palace, countless ships must have anchored off our coast and deposited soldiers throughout the land. My camp was hopelessly outnumbered, our only advantage our secrecy. If there were other Alrenian encampments, other Alrenian soldiers prepared to fight for their empire, my own army and I didn't know where they were.

As far as we knew, we were alone.

And, with the arrival of Kovi and the Teramese officer, it seemed even our secrecy was lost. I couldn't trust that they hadn't sent word, that they hadn't been led here by Teramese scouts.

I gritted my teeth, feeling my blood boil. *Of course you knew Kovi wouldn't hesitate to kill you,* I reminded myself.

But then I thought of the way he'd looked at me when I'd visited him last night, how he'd promised not to use his magic against me. It felt conflicting, all of it. I knew on some level, at least before I'd threatened him and escaped the palace on Ryke, Kovi had cared about me. I couldn't stop thinking about his confession the night of the Autumn Ball.

And yet, I wasn't sure if those feelings were enough to overcome his need to be a loyal soldier.

Maybe he had a different reason for holding his magic back. Did he truly hate connecting himself to his enemies' emotions, as he'd claimed? Or was his magic more limited than he'd made it out to be?

Then again, I hadn't killed him, either. The curse hadn't harmed him. *I thought Nesrelle said the curse would hurt anyone guilty of shedding Alrenian blood.* I remembered what Kovi had said, that he'd slain four of my people so far. *And yet...like he suspects, maybe deep down, I still have to want to harm them.*

That thought shook me a little. I remembered the anger writhing inside me when I'd lashed out at Lady Leanai, forcing her to bow before me, or when I'd strode after Keeper Yaelti and seized his wrists. The fear and rage that had consumed me when I'd found myself betrayed by an Alrenian—twice. Clearly the curse affected more than just the Forwyn people, so perhaps it made sense that it could also spare Forywn too.

And truthfully, no matter how hurt I'd felt by Kovi lunging at me with a dagger, I hadn't wanted to kill him when I'd touched him.

I shifted uneasily on my feet, glancing over my shoulder toward the line of trees near the foot of the closest mountain. There I could just make out Kovi's form, chained to a tree and left far removed from the camp. I'd ordered my soldiers to stay far away from him as a precaution, fearing he could gain control of them and force them to free him. Even fight for him.

Kovi's Teramese companion was chained to another tree several yards away. I didn't fully understand Teramese magic, so I hadn't wanted the prisoners too close together, either. Whether Kovi truly considered himself allied to the Teramese or not, I didn't doubt that with my army as their common enemy, they would work together.

"This is your chance," Nesrelle murmured.

I blinked to find her standing beside me, stroking Ryke's scales. The beast snorted and studied her with one huge, gleaming eye.

"Are you here to counsel me?" I demanded. "Tell me what to do with my prisoners."

Nesrelle's smile was calm, calculating. "I think you already know how you will use them."

I frowned at the sky. "Then help with this: The Teramese soldiers outnumber us, *and* they have our dragons. I can't lead my army to take back Inalgoth. It will be a suicide mission. Even if I find leverage to use against the Teramese soldier and Kovi, and force them to use their magic to fight for us, it won't be enough."

Nesrelle's smile widened. "Oh, little empress," she crooned. She settled a hand on my shoulder, her fingers so icy that I could feel their chill seep through my dragon scale armor to my bones. "I've given you the curse you wield. Didn't you ever think, if you wanted a dragon army, that all you had to do was ask?"

A strange mixture of hope and trepidation slithered through me as I turned to study her expression. "What do you mean?"

Her grin was somehow comforting and vicious at the same time. "Your people have always prided yourselves on being Dragon Keepers, able to tame and ride and command the dragons. But why not *be* the dragons?"

I frowned and gestured to my dragon scale armor. "You'll dress us in scales and teach us to breathe fire?"

Her lips curled until she showed her teeth, which shone unnaturally white and too long, too sharp. "Something like that," she said. "Command your people to gather out at the training grounds." She nodded toward the open space left within our campsite for the soldiers to go through daily exercises and sparring matches. "We will speak to them, rally them."

My eyes flicked back toward Kovi. "And the prisoners?"

"You've already decided they'll be useful, or they'd be dead, wouldn't they?" Nesrelle laughed lightly. "Or at least, the Teramese mage would be. I know your weakness for that Forwyn soldier."

I swallowed thickly and glared, but she only smiled demurely back.

"Just don't forget who he is," she cautioned. "Now, gather your army."

The soldiers stood in rigid rows, eyes staring straight at me with deference and a hint of fear. My skin fairly tingled with the sense of power it gave me, to know I commanded my people and their respect. To know that perhaps, at last, my mother could look upon me from the afterlife with something other than shame.

When Nesrelle manifested herself before them, however, they couldn't contain their surprise, eyes widening and soft gasps running through their ranks. The breeze kissed my cheeks as it swirled around Nesrelle's midnight blue skirts and ran through her tumbling red hair. With her pale skin and formal attire, she was starkly out of place, and yet her own commanding power was evident. I could taste it on my tongue, like the acrid flavor of dragon smoke lingering in the air; and I could feel it in the wind, like the crackling energy of a building storm.

"Who is this?" Daedra, positioned close to me, murmured. She was daring to break the silence I'd demanded of the army, but I let it slide this once.

"I think you already know who this is," I said, lifting my voice to be heard throughout the rows of soldiers.

A few shuffled, uncertainty or raw terror flickering across their faces. Some lowered their heads reverently, entranced by the Queen of Death's magnetic, powerful aura and stunning features. Most remained still and quiet as requested, their eyes darting between Nesrelle and me as they awaited my next order.

"You fear you've lost your empire," Nesrelle began, her words ringing out loudly despite the softness of her voice. "The Forwyn and now the Teramese have seized control of your palace and your dragons. You've called upon the Life-Giver and you hear no answer. Over the years, your greatest gifts have slowly vanished, leaving you feeling like you're less worthy than your ancestors of old, with their great tales of conquering kingdoms and commanding dragons. You're ashamed of what you've been reduced to, hiding from your former slaves and biding your time to build an army worthy to defeat the Forwyn.

"Now you fear you're forever outnumbered with the Teramese forces crawling across your land."

My heart hammered against my chest, eagerness thrilling through me. What could Nesrelle offer us to lay our enemies low?

"But I'm here to tell you that *I* have seen your plight," Nesrelle continued. She gestured one graceful hand toward me. "I'm the one who gifted your empress with the curse she carries, a curse to judge the Forwyn for the Alrenian blood they've shed. You have always taken pride in being the Chosen People. But I have chosen you for even greater things than you've ever imagined.

"Kneel before me, submit your allegiance to me, and you will become an unstoppable army against your foes. Their numbers will not matter. The weapons they wield and the dragons they ride cannot stop you. You will walk through fire and not burn. You will see into their minds to discern their deepest fears, and you will use those fears against them. You will bring the Forwyn infidels and Teramese invaders to their knees, weeping and begging for mercy. You will reclaim your empire and make your generation worthy of new songs, new stories. No longer will you shame the legacy of the Alrenian Empire. Instead, it will rise again from the ashes."

Slowly, I could see the expressions on my soldiers changing, their energy transforming from concerned or doubtful to hopeful. Eager. Hungry for power and prestige, for the world our mothers and fathers had known. And something even greater—the conquests of forefathers long gone to the afterlife. An empire rebuilt and expanded. Kingdoms laid at our feet. The world ours for the taking.

As if Nesrelle could illustrate with her words, I could see the images in my mind's eye: the forests and small towns of Misroth once again paying tribute to my people; the vast grasslands and caverns of Toryn open to my dragons to explore; the rich island kingdom of Forwyth offering up its resources. Teramyl paying for its crimes by becoming part of our empire. And other kingdoms across the Great Sea, all joining us. Never again would we fear invasion or the loss of our dragons, our luxury, our riches, our power. Never again would we be scorned for our weakness. Never again would we have to watch our fellow Alrenians captured and brutally murdered in horrific public displays.

"I ask you," Nesrelle continued, lifting her voice until she was almost shouting, "is this what you want? The glory of former days restored? Power that will make you never fear for your loved ones' lives again? Strength to subdue any who defy you?"

The army roared, fists punching the air as they cried out in unison. "Yes!"

"Then kneel to your empress, and to me!" Nesrelle cried.

Raw terror lingered in numerous pairs of gold-flecked eyes as the soldiers watched uneasily. It was clear from their expressions that most were torn, wrestling with their longing for vengeance and their lifelong fear of the Queen of Death. Every Alrenian, whether they thought her myth or real, knew the stories. Knew how she fed on despair and pain, how she reveled in all of humanity's destruction.

"What—what price do you require from us?" a man asked, quaking where he stood. His voice was tremulous, his eyes darting from Nesrelle to snag on me. I wasn't sure if he hoped for reassurance from me, the bearer of Nesrelle's curse—a survivor of her presence—or if he awaited my command.

But I wouldn't order my army to obey. They had to willingly make their choice, the same as I did. My heart hammered in my ears, uncertainty creeping down my spine. The curse seemed to buzz with power through my veins, yet I knew it, too, came with a cost. Anything Nesrelle bestowed would.

Nesrelle smiled at my ranks like a benevolent mother. "You are soldiers, accustomed to risks. You didn't hesitate to accept the sacrifices you will make by taking up your sword in your empire's name. But what I'm promising you is strength beyond your imagination: the ability to stare into the face of death and walk away unscathed. I'm offering you the blood of your enemies, stretching out in an endless ocean at your feet. I'm granting you power and glory and redemption. Isn't that worth any risk?"

A chill coiled in my gut even though her words were as sweet as honey. She refused to specify the price, because we already knew the ugly cost, deep down. The price would be our own souls.

Still, her words a mesmerizing siren song echoing in our ears, we listened and soaked in her promises. And my soldiers' expressions softened, lulled into a sense of security. Their eyes gleamed with hope and bloodlust as one by one, they made their choice.

The rows of Alrenian soldiers knelt before us, bowing their heads deferentially. Another rush of power swept through my body, electric and intoxicating. Tears burned my eyes.

"And you," Nesrelle murmured, turning to me so only I could hear her. "You must pledge yourself to me too. I need to know you are not afraid of the curse you carry. That you can wield your power without hesitation and lead your people to victory. I must know that I'm not entrusting this greatness to someone…unworthy."

Her piercing blue eyes burned into mine, as if she could see into my very soul. A shock of terror jolted through me as I remembered the stories about the Queen of Death and the demons she commanded. It was said her teeth were like daggers, her fingernails like claws. That she was a fallen Immortal, given to evil. That she would do anything to deceive and destroy mortals, feeding off their despair and pain.

Giver of Life, I thought, but it was more of a curse than a prayer. I'd long since given up trying to pray to the god of my people. *What have I gotten myself into?*

And yet…my throne waited for me. If I said no, I wasn't sure my people could stand a chance against two enemy forces. Ryke couldn't defeat all of the other dragons alone. I blanched at the idea of leading my people into a slaughter. Of being captured and murdered—or worse, imprisoned once more to watch my people languish and die as I was used in another political game. I would be abused and mocked, weak and alone forever.

I will never be weak again. My earlier vow swept over me. This was my chance to make it true, once and for all. To wield something even greater than the curse flowing through my veins. *I will never make my mother ashamed again.*

But at what price? a quiet voice whispered in my head. I swept it aside. This was no time for hesitation. My people needed me.

I lifted my eyes, and for one painful instant, my gaze pulled past the lines of kneeling soldiers, past the furthest tents, and toward the line of trees where Kovi was chained to a trunk. He was directly across from me, the yards between us seemingly shrinking to nothing as his eyes captured mine. His jaw was taut, his brow furrowed. His lips moved, as if he were trying to share a message with me. As if he were pleading. As if he cared, and did not want me to make this deal when the cost would be my soul.

Of course he doesn't want you to, I reminded myself sharply. *It will mean you can defeat his army. He came here to kill you, not watch you grow in strength.*

I turned to Nesrelle, ignoring the ache in my chest, the magnetic pull I still felt between Kovi and me.

"Yes," I said. "I pledge myself to you and accept the power you can bestow upon my soldiers and me."

Nesrelle's grin stretched wide.

CHAPTER EIGHTEEN

Lo

AFTER MY CONVERSATION WITH CAESIEM, I'd gone back to sleep, my first dreamless rest in far too long. When I awoke, my headache had all but disappeared, and my body felt stronger. The theslynik truly was miraculous, just as the healer had claimed. Other than a lingering light-headed feeling, I was almost back to normal—better than normal, if I was being honest. Rarely did I ever have as much rest as I had this past day.

Despite the threat Mio'e—and likely the other vigilantes—held over me, I was far too restless to stay confined in the palace again.

Since Caesiem had vanished again after bathing, it was all too easy to slip outside to the balcony, where the guards were still absent, and into the gathering dusk. The gardens' aroma was heavy, the slight coolness on the breeze comforting rather than chilling. I darted swiftly through the grounds and scaled the wall.

At the top, I waited one instant to take in the stunning view: the sea churning blood-red and foamy, the gulls swooping low over the waves, and the city streets spread out below. Inalgoth's stone buildings glistened red, orange, or gold in the waning sunlight, breathtakingly beautiful, as always. My eyes drank in the sight, both loving and hating it. Then the moment was over, approaching footsteps signaling my need to retreat. I descended the wall and crept down the winding path toward the city.

I wasn't quite sure where I was going, because I hadn't left with a particular destination in mind. I was simply…walking. I was falling into my old restless habits, the coming night drawing me out into the streets I'd so often wandered even when I'd lived within the peaceful abbey. It was a way to occupy my thoughts and flee the nightmares that would find me if I gave into sleep.

Eventually, I found myself creeping toward the abbey. Though I was no longer welcome within it, I had to see it, to reassure myself the sisters were safe.

Each street was eerily empty and still but for the Teramese soldiers crawling throughout Inalgoth. They patrolled every inch and chatted at every corner. I clung to the shadows to avoid their piercing stares, and from the buildings and houses I scanned, I could tell that, whether by decree or fear, they were keeping the citizens hidden away. Window curtains were drawn shut, with only the occasional Alrenian or Forwyn succumbing to curiosity and peering cautiously outside.

My path led me in the direction of the pub that Caesiem had once stayed at, using his musical talent to pay his room and board. The Broken Crown was a Forwyn business, owned by a man named No'ahim. Even though I'd only been inside a couple of times, seeing the warm glow through the windows sent a jolt of sadness through me. If only Caesiem truly had been nothing but an orphan seeking a new life.

As I stepped closer, I noticed a cluster of dark-uniformed soldiers muttering in the musical Teramese language, their words rolling swiftly like the notes to a song. My heart thundered in my ribcage as I tried to make myself unobtrusive. I lingered in the shadows before creeping carefully along a nearby alley. As much as I longed to use invisibility with the power of Elhani's magic, I knew he wouldn't listen to me. I could only hope my talent for going unnoticed would work instead.

"You there," barked a man, suddenly switching to the merchant tongue. My heart froze mid-beat, my steps drawing to a careful halt. I lifted my chin slowly to meet his eyes.

But his emerald gaze was not pinned on me, but on someone around a corner of the road.

"What are you doing out past curfew?" the Teramese soldier continued, stepping forward, his hand hovering near his sword hilt.

A soft, familiar voice answered. "Forgive me, sir. I'm a nun. We tend to some of the poor and sick in the city, and I am needed at the home of a very ill family tonight."

Pauni'a. Hope fluttered through me as I strained to listen to every word. The last time I'd seen my friend, she'd been sick herself with fever from aiding a family, but I didn't doubt that after several days of rest and Naina's careful nursing, Pauni'a was healthy again.

The soldier stiffened, as if uncertain. He tossed a glance toward his companions, then back down the street where Pauni'a apparently stood, waiting.

"Emperor Revaed said there were to be no exceptions," the Teramese soldier continued gruffly, taking another step forward, hand still on his hilt.

I shuffled closer to the alley's entrance, daring to slip partially out of the shadows to crane my neck and find Pauni'a. She appeared shorter and slimmer than ever, her small frame nearly drowning in the long cloak she wore to chase away the slight chill in the air. The dusk was quickly melting into velvety shadows, encasing Pauni'a. She stood perfectly still, her chin angled down and her lovely amber eyes exuding humility. The slight downturn of her heart-shaped mouth added to the effect of subservience and fear. Surely the Teramese soldiers wouldn't believe her to be a threat…

"Please, sir," she said, her voice dropping until it was almost whisper-soft. "They fear they are dying, and they have unatoned sins. They need me there to help usher their souls safely into the Golden After."

I pressed my lips together to contain my surprised laughter at my sister's lie. We nuns didn't help others atone for their own sins; we believed Elhani wanted us all to seek him as individuals about our misdeeds. It made me wonder why Pauni'a was *really* out on the streets past curfew.

The soldier rolled his eyes. "What superstitious nonsense is that?" he scoffed.

Another man, his appearance younger, his silver eyes gentler, laid a hand on the first soldier's arm. "I don't think…" he started, but the first man shook him off.

"Do you want to speak to a Xalenos about why you thought it was all right to disobey a direct command?" He sneered at his companion. "I'm sure you could wax poetic about this girl's pretty face as Lord Xalenos draws the blood from your body."

The young man trembled, his eyes widening at the thought. He shook his head rapidly.

Draws the blood from your body? I thought. A bout of dizziness gripped me as images flashed through my mind: Caesiem storming into his quarters, coated in blood that wasn't his own. His light blue eyes darkened with a conflicting combination of remorse and determination.

"You're under arrest," the first soldier declared, striding toward Pauni'a. Two of the other soldiers, an older man and a young woman, flanked him.

My brain went into action, churning through different possibilities. I couldn't let them drag Pauni'a away, likely to meet a swift and brutal sentence from the Teramese. But I knew my prayers to Elhani would fall on deaf ears. I had no magic to wield, and she and I were horribly outnumbered.

Before I could hurl myself into the street, straight into danger, the female soldier cried out in surprise. "Where did she go?"

One of the men unleashed a curse.

"Demonic magic," another soldier snarled, drawing his sword. The sharp ring of steel scraping made me feel like insects were scrabbling down my spine. "Split up and search the surrounding streets and alleys. She can't go far."

Before I had time to react, to race through the streets searching for my friend, something seized my wrist. I bit back my startled cry as the invisible fingers, soft yet firm, made my own arm vanish before my eyes. Elhani's magic coursed warmly through my veins as the hand tugged, pulling me back down the alley and away from the pounding steps of the searching soldiers.

Elation burst through my heart as I let Pauni'a guide me invisibly down the alley, dodging questionable-looking puddles and garbage piles. She wound a path through shadowy streets. I held my breath and tried to soften my steps as we skirted wide paths around other Teramese men and women patrolling the city. My feet were light, as if with just a little more effort, I could launch myself forward and I'd be airborne, free to touch the clouds and sail among the stars. Fear of pursuit and all my burdens fell away with the adrenaline, almost as strong as the joy I experienced from the feel of magic burning through me once more.

Even if I wasn't the one wielding the magic, it was an indescribable sensation, one I could never put into words. It was a soothing hand of comfort, or the grounding weight of a weapon making me feel invincible. Snatches of Elhani's song burbled through the air, ringing in my ears so beautifully I could feel tears stinging my eyes. Maybe he didn't hate me. Did I dare believe it? Did I dare imagine a world in which my god could forgive me? Could give me purpose and power again?

Pauni'a wheeled us around a sharp corner, and we were immersed in the overwhelming tang of the sea, the rush of the wind, and the lap of the waves. We were near the shipyard and the harbor, where low buildings gave me a clear view of countless rows of foreign ships docked in our waters. A lump of fear lodged itself in my throat. I'd caught a glimpse from a distance the night of the Autumn Ball, but even that hadn't given me an accurate idea of their numbers. The Teramese had brought a *fleet*. No wonder their people were everywhere, overwhelming us so suddenly and completely.

Here, though, the world appeared deserted and still. The ships were quiet, and no one else walked the narrow street that led straight toward the harbor. Panting, Pauni'a slowed her pace to a stroll, her grasp on my arm easing. The rush of magic faded, leaving me feeling cold and empty.

I turned to her, each of us blinking in wonder. Everything about my friend was utterly familiar and comforting: her oval face, her shining amber eyes, and her full lips, the corners upturned in an overjoyed smile. She burst into laughter and threw herself into my arms, her embrace surprisingly strong for her petite frame.

"Lo," she murmured, her voice still breathless. "I knew I'd find you."

"Find me?" I asked in surprise. "Why? You knew I'd left the abbey, Nia. I can't return…"

Pauni'a pulled back to stare into my eyes, her brow crinkled in a frown. "I knew your habit of running through the city at night, remember? It seemed only a matter of time before I'd find you out here. And I *refuse* to believe that anything you've done is unforgivable," she said solemnly, her mouth set in a stubborn line. "The sisters and I…our love for you will never fade, no matter what."

I could feel my eyes misting even as I tried to brush her words away with a shake of my head, with protests my open mouth couldn't seem to form properly.

Pauni'a ignored my silent disagreement and pressed on. "And if mere mortals can love you in spite of flaws and mistakes, then surely Elhani can too."

I scowled. "Nia, I—I *killed* someone. I forsook my vows." My voice was broken, entreating. I wasn't sure if I was pleading for her to agree with me or continue to fight her point. All I knew was that the mere sight of her made me homesick, opening a void in my heart I was afraid I would tumble into.

She set her hands on her hips. "I know you, Lo. You wouldn't kill anyone without a just cause. Elhani allows avengers of blood to mete out punishment, to restore balance and order by slaying murderers and unrighteous killers. You only vowed to never shed *innocent* blood. Was the person you killed innocent?"

I blinked at her, considering. Lost. Wilvhe had been my ally, and so I'd never questioned the wrongness of my actions. And yet… "He tried…he was going to kill me," I said haltingly. "I reacted to stop him."

A knowing smile tugged at Pauni'a lips. "See? Innocent," she proclaimed.

Heated guilt seared through me. "I'd planned to help assassinate the empress."

"Because the guidespirit led you to the vigilantes. And you believed the empress's death would save Forwyn lives." Pauni'a spoke the words assuredly, as if she'd been present to witness everything I'd done myself. I'd told her much about my plans, but not everything. She had filled in the blanks remarkably well. But then…she was right. She *knew* me.

"Yes," I acknowledged slowly. "But…I figured the choice would expel me from the abbey forever."

Pauni'a shrugged. "I still believe Naina would have forgiven you, if you had succeeded."

If. Clearly, word had spread throughout Inalgoth that the empress still lived. Perhaps hopeful rumors spread by the Alrenians.

I swallowed thickly. "Well, I wasn't sure," I continued. "I thought if I was already throwing away my life, it didn't matter, so I also kissed Caesiem. Twice." I bit back a grimace at my confession, feeling childish. Unworthy.

Pauni'a nodded slowly with feigned solemnity. "Well, if you were going to throw away your sisterhood, at least you chose a *handsome* man."

"Nia!" I scolded, slapping her lightly on the shoulder.

Pauni'a grinned wickedly. "How was it?"

Pain lanced through me as I remembered Caesiem's betrayal. "I'm not talking about it. It was wrong."

But her face had turned serious again. "I don't think you were ever meant to be a nun," she declared, the assurance in her tone so intense that I froze.

"What?"

She nodded toward my golden ribbons, braided into a necklace that concealed the scar on my neck. The mark that forever reminded me of the night Empress Karye had tried to murder me, and I'd exacted my revenge instead. The night I'd learned vengeance was empty, despite the sacred vows avengers of blood made to supposedly restore balance and bring rightness to the world, as my sister had claimed.

Evil had lived on, just the same.

"You have always been a fighter," Pauni'a murmured. "You have a fire within you I've always admired and envied." She smiled bashfully. "You love fiercely, and it's that fierce love for our people that fuels acts of bravery I could only dream of. Surely Elhani wouldn't give you a warrior's heart so you could spend all your days serving widows and orphans and nursing at sickbeds. He called you to something greater."

"Serving our people *is* our greatest calling," I argued.

Pauni'a nodded. "Some of us spend our lives serving a few, and it is important. And some people—*you*—are called to serve *all*. To change the lives of *every one* of the Forwyn."

I frowned. "How do you know this? How could you imagine Elhani would give me a purpose when I broke his trust already?"

"Don't be dense, Lo! I already told you he would forgive you. And your calling isn't about you. It's bigger than that—it's about all of us. Do you think you could make enough mistakes to throw Elhani's purpose off course?"

"No," I said slowly. "But how are you so confident about my purpose?" I bit back a sad laugh. "Even I'm not sure."

"I've had dreams," Pauni'a said in a low voice.

My eyes widened. "What kind of dreams?" I asked, but Pauni'a looked anxious, glancing about as if she'd heard a noise.

I froze. "What is it?" I whispered. Though the streets appeared deserted, I knew we'd lingered too long in one place, too caught up in our conversation.

"I thought I heard something," Pauni'a said, grasping my arm and tugging me forward.

"We've stayed too long. You should be back at the abbey," I said pointedly. "Are there really sick families you need to visit in the middle of the night?"

Pauni'a grinned. "Oh no, I had that lie ready. I was out looking for you."

I frowned, wanting to protest about how dangerous her search was, to ask why she'd felt it was so urgent. As thankful as I was to see her again, I didn't like the fact that she'd risked her life just to find me.

"If I've finally convinced you we don't hate you," Pauni'a went on, "you could return to the abbey too."

"But—" I began.

Pauni'a was still speaking, unimpeded by my weak attempt at interrupting her. "We have Teramese soldiers occupying the abbey," she went on with a cringe. "I know they're in homes throughout the city, but they've especially crowded the abbey because it's a larger building. We have had to share rooms just to make space, and don't even let me go on about trying to share the washroom…"

"What?" I breathed, my stomach curdling at the thought of those brutal soldiers invading my old home, sharing space with my friends, befouling our sacred space and interrupting worship and training times.

Pauni'a nodded, trying and failing to repress a shudder as she led me into a deserted alley. "I hate the way they look at me, Lo."

A sour taste filled my mouth, coating my tongue with bitter hatred. "Have they laid a finger on you? On anyone?"

Pauni'a shook her head. "No, but they make threats."

My heart slammed against my ribcage; my fingers twitched with the desire to fight. I couldn't stand the injustice of it all. *And Caesiem brought them all here,* I thought angrily. Any soft feelings I'd entertained after he'd saved my life were quickly drowning in a new onslaught of indignation.

"Nia," I whispered softly, yanking my hand free of her grasp.

She turned toward me, her face bathed in shadows. Over the lapping of the sea a short distance away, my voice was like a breath of wind, low even to my own ears.

"I can't go back."

"Lo, I told you—" Pauni'a blinked back the tears pooling in her eyes. "*Please.*"

"I'm…staying with the Teramese. I have a plan to work against them from inside the palace."

Pauni'a's eyes widened. "What?"

Before I could explain, a soft thud echoed in the stillness of the alleyway. My gaze darted over Pauni'a's shoulder, toward the shadows clinging at the far end. Jagged stone walls rose high above us on either side, each part of abandoned businesses. The vacant buildings reminded me of the place the vigilantes had gathered, and my stomach clenched. Here I was, dangerously close to the harbor at night. With my friend.

We're too close.

As if summoned by my thoughts, Mio'e herself materialized, stepping out of the shadows as smoothly and silently as a ghost. Her body was slender yet strong, her gait confident and assured. Her shorn hair and the scars lining her bare arms reminded me that she'd been a slave not long ago, and that she'd had the courage and wit to escape her fate. She already had her weapon drawn: a dagger that sparkled, wicked and sharp, in the starlight.

"I can't believe you delivered yourself right to me," she taunted, her mouth stretched in a cruel grin. Her teeth flashed, but her dark eyes burned with a quieter, more terrifying hatred.

She stalked forward, as silent as a predator as her eyes scanned first me, then Pauni'a with her clothes in shades of grey, proclaiming her status as a nun. "Although I'm sorry you brought a friend." Lifting her free hand to show off a bandage wrapped around her palm, she addressed Pauni'a. "This is your chance to do the right thing, nun. I've made the sacred vow of a blood avenger. Your friend Lo'laeni there is more than just an empress slayer."

My skin crawled as Mio'e's eyes bored into me. "She is apparently *also* a slayer of her own people, a shedder of *innocent* blood, a traitor to her allies." She spat the words out viciously.

"No!" Pauni'a retorted, squaring her shoulders. "She's not, and you will *not* touch her."

Mio'e's paused mid-step, assessing my friend in surprise. "What exactly do they train nuns?" she demanded. "You all have far more gumption than I expected from women who sit around and pray all day."

I bit out a harsh laugh. "You have no idea."

Mio'e sneered at me before rounding on Pauni'a once more. This time, she was dangerously close, her dagger still flashing as she hovered near my friend. My sister. Fear trickled down my spine like icy water. I couldn't let her touch Pauni'a.

"Now this is *your* chance," Mio'e announced. "You can leave and let me fulfill the promise I made before Elhani and all of his immortal guidespirits, or you can die with your friend."

"Go, Nia!" I snapped through gritted teeth. "Listen to her. Go home."

Pauni'a curled her hands into fists. "Never. I will not stand by and let you kill her. She's innocent!"

As she spoke the words, she launched herself at Mio'e, taking the other woman off guard with her aggression. Pauni'a slammed her foot into Mio'e's knee, dropping her with a groan.

"Run!" Pauni'a screamed. I was already on her heels, darting down the alley toward the nearest street. Distant shouts alerted me to guards who must have heard us and would soon be on their way to scope out the disturbance. We veered right, back toward the sea, a briny breeze tugging at my curls.

I couldn't look at the glint of moonlight on the water without once again seeing the huge water beast Caesiem had summoned from the waves.

My eyes scanned for a street or alley that connected to ours and would lead us away from the watery dead end we were charging toward, but there was nothing but cramped, abandoned buildings lining either side of the road. Just as I spied two narrow alleys, one to our left and another to our right, forms sprang from the shadows like phantoms.

My stomach tightened: it was just as I feared. Pauni'a and I were outnumbered and surrounded. Mio'e pursued with swift footsteps, prepared to launch herself at us. On one side, Nu'or emerged, dwarfing Pauni'a and even me with his tall stature and impressively muscular figure. On the opposite, A'elli with her gentle, freckled face had become a living nightmare. Jaw set in a terrible line, she stared daggers at me as she hefted a hatchet. Tears of grief and rage glittered in her eyes.

They hate me for what I did, I thought. Somehow, I hadn't realized how close the group was, how they all depended upon one another and protected each other. How much they, like Naina and my sisters, had become a family. And I'd ripped it apart, first by slaying Wilvhe and then by letting Caesiem kill Renni. My throat burned with renewed guilt, despite what Pauni'a had told me. Self-defense or not, I could practically feel the blood coating my palms, dripping from my fingers.

The thought nearly took me back to the horrors of my past, to endless bloody deaths. There was always so much blood…

"Lo," Pauni'a ground out, her eyes darting toward me, her sharp glance and firm voice drawing me back to the present. I'd been gasping, choking on my own air.

"This is for Wilvhe and Renni, you miserable traitor," A'elli cried, her voice wobbly yet powerful enough to echo in the street.

"Don't be fools," I said quickly, forcing my own words to be strong. "Listen." I raised a hand, as if to pause the three's advancing steps. For one instant, they did halt, tilting their heads to focus on the shouts in Teramese that were gradually growing louder as the soldiers ran nearer. They couldn't have been more than a few streets away. "They'll kill us all for breaking curfew. They don't care a demon's claw about your avenging oaths."

Nu'or sneered at me, his eyes shining with bloodlust. "Then we'll just have to be quick."

He lunged for us, shoving toward Pauni'a first, likely assuming because she was smaller that she would be the weaker target, the one to pick off first. He was wrong.

While the other women charged from different directions, closing in to surround us, Pauni'a dropped into a fighting stance, her body poised and ready. She moved as effortlessly as breathing, ducking as Nu'or swung his blade and seizing a handful of dirt off the dusty street in the same motion. As she rose, she hurled it into his eyes, forcing him to stumble back, blinking furiously when muddy tears streamed down his cheeks.

A'elli reached us next, a beat faster than Mio'e. She lunged at

Pauni'a and swung her hatchet in a slightly too-wide arc, her anger making her clumsy. Pauni'a dove for her legs, sending the woman careening to the ground. A'elli hit her back with a grunt, her weapon falling from her hand and striking the cobblestones with a clatter.

Before Mio'e could slice at me with her dagger, I'd scooped up the hatchet and turned to face her. The woman drew up short, eyes narrowing.

"You did such a good job playing the part of an innocent nun, too pious to commit violence." She scowled. "And look what a lie that was, how easily you hold a weapon. *Murderer.*"

I bit the inside of my cheek, letting the words roll off me. Letting Pauni'a's reminder take over instead. *I did it in self-defense. I did it to survive.*

As my friend leapt to her feet to fend off a recovering Nu'or, I took another step toward Mio'e. Despite her words, the hatchet felt heavy in my hands. I didn't want to be here, fighting against my own people, not when we had enemies we should have been uniting against.

The Teramese shouts were growing louder. We had perhaps a minute at most before they'd be upon us.

My stomach churned with revulsion. I had killed to survive, and I would kill again to survive, if I had to. But that didn't erase how much I hated it. How much I longed for things to be different. All I wanted was to seize Pauni'a's hand and flee before even more enemies were upon us. I longed to hurl this weapon into the sea, take my friend, and then run, run from this bloody city and never look back.

But that was impossible. I had to stay, to fight for the ones I loved. My sister panted behind me, the sounds of her and Nu'or's scuffle loud in my ears.

Mio'e inched closer, and I hefted the hatchet, letting its weight shift until it balanced more comfortably in my grip. Hours of chopping firewood for the abbey had prepared me for this moment just as much as any sparring or exercises had. I scanned Mio'e swiftly, searching for weaknesses and determining my best target.

Behind me, A'elli groaned but didn't rise to her feet. She lay still, knocked unconscious from striking her head against stone. She wasn't a threat, so I turned my full attention to the one who was.

My blood pounded in my ears as Mio'e bridged the gap between us, feinting a swipe with her dagger toward my head before ducking and plunging her blade low, toward my chest. I leapt backward not an instant too soon and countered with a swing of my hatchet. We circled one another, eyes narrowed in concentration as sweat beaded on our foreheads. My palms felt slick as I shifted the hatchet's weight once more.

Before we could spring together again, the Teramese were upon us.

An arrow whizzed overhead, narrowly missing my ear. I could feel the breath of wind from its passing against my cheek.

"Break it up!" a male voice barked in the merchant tongue. "That was your warning! Drop your weapons and surrender, or be sentenced to death for defying the authority of His Imperial Majesty!"

Mio'e bit back a cry of rage. She cast her eyes toward Nu'or, and they shared a silent message. Both their gazes flicked anxiously to A'elli before they turned back toward one another.

"A'elli, forgive us," Nu'or breathed. "We can't save you."

They were forsaking her, leaving her to a fate that likely ended in imprisonment and torture—or death.

Without a backward glance, they sprinted down the road, away from the advancing Teramese soldiers and toward the water. Heart in my throat, I caught Paunia's nod, and together, we raced after our enemies.

Help us escape, I pleaded with Elhani, trying and failing to catch a note of his song around me. Besides, what good was disappearing now when we were trapped between soldiers and the sea? We wouldn't be able to exit this street unless we could scale one of the buildings or swim further and faster than the pursuing soldiers. Even now, they were surrounding us, cutting off any possible escape routes by swarming the alleys intersecting with our street.

There was nowhere to go but the water. Perhaps we could vanish beneath its surface and come up for air far enough away they'd lose us. Maybe…

Mio'e and Nu'or reached the edge first, sheathing their weapons and plunging into the harbor. More arrows flew through the air, one cutting dangerously close to Pauni'a's head.

"We should let Lord Xalenos summon one of his water beasts!" a woman shouted, laughing cruelly as Pauni'a and I darted to the end of the street and slowed to peer into the harbor.

The twang of more bowstrings filled the air, and I knew we had only one choice. One desperate chance. I dropped my hatchet to the cobblestones with a clatter. "Now!" I cried to my sister.

With a final gasp of air, I seized Pauni'a's hand and leapt into the water.

The force of impact yanked Pauni'a's and my hands apart, wrenching us in different directions. The water was surprisingly cool given the warm night, churning and foaming around me as I sank. Arrows followed, splashing and slicing paths through the water.

Though the harbor was calm, the water still tugged me, pulling my weight down into its murky depths, where it was too dark to see the sandy bottom. A memory of swirling tentacles flashed through my mind and I kicked furiously toward the surface.

As my face broke above the gently lapping waves, I gulped in the briny air. I scanned for my sister, for my enemies, and for a glimpse of the line of Inalgoth stretching behind me. I needed a direction to swim that would take me away from danger, and I needed to know Pauni'a was all right.

A cry of pain made me crane my neck to the side, where Nu'or flailed in the water, an arrow shaft protruding from his shoulder. Blood stained the frothing water pink as he struggled to swim away, diving beneath the surface once more. I ducked back under and searched again, but saw nothing.

"Nia!" I shouted, but the Teramese were already standing in a row at the harbor's edge, drawing their bows.

Hide us, I prayed, straining to catch the faintest notes rustling on the breeze and flowing through the water.

And then the arrows were flying.

I sucked in more air and dove deeply, shoving all thoughts of Caesiem and his water creatures from my mind. I steered myself, as best as I could in the dark waters, toward what I thought was a point further along the shore, away from the streets occupied by the shooting Teramese. My arms ached, though I could feel Elhani's magic coursing through me, warm and sustaining, keeping my exhaustion at bay.

A minute passed. Two. More. Without air, my lungs burned, but not as much as I expected. The song running through my heart and mind rang out clearer, stronger, and it was as if it became my air, my strength, my protection. I felt a supernatural surge run through me, keeping me from growing light-headed and weak. Somehow, I didn't need to resurface, even though I knew at least five minutes must have passed.

Impossible, but for Elhani's power. A thrill rippled through me. He'd forgiven me after all, just as Pauni'a had believed.

Thank you, thank you, I prayed, swimming fast and far, knowing I was out of range of the arrows. The Teramese would believe I was dead, having gone too long without resurfacing.

At last, I dared to rise toward the surface and survey the shore. I drew in breaths of sweet air and listened to…stillness. Silence. I peered behind me to see the streets where the Teramese had waited were no longer visible, all but a smear of darkness in the night, which was quickly fading into the pale grey light of morning. There was no sign of Mio'e or Nu'or, who'd either perished or already fled to shore. But there was no sign of Pauni'a either.

Fear lanced through my heart, jolting my concentration on Elhani's song. The warmth and strength vanished, leaving my muscles aching, my head pounding with fear and weariness. Nearer than I expected lay a more rugged coast: golden sand and then stubbly grass and palm trees. The city walls rose tall and foreboding a few hundred yards away.

I swam past the city limits, I thought in amazement.

This knowledge bolstered me with hope. Surely Pauni'a wouldn't have gone so far. She would have swum ashore many yards back to slip into one of the quieter streets and find her way back to the Akytha District and our abbey. *Her abbey,* I corrected myself.

My eyes darted toward the rising city streets that climbed in one gradual incline toward the sprawling palace, its grounds, and the Keep with its cliff's edge for the dragons. A golden glow emanated from all the buildings' many windows, visible even from here. It was surprisingly beautiful—not only all of Inalgoth, spread out before me in the gathering light of an approaching dawn, but also the palace, with its carved, glistening white walls and details. Though it was tempting to slink back toward the abbey and never face Caesiem or Emperor Revaed again, I knew what I had to do.

Find Pauni'a and make sure she's safe, I thought.

Then return to the palace…and somehow, find a way to help my people.

CHAPTER NINETEEN

Kovi

E VERY TIME I CLOSED MY eyes, the horrors of the Alrenian camp and their deal with the Queen of Demons faded, giving way to the horrors of my past. The courtyard of Aerekni Academy rose in my mind, my boots pounding against the smooth cobblestones beneath me, my footsteps echoing off the huge stone walls. Disciplined rows of my peers, in perfectly pressed uniforms and polished boots, stood with backs straight and eyes trained forward as they awaited their moment to prove their worth and graduate the academy.

But for now, it was my turn.

When I passed my friend Rhi'il in the front row, I was tempted to turn my head and try to meet his gaze, though I knew he wouldn't ever shift his eyes or change his masked expression. There were too many hopes and dreams, along with the weight of our parents' expectations—those of us who had any living parents, anyway—riding on this moment for everyone. The moment we became true soldiers, ready to be recruited into the army, the guard, or even among the ranks of the Dragon Keepers, and serve our people, protecting them from the merciless Alrenians. Avenging dead loved ones.

A dim memory of my mother flashed before my eyes, from a time long ago when I'd been a palace slave. *Lift your head, Kovi.* I sucked in a breath, pushing the stab of grief away. I had to remain focused.

Before me stretched a line of condemned Alrenians, some with their heads hung low, but many studying the soon-to-be Aerekni graduates with malice shining in their gold-specked eyes. Their gold-sheened skin gleamed in the afternoon sunlight, hurting my eyes if I studied them too closely. No wonder they were such a fearsome race, with their shimmering skin, their tall, lithe bodies, and greedy, cruel nature. Hatred simmered low in my gut, making it all the easier for me to imagine drawing the blade at my side and shoving it through one of these prisoners' hearts.

All I could see was my mother. All I could hear were my father's words when he'd visited the academy and told me her fate. His voice had cracked as he'd explained that Karye had slit her throat, all for the simple crime of spilling tea.

These brutal Alrenians deserved their fate.

"Bring the first prisoner forward," General Ilowhe ordered two Aerekni students, both at least a year away from graduation still. They shuffled forward, seizing the first chained prisoner in the row and dragging the captive forward. Toward me.

My eyes landed on the form and my heart stilled, the breath in my lungs seizing. At my side, my twitching fingers stilled, frozen on my sword hilt.

The captive was younger than me, closer to boy than man. His green and gold eyes sparkled not just with hate and anger, but also with fear. A muscle worked in his jaw as he studied me, trying to brace himself for the inevitable. Trying to make himself face the end with the fearless dignity his people admired so much.

My throat was dry, and my tongue cleaved to the roof of my mouth. Surely this was a mistake. This couldn't be the final, honorable act of an Aerekni graduate, to cut down a man not even my size and claim it a great victory for my people.

This is a trick, I thought. *A different sort of test. This isn't an act to determine your mettle, your determination in battle. This is something else, a test of your virtue and self-control. To see if I can show mercy as easily as I can kill.*

Right?

I glanced toward General Ilowhe, whose great height, broad shoulders, and square jaw demanded attention and respect, wherever he went. It was clear from his every feature, down to his stern eyes and commanding voice, that he'd been born to lead armies.

"This Alrenian is guilty of breaking curfew, armed robbery, and murder. He didn't even deny that he'd killed Forwyn citizens."

As he spoke, I could feel my heart harden. *Just like all the others, then, growing up to be a monster,* I thought. *Another ruthless killer who thinks only of himself.*

"His sentence is death, Officer Ettonou," General Ilowhe continued. "It is your duty to carry it out and prove your loyalty to your superiors, your government, and your people." His eyes cut into mine. "Are you loyal?"

I saluted. Steel scraped, echoing through the courtyard as I drew my blade. It shimmered in the light, glistening in its spotless glory. A weapon that had never yet seen battle or shed blood.

"Always, sir!" I vowed.

And I plunged my sword through the young man's chest.

At least his death wasn't one I had to feel.

I opened my eyes to find the Alrenians showing off fearsome new abilities that made chills run down my spine. A trusting soul stepped straight into one of the still-burning campfires, everyone marveling as the flames crept around his body and enveloped his leathers, yet never burned him. He emerged from the fire with flames still licking at him like a raging mantle, deadly and beautiful and mesmerizing.

After that, the others were quick to show off their abilities with fire, finding they could not only survive it without being burnt, but that they could also wield it as a weapon. They took flames from their bodies and tossed them like darts toward one another, laughing and rejoicing in their new power. But I could practically see the shadows twisting around them, curling like living snakes about their beings, as deadly and ominous as the flames they threw. They'd given their souls to Nesrelle for these abilities, and I could only imagine the terrifying results.

"What is this madness?" Vander said from the tree he was chained to, yards away. I could just make out his voice over the soldiers' raucous laughter and shouts.

"This is what happens when someone makes a deal with the Dark Immortal One," I responded.

Unable to tear his wide-eyed gaze from the Alrenian army, Vander pressed his lips together. I didn't think he could put his shock and horror into words.

I squeezed my eyes shut. *Elhani help us,* I thought.

When I looked again, Jalie and Nesrelle were walking side-by-side among the soldiers, encouraging them to square off and spar. To test other powers in ways I couldn't quite fathom. In the midst of a fight, the soldiers would often taunt one another, somehow sending their opponents into horrified shrieks or whimpers. I strained to catch snatches of their words, but there was too much noise from all the shouting and groaning of soldiers, the clanging of metal on metal as swords crossed, and the roar of flames as they licked harmlessly along the Alrenians' bodies.

Slowly, Jalie and Nesrelle drew closer to where Vander and I were chained. The empress lifted her eyes to meet mine, and an overwhelming ache shot through me. Her emotions were too strong for me to ignore, like a storm pounding against a windowpane, wild and relentless. *Fear. Uncertainty. Pride. Pain. Excitement.* And beneath it all, there was something else, an answering longing to mine, pierced through with a sense of betrayal.

Her feelings were so conflicting and powerful, that their sudden onslaught took my breath away. I tightened my jaw and stared back at her, studying the shadows that coursed from Nesrelle to Jalie. They pooled at her feet, writhed around her body, and swept over her arms, twisting among her fingers. Next to Nesrelle herself, Jalie's aura had the most shadows out of the Alrenians, and the sight filled me with sorrow and dread.

"Instead of practicing with their new powers on one another, which is all but futile, why not have your soldiers practice on your prisoners?" Nesrelle nodded toward me, her red lips stretching into a taunting smile. "It seems a shame to have perfectly good targets go to waste."

I sensed a jolt of fear and guilt shudder through Jalie like they were my own emotions. She tore her gaze away from me, unable to meet the condemnation in my eyes.

"But I need them," she said, glancing at Nesrelle.

I couldn't help but be impressed. She was either brave or foolish, to so openly and easily defy the Immortal One's wishes.

Nesrelle laughed lightly and waved her hand through the air, as if she were a noblewoman discussing something as mundane as guests at a party. "Only one of them." Her eyes sharpened, just a little, as she trained them on Jalie. "Don't tell me you're too attached to make use of the prisoners who tried to *assassinate* you."

Jalie swallowed and stiffened at her words. "No." She turned to me once more. Through my connection with her emotions, I could feel her uncertainty and fear harden into resolve and assurance. "Daedra!" she called, and one of the women sparring nearby stopped mid-swing, kicking her opponent to the ground carelessly before striding toward her empress.

"Yes, Your Majesty?" the soldier called Daedra asked, dipping her head reverently before her empress.

"Call off the sparring and unchain the prisoners. We have a new use for them."

Daedra bowed again. "With pleasure, my empress."

I met Jalie's eyes again, to find her staring directly at me, her mouth a firm line. Her emotions were so easy to read, it was almost as if I could discern her thoughts too. Overpowering the current of fear and guilt within her was a burning sense of confidence.

I knew exactly what she wanted me to do, what she expected I would do, and a cold knot formed in my stomach at the knowledge.

I stretched my neck and rolled my shoulders, trying to ease the ache in my muscles from the long hours bound to a tree. The weight of a sword hanging at my side was a welcome familiarity, even though I wasn't sure what good it would do against the unnatural powers the Alrenian standing across from me now possessed.

The soldier was a young man, perhaps a year or two older than me, with grey and gold eyes that shone with arrogance as he sneered at me. His dark hair was shorn in the typical style of a soldier, and his golden skin was paler than the tanner complexions of the Alrenians of Inalgoth, likely due to months living and training in the colder climate of the Aramith Mountains. He shifted fluidly on his feet, moving his weight from one side to the other as he lit a match. His leather armor dripped with oil that caught fire in an instant, dousing the man in a raging inferno that made him look…unearthly. Demonic.

My heart quickened as his eyes reflected red and orange flames. When he stepped forward, I could sense the heat radiating off him. A single touch and he could end me, stopping this fight before it had truly begun.

The soldier was swift and brutal in his movements, unsheathing his sword and launching himself at me almost before I had time to draw my weapon. But I had trained for this. I parried his flurry of attacks, the motions coming to me as easily as breathing. I knew the vicious, graceful way the Alrenians fought, as I and most of the other Forwyn soldiers had been trained in the same methods at Aerekni Academy. It was almost like dancing: graceful movements of ducking and weaving, leaping and dodging. And yet, it was brutal too, with feints to deceive one's enemy and brutal, deadly strikes.

Now it was even worse, the heat of the other soldier's flames making sweat slither down my back and trickle into my eyes. Soon my shirt was drenched, while the soldier in his thick leathers seemed untouched, laughing and taunting me. Stepping back, he lowered his sword and flung his free hand toward me, hurling a ball of fire straight toward my face. I dove and rolled, tossing my sword to the side in the process to avoid cutting myself on the blade. As I leapt to my feet, my opponent smirked at my empty hands and stepped forward, lifting his sword for the killing strike.

All around me, soldiers roared. "Kill him, kill him!" they chanted, clapping their hands and stomping their feet.

But I was ready.

Instead of retreating, I charged him, ducking low and slamming a kick at his groin. The onlookers booed, screaming obscenities and insults at me. As I reared back, flames licked at my boot, lashing at the leather. While the soldier groaned and stooped low, trying to recover from my blow, I stomped my foot to put out the fire. The flames winked out and I retrieved my sword just as the man let out an infernal roar, like an enraged animal. I'd humiliated him in front of an entire army, and now he was out for blood. Now, he didn't just want me to die. He wanted me to suffer.

He lifted his hand and more flames leapt from his fingers, blasting toward me with the speed and strength of dragon fire. I dodged, just barely, feeling the heat singe my shirtsleeve. Wisps of smoke curled in the air around me, leaving an overpowering stench that scorched my nose. My throat ached and my eyes watered. I coughed and tried to suck in a breath of fresh air, but the clouds of smoke were thickening, encircling my body.

Opposite me, my enemy seemed unaffected, his breathing normal. His eyes gleamed wickedly in the flickering light as he lifted his arms. The flames danced down his shoulders to his hands, rippling fluidly. Beautiful. Deadly.

I blinked furiously to clear my blurring vision, and my eyes landed on Vander, where he stood, unchained but surrounded by guards in the crowd. He stared at me intently before lifting his hand, just barely. I knew what he was doing before I felt the fresh air rush across our makeshift arena, making the long strands of grass swell and undulate around me. The smoke rushed away on the wind, leaving behind blessedly sweet air that my lungs drank greedily.

When I flung my gaze back to my opponent, his flames were dancing wildly, caught in the growing breeze.

Jalie snapped her eyes toward Vander and the soldiers surrounding him. "Stop him!" she demanded.

One of the soldiers understood immediately, clamping a hand on Vander's wrist and forcing his arm down to his side. I wondered if any of them knew about the Teramese pendant hanging from his neck, hidden beneath his jacket. None made a move for it, so I assumed not.

I spun back to my opponent as he went again on the offensive, gathering another ball of flames in his hand. He smirked as he tossed it at me. Then another. Another. They came in a flurry: high and low, to the right and left, whirling around and landing in the grass just behind me, until I was hemmed in by a wall of fire.

Doubt coiled in my stomach. I wasn't afraid of death, of exploring the Golden After. But I was afraid of failure. I couldn't bear the thought of dying here, leaving my people to face the Teramese and this new, nightmarish Alrenian army without a chance to warn them or fight beside them. I squeezed my eyes shut and thought of my friend Rhi'il, still residing with the army at Aerekni Academy and with no idea what he was about to face.

"Not so confident now, are you?" the Alrenian jeered, throwing another cluster of flames at the grass nearby.

It was clear his plan was to completely envelop me, until I was either cornered and left at the mercy of his blade, or simply burned alive by his fire. .

You have no choice, I thought. *Focus your magic. Control him. Stop him.* My mind rebelled as memories flickered through my head. I'd done this to enemies before, right before my fellow soldiers had slain them. I'd experienced their rage and fear; I'd tasted death as they'd drawn their last.

No, I wasn't afraid to die myself. I was terrified of experiencing my enemies' deaths in an endless, horrifying loop. First as I felt their emotions. Then forever after as the memories haunted me.

What kind of soldier can't use his greatest weapon to kill his enemy and help his people? I berated myself.

I drew a deep breath through my nose despite the gathering smoke, and lost myself in a coughing fit. Fire leapt and crackled at my back, the heat merciless. My uniform clung to me as sweat snaked along my spine. The flames were closing in, and so was the Alrenian soldier, who was still laughing, still taunting as he stalked nearer, raising his blade. Apparently he was determined to give the killing blow himself, before the growing blaze could consume me.

Though the roar of flames was loud in my ears, the notes of Elhani's song were stronger, weaving through the air, through my brain, and through my very bones. I clung to them and focused all of the power burning through me, hotter and greater than the unnatural fire threatening to devour.

"Stop!" I cried, my voice raspy as I raised my sword. It flashed in the firelight, glowing the color of blood. "Don't move. Drop your weapon."

The soldier froze, his eyes widening as his body worked against him, obeying my every command. All around us, shocked and angry shouts arose. The crowd was disappearing in the haze of smoke permeating the air. I met my opponent's eyes, refusing to flinch even as I felt his fury and a hint of fear trickling through me. Swallowing back guilt, an emotion wholly my own, I stepped forward.

"Dishonorable murderer," the soldier spat, his hands hanging limply at his sides, his blade lying at his feet.

I ignored him and the bile burning the back of my throat.

He would kill you without hesitation.

I raised my blade.

He would kill your people without hesitation.

I tensed my muscles, gathering my strength for the strike. Shoving aside all emotions, both his and mine. Still, some of the tears blurring my vision weren't merely from the smoke.

It was easier to slay an enemy when you could remind yourself they weren't human. When you couldn't experience their very human feelings. When they were brutal monsters trying to murder you, and not helpless victims staring back as you went in for the kill.

I plunged my blade through his chest.

His pain and terror and rage burst through me like an explosion, nearly knocking me off my feet. He screamed, and I lost my hold on my magic. Loosened from my power, he lifted his arms and slammed his palms against my chest, setting my shirt ablaze.

With a grunt I yanked my sword from the man and leapt back, dropping to the grass and rolling until I'd put out the flames. Pain seared at my skin as I stood, staring at the holes in my uniform and the red, raw skin revealed beneath them. My head pounded and my entire body ached.

All around me, the unnatural fire had vanished, leaving behind a semicircle of scorched grass. The smoke was already clearing on a stiff breeze, giving my burning lungs relief. I blinked away fresh tears from my stinging eyes to find the entire army staring at me, their eyes wide with horror and fear and rage.

I glanced over at my enemy, who'd collapsed in his own blood, motionless. Dead. His emotions winked out, but my guilt did not.

I could still feel the way death had closed in on him, the way he'd fought, refusing to believe it was the end. His blood coated my hands and dripped from the Alrenian blade Jalie herself had brought to me.

When I lifted my eyes again, I found Jalie in the crowd. At some point in the fight, Nesrelle had disappeared from her side, but the shadows clustering around the young empress and her army hadn't dispersed.

Jalie's face was unnervingly blank.

As the shock wore off, the pain in my chest shuddered through me, intense and consuming. Darkness crept in at the edges of my vision and my legs went unsteady. I felt myself collapsing, and then— nothing.

I opened my eyes to the peaked, canvas ceiling of a huge tent. Flickering lantern light danced across its surface, painting it a buttery shade of yellow and casting strange shadows.

My whole body ached, muscles weary from the fight, wrists raw and cut from the shackles, and chest throbbing from the searing pain of my burns. In fact, it felt like I was on fire, burning from the inside out, my throat tender and dry and a sheen of sweat coating my face. Nausea roiled through me as I tried to sit up, fighting against the pain.

I was reclining on a cot, my chest bare without my ruined uniform in sight. My burns looked ugly and untreated. When I glanced at the angry red skin, I bit back a groan and flicked my eyes away.

"Don't move," came a firm yet gentle voice. Jalie.

I glanced toward the center of the tent, where the empress stood, backlit by several lanterns set on the table she was bent over. She hadn't bothered to turn around, leaving her back to me as she pored over papers scattered across the table. No longer clothed in her sparkling dragon scale armor, she wore a loose white tunic and brown leggings, likely the plainest outfit I'd ever seen her in. Her golden hair hung in a curtain down her back.

My brain was hazy from pain as I studied her, waiting for her to spin around and shove a dagger to my throat. I wasn't sure why else I'd be here, inside her tent, after I'd slain one of her soldiers so dishonorably.

He wouldn't have hesitated to use his advantage to kill you, a voice inside me argued.

"Why am I here?" I asked, my words coming out gravelly.

At last, Jalie turned to face me, her eyes widening for a moment as if it were the first time she'd seen me since she'd had me brought to her tent. Her gaze lingered on the muscles in my stomach before snagging on the burn wounds across my chest. A jolt of guilt coursed through her, so strong and clear I could feel it as easily as if it had been my own emotion.

"To have your wounds treated," she said coolly, jerking her gaze away and striding toward the tent opening.

I could see now that a low table rested there, with a tray covered in medical supplies: rolls of gauze and jars I assumed were full of ointments and perhaps, if I were fortunate, medicine for the pain.

As she lifted the tray and approached the cot I occupied—*her* cot, I realized, surprised she'd given it up to me—she offered me a tight-lipped smile. "I can't have my valuable prisoner dying on me."

I quirked an eyebrow at her. "Valuable?" The word came out strained, ending in a cough. When I'd caught my breath, I continued, "The Teramese don't care one way or another what happens to me. They only wanted to use me to get to you."

It was her turn to look skeptical. "Your magic makes you valuable, and you know it. And the Teramese didn't want to use you to *get* to me, they sent you to *kill* me." Though her face revealed nothing as she studied me with an air of haughty indifference, I felt the ache of betrayal shudder through her.

"I wouldn't have killed you," I said gruffly. "But I don't know why you're worrying about me dying *now*. You didn't hesitate to pair me against a soldier who wanted to murder me earlier."

Jalie set her tray on the cot's edge, her fingers halting mid-reach for one of the jars. "Because I knew you would win," she said, a furrow between her brows. I could sense the truth of her words based on the conviction she felt. "Even with our new powers, how could we be a match against someone who has the magic to control others' actions? You could have commanded him to cut open his own throat, and he would have obeyed." There was fear and bitterness there, mixed with something darker. Anger. Perhaps hatred. She despised what I could do, and I couldn't blame her. What I'd done seemed like a blasphemous use of Elhani's power.

But I'm a soldier, I reminded myself stubbornly. *My survival helps ensure my people's survival.* At least, that was the motto that had been drilled into me at Aerekni Academy, as I'd been trained to slay Alrenians without mercy.

"I didn't want to use my magic," I muttered.

"I know," Jalie said, opening the jar and dipping her fingers into the ointment within. It smelled strong, fresh and crisp. "It's the thing you fear the most, next to failure."

Her eyes met mine, and some of the hardness in her expression relented. She looked more like the woman who ached to save her people, who feared death and hid her loneliness. She seemed vulnerable. Gentler.

Reaching out, she ran her fingers along the burns marring my chest, applying a generous coating of the ointment. I repressed a grunt of pain, but that sensation quickly disappeared as the ointment went to work, cooling the fire in my skin and easing the throbbing ache. Her touch was tender, her eyes deliberately avoiding mine as she worked. Beneath the golden sheen of her complexion, a hint of a blush crept across her freckled cheeks.

As the pain receded, every muscle in my body tensed for a new reason, finding myself hoping for this moment to last forever. Wishing futilely that this version of Jalie could remain.

Here in the privacy of her tent, just like in the privacy of her palace chambers, we were reminded of all the things that connected us. We could pretend everything that divided us was a distant memory, part of the outside world that we'd shut out. We could pretend we could stay in this sanctuary forever, where we weren't on opposite sides of a coming war, each of us devoted to people who would eternally despise one another.

But I couldn't ignore the thick shadows that perpetually clustered about her form. A reminder of her pledge to the Dark Immortal. And I couldn't shove aside the question filling my mind, demanding an answer.

"How do you know I fear using my gift?" I asked, catching my breath.

Jalie pulled her hand away and reached for the gauze, unspooling it methodically, keeping her eyes trained carefully away from mine. "I can sense others' fears," she said. "It's part of the…new power."

I repressed a shudder at her words as I studied the shadows dancing over her skin.

"Jalie," I said, my voice low and gentle, but unable to hide my concern.

Her eyes narrowed at my tone. "No," she snapped. "You don't

have a right to judge my choices. You're a soldier who has killed for your people. Your father controlled and abused me."

I tensed, a retort forming on my lips. I didn't want her to think I condoned the cruelties my father had comitted—that I'd known about them before I'd seen him attack her in person.

But she ignored my expression, pressing on. "So you can't look at me and what I'm willing to do for my people and pretend you're above it all." She swallowed, tears glistening in her pale, gold-flecked eyes. "I told you. I'll be a monster like my mother, if that's what it takes to keep my people safe. I'll make this deal with the devil, if it means I never have to watch another Alrenian burn in dragon fire or bleed out on my rug." Her voice cracked at the end.

"I'm not judging you, not when I can see myself in you. You carry the same dedication to do whatever you must for your people. But the deal will cost you much—probably more than you know," I said, keeping my voice level and calm as I extended my hand. "I don't want…I don't want to see you hurt."

She didn't shudder away when I ran my fingers over the back of her hand, didn't pull away when I threaded them through hers. Instead, she stared at our joined hands, frowning, her tears catching in her eyelashes and threatening to fall. "I never came here to fight against you," I went on, my words picking up speed. "I didn't want them to send someone else to kill you. I came hoping to save you. We don't have to be enemies. I think you saw that too, back at the palace. And I can sense your emotions enough to know you no longer hate me."

I needed to say everything on my mind before she retreated into herself, before she yanked her hand from my touch and pushed me away.

You're a fool, a voice in my head warned, but I couldn't stop myself.

Heart pounding, I squeezed her hand and blurted out the words.

"Have you considered an alliance between…*us*? We have a common enemy now, and you can't pretend things haven't changed between you and me. We've found we aren't that different…and if we can cross the divide separating us, couldn't both our peoples? If they witness us working together to defeat the Teramese, protecting and defending one another in our fight against them, we could see the united empire the Elders used to talk about."

"You want to be my ally?" A sad, twisted sort of smile flitted across Jalie's mouth.

She didn't jerk away from me; instead, she drew her hand from mine so gently it was almost like a caress as her fingers swept across mine. My hand felt cold with the absence of hers.

She turned to her tray again, lifting a pair of scissors to cut strips of gauze, moving swiftly and gracefully. "That will never end well. It's nothing but a child's dream to imagine our people ever standing side-by-side, common enemy or not. If they saw us together, what would they say, truly? Likely that I'd seduced you into serving me, or that you were using me to regain the empire somehow. Even if they believed our alliance…it wouldn't last. My people would rise against yours, or yours against mine. And in the end, who do you serve? Who would you choose to defend?"

I averted my eyes, staring at my empty hands. I didn't need to speak the words; she already knew.

"And it's the same for me," she went on. "It always has been. We'll always put our people first. We have to. It's who we are."

She leaned in close—too close—to wind the first strip of gauze across my chest, wrapping it tightly and then binding it at my shoulder. Her breath was warm against my neck as she focused on her task, refusing to lift her head and meet my eyes. If she did, our faces would be too near, our lips only centimeters apart.

Despite the memory of how our first and only kiss had ended, I couldn't help but think of it again. I knew from the desire and fear beating through her—like a frantic, caged bird—that her thoughts were similar.

They were foolish thoughts, ones I hated myself for entertaining. *Your feelings for her can't get in the way. Not if it comes down to a choice between all of the Forwyn and her. You can't choose her over an entire race of people.*

"What if we didn't have to choose?" I insisted. "What if the Forwyn and Alrenians were on the same side? What if we *did* manage to make that happen?"

Jalie hesitated, her fingers splayed against my chest, where my heart beat erratically. "I don't think that's possible."

"So maybe it doesn't work permanently," I pressed on stubbornly as she reached for the next strip of gauze, once again leaning in close to tie it in place. I concentrated on keeping my breathing even, on making my voice sound natural. "At least we both know where our greatest loyalties lie. Any agreement between us is over the moment we need to defend our own people, or when we defeat the Teramese. Whichever comes first. But don't you think we could be stronger together?"

"You don't even want to use your magic," she cut in, but her protest sounded weaker this time. She'd finished tying the gauze, but her hand lingered on my arm, almost as if she'd forgotten she'd laid it there.

"I *will*," I vowed, my words a low rumble. And I meant them. "In the end, you saw that I will. Anything to protect my people. *And* you." With a wistful smile, I finished, "I'll fight for you, Jalie. As long as you let me."

Jalie sat back, laying her hand in her lap. Her smile was wry, and she still refused to look directly at me. "Fight for *me*? You would ally yourself with the woman who made a deal with the Queen of Death?"

I frowned, my muscles tight. "I won't pretend I like your agreement with her, and I won't follow her. I follow Elhani alone, and my alliance with you is apart from your deal with her. I won't follow her commands or partake in any power she offers." I paused, breaking into a grin. "But think of what we could do together."

An answering smile tugged on Jalie's lips. "You're only tempting me because you know I can't resist power. But alliance or not," she added solemnly, "you still have to play the role of my prisoner. I can't have you parading about among my soldiers or bedding in a tent next to them. They'd try to kill us both for that."

"Of course. I would want to keep up appearances around Vander, too. Even if…even if I'll probably have to kill him later." True regret swept through me at the thought. He didn't deserve death, even if I knew we would both be fighting on opposite sides someday.

She turned to meet my gaze again. "What do the Teramese hold over you?"

"The lives of every Forwyn remaining in the palace," I said, the weight of the words settling over me like a heavy blanket. I thought of my father, and despite the anger that seethed within me whenever I remembered the things he'd done, I also felt a stab of worry. I didn't want to watch him, the only family I had left, being harmed or killed.

Jalie didn't comment, even if I could detect her rising anger at the thought of my father and the ways in which he'd hurt her. Instead, she distracted herself by assessing her work on my injuries. Already my pain had eased, soothed by the cooling ointment she'd applied. As if realizing that she was staring at my bare chest, her cheeks reddened. "Put on a shirt," she added, pointing toward a fresh shirt folded at my feet.

I stifled a laugh. "Tempted to try kissing me again? Sounds like an agreeable way to seal our alliance."

Jalie rolled her eyes. "That didn't end well for you last time."

Despite our attempt at levity, the air grew heavy between us. She didn't pull back, her face temptingly close to mine. When I reached out to brush a strand of hair behind her ear, she inhaled sharply, but she didn't break my gaze. Didn't flinch away.

This will never end well, I thought, my mind echoing Jalie's warning, even as I leaned in closer.

If our first kiss had been full of passionate denial, this one gave away every word we didn't dare speak. We were hungry and a bit desperate, each brush of our lips familiar and yet foreign. This was a kiss in earnest, not a game.

I could sense every emotion roaring through Jalie as powerfully as my own. Every other complication fell away in the growing understanding of what was between us. What we felt.

Grasping her waist, I tugged her closer, and she responded by throwing her arms around my neck. I drew one hand up, running it through her hair, as I tried to memorize the way she tasted, the way she felt in my arms. Gently, I bit her bottom lip, and I felt her smile as she responded by deepening the kiss. She tugged one of her hands from my neck to run it along my chest, once again feeling my pounding heart.

We finally pulled apart, both breathless. When our eyes met, Jalie's mask was gone, her expression open. I leaned my forehead against hers, savoring her nearness, and whispered the only words I dared admit in that moment. "I *will* fight for you."

From the way hope shone brightest among her emotions, I was sure she understood what I really meant. It was a promise I prayed I wouldn't ever be forced to break. A vow to fight as hard for her as I fought for my own people, even if the Alrenians and Forwyn never battled side by side. And it was a confession of what both of us felt yet dared not name.

Jalie seemed at a loss for words, instead rising quickly, her cheeks still flushed. She tossed the extra shirt at me, and I couldn't help but grin again. As I pulled it over my head, thankful for the gauze that kept the material from rubbing at my wounds, she strode back toward her table. Her eyes once again scanned over the documents laid across its surface.

Clearing her throat, she asked, "If you're to be my ally, you'll answer my every question about the palace and the Teramese occupying it. And explain more about Vander's magic." She smirked. "I did tell my soldiers that this was an interrogation, after all."

I smiled in return, spreading my arms wide. "Of course, an *intense* interrogation." Jalie's blush deepened at my words. "Go ahead, ask me anything, if you're agreeing to my proposal."

She nodded thoughtfully. "All right. We can be allies."

"Allies."

CHAPTER TWENTY

"YOU'RE A SOFT-HEARTED SOUL, TOO good for this world," Revaed said, his brow crinkled in sadness.

I sat numbly in his presence, surrounded by shadows that were just now gradually giving way to the grey light that announced the approaching sunrise. After fleeing the dungeons and cleaning up in my chambers yesterday, I'd wandered outside for too long, lost in my own thoughts, shirking my duty.

I hadn't had the heart to face Revaed, not until I'd awoken in the darkness this morning to find Lo once again absent. Being alone with my thoughts was worse than facing my guardian's possible disappointment.

I was consumed with guilt and shame.

Instead of the turmoil inside me, I tried to focus on my surroundings, drinking in their beauty. The air was cool, a tangy sea breeze rustling through the palm fronds and making the flowers bow like loyal servants before Revaed.

In the palace gardens, lush with vibrant plant life and colorful flowers foreign to my Teramese eyes, I could find a measure of peace. When the wind swept through my hair, it brought notes of a song to my ears: cicadas and other insects buzzing, a few early birds beginning to greet the day, and the whisper of leaves. When I drew in a fortifying breath, fragrances of floral and brine, citrus and earth all mingled together into something soothing. A hint of the familiar and the foreign, all tangled together into something enticing. Distracting.

Do not think about it, I told myself for the thousandth time, squeezing out memories of the way I'd drawn the life from those Alrenian prisoners. Instead I made myself concentrate once again on the sounds and scents and sights around me. Golden flowers bouncing in the breeze. Oranges hanging from a nearby tree, filling the air with their intoxicating smell. Palm fronds rustling. Revaed's footsteps thudding along the cobbled path before me as he paced.

"But you know," Revaed went on softly, wistfully, "we don't have a choice. Weak rulers never survive. And to hesitate is to be weak. I'm glad that you chose to be strong."

The man's screams. Blood splattering against my face.

I swallowed the lump in my throat and watched a lizard scurry up an orange tree.

"If you hadn't killed those men, they wouldn't have hesitated to kill you and any other Teramese man or woman as soon as they had the chance. We can't let dangerous men like them live."

Lo's wide eyes. Scrubbing the blood off my skin until it was red and raw…

I forced myself to study the way the sunlight danced, warm and golden, on the white flowers across the path.

Revaed paused in front of me, his hands folded behind his back. "We have to ensure our people survive, Caesiem," he said solemnly, his violet eyes piercing. There was regret and pain and darkness in their depths, cutting me to the core.

The memories of the devastation we'd left behind—the charred remains the wild dragons had turned so many Teramese cities into— were seared vividly into my mind. I could never forget the ash-covered people, sifting through the wreckage of their homes and businesses, cradling limp and broken bodies, sobbing as the flames turned to embers, as their cities turned to ruins. The acres of destroyed crops, burnt to a crisp in the relentless sun. Even whole sections of thick jungle vegetation had been blackened, wasted.

When I looked into Revaed's eyes, I could see the way he was haunted by these memories, by the burden of saving his people, just as I was.

He laid a calloused hand on my shoulder, warm and reassuring. Though he was my official guardian, and I his heir; though he had raised me since the day he'd taken me in from the streets, after I'd been nothing but a thieving orphan, he never called me son. He was my father, in every sense of the word, but the small gap in our ages made it seem strange for us to call each other by those titles. We were like father and son, and yet closer, friends who could relate to and understand one another. Friends who could rely on each other, supporting and encouraging each other. Revaed wasn't one to coddle me, and with my background, I wasn't one to depend on anyone.

But now, I had an overwhelming urge to stand and fall into Revaed's embrace. To weep and let him pat me tenderly on the back like a father would. To find refuge from the nightmares and guilt plaguing my mind, from the burden I carried.

Lord Xalenos shoulders his burden alone, I thought gruffly, *as all Xalenos men do. I must be strong and prove I'm capable to someday lead the new Teramese empire. I'm a man, not a child.*

And with those thoughts, I swept away my regret and horror. What was a bit of Alrenian bloodshed if it could relieve my people's suffering? If it could finally stopper the sound of their cries, their pleas for help from the throne, that forever echoed in my ears at night?

"You're right," I said, my voice low and raspy. I smiled at Revaed, and he smiled back, clearly relieved to see me come to. "I take no pleasure in violence, but I don't regret doing what I must to save my people."

Revaed dipped his head, pride glinting in his eyes as he retracted his hand and stepped back to assess me. "You will make a fine leader, Caes."

I stood, brushing invisible dirt off the front of my jacket. "You said there was much to do yesterday, before I fled like…" Averting my gaze, I cleared my throat in growing embarrassment. "Well, like a frightened child." I flicked my eyes back to his, but there was no judgement in his expression. "What do we need to accomplish next?"

Revaed's grin broadened. "I'm glad you're ready to help." He swept his arm, gesturing toward the path before him. "Come, let's walk and discuss some matters."

Falling into step beside Revaed, I drew in another breath, my body already feeling lighter. *Thank you for reminding me of my purpose,* I thought, though I didn't speak the words aloud, not wanting to interrupt my guardian. Ahead, one of the guards patrolling the grounds crossed our path, saluting as he passed.

"While you were away, I had some good news," Revaed announced.

"Vander and Kovi Ettonou have captured the empress?" I asked, hope buoying my spirit.

Revaed sighed. "No, still no word from them." He frowned, pausing as if mulling the matter over, before recollecting himself. "But I received word from General Xelia. Her forces have taken Aramith, and she has enough to press westward and join those marching toward

Hemlaen. I've also heard that General Thelos' men took Brema and some of the smaller villages to the north." He glanced side-long at me, grinning and hopeful. "Once we have the entire empire securely under our control, it will be easy to gather and ship resources to Teramyl."

"That *is* good news." I hesitated a beat. "And…are the citizens…resisting?"

Revaed clasped his hands behind his back once more, his brow furrowed in concentration as he walked. "Yes," he admitted, slowly, "all reports indicate that our forces have been met with hostility. There have been casualties on all sides, ours, Alrenian, and Forwyn." He glanced toward me, violet eyes alight with curiosity. "Do you think your girl will truly work to convince her people that an alliance is in everyone's best interest?"

Fidgeting with my jacket sleeves, I drew a deep breath, trying to dispel the memory of Lo's eyes on me earlier, all at once cutting yet gentle. Concerned about me, but clearly loath to be. "She said she wants to speak with the general at Aerekni Academy," I announced hopefully. "I know our efforts there have been…slow."

Revaed scratched his chin. "That's encouraging, at least on the surface. I'd want you to go with her, of course. Listen to any discussions she has with the Aerekni general. But maybe she can make more headway with him than we have. We need to ensure the academy won't decide to move against us. That's too many Forwyn soldiers too close to the capital for me to feel comfortable until we can trust they aren't a threat."

I nodded. "Of course."

Revaed brightened, loosening his stance and picking up his pace. "You're a good man, Caes. I knew with you at my side we could save our people."

I tried not to let my lingering doubts take hold and drag down my hopes. Imagining a world in which the Forwyn and Teramese worked side-by-side, in which neither my people nor Lo's need ever suffer again, seemed like too much to dare, nothing but a distant dream.

"What else is on the agenda today?" I asked instead.

"Well," Revaed said slowly, "if we don't hear word from Vander soon, I'll send more scouts to the Aramith Mountains to see if our suspicions about an Alrenian army are true. Even if they're not, it seems only a matter of time before the natives' resistances become more organized." He sighed before a mischievous glint returned to his eyes, and he nudged me playfully. "We'll need the dragons. If your girl is recovering from an injury, I'd hate to delay your work with the beasts any longer. After we train with the soldiers, what do you say to you and I trying our hands at some dragon taming?"

Earlier, Darix had relentlessly teased me, making nasty remarks about Lo. But now, he'd stopped, whether because he'd grown jealous, or because I'd defeated him in four rounds of hand-to-hand combat already, I wasn't sure. All I knew was that it was clear from the lethal glint in his eyes and his reddened cheeks that he wasn't in the mood to hide his outright hatred of me any longer. Smearing the trickle of blood from his nose with one meaty fist, he assessed me from across the training room like he was planning how to murder me in plain sight of my guardian.

Pretending I hadn't observed the way he was staring, I rolled my shoulders casually, stretching my neck until it popped. I held out my hand, acting as if I didn't even notice as water rose up from the jug on a side table, rising in a glistening stream and flowing across the room to hover over my palm. It danced from finger to finger, leaving a few shimmering droplets behind before I sent it back across the room, splashing into several of the cups laid out for the men.

Pados, who'd just won a round against Valentra, grinned and clapped appreciatively. Most of the others froze, round eyes studying me cautiously.

Darix grunted. "I thought we'd agreed not to use magic when we're practicing hand-to-hand combat, my lord," he said, the derision clear in the way he spat my title.

I tapped the chords to a jaunty Alrenian tune I'd learned across my palm, pausing suddenly, as if I'd just realized Darix had spoken. "But I'd already won," I said, tossing him a careless smile. I flicked my eyes toward Revaed, who had taken a break from sparring with this group, some of our prime officers, to stalk back and forth across the lines and assess our efforts.

As he approached where Darix and I stood, Revaed offered me an indulgent smile, perhaps to dispel the clear hostility rising off my opponent. "Well done, Caes," he said. "It's always good to ensure all of your skills are sharp for battle. I appreciate that even your breaks between fights are filled with practicing." He winked at me and spun on his heel to stroll back down the line again.

I turned to Darix and shrugged. "What can I say? We Xalenoses enjoy our power." As I met his gaze head-on, I let my unspoken threat burn through my words, adding weight to my lighthearted tone. *We hold the power here. Cross the line and you'll pay the price.*

Darix scowled as he stepped forward to square off against me for the fifth time. "You also enjoy your women," he sneered, angry enough to return to his taunts. "Is it right, when all of us fought and bled for Teramyl, that the emperor shows such obvious favoritism toward his heir and his heir alone, by granting him a Forwyn whore?"

Heat seared through me, making me bunch my hands into fists prematurely. Normally, the traditional Teramese fighting stance dictated that we held our hands loosely in front of us, ready to block, grab, or punch at a moment's notice. Tightening the muscles made for jerky movements and sloppy mistakes.

"*What?*" I snapped, breathing as much malice as I could into a single word.

Darix took a step closer, using his excessive height to glower down his nose at me. "You heard what I said. There are plenty of Forwyn women in the palace. When do we get our pick?"

"You pig!" I launched myself at him, throwing a wild punch that he blocked easily. "You heard Revaed at dinner—she's my betrothed. It's a political arrangement. The Fowyn women are not our whores or slaves." I aimed a kick low, toward his groin, but he sidestepped me.

Darix chuckled darkly. "Really?" he drawled. "How naïve could you be? Did you think the Xalenos family would conquer the great Alrenian Empire and then make friends with its people? Did you think the Forwyn who surrendered to us are serving us willingly…or out of self-preservation?"

I gritted my teeth, equal measures of shame and rage coursing through me, making it hard to think clearly. Was Darix trying to imply Revaed had lied to me? Or was Darix simply the nasty man I'd always judged him to be, eager to use his power to abuse those around him?

A hundred retorts fluttered through my mind, but they all seemed foolish. Darix would either dismiss them or try to use them against me. I didn't need to further fuel his belief that I was unworthy of my title, of the leadership that would one day be bequeathed to me. I didn't want him to assume he'd found some weakness and attempt to use it.

He doesn't know Revaed as I do, I reminded myself, taking several calming breaths through my nose. *He wasn't present for our talks of peace with Lo. He doesn't know our plans. He's an ignorant, bull-headed pig of a man who thinks only with his fists and his genitals.*

But I couldn't fully dismiss the unease rushing over me, the growing fear that perhaps Revaed didn't *always* tell me everything.

After Revaed and I cleaned up, I insisted on making rounds through the palace to see where the Forwyn were being moved. Despite my guardian's complaints of hunger, he'd humored me, escorting me to the southern wing where rows of unoccupied servants' quarters were already full of Forwyn.

With my discomfort abated slightly, Revaed and I returned to his luxurious rooms, where we could discuss everything we'd observed about our officers over breakfast.

"Some have grown lazy," he observed wryly. "They fought with their soldiers when we took over the palace, yes, but mostly they direct others and sit about discussing war strategy."

I prodded at a piece of fish on my plate, finding the day's events had killed my appetite. Though I'd combated the ridiculous doubts Darix's ugly words had inspired, they wouldn't stop occasionally dancing through my head. The idea that he considered Lo to be little more than my property, a finely dressed slave I used for my pleasure, made my stomach sour. Even worse was his expectation that he could claim a Forwyn woman like that, that he and all the Teramese soldiers were entitled to taking their defeated enemies as slaves.

Do other soldiers think that way? Do their commanding officers encourage those sorts of ideas? Even now that the Forwyn have been moved into palace quarters?

It took me a moment to realize Revaed had continued to speak while I'd been occupied, going on about possible strategies to keep the officers in top shape. Now, as he changed the subject, my mind jolted back to the moment.

"Darix seems to be holding quite a grudge against you," Revaed was musing aloud, studying me thoughtfully. "Another petty man who thinks he's better than you, more deserving of my crown when I pass on?" Though his words were light, his smile carefree, I could hear the undertone in them, the angry, protective edge to his voice that reminded me he would never hesitate to defend me. His punishment upon anyone who dared defy or harm me would be swift. Brutal.

"Maybe," I said slowly, still staring at my plate. My thoughts were so heavy that even considering the words weighed down my tongue, but I couldn't hold them to myself forever. I shifted in my seat, tapping my foot on the floor in a steady beat—to Revaed's clear annoyance.

"It seems," I added at last, clearing my throat, "that he thinks Lo is just a…reward to me. Little more than a slave, just there to serve me however I wish. A sign of your favoritism despite others' loyal service to you in our operations to overtake Alrenor." I squeezed my fork a little tighter, lifting my eyes to meet Revaed's steady gaze. "His claim was that all soldiers should have their pick of Forwyn women to use, and that we should have all the Forwyn enslaved and serving us. Letting us live in luxury, I suppose."

Revaed burst out laughing. "A petty man who also longs for an easy life, then," he said, lifting his mug and taking a deep gulp of his coffee. "It seems our good Captain Darix grows weary of the hard work of a soldier." He smirked, setting his mug down and clapping his hands together. "So how will we torment him? Extra running in the mornings? The lure of a promotion if he actually sweats and bleeds for his new empire?"

I bit back my own growing smile. "It would be fun to see that large oaf try to run more laps. I think you're right. He's gotten lazy."

"Lazy and entitled," Revaed drawled, setting down his fork and throwing his napkin across his empty plate. He eyed my own untouched meal. "It's not like you not to eat, Caes. Are you sure you're all right?"

I shrugged. "Nothing about this has been easy."

Regret dimmed Revaed's eyes. "I know," he muttered. "I think you've had the hardest job of us all, and I'm sorry."

Forcing a smile, I shook my head. "Don't be. I wanted to help. This was my choice."

Revaed nodded slowly. "Maybe the dragons will cheer you up?" he suggested.

Abandoning my plate, I stood and nodded. "How could they not cheer me up?" I said lightly.

Revaed waved aside his bodyguards when they tried to fall in line behind us. Instead, we walked, leaving the late morning light gilding the gardens to delve deep into the heart of the cavernous Keep.

The Dragon Keep was all but empty, its occupants having already been fed for the morning by the Forwyn. After Lo had so easily entered the Keep, Teramese soldiers now closely monitored it around the clock, as the dragons were our most powerful weapons. But, from the peaceful stillness reigning throughout the tunnels, it was clear no trouble had occurred since Lo's failed infiltration.

Our boots echoed dully against the tunnel floors, bouncing off the cavern walls. Torchlight left behind from the earlier feedings danced across the space, elongating our shadows to ridiculous proportions.

As we passed rows of den entrances with dragon names carved above them, I noted the muffled shuffles of their occupants. The creatures seemed restless, and I couldn't blame them. They lived in spaces too small to fly within, and they were forever tempted by the small glimpses of sky afforded them by the holes in their ceilings. Holes that were too small for them to escape through.

Without discussing it beforehand, Revaed and I both halted outside of Karos's den. We would start with the most challenging and intimidating dragon. If I could tame a powerful, unpredictable beast like him and survive to tell the tale, then none of the dragons would be too difficult to handle. And that meant that the strength of Teramyl's army would be limitless.

I didn't need any buckets of water this time—not with so many holes in the Keep's ceiling to act as vents for dragon smoke. It would be easy to draw on the sea's contents, even from this distance, when it could literally rain through the ceiling.

Revaed stepped forward to work the pulley system, lifting the heavy metal door from the ground. It creaked and groaned, inch by inch. I hovered before it, studying the details of the dragon waiting within as the door rose, leaving me standing, empty-handed and vulnerable, directly before the fire-breathing creature.

Karos was one of the most intimidating dragons of the bunch, with scales in shades of black, red, and umber that shifted and undulated in the moonlight, as if he were darkness and flame, comingling in a beautiful contrast. Massive spikes lined the back of his neck and trailed down his tail, each as sharp as a knife's point.

When the door lifted, Karos shifted his huge head, tilting it so that his ear hole could take in every sound. His great eye fell directly on me, piercing me with a fiery gold stare. A forked tongue flicked from his mouth for an instant, like he was tasting the air, testing my very scent to determine if I was edible. Then his pupil dilated, and his muscles rippled beneath his scales.

My heart froze and my body tensed, mind flying into action. Before Karos could shift to face me and attack, I was focusing all my thoughts on the sea outside. In my mind's eye, I could imagine the waves rushing toward shore. I could taste the salty water, could smell its tang on the wind. Its coolness embraced me, and its currents drew me in, pulled me under.

Karos opened his maw, revealing rows of dagger-sharp fangs glistening with saliva. A blast of fire hurled into the air, great fingers of flames extending forward to consume me in their deadly grasp. I lifted my hands and a flood of water fell through the ceiling in Karos's den, sweeping through the air and descending like a rushing wall between the flames and me.

The roar of fire and water was nearly deafening. My ears popped as the two elements met, sending a cloud of thick smoke billowing through the tunnel. For several long moments, I could do nothing but cough and blink, trying to clear the water from my burning eyes. Somewhere beyond the smoke, Revaed was coughing too.

Slowly, the smoke cleared through the vent in the ceiling, leaving nothing but Revaed, Karos, and me facing one another in the tunnel. Revaed gaped at me, wiping at his watering eyes. If dragons could look taken aback, Karos might have been gaping too. I continued to hold my hands aloft, letting the water I'd called upon ripple and dance in swirling circles around me, glowing like a silver thread in the sunlight.

I lifted my stinging eyes and stared directly at Karos. The dragon grunted and turned away, retreating further into his den.

Revaed's voice was raspy as he spoke. "Reminds me of when you saved my life from that dragon." He swallowed. "This is progress, right? When a dragon walks away rather than tries to kill you?"

I grinned wryly, sending the water back up through the ceiling, back toward the restless sea. "He didn't bow to me as befitting the prince I'll soon be," I quipped. "But yes, I think that could be called progress."

CHAPTER TWENTY-ONE

Jalie

AFTER I'D FINISHED QUESTIONING KOVI, I'd ordered some of my soldiers to bind him and his Teramese companion in our supply tent and guard it vigilantly. Despite their newfound fear of Kovi and his unnatural abilities, their own powers gave them confidence, and they obeyed me without question.

Now I lay on my cot, which unfortunately still smelled like him, and tried and failed to sleep. The wind whispered through my tent like the pleas of lost souls, making the canvas tremble. In each corner that my flickering lamplight did not touch, shadows clung so thickly that I was convinced there were eyes peering back at me. Wraiths? The ghosts of those I'd killed? Nesrelle, waiting to see if I'd turn my back on my deal with her because of my tenuous alliance with Kovi?

An alliance that will most likely end with at least one of us dead, I thought darkly, an ache settling in my chest at the thought. Still, despite the confusing feelings I had about the Forwyn soldier, it was somewhat comforting to be speaking more plainly with one another. At least now we weren't hiding behind games or pretending our mutual connection didn't exist. We could openly admit to using one another. Because that was all this was.

Or that was what I told myself as I tossed and turned on my cot, the murmuring wind and my own restless thoughts making it impossible for me to sleep.

But I couldn't stop hearing Kovi's laughter, filling my tent with its music when he'd teased me. I couldn't stop feeling his warm mouth on mine.

You're just lonely, I reasoned. Never mind that there were endless young, handsome Alrenian soldiers here in camp that would gladly receive my attention, and none had so much as captured a second of my interest.

I rolled over, trying to concentrate on something—anything—else.

The whispering wind seemed to rush a little louder through my tent, until I was certain I heard my name on the breeze. *Jalie. Jalie.*

Heart pounding in my throat, I sat up and searched the shadows, my eyes landing on movement on the opposite side of my tent. The clank of dragon scales and chains struck my ears as a figure stepped forward, tall and lithe. Long golden hair swept down her back and fierce blue and gold eyes met mine.

A mixture of longing and fear tore through my heart, threatening to shred the last ounces of my strength. Unshed tears burned my eyes as I stumbled from my cot, knees weak.

"Mother?" I whispered.

She frowned, as if confused. "I…was that once, wasn't I?" she murmured.

Her appearance and voice were that of Empress Karye, but everything else was off, enough to prevent me from rushing forward and throwing my arms around her neck. The far-away look in her eyes seemed to stare straight through me. Her posture was uncertain, at odds with her familiar confident stance. Everything about her seemed diminished, rather than the force of nature I remembered her being. The way she'd always managed to command the attention of an entire room, her very aura demanding respect and fear.

Worst of all was the jagged, still-bloody slit in her throat, a morbid echo of her blood-red lips. My breath caught in my lungs at the sight and tears threatened again, but I swallowed them back. Fury consumed me, filling me with a wild and irrational desire to draw my sword and slash the tent surrounding me to shreds. To scream until my throat bled. To light a fire that burned down the whole world.

I ground out the words. *"Who did this to you?"* I hesitated before forcing myself to speak the words. *"Who* killed you?"

Mother tilted her head slightly, blinking to focus her eyes on me. Her gaze swept from my head to my toes, taking in the simple tunic and leggings I wore, so unlike the gorgeous gowns or regal dragon scale armor I was used to. A shrinking feeling weakened my anger, just a little, as a new fear struck me. What if Mother was ashamed of me? What if she looked at me and saw a pathetic little girl, lost in fear and confusion and doubt, a mere shadow of the great leader she had been?

"I…" She blinked once. Again. Recognition lit her eyes and a tremble crossed her firm mouth, loosening that lost look into something equally unrecognizable.

She looks broken. The thought took me off guard, shaking me to my core.

"Jalie?" she whispered, the sound both tremulous and gentle. Then she blinked again, and the softness vanished. Her eyes darkened into pools of blackness, her stare becoming chilling and empty.

Desperate, I took a step forward, not caring that my mother didn't exactly look like my mother anymore, but a pallid corpse overtaken by those unnatural, ink-black eyes. "Mother. Talk to me," I demanded. "Tell me what to do. Tell me how to save our people and stop our enemies." My brow furrowed. "Tell me how to avenge your death."

Mother stepped forward, gripping me with vise-like fingers as cold as ice. At this proximity, it was easy to smell the sickly-sweet stench of decay lingering about her, to see the congealed blood clinging to her wounded throat. Nausea swept through me, but I didn't try to back away.

"Stop being afraid," she hissed. "Stop shaming me. Destroy them."

And then she was gone. Wind whispered through my tent, fluttering the canvas and murmuring. *Jalie,* it taunted. Shadows swirled near, clinging close to my skin. I shuddered at the memory of my mother's touch.

Not my mother anymore. A monster.

And yet, wasn't that exactly what I was now too—a monster? Wasn't that the price I'd said I was willing to pay to help my people and make my mother proud?

Destroy them.

A strange sensation chilled the skin by my right shoulder, and I frowned, drawing back the collar of my tunic. There was something odd marring the skin near my collarbone, appearing like a dark blotch where once there had been only gold. I ran my fingertips along the patch, which was no larger than a coin. It felt smooth and hard, cool at first but swiftly warming with my body heat. Like armor, but different, like a shell or…a *scale.*

I squeezed my eyes shut and tugged my collar back into place, trying to ignore the new fears darting through my mind. The concerns Kovi had voiced.

Now my body itself was changing and I was seeing ghosts in the night. I repressed another shudder. What was happening to me?

Yes, I wanted to destroy my enemies, but would I destroy myself in the process?

Wind tugged at my braided hair as Ryke soared over the Aramith Mountains, rising until all but the uppermost snowy peaks were swallowed by thick clouds. These gleamed in the rising sunlight, glistening shades of red and orange and gold, almost blinding in their rugged beauty.

The air at this altitude was thin and bitterly cold, and would have bitten at my skin until it was frozen if not for the comforting heat Ryke gave off and the shielding effect my dragon scale armor and helmet gave me. The scales not only protected one from being scorched by heat as strong as dragon fire, but also insulated one from the frigid temperatures riders often faced on dragonback.

Under my helmet, only a portion of my face was exposed to the elements, and I'd covered it with a wrap, leaving only my eyes free to take in the sights around me. They watered in the wind, making teardrops freeze on my lashes, but the warmth enveloping me prevented the temperature from doing anything worse than that.

I'd been out since before sunrise, first soaring near enough to Wynlaen to scout out the town, and then practicing aerial maneuvers with Ryke and relishing the quiet, with nothing but the roar of the wind and the thunder of his wings in my ears. It was almost enough to drown out my tangled thoughts, to make me forget the unsettling visit from my mother and my fear I'd disgrace her. Enough to make me forget about whatever was happening to my own skin.

A new manifestation of the curse? A result of the strange powers Nesrelle granted because of our agreement? A million similar thoughts had tumbled through my brain until I'd reached Ryke's side, stroking his snout and eagerly saddling him. He'd been just as impatient to be out and about. Though I'd let him fly—always under a strict command that his intelligent mind understood: *no killing my people or their animals*—he seemed to prefer having me with him. There was a bond there, one I didn't fully understand. We were loyal and protective of one another, but it went deeper than that. It was as if we understood one another.

"If you could speak to me," I murmured, patting Ryke as he swooped closer to the coast and the dazzling sea stretching out toward the horizon, "what would you say?"

Of course, he couldn't speak, a fact which only increased the painful loneliness creeping over me. I wielded unspeakable power and had a loyal army prepared to lay down their lives for me, if necessary. I was a member of the Chosen People, a people with a heritage of victory and strength and courage. And I was the heir to an empire. All the stunning land sparkling beneath the sun was mine.

And yet, I was as alone as I'd been in the palace, imprisoned and used by the Forwyn. Even my tie to Kovi was doomed.

I ordered Ryke to turn back, having him land on the outskirts of the camp. Smoke curled up from fires and the scent of meat wafted on the breeze. Most of the soldiers were already stirring, preparing or eating food and readying themselves for the day's training. Talking and laughing as if, even with their strange new powers, life went on much the same for them. They weren't plagued with doubts, only confidence that we were now invincible, and everything our people had lost would soon be ours again. They weren't lonely, and they certainly weren't afraid of their own shadows.

Dismounting Ryke, I went about removing his saddle and running my fingers down his sides. He grunted and nuzzled me, snorting a puff of grey smoke into the air. I leaned into him, relishing his warmth and his soothing presence. It was as if he were telling me I wasn't alone, not with him there. That I needn't ever be alone again.

"Thank you. I think you're my only true friend," I whispered, even if I wondered at my sanity. Did other people speak to animals—to these beautiful beasts—the way I spoke to Ryke?

But Ryke's large, intelligent eye blinked back at me, seeming to understand every word I shared with him. Leaning into my palm, he nuzzled my shoulder as if to offer comfort.

With a grin, I gave him the releasing command to go hunt for his breakfast. I stepped back and watched in awe as he sprang into the air, his great wings unfurling and thrusting a rush of air back toward me as he rose up, up, until he was only a dark blot against the grey sky.

"Wynlaen is overrun," I said as soon as my trusted soldiers had gathered together in my tent. Clustered around the table at the center of the space, they watched intently as I overlaid a rough sketch atop the town on one of the numerous maps spread out before me. "The Teramese arrived and are already swarming all over it. Soldiers are posted and watching the borders, and it appears they may be occupying many of the homes and shops." I pursed my lips, anger swirling through my stomach. "The rest of the army is encamped in the surrounding countryside."

"How great are their numbers?" Daedra asked, tapping her chin thoughtfully as she stared at the map.

"For taking a mere town?" I grinned. "It appears they sent less than a thousand soldiers."

Zakren, a barrel-chested man with deep brown and gold eyes, laughed heartily. "For our thousands? We could have taken them easily even without our new…strengths." He smirked at the word, pride and confidence practically billowing off him.

I wondered if any of my soldiers had noticed anything strange lately. Had their sleep been interrupted with ghosts? Was their skin changing?

"But why waste our time on a skirmish, when we could march straight for the capital?" Daedra asked. "They'll have seen your dragon and expect us. We'll lose valuable time *and* risk losing a few Alrenian lives for…what? Wynlaen is insigni—"

I slammed my fist on the table, my stare burning into Daedra's widened eyes. "*None* of our people are insignificant," I countered. "I will show them that none are forgotten, that none are too lowly. We are the Chosen People, warriors of old. I will *never* abandon any of my people like that. First we take back Wynlaen, and then Aramith to the south. Then we move on to Inalgoth. Do you understand?"

Daedra blinked several times before swallowing and dipping her head. "Yes, Your Imperial Majesty," she murmured. "Of course."

I turned to scan the faces of the other men and women surrounding me. Zakren. Breyna. Elvik. Merev.

"Does anyone else have a problem with freeing our fellow Alrenians in Wynlaen? Does anyone else doubt the value of *every* Alrenian life?"

There was a chorus of "No, Your Imperial Majesty" spoken deferentially. Despite their newfound powers, they still respected the curse I bore.

Without further protest from my officers, we worked together to assemble a plan of attack.

"We are ready," Zakren said as they all prepared to exit my tent and help with training for the day. "Your army is anxious to begin retaking Alrenor."

I grinned. "As am I."

They filed out, all except Daedra, who lingered, watching the tent flaps close behind Zakren as he marched away.

"Is there something else you needed, Daedra?" I asked, picking at my nails. I hadn't appreciated Daedra's attempt to oppose me earlier, and feigning indifference to the way she stayed behind now seemed the best course of action. I needed her to remember her place.

"You spoke of your plans with the Teramese prisoner, but what of the Forwyn one?" She didn't meet my eyes as she spoke, but I could practically hear the hatred rolling off her words.

An urge to order her never to lay a finger on Kovi burned through me, but I didn't dare speak the words. I couldn't justify that command to my people. They'd question my loyalties, suspect my motives. Instead, I swallowed, the action of holding back that order slipping bitterly down my throat. I was tempted to bring him to my own tent, where I could ensure none of my people dared go near him, but that would certainly draw suspicion.

He can take care of himself. Ally or not, why are you wasting so much energy worrying about his safety? I berated myself.

"Don't concern yourself with him," I said. "I have already begun interrogating him, remember? I know how to put him and his power to use."

Wordlessly, Daedra saluted and swept out of the tent, but something about her searching expression left me feeling empty and chilled.

CHAPTER TWENTY-TWO

Lo

CAESIEM'S QUARTERS WERE AS EMPTY as I'd left them when I finally returned that morning, after ensuring Pauni'a was safe. Still damp and cold from my plunge into the harbor, I'd waited to check for a guard posted on the balcony—and had found none—before clambering up. When I slipped quietly within the bedchamber, my heart leapt in a strange mixture of fear and anticipation to see the breakfast tray still waiting for me.

If Caesiem had eaten, there was no sign of it—no dirty dishes left, and the pastries and fruit all appeared untouched. The pot of coffee had long gone cold, but I poured myself a cup anyway, desperate for a bit of energy after my exhausting night.

As I'd hoped, there was a note waiting for me, resting beneath the pot. The handwriting was small and cramped on the tiny scrap of paper. In Forwyn, it said: *We are ready to train the dragons, but we need your help. Only a few of us were hired to work in the Keep. Most of the Forwyn Keepers trained and worked with their own dragons without extra help. The dragons won't know us like they know you. If you can't risk being seen around us, send information about them in future notes. Teach us how to earn their trust.*

I tore the note up immediately, struck a match, set the paper alight, and tossed it into the unlit hearth. As soon as the flames sputtered out, I knelt and buried the charred scraps in the ashes. The nights hadn't been cool enough yet for a fire to be lit, and I didn't want Caesiem to realize I'd burnt something in the hearth.

As I crossed the bedroom to claim another piece of paper, ink, and a pen, I drew close enough to the sitting room door to detect heated voices coming from within. I froze, pen clutched tightly in my fist, and listened.

"Oh, so you think the rest of us don't see this supposed marriage alliance for the farce it is? Like I said, you clearly can't control your *whore*. But I bet I could control her for you," an angry, unfamiliar voice snapped. The man's tone was guttural, and full of utter hatred and derision.

I bristled, freezing in place as Caesiem raised his voice in response. "Call her that again, and we'll see how long you can breathe underwater," he snarled. "I think I already proved to you earlier that you won't win in a fight against me. And don't think you can get away with these threats and this disrespect, Darix."

Darix. The burly man from the formal dinner I'd been made to attend. I drew a deep breath, heart pounding furiously.

But Darix was laughing. "Revaed can't risk the safety of one of his mages. He'd have to punish even *you* if you harmed me. You can't do anything."

"I could say the same about you."

"And yet, when Revaed dies and you claim the throne, who will be loyal to you?" Darix demanded. "Who will you cower behind then? No one. You're *no one* without him, just a brat off the street who was lucky enough not to starve to death. Your magic doesn't make you noble."

Caesiem's tone was deadly. "Get. Out."

Darix must have chosen to listen, perhaps realizing Revaed *was* still alive and there could be repercussions for his behavior, because I heard the door slam. A chill swept down my spine. Had he barged into Caesiem's private quarters to hurl threats? If some of the other Teramese despised Caesiem, what would they do when Revaed wasn't around to keep them in line?

There was a quiet moment, and I realized this might be all the time I had before Caesiem walked in and found me. My heart fluttered somewhere in my throat as I dipped the pen into the ink and scrawled out my message as fast as I could.

Use the times the Teramese are not present to your advantage. When you feed the dragons, enter their dens without showing fear. They can sense it on you, and that's what makes them think you are prey. Look them straight in the eye and walk proudly. Believe they will submit to you, and they will.

They are intelligent creatures who notice those who respect and care for them.

Torla has a weakness for chin scratches. The surest path to Ivez's heart is food—he's always loved bacon. Ziltha is slow to trust, but eager to be in the sky. Her restlessness will be what earns you loyalty, when you take her out to fly.

I heard footsteps pacing in the sitting room, forcing me to cut my message short. Scrawling quickly, I added:

Leave Karos to me.

I dashed across the room to tuck my message beneath the coffee pot. Then I left the rest of my cold cup of coffee on the tray and seized a new outfit from the wardrobe—leggings and a tunic, procured specifically for me—and strode into the washroom. Turning on the hot water, I let it spill into the tub until steam curled around my face. By the time I'd filled it to the brim, adding soap until it bubbled invitingly, Caesiem was knocking on the door.

I scowled, but stalked over to open it, meeting Caesiem's own frown. His bright eyes swept over me, taking in the sopping curls clinging to my face and my dirty, soaked outfit.

"You might feel back to normal after the theslynik, but that doesn't mean you should be running around the whole city. I thought the healer told you to rest." He sighed. "Where have you been?"

I stared back at him, noticing his clothes were dry but his hair was damp. The scents of sea and smoke enveloped him. Dragon smoke—unique from any other kind because it had a unique scent that made it extra acrid.

I narrowed my eyes. "I could ask the same of you." I hesitated a moment. "What was that conversation out there?"

Caesiem scowled. "Nothing. Just Darix being an ass, as usual. He's angry I convinced Revaed to stop assigning guards to watch you and that I'm not treating you like a prisoner. Don't worry about it."

Biting back an anxious laugh, I stared into the tub. "He said he was a mage."

Caesiem's tone was steady, but dark. "And I'm a more powerful one."

"Is water magic the most powerful magic in Teramyl?" I asked, turning to study his face.

He was leaning against the entryway, his arms crossed. Slowly, he shook his head. "Not necessarily, though it is most revered because it usually protects us best from wild dragons. But some mages are more powerful than others, and I am... Well," he said, smiling in a way that didn't quite reach his eyes, "there's a reason after I saved Revaed's life from a dragon that I became his heir."

I stared at him.

Caesiem lingered a moment longer in the doorway. "I'm glad you're all right," he said, and I couldn't miss the sincerity in his eyes. It took me aback, loosening a bit of the tightness lodged in my chest. He truly did worry for my wellbeing. It was strange, confusing. Didn't he know how his soldiers were oppressing my people?

As he left me alone to strip out of my wet clothes and sink wearily into the hot water, I considered the events of the night. After emerging from the harbor, I hadn't found a sign of Mio'e or Nu'or, but I'd discovered Pauni'a not far from the abbey. Though she'd embraced me tearfully, reluctantly, she'd understood the importance of my need to return to the palace.

"Stay safe," I'd whispered. "Do whatever you need to do if those soldiers try to lay so much as a finger on you."

She'd smiled at me mischievously. "I'll make them fear me," she promised with a wink.

Now, my mind whirled. If they'd survived the Teramese arrows, Mio'e and Nu'or wouldn't be satisfied until either I was dead—or they were. Caesiem was an enigma I couldn't—or perhaps simply didn't want to—unravel. Most of all, Pauni'a's words echoed in my head. Her certainty that I was not damned, that Elhani could not only forgive me but also love me and let me serve him again.

I sank back into the water, filled with the first true relief from guilt I'd felt in far too long.

I tried to rest like Caesiem had advised, but I only managed a short hour. I awoke with my heart thundering in my chest and sweat coating my skin. It was always disorienting awakening this way, even though I did more often than not. My mother's or Edi's voice would be ringing in my ears. Their losses were a continuous void in my heart. Edi's bloody, violent death was forever seared into my memory, haunting my dreams even when I tried to dispel the images from my waking thoughts.

This time, Pauni'a's earlier words helped assuage the pain. Rather than give in to tears or anger, I shoved the grief away and concentrated on what my friend had told me.

I am not condemned.

And wilder still: *Maybe she's right, and I was never meant to be a nun. The vows I broke were never mine to make.*

Sitting up, I breathed a soft sigh. I'd known what I needed to do for hours, but now it was time.

Purpose burned in my heart, lightening my body as I swung my legs over the side of the bed and shuffled across the plush rug. Caesiem was once again absent.

Stomach aching after my missed breakfast, I approached the side table where a tray with lunch dishes awaited me. I was surprised I'd managed to sleep through its delivery, but pleased to find another message beneath a dish of shrimp. *The dragons seem to be warming to us, but we are always watched. We don't think the Teramese have their loyalty, however, since they are present but never the ones doing the feeding or even touching the dragons. They hope to ride them with us soon, but what next? Even with the dragons, we are outnumbered by the Teramese and Alrenians alike. We are not warriors. Please tell us you have more plans.*

I shoveled food into my mouth as I scrawled a quick response. *I'll be in contact with the academy soon. We won't be alone.*

Settling the message beneath an empty dish, I seized a knife from the tray. It wouldn't be much of a weapon against another person, let alone a soldier, but it was sharp enough for what I had to do. With no guards monitoring Caesiem's balcony any longer, I slipped down into the gardens without issue. It didn't take long to find a plump rabbit, too accustomed to nibbling on vegetables and approaching the people who forever roamed the grounds to be afraid of me.

Its heart pounded frenetically against my hand as I carried it, its warm body nestled against my chest. My soul ached with remorse for what I had to do. I wove a path back toward the very same cliff that Renni had tried to fling me over. For a moment, I watched sunlight dance on the waters far below.

The climb down to the beach was lengthier than I'd expected, especially because the only available path was steep and narrow, riddled with loose rocks and dirt. When I stepped onto the smooth stretch of sand, I drew a deep breath of the briny air tugging at my curls. Removing my sandals, I waded out into the shallows, foamy waves crashing around my knees.

I grasped the rabbit firmly yet gently by the scruff. With my other hand, I lifted the dagger, naked and glistening like just another shard of light.

My stomach tightened. I caressed the rabbit again as I prepared to slit its throat.

"Thank you, sweet, innocent friend," I whispered. Tears clinging to my lashes, I shut my eyes and lifted my voice in prayer. "Please accept my offering of innocent blood, shed to atone for my sins. Forgive me for dishonoring you by breaking my sacred vows." I swallowed. "I thank you for your forgiveness, so readily bestowed, and I accept it with my whole heart."

"I think that's unnecessary," a male voice said gently.

I dropped the knife and it splashed into the water, sucked out to sea. Cradling the rabbit against my chest, I marveled that it seemed calmer, almost relaxed in my embrace.

Turning, I found a man standing on the beach. He appeared Forwyn, with warm, dark skin and kind eyes. There wasn't anything notable about him—his clothes were plain, in muted shades of green and brown. Leaving the water, I returned to the beach, sand clinging to my wet feet as I approached.

Hesitation slowed my steps, but not fear. Nothing about this man seemed threatening—not his posture or his smile. And he was unarmed, his hands thrust into his pockets as he alternated between watching me and studying the sea.

When I stopped before him, his smile broadened, and I was struck with his *power*. It was a strong sensation, emanating from his very aura. He looked like a humble Forwyn man, but my skin tingled and insisted he was something…other. An Immortal.

Cautiously, I knelt and lowered the rabbit to the sand. It hopped further inland, toward the stalks of grass waving in the breeze, as if it hadn't a care in the world.

"What do you mean? Are you a guidespirit?" I murmured, eyes darting over his form once more. No otherworldly light flickered around him, and nothing about his features made him seem extraordinarily handsome or different. He appeared to be older than me by at least a decade and a half, but still able-bodied and strong, with a tall, muscular frame. An earthy scent that reminded me of trees and other living things clung to him, mingling with the tang of the sea breeze.

Instead of answering me directly, the man's lips twitched in amusement as he stared out at the horizon. "Why are you so full of questions and doubt when deep down, your heart is confident? You have always carried a fierce love for your people. You have always been a fighter. Not because you want to shed blood"—he nodded toward where I'd released the rabbit—"but because you want to protect the innocent. Do you think that honorable desire is wrong?"

I frowned. "The nuns are honorable in their quest to help our people and cling to peace," I protested.

He turned, his eyes boring directly into mine. I had the uneasy sense that he could see straight into my soul, that he knew everything I'd ever thought or said or done, and everything I ever would think or say or do until the end of time.

The notes to Elhani's song swept over me, the loudest and clearest I'd ever heard them. In my bones, I knew. This was an Immortal, the most powerful one known to my people. This was my god, standing before me and communing with me like a friend.

Grateful tears burned my eyes.

"Some people are called to help a few, to change their lives. But others? They are called to do even more. You are a world-changer, Lo."

I stared at him, heart thrilling with his words. Doubt clung to me. "I've made so many mistakes."

He smiled gently. "I forgive them. You don't need to shed an animal's innocent blood to cover your mistakes. You don't even need to offer penance—not to me. Pauni'a is right. You didn't damn yourself with your choices. You followed the path I called you to when I sent a guidespirit to lead you."

I rocked back on my heels. "But I'll make more mistakes. I'll say something stupid—I'll hurt people. I do the wrong things all the time."

His mouth quirked again, as if he were holding back a chuckle. "And I'll forgive you all the time."

A hundred questions darted through my head, but it was impossible for me to focus on just one. Finally, the most terrifying question, the most persistent one, spilled from my lips. "What if I fail you? What if I fail my people?"

"How can you fail at what you were born to do?" the man demanded. "At what you already do, every day?"

I stared back at him, struck speechless. It was all so clear, the way I'd always felt a fire and fearlessness inside me to fight for my people, no matter the cost. The way I loved them and wanted to see them safe and prospering, with a longing so huge it felt bigger than my heart could contain.

I can't fail my people because I am called to love and fight for them, and I've already been doing that.

"Free my people, Lo," he said, and then he was gone.

I collapsed to my knees in the sand, weeping. Laughing. Burning with confidence and purpose and power as I'd never felt it before.

I will free them, I vowed, *or I'll die trying.*

Only a couple hours later, Caesiem returned to find me waiting in his rooms, and explained I'd been invited to a trial.

I'd changed into a simple dress and tugged my hair into a single thick braid to prepare, eager to know if I'd have a chance to influence the outcome, as the so-called alliance between the Teramese and Forwyn would claim. I hadn't even minded when I'd walked in on Caesiem's arm and Revaed had once again announced me as Lord Xalenos's betrothed, not when it had compelled the Teramese to stand at attention and bow their heads in a show of respect toward me. *Let Darix storm into Caesiem's rooms and make threats now,* I thought as my eyes lingered on the officer, whose face looked etched from stone as he forced himself to dip his head.

As soon as Caesiem and I found our chairs, I studied the Forwyn, men and women who must have once been among the Council of Elders' advisors and assistants, seated across from me. Shame made a lump form in my throat as I wondered what they thought of me being announced as Caesiem's future bride. Did they think me the worst sort of traitor? Or, being among those who had surrendered to the Teramese, did they think I too was agreeing to this for survival?

Among the Forwyn in attendance were the surviving Elders themselves. Once again, my stomach soured at the sight of them. Elder Ilhoa, Elder Ettonou, and two others, a man and a woman, that I didn't recognize. They'd spent far too long turning a blind eye and deaf ear to the Forwyn cries for help as Alrenian insurgents plotted against them. Secretly enslaved them. Murdered them.

Now they wore fine clothes and willingly worked alongside the enemy and plotting my marriage into the Teramese imperial family, all to ensure their own survival and comfort.

All along, it seemed their motives had been purely selfish.

Leaning back in my uncomfortable wooden chair, I scanned my surroundings one more time, taking in the thick rug covering the marble floor, the elaborate carvings in the ivory painted wood paneling, and the unnerving statue of the Alrenian Giver of Life that stared us all down.

Chiseled from marble, his face was stern. His eyes appeared inhuman, set with shimmering sapphires. Rather than lend the piece of art a sense of opulence, it added a chilly aspect that made my skin crawl.

As if a withdrawn, angry, heartless god watched the proceedings.

During my enslavement in the palace, I hadn't had to enter this room often. Karye rarely held formal trials and sentencings, preferring to either execute those who angered her immediately, or to allow the victims a chance to fight against her dragons. When I had been ordered to this room, it had usually been with a handful of other slaves to find it empty and cold, reeking with the stench of blood from the puddles we had to clean up.

The rug beneath my feet was a replacement, after the previous one had been burned.

Now I drew in a deep breath, relishing the fact that the air was mercifully fresh and free of any lingering stink of death. Murmurs from Forwyn and Teramese alike drifted throughout the room. Numerous eyes—enemy and ally—darted toward me, inspecting me with open derision and hate.

"I suppose we're ready to begin," Revaed drawled, his violet eyes sparkling in the morning light sweeping in through the floor-to-ceiling window behind him. Just like every other time I'd seen him, he was dressed in a Teramese military uniform rather than in royal finery. Despite his casual air, not a hair was out of place on his head, and every button on his jacket was perfectly polished.

His charming smile made my blood simmer.

Leaning forward, Revaed addressed the soldiers positioned on either side of the heavy doors across from him. "Bring in the prisoner," he ordered.

The doors creaked open and footsteps thudded across the floor. Rather than watch, I turned my gaze toward the man seated directly opposite me—Elder Ettonou. Dressed in immaculate clothes in vibrant hues of red and green, he hardly looked like a man who'd recently been removed from power. He certainly wasn't a prisoner himself, nor was he serving the Teramese as payment for having his life spared.

Snake, I thought bitterly. *What sort of deal did you make with this devil of a man who stole our homeland?*

Elder Ettonou's dark eyes met mine, assessing me with cold calculation. I swallowed against the burning sensation in my throat.

The sudden rise in the voices around us drew both the Elder's and my stares away from one another and back toward the center of the room, where two Teramese guards stood, holding an Alrenian boy between them. Together, the guards shoved the boy to his knees, right in the middle of the space. Right on the plush carpet that so often had been stained with blood.

My back stiffened, spine rigid and shoulders taut. When Caesiem had informed me I'd be taking part in a *just* trial involving an Alrenian assassin, I'd imagined an imposing figure, like the insurgents we'd once faced together. Someone who would be an even match against the Teramese soldiers. Someone who would have innocent Forwyn blood on his or her hands.

Someone like the Alrenians who'd been murdering Forwyn citizens and then leaving their bodies on pikes with painted messages. *Avenge the empire.*

This boy was thin and scrawny, his appearance so ragged he was likely a street beggar or thief. His hair might have been sandy blond or a light shade of brown—it was so dirty and greasy that it was impossible to tell. Despite the harsh set of his jaw and the flashing anger and contempt in his eyes, he couldn't conceal his fear.

It took everything in me not to leap to my feet and shout my protests. *Patience,* I cautioned myself. *You're nearly as much a prisoner as this boy. You won't convince anyone by screaming like a madwoman.*

I could feel the way Caesiem tensed, his discomfort palpable. Casting a sidelong glance his way, I scanned his face, noting the furrowed lines of his brow. It made a glimmer of hope blossom inside me. Maybe I wouldn't have to work too hard to convince the Teramese to be humane.

Across from me, Elder Ettonou's dark eyes bored into the Alrenian boy as if his stare itself could set the prisoner aflame. I wondered if he was imagining the times he'd convicted other Alrenians to death by dragon fire. Once again, I dragged my gaze away from the horrid man.

One of the Teramese officers, seated near Elder Ettonou, shifted in her seat. I remembered her from the dinner I'd attended, and I was fairly sure her name was Valentra. "Forgive me, Your Imperial Highness," she said, not daring to lift her golden eyes to stare directly at Emperor Revaed, "but my understanding was that we were gathered to try a dangerous criminal."

Still clutching the boy in a vice-like grip, one of the guards turned scornful eyes upon Valentra. "This boy was plotting to assassinate our emperor with vylae. We found the vial on him and he didn't even try to deny it."

"Enough, Malec," Revaed cut in, his voice sounding almost bored.

The guard frowned, but lowered his eyes to stare at the floor.

Revaed turned to Valentra, who was twirling one of her long, dark braids through her fingers furiously. A row of daggers lined the belt at her waist, and when she shifted again, I glimpsed some embroidery decorating the shoulder of her uniform jacket. I couldn't remember her ranking in their army, but it was clear her word held at least some weight with Revaed.

"What our good Jevoro Malec said is true, Lieutenant Valentra." He gestured with his arm toward the two guards. "Show us the vial."

The guard named Malec produced it with a flourish. It was such a tiny thing, a little glass cylinder filled with clear liquid that could have been nothing but water.

Another Teramese officer, a man with a nasty sneer, leaned forward, his wide eyes drinking in the sight of the vulnerable boy as if he hoped to snap his neck himself. "And you say he confessed to everything?" he asked eagerly.

Malec nodded smugly. His fellow guard shoved the boy roughly between the shoulder blades. "Tell them what you told us," he commanded.

The boy lifted his chin to meet Revaed's eyes. "Gladly," he said, his voice ringing out surprisingly loud and clear. "My name is Sirev, son of Verlek, who was a Dragon Keeper in service to Empress Karye herself. Since the day he was killed by Forwyn slaves" –he spat on the ground– "I have lived as an orphan on the streets, struggling to find scraps of food. There has been no mercy from the Forwyn." His eyes filled with hatred.

"And I have no interest in seeing my empire fall into the hands of merciless alliance-breakers," he added. "Teramese *traitors!*" He spat again before lifting murderous eyes back toward Revaed. "I will gladly serve my empire by killing the likes of you."

For half an instant, silence consumed the room, every eye staring at the boy before us.

Then, someone dared to break it.

"Kill him!" Elder Ettonou barked. "He's admitted he hates us all. Admitted he is a would-be murderer, and a descendant of a servant of that murderess and monster, Empress Karye." A vein popped in his temple, his cheeks puffed with his rage. His eyes held no mercy, no hesitation. "His life is forfeit."

This time, I couldn't refrain from standing, from glowering at this man who proclaimed himself one of the Chosen Followers of Elhani, yet was so eager to shed blood.

"He's a *child*," I snapped, scarcely able to keep my voice from trembling with my building emotions. I gestured toward the boy without tearing my gaze from the Elder's. "And a half-starved one, at that. As a leader of our people, I thought you were also supposed to be a man of god. But, for a pious man, you seem awfully eager to play the roles of judge and executioner."

I could feel Caesiem's eyes boring into the back of my head, as if he hoped he could silently command me to sit and hold my tongue, but I ignored him. None of the others—not even their self-proclaimed emperor—so much as moved a muscle, their eyes darting back and forth between Elder Ettonou and me. Further back in the crowd, Elder Ilhoa shifted in her seat, scanning the entire room as if she were more interested in weighing the motivations and opinions of others than she was in voicing her own.

Elder Ettonou stood to his feet slowly, his eyes smoldering like dragon fire. "You know what his kind did to us. You know exactly what he and his people are capable of. How dare you question me and my motives, when you are discussing the *lives* of our *people!* Do you value your people—god's people—so little that you would put this unbeliever before them?" He sneered. "You are a disgrace." His eyes flicked toward Caesiem and back to me, the implications of his words searing deep. He thought *me* the worse traitor, even if he was just as guilty of working with the Teramese. Even if he was the one who'd been part of arranging Caesiem's and my betrothal. "I'm ensuring our people's survival always comes first."

"What about mercy?" I blurted out. "What about forgiveness? What about choosing a better path? What about choosing humanity rather than becoming as guilty as our enemies?" I took a step forward, raising my voice until it echoed throughout the room. I could feel every eye staring at me, and I hoped my words rang true, that they sank deep into their hearts and souls. "If we continue the cycle of killing, *when will it stop?*"

"You want to speak to me about *guilt?*" Elder Ettonou cried. "Do you have any *idea* of the long list of atrocious crimes Empress Karye alone committed against our people?"

White spots danced across my vision as a roaring filled my ears.

All I could see was Edi's face, all I could hear was his gentle, reassuring voice. *She can't separate us, not really.* For a moment, I was struck breathless, and then rage filled me instead. Pure. Blinding. This arrogant, cold man knew *nothing*, and despite my earlier argument for mercy, I had an overwhelming urge to bridge the gap between us and seize him by the shirt collar.

Without quite realizing it, I must have taken a step forward, because Caesiem sprang into action. He cursed softly and seized my arm. He tugged me back, as if he thought he could make me sit and this entire heated conversation would blow over. I tossed him a livid glance over my shoulder. With another muttered curse, he released me.

Before Elder Ettonou's and my conversation could escalate, Revaed stepped forward. "Tensions are high among the Forwyn and Alrenians, I know," he said, his voice measured yet forceful. "You both make great arguments, ones that are both worth listening to." He scanned the rows of Teramese and Forwyn sitting in a semicircle around him. "It's important that we never lose our grip on our humanity, that we always cling to mercy and never kill without warrant." He shot me a smile, and I stared blankly back.

Elder Ettonou grumbled softly. For a man who'd surrendered to these people to save his own life, I was a bit surprised by his audacity. Perhaps, like me, his anger was making him brash.

"However," Revaed continued, his eyes flitting to the Elder and settling on him. "It is also true that mercy should never become more important than the safety and survival of the innocent."

A chilling sense of foreboding washed over me. His words weren't ones I could disagree with, not outright, and yet they felt all wrong. Twisted. Off. Like the moment a bite of food just gone bad went from tasting palatable to turning sour, his speech started out sounding right and ended in a way that felt rotten.

I hadn't even bothered to sit again, instead standing with every muscle coiled tight, my hands fisted at my sides.

Revaed halted directly before the boy, who continued to stare with defiant eyes despite the obvious threat on his life. "This boy is nearly a man, and he has made the decisions of one. He poses an obvious threat to our lives and the lives of those we care about."

To your life and your rule, you mean, I thought darkly. Although the boy might truly pose a threat, I couldn't ignore the possibility that maybe he could change. That he was young and desperate and starving, and some mercy could turn him from a criminal and assassin to an ally.

At the very least, he could serve a prison sentence for his actions, rather than die.

He's too young, I thought. *Younger than I was when I slew Empress Karye. Younger than Edi when he was murdered. So young.*

Lost in my thoughts, I hadn't realized Revaed was still speaking. "…above all else," he announced.

All around me, every Teramese citizen, including Caesiem, repeated the phrase, leaving me in no doubt as to what their emperor had been saying. "Survival above all else."

And with that, Revaed drew a dagger and plunged it straight into the boy's heart. Blood burst from the wound, splattering across the emperor's pristine jacket and perfectly polished buttons. It drenched the boy's rags and pooled onto the carpet at his feet.

Someone else will have to burn that rug, I thought numbly.

As the boy collapsed in his own blood, I couldn't stop staring at the scene before me, watching it as if I were no longer in my own body. The Forwyn Elders stood alongside Teramese officers, bowing to the emperor as if he'd just done something heroic. Their own faces bloodied, the guards grinned and saluted, as if relieved to be rid of the nuisance they'd been burdened with.

Horror swooped low in my stomach and bile rose up my throat. I was frozen, lost.

I was trapped in a sea of monsters.

I was barely aware of Caesiem, the only other person who hadn't stood or applauded, gently taking my arm and guiding me out of the room. There was a sound that could have been his voice, low and melodic in my ear, but I couldn't make out the words. I wanted to spin and punch him, yet I couldn't even focus.

The rushing in my ears was back, louder than ever.

How can I save my people when they can't save themselves? When they choose this darkness?

CHAPTER TWENTY-THREE

Kovi

WIND WHISPERED THROUGH THE TENT Vander and I were chained within, brushing chill air against our faces. The rustle of leaves and canvas filled my ears, muffling the distant hoots of owls and cries of coyotes.

After the Alrenians had brought me here, chaining me to the middle tent pole right beside Vander, the Teramese soldier and I had barely spoken. Back to back, we couldn't see one another's faces, but I could practically feel the anger and suspicion pouring off him in waves.

An entire day had passed with little event. Jalie hadn't tended to my wounds again herself—she'd sent one of her healers, a stern-faced woman who'd applied the ointment none too gently.

My entire chest still hurt, every movement tugging on the bandages and igniting pain across my skin. Thankfully, I'd called upon Elhani's magic to help heal myself, and even if—despite my focus and ability to command others—I wasn't particularly skilled in that area of wielding Elhani's power, I could feel the difference. My wounds would heal faster this way, and I knew I wouldn't have to worry about infection.

Jalie's absence made me wonder if she was occupied with preparing her army to move. Were we to march soon? She hadn't shared details when we'd spoken, as she'd still been planning and scouting Wynlaen.

At last, Vander cleared his throat, breaking the silence. "Your magic gives you the power to…command people." It wasn't a question.

"Why haven't you used your power to force the Alrenians to free us? To command the empress to fall on her own sword? To stop her army with their unnatural demon powers?" Fury thundered in his words. "You know what they will do. Your people are in the capital as well. At the very least you could force them to let us escape and warn our people before the Alrenian army overwhelms them."

Squeezing my eyes shut, I tried to block out the memories flashing through my mind. *Rage. Denial. Horror. Fear. Agony. Lifeblood draining past my fingers. My soul slipping away…*

"You don't know the price of the power I carry," I murmured, and I didn't try to conceal the heat of my own anger burning through me, either. "And you don't know its limits. What you're claiming I could do? To control that many people, for that long? It's not possible…"

What I'd said wasn't exactly a lie. I couldn't control an entire army, and I certainly didn't want to feel a connection with that many Alrenians, even if I could.

"What did the empress want with you yesterday, in her tent?" Vander cut in. I could feel him shaking now, tugging against the chain securing him to the pole.

"To question me," I said, keeping my tone level. Deadpan. "To know about my magic, especially." The memory of her fingers brushing against my skin tumbled through me until an entirely different type of heat filled my chest, but I shoved that feeling aside.

There wasn't room for desire in anything I had to do. She was an ally, a means to an end to protect my people. It was foolish to imagine we could ever be together. Foolish to imagine our paths wouldn't eventually lead to opposing ends.

I prayed that this way, at least I wouldn't ever have to watch her die.

Vander was quiet for a long while. "It's strange she didn't have someone else do that for her."

"Likely she wanted the information for herself, because she trusts very few people," I muttered. "Even among her own." I drew a deep breath. "And she knows me, a little. I guess she was confident she knew how to get me to talk."

"Did she?"

I offered a scornful laugh, as if the idea were preposterous. I didn't remind him I was an Aerekni Academy graduate, a member of the most elite fighting force in Alrenor. I didn't tell him of the years of intense physical and mental training I'd undergone. It didn't matter, because it was all a lie anyway. With Jalie as my ally and the Teramese still my enemies, I'd told her everything she'd wanted to know.

But Vander didn't need to know that.

"No," I said instead.

Movement at the front of the tent jerked my gaze up. At my back, Vander squirmed, struggling to look over his shoulder and see behind him. A dark form entered, silent as a shadow. It fumbled in the corner before lighting a lamp—illuminating stacks of crates and barrels filled with food and supplies—and turning back toward me.

It was one of Jalie's female officers—Daedra, I believed they'd called her. Her dark, gold-flecked eyes inspected me with narrow focus, and an uncomfortable feeling settled in my stomach. I could see the shadows dancing around her, alive and threatening and powerful.

Was she here to question me more? To torture me? The Alrenians made no secret of how much they despised us prisoners. Surely they were itching to see us suffer.

Slamming the lamp down, Daedra seated herself cross-legged across from me and scowled. "What's your name?" she demanded.

I stared at her, silent. Assessing.

Behind me, Vander chuckled darkly. "What's yours?"

Daedra turned and spat off to the side. "I didn't ask you a question yet, Teramese scum. Shut up or I'll cut out your tongue." She turned her dagger-like gaze back on me. "And *you*. Answer me, or I'll show you what my power can do."

"I could command you to cut out your own tongue right now," I said instead, keeping my face a mask of dark indifference. My voice was low and measured, letting my words alone be threat enough. "Do you really want me to keep speaking?"

Daedra stiffened, a hint of fear flashing across her face, before she regained control of her expression and blinked. Offering me a carefree smile, she waved her hand. "I don't think so." She narrowed her eyes still further as she studied me from head to toe. "If that were the case, and your power truly was that unlimited, why are you still a prisoner?" She hesitated, her grin widening. Sharpening. "Unless…you *want* to be a prisoner."

My mind whirled at the accusation, but I refused to give anything away. I was trained for this. Without flinching or averting my eyes, as she likely hoped I would, I barked out a harsh laugh.

"You would like that, wouldn't you?" I responded, smirking just to make her livid.

Behind me, Vander was quiet, his breathing shallow and even. He was clearly listening to every word, every inflection in my voice.

Chewing her lip, Daedra considered my answer, clearly unsatisfied. And then, without preamble, she lunged, pressing a dagger against my throat. I didn't move, didn't blink, as the cold metal caressed my skin. I stared straight back at her.

"A quick death is too good for you," she breathed, her voice strained. "You're an unbeliever, a blasphemer who follows a false god and wields unnatural powers."

I couldn't ignore the irony of her words. Did she think her alliance with Nesrelle, Queen of Death, wasn't blasphemous in the eyes of her god, the Life-Giver? Did she think her own powers were any more natural than mine?

"What about your alliance with Nesrelle?" I demanded, my voice guttural.

Daedra sneered. "The Queen of Death was created by the Giver of Life. Death is just another part of life, after all. Her powers are a gift to us, the Life-Giver's appointed Chosen Ones, to help us regain our glory and power. He's finally blessed us once more, after far too long without any sign of the courage and war gifts of old." She smiled, and everything about it was wicked and terrible. In the flickering lamplight, her teeth flashed orange and looked sharp as fangs.

Fangs. A hint of fear trickled through me. I blinked, and Daedra's teeth looked normal again. *A trick of the light,* I reasoned.

"Has the empress ordered my death?" I demanded. I knew Jalie hadn't, but I wanted to know what this woman was planning, why she was going behind Jalie's back.

Daedra's grin turned to a scowl. "No, and she's a fool for tending to your wounds and letting you live after you murdered Corvath." Her voice shook a little on the man's name—had the soldier meant something to her? She drew a deep breath, her eyes hardening once more. "But if I can't kill you, and she wants to be the only one to interrogate you, then I can make you suffer."

Before I could fully register her words, the shadows swirling about her began to writhe, gathering until they coalesced into a great cloud. It rushed toward me, consuming me in a dark, cold embrace that plunged me into my own memories.

I was immersed in the streets of Hemlaen, an Alrenian city near the western coast, surrounded by countryside and lush, rolling hills. An afternoon sun beat upon my back, the heat already hinting at a stifling, humid summer to come. All around, fellow Aerekni Academy graduates—who, like me, were being forced to prove themselves—shouted while they drew their weapons. My sword felt familiar in my hand, though the chaos and noise of battle did not.

In that moment, a memory coursed through me as Rhi'il cried out beside me, fending off a wild-eyed Alrenian. I could hear the warmth in General Ilowhe's tone as he praised me. I've never met anyone else with a mind and faith as strong as yours, able to focus Elhani's power as you do. No other soldier can command others—either they lack the focus or the courage to make such a connection with their enemies. But you? You will be a great and powerful warrior... Remember that. Use your power. Serve your people well.

Forcing the memory away, I plowed toward Rhi'il, swinging my sword to block his enemy's attack. I threw myself into a flurry of counterattacks, refusing to let the bloodthirsty Alrenian threaten my best friend. Sweat drenched my back and trickled into my eyes until they burned. Enemy after enemy leapt toward me, relentless.

As a rule, the Alrenians tended to be taller and stronger than most, as if their race had long been bred for nothing but war and bloodlust. I could hear the arrogance in their cries. It only served to fuel my rage, lending strength and speed to my limbs. I fought like a man possessed, every hour of training returning to me effortlessly, as if I'd been born to do this. I was meant to be a soldier. Meant to protect and defend my people until I breathed my last. Meant to wield the power flowing around and through me in a sweet melody that, even in its softness, somehow managed to overpower the screams of fear and death.

The Alrenians outnumbered our ranks: that much was clear. And as I lifted my eyes to scan the field of battle in a rare moment of reprieve, I noticed with a gut-sinking feeling that my companions and I were losing. *Bodies were piling up, bodies of young men and women I'd trained and ate and laughed with. Bodies of soldiers who'd recently graduated and were meant to spend their lives serving their people, not dying in their first assignment. The scent of blood permeated the air and I felt sick, my fury threatening to be quenched in an onslaught of despair.*

Our training might have been superior, but this force of Alrenian insurgents seemed unstoppable. It was as if the entire city of Hemlaen had joined in, flooding the streets. Rushing forward with any weapons they could find—from beautiful blades and axes to huge branches wielded like clubs or fire pokers thrust like spears. Worst of all, they were closing in, pinning those of us Forwyn who were still alive and not too gravely wounded into a tight knot. The buildings seemed to tower over us. There was no way out but to kill our way through.

Rhi'il's dark eyes met mine, and without a word, I could tell exactly what he was communicating, even if he hadn't mastered the magic that would allow him to project his voice into my mind. No, I could read his thoughts in his expression: It's time. Don't hesitate. Save us.

I threw every ounce of my mind into the focus it needed to draw on the power flowing through everything—my blood, the earth, the air. Warmth rushed across my skin and through my very being, filling my soul with courage and strength that offset the weariness and doubt that had been clinging to me. I thrust aside the unease I felt at what I was about to do, the thoughts that asked, Is this a dishonorable way to fight? To kill? Is this a misuse of Elhani's magic?

Instead, I raised my voice and shouted above the tumult, forcing the battle to a standstill. None of the Alrenians could resist the power of my words. "Stop!" I cried out. "Drop your weapons."

Half a dozen of them, man and woman alike, tossed their swords and axes and bows and fire pokers and sticks to the ground. They stared at me blankly, as if waiting for another command to fall from my lips. Arms hanging limply at their sides, they held their bodies still. For one strange moment, quiet and peace reigned through the city of Hemlaen, almost oppressive after the constant assault of sound and movement before. The air stank of sweat and blood and death and fear, but a breeze that tasted of the sea brushed through the street, as if trying to cleanse Hemlaen of the violence it had witnessed.

And then my fellow soldiers moved, plunging blades into enemy hearts, lobbing off heads. Cutting the nearest Alrenians down where they stood, helpless and vulnerable. I could feel every emotion, the hatred and terror, the pain and disbelief. As I watched my enemies bleed, I died multiple deaths in a single moment.

My heart stuttered as the bodies thudded to the ground, creating a wide circle of death between us and the remaining Alrenians. I swallowed back the guilt and horror and lifted up my voice once more.

"Lay down your weapons and surrender. Do not resist."

Wiping his sweaty, blood-splattered brow, Rhi'il glanced toward me, offering me a single nod. His mouth was a solemn line, his body taut. I could tell he was as uncomfortable as I was with the results of the fight. It had been about survival, and yet…

It felt ugly. Like we'd been no better than the Alrenians.

Serve your people, *I told myself, wishing I could block out the memories of the dead Alrenians' last moments.*

Choking back a cry, my eyes sprang open to find myself staring into Daedra's cold gaze. Something about her eyes seemed all wrong, though with my racing heart and sweaty palms, it took me a moment to calm myself and identify it. Her pupils were too large, too dark, like endless pits of emptiness overtaking her irises. There was the shadow of a gloating smile on her face, twitching her lips, but for the most part, her expression was emotionless. Unnatural.

Then she sucked in a breath and she chuckled. "You fear your power," she said triumphantly. She laughed more, as if the thought was unbelievable to her. "You *fear* it!"

She seemed ready to do more, perhaps sever my neck from my shoulders or find some new way to torment me, but the tent flaps opened. Two gruff-looking guards poked their heads in, frown lines etched across their foreheads.

"Time's up," one of the men said. His eyes shifted, as if studying something outside, before darting back to Daedra. "Unless you want to speak to the empress about this visit."

Daedra stiffened, scowling at me before withdrawing her blade and shoving it back into its sheath. As she rose, taking the lamp with her, she threw me one last threatening smile.

"I'll discover your other fears, soldier," she taunted. "I'll learn every one of your weaknesses. And then I'll use them against you."

CHAPTER TWENTY-FOUR

DURING THE EARLY YEARS OF my life, the older orphans who had found me took compassion on me, keeping me alive despite their own desperate circumstances. They fed and cared for me, keeping me safe from the numerous dangers that could befall a child in Vicidor, the Teramese capital. Some days, the list seemed endless. There were other homeless thieves and orphans, whose empty stomachs made them desperate enough to kill if they found someone else with even a scrap of food. There were incessant mosquitos that pestered those of us in the crumbling ruins on the outskirts of the city, nearest the jungle—mosquitos that often brought fever and death. And there was the flooding that came with the rainy season, threatening to drown anyone who was foolish enough to be caught in the storm or to live in a home that wasn't lifted off the ground with sturdy stilts.

Not to mention, there was always the threat of wild dragons. Though they generally stayed further north in Teramyl, preferring the drier climate, tales were often told of how some had occasionally wandered toward the capital, bringing chaos and death on their wings.

The other orphans defended me with weapons and hung netting in our glassless windows. They made sure the old, abandoned home we'd made our own remained secure, replacing wooden beams that threatened to break away due to age and rot. They stole food and gathered fresh water from a burbling spring not far down one of the jungle paths. And then, when I was old enough to sneak about the city with a measure of confidence, to understand their commands and know when to be quiet and how to go unseen, they'd taught me to steal.

Elyxia and Jarex were orphaned siblings whose parents had once lived—and died—in the ramshackle house we resided in. Over the years they'd welcomed other orphans into their group so they could all work together to survive, subsisting on whatever we could gather in the jungle or steal in the city. Despite our rough circumstances, Elyxia and Jarex had managed to create something that had felt like a haven. Though they weren't many years older than me, I'd looked up to them almost as a mother and father. I'd been eager to please, eager to add a share of food and supplies to the pile the rest of my "family" brought in.

So on the day Elyxia had led me toward the tolling plague bells, my heart had thundered with anticipation and excitement. In all my four years of life, I'd never once had a chance to open gifts as part of the Festival of the Elements, but I'd heard stories of how wonderful those celebrations were. And I could imagine that my excitement rivaled that of children who awoke on a festival morning to endless spectacular gifts.

I'm growing up, I'd thought eagerly, my wide eyes scanning the streets, drinking in the sights and smells and sounds around me.

With the bells continuing to ring throughout the streets, pulsating a strangely cheerful warning, it was pure chaos. Nearby, a woman wept while masked guards pushed her back gruffly, urging her back toward the home behind her.

"You need to stay inside!" they ordered. "You spread the disease bringing yourself out here!"

Other citizens dashed across the street, murmuring and gaping at the scene unfolding before them. The healers were masked and gloved, like the guards, working with tense frowns on their brows as they swung a man onto a gurney. His skin was unnaturally pale and coated in a layer of sweat that made his grungy clothes cling to him. He moaned through cracked lips, blinking at the hazy afternoon sun with bloodshot eyes.

Fever. Delirium. A feeling of dread threatened to quench my anticipation as I stared at the man. Even at my young age, I knew what the bell and the masked healers and gruff guards shoving a woman into quarantine meant. Though the plague didn't seem to threaten anyone as young as Elyxia and me, it still filled me with terror. After all, it was what had orphaned Elyxia and her brother, and far too many of our other companions. It was, in all likelihood, what had orphaned me.

Elyxia grasped my elbow and drew me close, whispering in my ear. "This is the perfect time to act," she said. "Use the chaos and everyone's distraction to your advantage. Pick your target."

Tearing my gaze from the dying man, I tried to focus on my task.

Pick your target. For many nights now over a meager supper of dry bread or thin stew, Elyxia and Jarex had been coaching me. I knew this first step meant to find someone who appeared to be carrying something worth stealing. Even if it was simply a loaf of bread. But it also meant picking someone who would be easy to steal from. Like the preoccupied man I spotted near the edge of the crowd, whose clothes looked clean and fine, dyed in rich hues, and who seemed lost in his own thoughts as he gaped at the somber scene before him.

Before Elyxia could say another word, I crept toward my target, as silent as a wraith. Perhaps I'd been young and overly confident, but I'd had much practice in stealth and sleight of hand under Elyxia and Jarex's tutelage, and my speed and small size both aided my cause. It was almost all-too effortless to slip behind the man and pluck the pouch of coins from where it hung from his belt.

As we'd strode away, gleefully counting the gold and silver pieces I'd obtained and dreaming of all the food we could buy, Elyxia tossed me a toothy grin. "You're a natural," she said. "And that means you're a survivor."

Striding through the palace halls with Lo, I forced the childhood memory away. It left an ache in my chest. By now, after leaving behind my orphan family for a life of luxury, they probably hated me. For all I knew, they could have perished in the time since I'd last seen them, falling prey to the dragon that had wrought so much destruction when it'd entered Vicidor, or simply starving to death in the wake of all the destroyed crops and homes. Anything could have happened to them, and as much as I told myself that I now strove for their survival as well as that of the rest of my people, I couldn't guarantee my actions could help them. Couldn't convince myself my choices could atone for the lousy decision of abandoning them when it came to my own survival. Of course, being summoned to the palace by the imperial family was hardly an order a citizen could decline—but my guilt lingered, nevertheless.

Maybe it was that guilt that had made me recall that memory now, as I led Lo back toward my chambers. That Alrenian boy had reminded me entirely too much of myself, and Revaed had killed him without an ounce of remorse.

But sometimes, survival had to look ugly, like stealing or ransacking plague homes or tricking a compassionate citizen.

An ominous silence hung between Lo and me now. I ground my teeth, praying to every god I could think of that she wouldn't lose her cool and…

And what? a persistent voice in my head demanded. *Race back to Revaed and speak more words of mercy?* It wasn't as if she were crying for bloodshed. No, the Empress-Slayer was the opposite of everything I was used to, everything I expected in this rough, kill-or-be-killed world. She was fierce in a way that made me wonder if, perhaps, my lifestyle of putting survival above any other motive was…empty.

She just doesn't understand, I thought fiercely. *She was a slave, but she's never had to choose between stealing or starving with her friends. She's never had to choose between making her enemies fear her, or letting her friends perish. She's spent too many years living in the nuns' fantasy world, where they think love and peaceful ways can change people.* I scowled as I reached my door and flung it open, ignoring the looks of the guards stationed in the hall.

As soon as the door clicked shut behind us, Lo pulled away from my grasp and whirled on me. Her dark eyes shone with a feverish light. Despite the shock and horror that had left her looking almost numb earlier, her inner fire couldn't be quenched for long.

"Is that the sort of man you want to serve? Someone who stabs a mere *boy* in the heart without regret?" she demanded.

She was so close I could feel the heat of her breath on my face, see the flecks of green in her eyes. I blinked away a wild, absurd desire to brush an unruly curl behind her ear and lean in even closer. Instead,

I gave myself to the anger building inside me. I couldn't help it. Maybe it was my own horror and doubt, or the constant guilt and fear for my people that weighed on me.

"He wasn't a boy, not anymore," I said. "He became a man the moment he made the decision to try to take a life. And that means he deserved to be punished as a man."

She stepped back until she was pressed against the door, and I settled a hand beside her. Not hemming her in—my other arm gave her space to leave, to back down from this argument if she wanted. But I wouldn't let her force *me* to back down, to doubt, to show weakness or question my guardian.

Revaed had *saved* me. He loved me like a father or older brother, as no one else had ever bothered to in my chaotic life. Though I'd been a nobody, a thief off the streets, a boy with no surname and no purpose or future aside from stealing to fill his hungry belly day in and day out, he trusted and respected me.

"That was barbaric," Lo said, the first hint of sorrow slipping into her voice as a tremor overtook her livid tone.

I swallowed the burning sensation in my throat and stared at her, unflinching. "No less barbaric than the executions your Forwyn Elders sentenced Alrenian criminals to. Burning by dragon fire?"

She ground her teeth. "I didn't condone their actions either. But don't you think that if someone doesn't stop it, the killing will never end?"

"Do you honestly think that what Revaed did was that different from what you did? He was killing to protect his people from a threat, same as you did when you slew Empress Karye."

Lo's eyes widened in horror, before she glared at me, fisting her hands at her sides. "The empress had a blade to my throat. That boy? He was already a prisoner, shackled and half-starved and nearly harmless."

"*Not* harmless. A would-be poisoner with *vylae*…"

"He was desperate!" she cried, her eyes fiery. "Revaed invaded *his* home. Threatened *his* people. In his mind, it probably was self-defense."

My jaw hardened, and though the words felt ugly and bitter, I couldn't stop them from tumbling out of my mouth. "Are you saying you would also spare the lives of the Alrenians who butcher innocent Forwyn and skewer their bodies on pikes as a message? Are you saying if they tried to kill one of your sisters, you would let them go free?"

Lo's eyes flashed with unshed tears. "I…" She hesitated. "I don't *know*. All I know is I'm sick of the killing, of the death, and *someone* has to stop it!" She pursed her lips. "And it clearly won't be your precious Emperor Revaed."

I stared at her for a long moment, too frustrated and angry to pull my thoughts into order. All I could hear were the pleas of my people. Images of burned homes and weeping, ash-streaked survivors filled my head. What Revaed and the rest of us invading Teramese were doing…it *was* about saving lives. About stopping death. But Lo didn't see that, because she only knew about the struggles her own homeland faced. If I tried to explain Teramyl's fight for survival, would she understand? Would she even care?

Before I could speak, Lo sighed and turned, slipping away from the door and sinking into the settee by the couch. She dropped her head in her hands, her shoulders slumped in weariness. The fight had left her as swiftly as it had begun. "I think," she said softly, refusing to meet my eyes as she stared into the empty hearth, "that you have lived with ruthless men for so long, you can't even recognize what they look like anymore."

"What?" I asked, keeping my voice low. I shook my head, trying to clear it.

"You heard what I said," she responded, keeping her words measured and emotionless.

I gazed at her back. A thousand furious responses soared through my mind, but as I sifted through them all, I realized it was pointless. Lo hadn't seen what I'd seen: whole towns and great cities laid low, charred corpses, people begging for help.

I had to think of everyone, of the greater good, while she had the luxury of worrying about individuals. She could take meals to hurting Forwyn and tend to the sick. I had to extinguish threats and conquer an empire, to walk in dark places and make the difficult decisions in order to save all of Teramyl.

Biting my cheek until it bled, I whirled on my heel and left.

"How do you bear it?" I asked, my voice strained. Anger had dissolved into a feeling of numbness, of sorrowful acceptance. Lo would always hate me. I would always have to live with blood on my hands, would always have to make the complicated choices, because I was a lord, a future leader of an empire. My people depended on me for their well-being, for their very survival.

Revaed peered up at me from his desk, where he'd been poring over his seemingly endless pile of paperwork: correspondences with the generals spread out across Alrenor, maps to track our army's progress and guess at the location of the Alrenian army. Not to mention messages from his father across the sea. Formal documents to sign into decrees.

I blinked and could imagine my future, a lifetime hunched over papers and attending meetings with military officers and advisors. No wonder Revaed relished his morning trainings, his chance to spar with me or another of his men and exercise his muscles and skills with the blade. When else did he experience such freedom?

Revaed's eyebrows rose as his violet eyes scanned over me. I wondered if I appeared as empty as I felt. "Bear what?" he asked.

I swallowed, leaning against the doorway. "The..." I hesitated. "Being feared. Hated. Isolated. Forever making the hard decisions that make people question you, or terrified of you, or wish you were dead." I shrugged. "How do you bear ruling, knowing you'll always have enemies, people who want to backstab you literally, or simply with their words? People who will pretend to love you and speak highly of you, only to get in your good graces? You're so..." I swallowed again. "*Alone.*"

Revaed's smile was wistful and soft, but not entirely without hope. "I have you, Caes."

"Don't you wish for more?"

Revaed snorted. "An arranged marriage with some woman from an enemy land—or some greedy family in Teramyl—who doesn't want me? The company of false friends?" He chuckled, though his laughter sounded hollow. When he met my eyes, though, his gaze was steady and confident. "You're the best family I could ever ask for. Better than any son I could have fathered myself, and you know I was never interested in that." He sighed. "But I understand your longing for more. Maybe instead of settling into a forced marriage, you could do as I did, and find your own heir. I wouldn't fault you for that."

I frowned at the floor, unable to banish the memory of Lo's shocked, hurting expression. "I wish that was all I wanted," I muttered. I lifted my head. "Are you saying...you don't care about the marriage alliance?"

"I'm saying if it will make you miserable, you can refuse it. You've always had a choice, Caes. I won't force anything on you. We don't need to marry you off to build an alliance or save our people. I'll convince the Elders. It's not like they can really deny any of our requests. They'll help us gain Forwyn cooperation, with or without a marriage." Revaed rose, striding toward me and settling a warm hand on my shoulder. I glanced back at him, awash in the compassion written across his face. "I love you like a son. Does that make you feel less alone?"

I nodded quickly. "Yes. Of course." I hesitated, my tangled thoughts diverting to a new topic. "I...I could see myself in that boy. Half-starved, desperate to do anything to survive." My voice sounded broken, even to my own ears.

Revaed nodded thoughtfully, his own expression taut with pain. "I thought as much. But, Caesiem, you never tried to *murder* me, or anyone else, for that matter." He grinned. "You *saved* me. I owe you my life." His fingers tightened, still gentle, but firm and reassuring. "There is no joy in killing. Sometimes we have to do the hard thing to survive. What would have happened if we'd offered mercy to that boy, and he escaped? Killed me...or you? Our deaths don't affect only us...they affect all of Teramyl. Our people need us to live so we can save them."

I drew a deep breath, taking comfort from his words, letting them ground me once more in my purpose. Letting them wash away my doubts like scattered sand on a wave-tossed shore. "I know. You're right."

"It's good you have such a compassionate heart, Caes," Revaed went on. "It's not even a bad thing that you wish all could like you. It means you care about your people, and that you'll do everything you can for the good of all. I'm proud of you."

When I left Revaed later, feeling more settled than I had in days, I couldn't quite banish the echo of Lo's earlier words. *All I know is I'm sick of the killing, of the death, and* someone *has to stop it!*

I squared my shoulders. I wouldn't flinch away from my purpose. My unspoken retort brought courage and strength to my every step: *Sometimes there are people who have to die to save countless other lives.*

When I returned to my quarters, I was surprised to find that Lo was still there, sitting on the settee with a tray for dinner resting on the table before her. Despite the generous spread of food awaiting her, she wasn't eating. Instead, she cradled a steaming mug in her hands as she skimmed through a book.

My eyes fell to the words on the page. Alrenian. It was a jolting reminder of how unworthy I was of her—Lo wanted to cross the divide between herself and her enemies. She was kind, intelligent, brave, and unwavering. *She* did not seem plagued with the doubts I felt.

All at once, the comfort I'd experienced after speaking with Revaed began to dissolve.

Oblivious to the hard knot of pain and confusion forming in my stomach, Lo lifted her eyes and met my stare evenly. Contrary to how I'd last seen her, she appeared composed. At peace. Not at all upset in my presence, and certainly not prepared to launch into another argument. She didn't smile at my entrance, but she didn't scowl either.

"An Alrenian book?" I asked, feeling foolish for my hesitant question.

"Know your enemy," Lo said with a shrug, and took a long sip from her mug.

As I stepped closer, I inhaled the scent of coffee. It made sense she'd be drinking more even in the late afternoon—I wasn't entirely sure I'd ever known Lo to sleep through an entire night. *Nightmares*, I remembered. *The memories from this place haunt her, and yet here she stays, for love of her people.* Another pulse of guilt coursed through me.

I lifted a plate from the tray and began to serve myself a helping of the still-hot fish and fresh greens. For dessert, sugared berries rested in a little bowl. No one had exaggerated Alrenor's wealth of fine food.

"You're not going to eat?" I asked after a long pause, when I'd finally settled in one of the seats closer to the empty fireplace. The autumn days were still hot; the nights not even cool enough yet for a fire.

For a brief instant, Lo's jaw tensed as she watched me shovel a forkful of food into my mouth, but then her eyes flicked away. "I'm not hungry."

The memory of the boy's death flashed before my eyes before I could banish it. Dropping my eyes, I hesitated, the plate still balanced in my hands. "I understand," I said at last. "But…I went too long not knowing if my next meal would be enough, or where it would come from. Even seeing the riches of Alrenor spread out all around me, I can't quite shake the feeling that at any moment it could all be ripped away, and my people and I will be starving again."

Lo watched me, a crease forming between her brows. Finally, she took another sip of coffee. "You really *were* an orphan living on the streets." It was more of a statement than a question, but I nodded anyway. There was a calmness to her words as she went on. "I never can be sure if you're telling me the truth or offering up some new lie you think you want me to hear."

I stilled at her words, guilt making my stomach feel like it was made of stone. "I know I lied to you before, Lo, and I'm sorry for that." My words came out sounding hoarse, forced through my tight throat. "But I promise I'm not lying to you now. I thought…I thought I was justified in what I was doing back when I lied to you, because I was doing it for my people." I stared into her eyes, and she didn't flinch away. "But you deserve the truth, always. And you may always hate me, but for as long as you have to tolerate my presence, I want to offer you everything you deserve."

Something softened in her expression before confusion flickered across her face. She glanced away, clearing her throat. "When did you…How did you become a lord?"

My lips twitched in a fleeting smile. "Like I said before, I saved Revaed's life from a wild dragon."

As she frowned thoughtfully, I glanced toward the pitcher of fresh water and concentrated on my magic. I could feel its power thrum through me, full and unrestrained after going unused for hours. A stream of water burst forth, rushing up into the air like a fountain until it coiled like a river, twirling and glistening.

It flowed around Lo, close enough for her to lift a hand and touch it, her eyes unable to conceal her wonder. The water reflected in the deep pools of her gaze, once again bringing to life those green flecks. She grinned, letting the water play across her fingertips.

Lo was mesmerized by my magic, while I was mesmerized by her.

"You stopped the dragon with your magic, and Revaed knew what you were," she breathed. She turned to me, her expression more guarded, as if she were afraid to reveal her awe. "It's…beautiful. I suppose I've only ever thought of Forwyn magic as beautiful, coming from Elhani himself, while the Alrenians seem to always be using their gifts to harm. And…I know almost nothing about Teramese magic."

"It can be beautiful," I agreed. *Depending on how it's used.* The unspoken words hung between us, but I let them fall. Let myself forget.

I closed my eyes and smiled, enjoying the feel of my magic coursing through my veins, the same way I relished the sound of music as I played or sang. It was passion and beauty and joy and life.

In moments like this, I remembered what I loved about my magic, and the dark moments—the lives I'd taken in gruesome ways, the guilt I carried—all vanished. It was temporary, but it was something.

It felt almost like peace.

Like home.

Opening my eyes, I met Lo's gaze and matched her tentative smile. I couldn't help the well of joy inside me. It couldn't last, this moment. This instance of…something almost akin to understanding between us. But I would embrace it while it was mine to enjoy.

CHAPTER TWENTY-FIVE

AFTER ANOTHER LONG NIGHT WITH ghosts whispering in my ear, the early morning light glared viciously through the tent canvas. I blinked my bleary, aching eyes and sighed, rolling over. My cot wasn't particularly comfortable, and the chill I was so unaccustomed to crept its unwelcome fingers through my blanket, yet I didn't quite want to face the day. The uneasy knot in my chest had only grown.

Drawing a deep breath to steel myself, I steadied my fingers and slipped them beneath the collar of my shirt. Once again, they brushed against that hard, scaly growth along my skin. I squeezed my eyes shut and shoved my fear away.

Alrenians do not fear anything, my mother had always declared. As a child, I'd taken that statement to heart as an irrefutable truth. If I were to fear anything, it was because I was something lesser than the glorious blood and courageous heritage I bore.

But I couldn't ignore the fact that I wasn't only chilly from the cold air, not anymore. The gooseflesh along my arms made me avert my eyes and rise. Tearing off my nightclothes, I dressed swiftly. When I'd donned the last piece of my armor and fastened a curved Alrenian sword to my belt, I braided my hair back from my face.

Someone cleared his throat at my tent entrance. "Your Imperial Majesty?"

"Enter," I called.

One of the camp cooks stepped inside, bearing a tray laden with food. Compared to my usual palace fare, it was nothing to delight in, but my sleep-deprived body rejoiced at the sight of a steaming pot of tea, freshly heated over one of the campfires. My stomach even growled at the rich scent of roasted hare, even though I much preferred my fruit and pastries in the mornings.

As soon as the cook departed, I sank into the chair at my table and poured myself some tea. The army had a small reserve of sugar, and I stirred a couple cubes in eagerly. Anything for something sweet.

I paused as I took my first sip. *Would Mother think me soft, hating camp food and shivering in the mountain chill? Dreaming of my soft bed and hot baths and tantalizing sweets?*

Scowling, I set the mug down and dug into the hare, taking a greedy bite. *I'm not weak. I'm not soft. And Mother, if you're going to continue to haunt me, I'll prove it to you.*

Someone shuffled through the tent entrance, and for an instant, I thought it would be another ghost even in daylight hours, or Nesrelle herself.

"Empress?"

Daedra.

I plastered a smile on my face before I turned around, relaxing my shoulders and gesturing toward the tray at my side. Rather than let her think me chilly or suspicious, I would be especially accommodating.

"Come, eat with me and tell me why you've come," I said with forced warmth.

She ducked her head in a hasty bow and plodded over to the table, sitting straight-backed in the chair across from me. When I again gestured toward the tray, she helped herself to one of the extra mugs the cook had so thoughtfully brought. She poured the tea slowly, her eyes trained on it intently as if it were the most fascinating thing she'd seen in a long while.

As she avoided my gaze, I stared openly at her, assessing the taut line of her mouth and the carefully neutral set of her brow. The blank way she focused on her beverage only added to my unease. Just as before, there was something troubling her. Something she'd come to disagree with me about.

Kovi, I thought, my heartbeat picking up in rhythm. I took another gulp of tea, and it burned on the way down.

I continued to play the role of polite, generous empress. As if I were hosting a ball or feast at the palace and speaking to a lady, rather than sitting in a tent addressing a soldier, I smiled. "To what do I owe the pleasure of your company?"

Daedra cradled her mug in her hands, inhaling the steam for a moment before finally raising her eyes to meet mine.

"I believe..." She hesitated, and for the first time I noticed the way her fingers trembled. "I believe the Forwyn prisoner you keep is the one who helped murder my father."

My hands stilled just as I'd moved to cut another piece of meat. "What?"

Daedra set her mug down, all pretense of drinking gone. "My family is from Hemlaen. It is a smaller city, half-forgotten and tucked away in the countryside, but it is a proud one. When the Forwyn murdered Empress Karye, a large rebel group was formed. They resisted Forwyn occupation for a long time before the dragons were sent and…" She swallowed. "Anyway, this past spring the rebels regrouped. My father was one of them. The Forwyn sent Aerekni Academy graduates to fight and prove themselves."

Dread curled through my stomach and crawled up my throat. Somehow, despite the fact that I'd known what Kovi had done, hearing this account made it much more real, and therefore more abhorrent.

How many of my people have you killed? I'd asked. At the time, he'd answered, *Four. Directly. Indirectly…many more.*

Nameless people, but they were *my* people.

And yet, in his place, would I have done anything different?

"It was a massacre," Daedra continued, a glassy look in her eyes as she stared over my shoulder, at some invisible mark. "The survivors said that the Forwyn used their demonic magic, but that the worst was from a young man who could command some of the Alrenians around him to stop, all with the simple power of his voice."

A chill rippled down my arms, but I kept my face impassive.

Daedra reached once more for her mug, gripping it with white knuckles. "My father was a good man, and the reason I fight and serve you today," she said steadily, meeting my eyes again. She didn't shed a tear, didn't abandon her stoic expression and disciplined posture, and yet I could hear the raw agony in the rhythm of her words.

There was a haunting melody to grief, one that no one else understood unless they'd experienced it too. And unfortunately, within her own story of loss, I could hear my own, echoing endlessly in my ears. It sounded like loneliness and emptiness and bitter tears, like the absence of my mother's voice and laughter. It sounded like Forwyn cries of victory, of Elder Ettonou's jeering voice announcing my mother's death.

"He was strong and brave, but also kind and gentle," Daedra went on. "He served the Giver of Life faithfully, and even bore the storytellers' gift." She blinked, though her eyes remained dry. "I know it was never as revered as the war or courage gifts and their power, but as a child…it was…he was magical."

My smile was brittle. Though Mother hadn't been supernaturally gifted in storytelling, in a way that apparently made the stories seem to come alive to the listeners, she had done it well for me just the same. A childhood memory of her snuggled against me, recounting a tale about dragons, made my chest ache. Even not long before she'd died, when I was nearly a woman and much too old for bedtime stories, she'd still come to my bedchamber each night to talk about our days and even share a story.

Finally, I took a long sip of my tea, steeling myself. "I've kept the prisoners alive because I have use of them," I announced, keeping my voice even. I would give nothing away.

Daedra stiffened, unable to fully conceal her anger. "Your Majesty…he's a murderer. He slew Corvath right before our eyes…"

"In a fight to the death that I ordered," I cut in.

I set my jaw. Despite the ache pulsing in my chest, I knew I couldn't blame Kovi for any of the kills he'd made. He'd only done what I would have if I'd been fighting for my own people under similar circumstances. And his power to command was no more chilling than mine.

Daedra swallowed, clearly trying to get her emotions under control. She didn't dare disrespect or defy me…not openly, at least.

"I'm sorry, Daedra," I added, allowing a hint of gentleness to leak into my words. "We've all experienced loss at the hands of the Forwyn. They've stolen so much more from us than just my throne or our way of life." I pressed my lips together firmly. "But this man is currently more useful to our cause as a living pawn than a corpse. You have to trust me."

Slowly, Daedra extended her hands, palms up, across the table, and then dipped her head in a show of submission. "I will trust you, Your Majesty," she muttered.

I nodded curtly, able to see she was eager to go and leave this farce of a breakfast behind. Perhaps, like me, she didn't have much of an appetite left. "You are dismissed."

When she exited the tent, I leaned back, pressing a hand to my temple and squeezing my eyes shut. Somewhere along the way, maybe when he'd saved my life or comforted me when I'd wept or held me when we'd danced, I'd started to forget exactly who Kovi was. This conversation, in which my feelings had all too readily defended him, made that much very clear.

I stared blankly at my food, suddenly unable to eat. My heart thudded dully in my ears. Just the thought of Daedra threatening Kovi's life, or of my army demanding I execute him before their eyes, turned my stomach and left an ache in my chest.

It wasn't just an alliance. It wasn't just attraction. There was something connecting Kovi and me together, something that had begun in the confines of my quarters when we'd only had one another's company. Something that had grown as we'd realized we were, in some ways, startlingly alike.

It was impossible for us to be together—I knew that. But perhaps keeping him alive wasn't as impossible. Because it was painfully obvious to me that a world without him would be dark and dismal and empty.

Something snapped in my chest as I finally recognized the truth. It wasn't simply that I no longer hated Kovi. I *cared* for him.

Zakren and Breyna—soldiers I'd sent ahead to Wynlaen yesterday—returned as we were packing up camp. The frosty air was still permeated by the morning's golden light as they rode up to where I tended to Ryke. When I turned, I could see even the large, muscular Zakren shifted uneasily astride his mount as he studied the dragon. Neither led their horses too close.

I didn't bother to repress my smile as I scanned the third horse Breyna led behind her. On it, a bound and gagged rider watched me with wide green eyes, her raven hair a wild tangle about her soft face.

I'd sent my soldiers into Wynlaen in the night, ordering them to overtake one of the Teramese I knew would be on watch. Someone I could use as leverage.

"I see your mission was successful," I said, still running a hand along Ryke's scales, relishing his warmth and the way it staved off the chill I felt. A chill that seemed to run bone deep.

Ryke leaned forward, nuzzling against my palm.

Breyna nodded sharply, the ghost of a smile darting across her face before she noticed the plumes of smoke curling from Ryke's nostrils.

"Perfect," I said. "Leave her to me and go help pack up camp. We'll leave by noon."

It was clear by the way the captive woman attempted to shy away from me that my reputation had spread far even among the Teramese. She shuddered when my hand drew near, as if she thought I'd send my soldiers through all the trouble of quietly retrieving her only to execute her so unceremoniously now.

"Oh, don't be afraid," I said, rolling my eyes. "I'm not going to kill you unless I have to." I smiled slowly. "But don't even think about escaping, unless you want my dragon to eat you. Follow me."

Her bronze complexion appeared a shade paler as she jerked her head toward Ryke. At that moment, with his contented rumbling and snorting as he curled up to take a nap, he didn't look particularly terrifying, but apparently dragons didn't need to bare their teeth to scare the life out of both my prisoner and my soldiers.

I turned impatiently, striding toward the supply tent where Kovi and the Teramese soldier were imprisoned. The woman stomped and mumbled in Teramese as she trailed after me, though only her hands were bound in front of her. She was a soldier—it seemed Teramyl was full of nothing but soldiers with the sheer number that had invaded my homeland—but she'd probably never expected to be captured in such an undignified manner.

Biting back my victorious grin, I opened the tent entrance with a flourish and swept inside. Kovi and Vander had their hands bound behind them, each tied to the tent pole. From here, I faced Kovi, who lifted his chin to meet my gaze. His expression was guarded, giving nothing away, but I knew he couldn't—not with our Teramese audience.

I led the woman around the pole, toward Vander. "I've come to show you my latest prisoner, taken from the town she helped conquer," I said, gesturing behind me. "I think you know her."

Satisfaction thrummed in my chest when Vander's eyes widened. My power hadn't failed me. I'd managed to pluck a fear from the man's mind without even coming near him the day before. With concentration, I'd seen a mental image of the woman he cared and worried for—a woman marching on Wynlaen itself. His deepest fears involve her suffering or dying, fears I could now capitalize on.

"You *monster*," Vander spat.

The woman dropped to her knees, her words an incoherent garble as she tried to speak through her gag.

Vander turned frantically to her. "Tayla. It'll be all right. I'll get us out of this mess. We'll be all right."

"Yes," I agreed smoothly. "You'll both be all right. If you do as I say." I reached out and seized Tayla's arm, eliciting a startled gasp. She writhed and struggled against me, but I held firm. Perhaps it was true that Alrenians tended to be stronger than other races. Or maybe my strength came from Nesrelle's unnatural power flowing through my veins.

Effortlessly, I yanked her to her feet and dragged her toward the tent entrance. She growled and thrashed, crying out through her gag in muffled words for the man she loved.

"I'll kill you!" Vander shouted, tugging fruitlessly against his own binds.

"No." My voice was sharp, ringing out loudly in the small space. Both Tayla and Vander froze at my words, listening intently. "You'll fight for me, Vander. You'll join my ranks of soldiers and use your wind magic to help us, or Tayla dies." I waited a beat, letting my words sink in. I didn't need to see Vander's face to know when he resigned himself to his fate, his shoulders slumping in defeat.

Across from me, Kovi's face was inscrutable, his dark, gold-flecked eyes intent. He'd known I would use Vander, and I believed the soldier in him would approve, but would the part of him who longed for mercy approve also? Everything in me wanted to go to him, to ensure he didn't hate me, that he wasn't disappointed in me for the times I had to be cruel for the sake of my people. To reassure myself that he understood that sometimes, I had to be a solider too, just like him, and set aside any inclinations toward mercy. But those thoughts were folly. Alrenor needed me to be strong, not a silly, sentimental girl.

"Understand?" I demanded of Vander.

His words sounded strangled, hopeless. "I understand."

The sky was a cloudless blue as we set forth, a long line of impatient horses and eager soldiers cutting a path through the grass toward the mountain pass. I'd let Ryke soar alone overhead, where he swooped and swirled, his great wings thundering like a herald for a storm. His body cast a huge shadow across the army, half of us engulfed in daylight and the other half shrouded in darkness.

I rode near the front of the line, Kovi and Vander flanking me on geldings I'd insisted we offer them. Though I'd received a few dark looks, when I'd proclaimed the two would fight for us, my soldiers had relented. Tayla was still bound, riding behind Zakren on his horse just a short distance behind, as a constant reminder for Vander of what the cost of his disobedience would be.

On a mare nearby, Daedra shot Kovi a tense look, her hand wandering toward her sword hilt.

For our people, I mouthed, my eyes cutting toward hers sharply, trapping her in my gaze.

She swallowed visibly and nodded, returning her hand to the reins.

The ranks of my army trotted their mounts and marched their boots in a steady beat, pulsing with the rhythm of Ryke's wings. As the sun continued to climb, we wound along the narrow path down the mountain. Our breath fogged before us, but I didn't notice the chill. With the approach of battle, fire burned through my veins. All I could think of was my people, trapped in a town full of Teramese soldiers.

When we'd left the mountains and I spotted the dark smudge that was Wynlaen on the distant horizon, the sun was already sinking in the west, staining the sky a deep orange. Riding out before my army, I wheeled my horse around in the grass to face them. Men and women stared back at me, jaws set with determination, eyes glinting with eagerness. Their dark leathers stood out starkly in the dying light, while my dragon scale suit flashed a bright emerald. Wind tugged at my hair, pulling strands loose from my braid.

"Today," I announced, my voice loud and clear as a bell despite the wind whistling in my ears, "we take back Wynlaen. We show our people that none will be forgotten or abandoned. We show them that their empress is here, to reclaim her throne and restore our empire to its former glory!"

Cheers erupted from my soldiers, who shot fists into the air and brandished swords.

Smiling sharply, I gave my last command: "Annihilate our enemies. Show them how fearless and ruthless Alrenor truly is!"

Amid the shouts of *Avenge the empire!* and other battle cries, my army surged forward, following my lead.

Without even turning my head, I sensed the moment Kovi's horse pulled up alongside mine. As before, he maintained a tense silence, unwilling to let my soldiers know that he was anything but a prisoner.

I shot him a quick look. "Stay close to me," I muttered, my voice lost in the pounding of horse hooves and Ryke's flight.

But as I'd hoped, he had read my lips. Kovi gave a curt nod before flicking his eyes back toward Wynlaen.

The Teramese didn't stand a chance as we rushed toward them. Following my earlier orders, Ryke didn't unleash a blast of fire on the town, but toward the tents set up on its outskirts. He opened his maw, revealing his gleaming fangs, and belched a ball of fire that utterly consumed canvas and human and beast. Screams erupted as the soldiers attempted to save one another or flee.

My army and I didn't have to fear the flames. Without missing a beat, I dismounted and charged directly through the fire, the tongues of heat licking at my armor, my face, my hair—but never touching, never burning. It was kept at bay by an invisible force that didn't even let me feel the heat as anything more than a comfortable warmth against my skin.

Nearby, Kovi was running, weaving around the roaring wall of fire, darting through the camp and swinging his blade. Though he'd explained he could use magic to protect himself from the searing heat, my pulse thundered as I watched him. I picked up my pace and followed, unwilling to lose sight of him, trusting my fellow soldiers would keep watch on Vander.

The world dissolved into nothing but raging tongues of flame. Screams of agony and terror rang out over the low rumble of fire. Adrenaline pumped through my veins as I dodged charred corpses and sucked down an acrid lungful of smoke, leaving my chest burning and my throat feeling scorched. It didn't seem to hurt me, but my body wasn't entirely immune to it, either, unlike the fire itself.

Through stinging, blurred vision, I noticed the lurking shadow just before it unleashed an arrow. It slammed into my shoulder, glancing off my dragon scales, but striking with a force that bruised.

Dropping his bow, the Teramese soldier was already attacking before I even had a chance to draw my sword. Easily twice my size, he towered over me as he lunged, slamming me to the ground. The air rushed from my chest and my lungs seized, gasping for air that wouldn't come. His bronzed face was painted in black designs meant to intimidate and call upon the help of his gods. Leering at me, he raised his sword, and I realized with a cold wash of horror that my arms were trapped under the weight of his body. I was pinned, defenseless, doomed to die a dishonorable, pathetic death.

Fury ignited in my heart. *I won't go this way.*

I called upon all the unnatural power Nesrelle had gifted to my army and me. I could feel it coursing through my veins like a consuming shadow, dark and hot and full of intoxicating strength. The man's blade flashed red in the flames as he lifted it over my neck, prepared to swing it down and sever my head from my body.

But I was too powerful.

Kill him, Nesrelle's voice commanded in my ears, and I happily obliged.

With a cry, I wrenched my right arm free and slammed it against the soldier's chest. Even through my armored gloves, my curse couldn't be stopped. This man was a threat, was guilty of shedding the blood of my people. Of storming into their homes and businesses, and then taking everything from them. Livelihood. Freedom. Loved ones.

And I was here to be their bloody revenge.

Silver eyes widening, the man froze before he could swing his weapon. I gazed into his face, watching as his shock melted into agony. He opened his mouth and shrieked as the curse consumed his skin beneath his dark uniform. I couldn't see it, not at first, not until it rose up his neck, spreading like a black stain from his throat to his face. It was a living shadow, rending flesh from bone until he was a bloody mess. Until he'd stopped screaming and collapsed, dropping his sword to the ground.

Until, with shaking, blood-stained hands, I was shoving nothing but a disfigured, unrecognizable corpse off my body.

For one weak instant, bile coated my tongue and my stomach lurched. But I would not be consumed by my horror or my fear of this curse I carried, not this time. This time, I would embrace it. I would be the monster my people needed.

I ripped my gaze away from my kill. Rising, I drew my sword and sprinted into the camp, seeking any living enemies, prepared to annihilate every last one of them.

CHAPTER TWENTY-SIX

Kovi

I'D DIED A DOZEN TIMES over. I'd felt the bitterest pangs of regret, the sharpest edges of anger and despair, and the coldest chills of paralyzing fear. I was intimately acquainted with death, and the many ways in which people faced it.

Perhaps that was why the idea of facing my own death held no fear over me. Despite the choking smoke that should have scorched my lungs and the leaping flames that threatened my skin, Elhani's magic protected me. Even though all it could take was a single instant in which I lost my focus, I wasn't afraid of rushing toward this possible death. Whether I lived or died, I would take some of my enemies with me, and that would protect my people. It was my only purpose, and—perhaps—my only redemption for the ugly atrocities I'd committed by controlling and killing my opponents in cold blood.

But you'd leave Jalie behind. The thought seared hotter than the flames enveloping me. I didn't only want to live for myself or for my people now. I wanted to live for her. As impossible of a dream as it was…I wanted to survive long enough to experience a future with her in it.

As sunset deepened to night, the scent of burning canvas, wood, and bodies churned sickeningly through the air, part of an onslaught against the senses that made it difficult to concentrate. Elhani's song was gentle, a quiet chorus amidst the din of death. As well as I'd been trained and disciplined to focus in battle, the blinding brightness of dragon fire, the overpowering smells, and the constant roar of the flames were enough to almost drown out all conscious thought. Added to that were the wails and screams of the Teramese either dying or fighting to survive.

But I was stubborn. I clung to my magic, clung to survival.

This is hell, I thought darkly, *but for killing and threatening our people, they deserve it.*

Ducking my head low, I gasped for the clearest air I could find, blinking back the sting of smoke. The heat made rivulets of sweat snake down my temples toward my eyes as I wove a precarious path through what was left of the Teramese camp. It was clear from the flashes of fleeing shapes in the chaos that the surviving soldiers were charging toward Wynlaen, hoping to find sanctuary within its streets. It wasn't a bad plan. Jalie wouldn't let her dragon burn down a town with her own people in it.

I gave chase. The walls of this town were insignificant after living my life behind the towering partitions enveloping Inalgoth, and their gates seemed flimsy. Other Teramese occupants had thrown them wide to give entrance to the soldiers fleeing camp, making my own passage easy.

Within moments, I was racing down the main street, only a few paces behind the rearmost soldier. Silent buildings stood sentinel on either side of the otherwise empty road. The Alrenian citizens and their Forwyn slaves would be hiding from the Teramese occupants anyway,

I reasoned. But where were the other Teramese?

A prickle of foreboding jolted up my spine. My mind raced as the soldier just in front of me glanced back over his shoulder and sneered, halting to spin on me and draw his sword. I didn't hesitate, didn't lose stride.

If I were overtaking a town, I thought, even as my eyes scanned the man before me, searching for an opening in his defenses, *I would keep a force within its limits. Soldiers to enforce my takeover and keep watch over the citizens so they couldn't revolt behind my back.*

I was upon the soldier. Our swords slammed together, steel scraping against steel. Then I was engaged in the dance of battle once more, effortless and swift, beautiful and terrible: Sidestep. Swing. Jab. Parry. Duck and turn. Feint and land the killing blow.

They're here, waiting. The realization struck me as I watched my opponent collapse lifelessly at my feet, his body stirring up dust. Two more Teramese were already turning around from their retreat to attack me, their eyes flashing with rage and bloodlust at the sight of my dripping blade. Their dark war paint contrasted sharply against their bronze skin.

For the briefest second, I allowed my eyes to flick toward the buildings surrounding me again. Empty, darkened windows. Drawn shutters and curtains. Closed businesses, quiet homes. If smoke curled from any of the chimneys, it would be impossible to tell when an entire cloud of smoke was pouring over the city, gathering like an ominous portent and choking out the dying sunlight.

Everything appeared as if Wynlaen was a sleeping, harmless town, unprepared for our attack. But we hadn't made our presence a secret. The Teramese hadn't been foolish in their invasion, and I didn't think they would be now. There would have been soldiers stationed on the walls as lookouts, men and women who would have seen our approaching army. They would have heard the thunderous beat of Ryke's wings. And they certainly would have seen Jalie scouting Wynlaen on her dragon in the days leading up to our attack.

Something is wrong, I thought again. Dread enveloped me.

The Teramese soldiers struck at the same time, and I launched into a flurry of attacks, all so familiar I could almost have executed them in my sleep. My reflexes were sharp and quick, despite the fact that my mind was elsewhere. It was easy. Too easy.

Wrong.

I blinked, jumping back before I plunged my sword into the man before me. My hand shook as I scanned him again, taking in his dark Teramese uniform. His thick black hair and blue eyes so vivid they shone, cat-like, in the shadows, reflecting the fiery inferno behind me.

But then—something flickered, as if my eyes were failing me or they were watering again, skewing my vision. His hair changed to closely shorn curls. His eyes darkened. The war paint vanished, and his skin...

No. Horror crawled up my spine. *Impossible.*

I dropped my sword with a clatter. "You're Forwyn!" I choked out, my eyes straying back to the corpse I'd left in an expanding pool of blood.

Forwyn.

The man in front of me stepped back, wide-eyed and horrified. He blinked dazedly, glancing first at the woman beside him and then back at me. As if the power of the illusion had shattered at my declaration, it was clear now that they both were Forwyn, with smooth, dark skin and the simple, tattered clothing of slaves.

Revulsion shuddered through me.

"You're Forwyn too." The man frowned and ran a hand across his eyes, drawing a shuddering breath before launching into a quick explanation in our native tongue. "We…I thought you were Alrenian." His eyes darted toward the flaming camp and more dread crashed into me. "The Teramese forced us to camp outside Wynlaen. They used us as bait."

"How?" I demanded. "How could they deceive us like this? Make us…see a lie?"

The woman blinked back tears as she took in the horrific sight of the burning camp. *We'd commanded a dragon to burn Forwyn.* The realization made me sick.

"I don't know," she breathed. "They have unnatural powers."

"So do we. We have Elhani's magic."

Before we could say more, the Alrenian army came charging through the streets, some pouring through the open gate nearby, their silhouettes backlit by the flames, and the rest entering from the opposite end of the town. They converged in a raging mass, many with tongues of flame licking at them, never hurting or burning them, but alighting them in an eerie, unnatural way.

The woman's eyes widened. "Alrenian *hilvoku*," she spat, lifting her blade to meet them.

"No!" I protested, but my words were lost in the chaos. Steel shrieked against steel. Cries of rage and agony tore through the air. Smoke curled and thickened, from the approaching dragon fire and the flames more and more Alrenians wore like armor and wielded as a weapon. The world reeked of fire and blood, sweat and ash.

Either fueled by their longstanding animosity or deceived by the same trick I was, Alrenians and Forwyn alike cut each other down viciously. Everything gave way to the din and stench of war. Bodies began to pile up, notably in favor of the Alrenians, who not only overpowered the Forwyn with their new powers, but also greatly outnumbered them.

All the while, there were no Teramese soldiers to be seen.

A figure stepped from the narrow, shadowed space between two buildings, and I turned, fully prepared to defend myself against a Teramese ambush. But instead, I found myself staring at…Nesrelle. Clothed in a long black dress that trailed the ground behind her, she looked shockingly out of place on the battle scene. Her skin was smooth and pale as moonlight, a stark contrast with her blood-red curls and lips. Her eyes were clear and bright as stars, and the freckles scattered across her cheeks made her appear deceptively young and innocent.

She leaned casually against one of the buildings and began peeling an orange. As if the chaos around her was mundane, and all she cared about was sating her hunger.

I gritted my teeth in rage. Her beauty was a mockery of everything sacred and pure in Elhani's creation. Though my mind warned me it was foolish to try to attack an Immortal, I tightened my grasp on my sword and lunged toward her anyway.

"What are you doing here?" I demanded, pressing the point of my blade against her throat.

Nesrelle dropped her orange and it rolled down the alley. She scowled at it for a moment before lifting her face and offering me a serene smile. "I've come to watch the show," she said in her breathy voice, lifting an elegant hand to gesture at the violence behind me. It was strange, how a voice could sound so gentle and soothing and yet make me feel like a thousand insects were crawling across my skin.

"Where are the Teramese?"

Her smile widened. "I made them a deal. As you must have already noticed, when you discovered their trick of sending Forwyn slaves to the outskirts of the city. Clever of them, to use them as pawns."

I reined in my anger in favor of getting answers. "I thought you were helping the Alrenians."

This time, she smirked outright. "Foolish little mortal. You think I've chosen a side amongst you pathetic humans? You're all pawns to me. Instruments to stir up chaos. I hate all of you equally." Her eyes seemed to darken, until they looked like deep pools leading to nothingness. "I'm here to watch you destroy one another."

A chill coursed through me and I let out an animal cry, shoving the point of my blade home. I'd cut her head from her body and see if she truly was immortal.

I blinked and somehow, she was stepping through my blade, like she was nothing but mist and the sword could not cut her. But when she slammed her hand on my arm, clamping her fingers around me like a vise, I could feel the solid weight of each finger. I could sense the icy cold she radiated.

Pain spasmed through every muscle in my body, so intense I couldn't even cry out. My sword dropped from my grip, thudding to the dirt street. I gasped, my mind blank with the agony shooting through me. And then…the pain vanished. I opened my eyes, and Nesrelle was gone, as is she'd never been there.

Find Jalie, I thought desperately.

I seized my weapon and scanned the battle. My eyes snagged on Ryke as he circled overhead, awaiting his chance to strike. Jalie wouldn't let him launch any more fire at the town, I knew, but there was plenty a dragon could do with its teeth and claws and mighty size. Tracking the area on which he seemed to be focused, I squeezed my sword hilt and sprinted in that direction, dodging strikes from hostile Alrenians and confused Forwyn alike.

Somehow, I'd missed Jalie's entrance into the town, but when I rounded the corner to face another street, she was impossible to overlook now. In her shimmering green dragon scale armor, with her pale hair and freckled golden skin, she was a sight to behold. Everything about her gleamed in the night's gathering shadows, like a small sun in the darkness. Though at first glance she held the appearance of a benevolent Immortal—like one of the guidespirits—she was anything but. She fought fiercely, her curved Alrenian blade spraying blood as it arced through the air. Her blue eyes shone like gems, glowing with rage and determination. Gore darkened her armor.

As I watched, she cut down an attacking Forwyn and lifted her eyes to meet mine. Horror curdled in my gut.

But…did she break our alliance, or is she deceived?

"Jalie!" I cried, racing toward her as another soldier leapt for her. I gasped in a breath of smoke and coughed, my lungs screaming in protest. This street was further from the thickest of the flame and ash, but still quickly being consumed by the cloud crawling over the city.

She ducked and kicked, knocking the man back. The Forwyn man reoriented himself and charged again.

"Jalie!" I tried again, my voice hoarse. "It's a trick!"

Brow furrowed in concentration, she stabbed for the man, who danced away just in time.

I pulled up mere feet from them, catching my breath. "He's not Teramese."

She and the man froze at the same instant, eyeing me warily. Out of the corners of their eyes, I could tell they were watching one another too, prepared to defend if one or the other pounced during my distraction.

"What are you trying to do?" Jalie snarled. "Do you want…" But then her words trailed off, at the very same moment that the man's eyes widened as he fully took in my appearance, perhaps seeing what I truly looked like for the first time.

"You're not Alrenian?" he breathed, rich brown eyes shining with something like relief. He started to relax his grip on his sword, before his eyes flicked toward Jalie and his expression hardened. "But *she* is."

Jalie stood still as a statue, her skin looking pale. Blinking rapidly, she brushed a gloved hand across her face, as if she could clear her vision. Her eyes darted to the bodies surrounding her—all Forwyn. Body trembling, she turned to me, her expression one of regret. "I—I'm sorry," she breathed. I was shocked to see tears sparkling in her eyes. "I thought they were Teramese. I thought they all were…" She dropped her arm, letting her blade hang limply by her side.

For a moment, I stood speechless, utterly baffled. Jalie hated the Forwyn, so surely she wasn't mourning their deaths. Perhaps she feared breaking our alliance too soon? But when I scanned the bodies again, I noticed a few Alrenian corpses strewn across the street as well. Disgust pinched my heart. Nesrelle was ruthless.

I opened my mouth to warn Jalie about the Immortal's deception, but that was when I sensed the oncoming attack. Countless black-clad soldiers, their faces smeared with dark warpaint to blend in with the night, shuffled almost soundlessly from every building, flooding the streets. Surrounding us.

The Teramese ambush had begun.

Soldiers swarmed the street, stabbing unsuspecting Forwyn in the back without hesitation, without mercy. Smoke swirled thickly about them, but the Teramese wore black scarves bound tightly over their mouths and noses, as if they'd prepared to face a dragon.

Which, of course, they had. While Jalie and her Alrenian army had expected the Teramese to flee, surrender, or be massacred, the Teramese had been planning all along to lure us in for their own slaughter.

"Watch out!" I shouted as a Teramese woman lunged for Jalie.

The soldier's movements were swift and graceful, almost like those of a dancer, as she sprinted forward and swung her blade.

Jalie ducked and spun in one smooth motion, slamming her gloved hand against the woman's arm. It took half a second for the woman's screams to pierce the air as she dropped her sword. Instantly, the woman's face was covered in blackened, dying skin. It rapidly devolved, turning into a bloody mess that hardly resembled a person at all as the woman's shriek cut short and she dropped lifelessly to the street.

Turning, Jalie's eyes met mine. Hers were wide, as if she were still a little shocked by her own abilities. But there was also a hard set to her mouth, one that told me she wouldn't hesitate to use the curse against the Teramese, again and again.

I clenched my jaw, refusing to be disgusted. Jalie's power was no more revolting than mine, and I'd already vowed to use it against these cruel people.

And I wasn't sorry. I couldn't be, not when I thought of their deal with Nesrelle and their cruel trickery. The burning bodies of Forwyn slaves sent as sacrifices. Forwyn I'd unwittingly cut down myself.

Flames from the outer campground licked closer and closer to the town, and when I took in the billowing clouds of smoke overhead and the dancing, eerie red light, I smiled grimly. The Teramese deserved this hell.

I stepped forward, grasping Jalie's arm to spin her so we were back-to-back. "We're not leaving until we kill every last one of these murderers," I promised. "They're not touching another one of our people again."

As the Teramese advanced on us, bloodied from killing both the innocent people of Wynlaen and Jalie's army, Jalie and I held them back effortlessly. Despite the skill and cunning our enemies possessed, they were no match for us. Not with Jalie's powers, which either dropped them screaming with a touch, or allowed her to pry into their deepest fears, as Daedra had done to me.

Somehow, that power was magnified for Jalie, because without even nearing them, she could send the soldiers into a panic. Wide-eyed and sweat-sheened, they'd throw their swords with a shout and curl up into the fetal position, weeping like children. Others turned on their comrades, running them straight through.

I'd never seen anything like it, and it sent fear through me when I realized those were the sorts of powers the Alrenians could also use against my own people.

However, the Teramese had the advantage of surprise. Many Alrenians had been struck down in the beginning, unaware of the enemies sneaking up behind them and slitting their throats. Now, it felt as if Jalie and I were battling atop a horrifyingly increasing mound of bodies, full of allies and enemies alike, trying to fend off a never-ceasing horde of Teramese soldiers.

"Ryke!" Jalie screamed into the smoky air, her voice hoarse. Her dragon scale armor appeared almost black, streaked with blood and ash. The dragon had circled to attack soldiers in another part of the town, and apparently didn't hear her. His bulky form had long ago vanished in the swirling sky. "Ryke!"

As I parried a strike and cut down another Teramese man before he could behead me, I scanned the street, eyes skimming over the blood and death and chaos. My chest burned and my eyes ached with the smoke swirling through the air, and all the while, I could see the flames licking ever closer. The dragon fire was hot and furious enough to burn along the dirt street leading into the town, even with little more than a few weeds to fuel it. Already it had touched the first wooden structures in Wynlaen—the gatehouses—and was growing in intensity.

Unless I wanted to suffocate in the wave of smoke rolling toward us, I would soon have to flee. I didn't have enough energy to call on Elhani's magic to protect me from the flames again for long.

But when I turned back to the fighting closer at hand, I caught a glimpse of Vander through the haze. He was flanked by some of Jalie's chief officers, whose burning, gold-flecked eyes found me amidst the throng immediately. Daedra was fairly dripping with blood, her face pulled back in a ruthless snarl. She studied me with outright contempt before her gaze turned on Jalie and she frowned.

My stomach lurched. I hoped Daedra and the other Alrenians assumed Jalie's close proximity to me in the battle meant she refused to let her prisoner out of her sight, and that she needed to be near to force me to fight for her. But Daedra's piercing stare suggested other suspicions.

As the Teramese charged for the newcomers, Vander lifted his arms. A roaring whoosh filled the air, and a fresh breeze coursed through the street, brushing away the stench of smoke and blood, death and dirt, steel and sweat. Tendrils of smoke blasted back toward the wall of fire, where it lingered like an ominous black cloud, held back by Vander's power and sheer force of will.

I couldn't help the sting of compassion I felt toward the man, even though he belonged to the enemy. It was a terrible thing to be someone's pawn in their bloody game. Although I'd used plenty of people—or rather, because of that fact—I knew exactly how it felt. He looked weary and sad, but his jaw was set in a hardened line, determined to protect the woman he loved. His dark hair was plastered to his face with sweat, his bronzed complexion paler than usual with his weariness. Blood darkened his black uniform even further.

Before the Teramese could attack him or his Alrenian

companions, they halted in their tracks with the force of another gust of wind, so supernaturally powerful it threw them back several feet.

Vander's eyes, like those of the Alrenian officers, darted to mine and then over to Jalie. His expression was unfathomable.

If the two of you ever escape, and he knows you made an alliance with Jalie, your agreement with the Xalenoses is over. They'll murder Father and the other Forwyn in the palace.

My heart thundered in my ears and for a horrible instant, I wondered if I'd made the wrong choice by allying with her.

Dozens of Teramese soldiers pressed toward Jalie and me, cutting us off from our allies. Behind me, Jalie was staggering on her feet, weary after using her power for so long. I glanced over my shoulder to see that the shadows that had been dancing around her all this time had disappeared. Were her abilities gone? Was she too exhausted to use them?

"Ryke!" she shouted again, swinging her blade to meet an onslaught from two soldiers at once.

At last, the thundering beat of dragon wings echoed through the air, and a huge form dove through the smoke clouds hovering overhead. Two Teramese soldiers dropped from Ryke's clawed feet, screaming and kicking in vain before pummeling to the street, not far from where Jalie and I fought. Something else fell afterward—it glinted pearlescent in the darkness and stopped at Jalie's feet. I saw her kneel to pick it up, tucking it away somewhere in her armor.

"*Rekkenah!*" she commanded in Alrenian. Attack. Clearly, Jalie was desperate to use a blast of dragon fire within the town.

The burst of flames came mere seconds later, consuming a whole line of charging Teramese soldiers in a flaming inferno. But...it was close. Too close. The heat hurled toward us, the fire extending devouring red claws to snag us in its grip. There was no time to run, barely even time to register that this was how I would die, by dragon fire. I braced myself for the end. I couldn't call on Elhani's magic this time.

Jalie must have realized this the moment I did. She spun and threw herself at me so forcefully we collapsed in the dirt, her arms wrapped around me. Her body hovered protectively over mine. Somewhere between the roaring of the fire and the fierce heat threatening overhead, I became aware of how she trembled. She was shouting something. There was a rush of wind answering the flames, a blessedly cool relief to the scorching heat and choking smoke.

When she pulled back from me, a few fingers of orange flame clung harmlessly to her, dancing across her armor and through her hair. They dispersed into the air as I watched, winking out and leaving her untouched.

And somehow, I was the same. Unharmed by the flame or the smoke that had miraculously disappeared, leaving only Alrenian soldiers, charred enemy bodies, and horrified Teramese survivors in its wake. Vander must have helped with his magic, but it was Jalie who had used her power, her new resistance to fire, to save my life.

"You…thank you," I murmured.

She was still so close I could feel her breath on my face. Her eyes sparkled with tears. Rather than hardening her expression or making some excuse for her actions—"I'm keeping you alive as long as you're useful to my people"—she drew in a shuddering breath and reached out, cupping my face in her gloved hands. The dragon scales were cool and smooth against my skin.

"I can't lose you," she confessed, her tone utterly vulnerable and broken.

There was something both freeing and burdening in her admission. I could feel the emotion rushing through her, how much she cared for me. It was the best and worst thing I could have ever imagined happening between us, ever since I'd been assigned to guard her.

I covered her hand with my own. "You won't," I said, a promise we both knew I was incapable of guaranteeing. But the ghost of a smile flitted across her face, telling me she knew what I meant.

As if recalling herself, Jalie pulled back quickly and leapt to her feet, putting distance between us.

I glanced toward the Alrenians, who were pressing further into the street, more and more joining us to fend off the remaining Teramese. It wasn't likely they'd overheard our exchange, but it was impossible they'd all missed the fact that she'd saved my life.

A hard knot of foreboding grew in my chest.

"Come," Jalie said, her eyes full of fire, her mouth a firm line.

There was no sign of doubt or fear in her tone. She was once again the removed empress, untouchable as the dragon fire she commanded. "We have a battle to win."

CHAPTER TWENTY-SEVEN

Jalie

IT BECAME CLEAR DURING THE battle that my powers—and those of my soldiers around me—were changing. Strength burned through me, fueling me with courage and a sense of invincibility. As I cut enemy after enemy down, gratefully drinking in the fresh air Vander continuously worked to bring sweeping through our battlefield, I started to grow numb to the death cries, to the blood dripping from my blade, to the lifeless eyes staring at me from the street.

For killing and threatening my people, you will die.

It was simple to peer into my enemies' minds and, seemingly instinctually, know their deepest fears. But my new power was my ability to convince them their horrors were coming to life.

I spun toward a Teramese man charging me, and with a mere thought I reduced him to terrified screams as I made him think spiders were creeping along his skin, biting and burrowing. He dropped his weapon and clawed at his own flesh, drawing blood. Weeping. Shouting.

A woman swung her sword to attack, and I fooled her into believing a gaping hole had opened in the earth, and she was teetering over its edge, falling into its endless dark depths. She shrieked, kicking and clawing at the air as if she actually were plunging to her death.

Make them all suffer, Nesrelle whispered, sounding as if she were standing just behind me. As if she were always with me.

And I didn't regret it.

But as the battle raged on, I began growing weary. My strength faltered and my power diminished, like I was trying to dip from a well that was running dry. Apparently even the supernatural had its limits. I would need time and rest to replenish, both luxuries I didn't have.

I didn't fear losing—no, as my men and women flooded into the street from other areas of the city, coated in the blood of our enemies, it was clear we still outnumbered the Teramese. Despite their unnatural disguise I didn't understand, these foreign soldiers were no match to our fierce resolve, or the abilities Nesrelle had granted us.

The trouble was that the Teramese were focusing their efforts on Kovi and me, apparently intent on killing the Alrenian empress. My dragon scale armor, even darkened with ash and blood, gleamed like a beacon guiding my enemies toward their target.

Muscles spasming with weariness, I whirled toward another enemy. "Kovi!" I shouted.

He knew immediately what I needed. Withdrawing his sword from a soldier's chest, he turned, eyes dark and intent. There was a cold fury on his face, one that had once been directed toward me.

Not now. Now, with the dregs of my power I could detect the carefully buried fear pulsing within him, clear as the anger written across his face. *He fears losing* me. The realization rammed into my heart. He feared losing me more than he feared using his magic. More than he feared perhaps…anything else.

Then Kovi spoke, his voice a deep, commanding shout.

"Stop! Don't move again." There was no mercy in those words, none of the gentleness I'd witnessed within him in his squared jaw and burning gaze.

My enemy faltered, and I lunged. While my new powers had been nearly depleted, my curse didn't seem to fade as easily. Maybe it was something that would never diminish with use. Instead, the more I used it, the more it seemed to grow in strength.

The intoxicating feeling sweeping through me almost drowned out the man's screams as he collapsed, finally stilling at my feet. Blood coated my gloves, dripped to the dirt street, and splattered against my boots.

None of the charging Teramese soldiers stood a chance. Apart, we were forces to be reckoned with, but together, Kovi and I were unstoppable. He could command anyone to pause mid-strike, opening them up for me to end them with my curse. A curse that condemned them all, because they were all guilty of murdering Alrenians.

In the end, the battle left the streets red with blood. Vander swept the smoke and fire northward, where it hungrily licked up the open grassland stretching between Wynlaen and the nearest towns. He collapsed in exhaustion, and I ordered some of my soldiers to shackle and carry him out of the city, all while continuing to keep careful watch over both him and Tayla. He had proved himself far too useful to lose.

I couldn't meet Kovi's eyes as I commanded others to secure him as well and lead him away. I didn't want him harmed, but I feared giving away the feelings tangled inside me, or the secret alliance we had formed.

It took hours of work to gather our dead and heap them into the dragon fire—which still burned us in death, we found—and tend to our injured.

When the first blush of sunlight tinged the eastern horizon, we tossed the final body into the roaring flames, and I cried out to Ryke. He nuzzled against me and I embraced him, whispering words of gratitude. Climbing atop his back, I commanded him to ride toward the coast, a short trip for the dragon. We dipped toward the vast waters of the Great Sea as the sun scattered its brilliant light across the world.

For Ryke, it was easy to fill his mouth with water and quench the angry flames. After a few trips to the sea, he left nothing behind of the fire but charred remains and swirling grey smoke. A fresh morning breeze sent the smoke and ash curling westward, away from Wynlaen. Away from the camp my soldiers were already setting up outside the city.

I dropped from Ryke's back to thunderous cheers from my awaiting soldiers.

When Daedra stepped forward, her face smeared with grime and blood, she offered me a fierce grin. "We did it, empress. We showed those foul traitors no mercy."

I smirked back. "They deserved none."

Zakren approached from my opposite side, appearing positively drunk on our victory. "Together we'll finally avenge this empire and return it to its former glory." He knelt right there in the blackened remains of the grass, palms up in a grand, traditional salute. His grin was almost feral. Others dropped around him, following his example. "We'll reclaim your imperial throne and raise it up higher than it ever stood, all on the corpses of the Teramese and Forwyn."

It was sunset before I had a moment alone in my tent to bathe, thanks to the water grateful Wynlaen citizens drew from their wells and brought to us. After, I changed into a fresh tunic and leggings. My armor I'd given to Zakren to clean and polish, along with my sword. In its place, I strapped a pair of daggers to my belt, along with the claw Ryke had lost amidst the battle.

For a moment, I ran my fingers idly along its smooth surface, contemplating when I might have use of this new weapon. The only thing that could pierce dragon scales were dragon claws and teeth. Otherwise, one would have to target a dragon's soft underbelly, its open mouth—which was usually spewing flames—or its eyes. And the carefully crafted dragon scale armor I wore was nearly as impenetrable as the dragons themselves. Which meant I preferred to have a weapon that could slice through it in my own possession. Plus, I might need to use it against a dragon.

I hated to plan for slaying any dragons, but with the other dragons in Teramese hands, it was likely that my army and I would have to face and kill some of our own. It was a grim thought, but a necessary one.

Weariness tugged at me, tempting me with my cot. Most of my army was settling down for some much-deserved sleep while a few took shifts to keep watch. But I had something I had to do.

No matter what Daedra might say now about the battle, she'd made her doubts about my plans for Kovi plain. And though no one had spoken of it yet, someone could have seen Kovi and me in that one moment in the battle…a moment that now, I wished I could take back. Fear curdled in my stomach. How could I have been so foolish? I could have given away everything.

I strode outside, winding a hasty path toward the supply tent. My soldiers didn't question me when I approached, only nodded and stepped aside to let me enter. Breath caught in my throat, I hesitated before slipping inside, blinking to let my eyes adjust to the darkness. I was relieved to find that both Vander and Tayla were curled up on the ground close together, sound asleep. Kovi alone remained awake and watchful. He gazed at me silently, his face drawn with weariness but his eyes alert.

"Pretend you're frightened when we leave," I whispered as I unlocked the shackles at his wrists with the key I'd demanded of the guard outside.

Kovi stood instantly and seized my waist, drawing me to his chest. I stifled a gasp of surprise, biting hard on my lip. Though he smelled of blood and sweat and smoke, I swore I could still catch a comforting scent beneath it all, one that belonged to him alone. His heart beat a steady, soothing rhythm beneath my ear.

"I just had to do that, once," he murmured against my hair. "I'm glad you're safe."

When he released me, I stepped back reluctantly, my eyes flitting briefly toward Vander and Tayla's forms. "That was risky," I said weakly.

"Worth it." He smirked, showing off that slightly cocky, dimpled grin that had once driven me mad when I'd hated him. Now, it made heat flood my body and settle in my stomach.

You're a fool, I chided myself.

Grasping his wrist, I made a show of dragging him out roughly. Kovi tensed, his hateful glare so convincing that for a moment I almost believed it.

The guards smirked when I led Kovi outside of the tent.

"Time to question him again?" one of the men asked, a nasty glint in his eyes as he laid his hand on his sword hilt. "I'd gladly do the job for you, Your Imperial Majesty. It'll be even more fun now that we can play with fire."

I smiled right back, all teeth and vicious promise. "The pleasure of making him suffer is all mine."

I guided Kovi toward a copse of trees away from camp. In the starlight, the leaves were edged in silver as they rustled in the breeze, whispering like lost ghosts. *Jalie.*

A chill snaked down my neck. *Go away, Mother,* I thought.

We plunged into the copse to enter a clearing large enough for my dragon. Ryke was nestled into a tight coil, his tail curled about his body. His breath was a deep rumble vibrating through his chest as he snored. Smoke rose gently from his nostrils, sending a steady plume into the air. Though dragon smoke was stronger than fire smoke, it left a comforting scent, reminding me of nights cuddled up with Mother near the huge hearth in her quarters, sipping mugs of tea or nibbling on slices of cake. She'd often smelled of dragon smoke.

Before she'd become the ghost that haunted me. Repressing a shudder, I shoved away the memory of the corpse-like spirit that had visited me before.

As soon as we were out of sight behind the trees, I released Kovi and faced him, my shoulders squared.

Despite our mid-battle moment and our earlier embrace—or perhaps because of it—tension thickened the air. Kovi didn't span the distance between us, but I could scarcely bear the intensity in his dark eyes. It looked like affection and desire and hope.

All things I couldn't afford to risk.

I longed to slam the door of my heart, but Kovi kept catching it before it could click shut.

"You have to leave," I blurted out, squeezing my eyes shut. My fingers brushed the hilt of one of my daggers, cool and smooth against my skin.

When I opened my eyes, his gaze was guarded as he watched my hand on my hilt, but his mouth twitched with the ghost of a smile. "Or…what? You're going to kill me at last?"

Rolling my eyes, I swiftly worked to unfasten my dagger from my belt and shove the sheathed blade into his hand. It was of fine workmanship, probably one of the best weapons my army possessed, one that had belonged to their former general. Its gold hilt was laden with a pattern of tiny rubies, likely imported all the way from Brevinn long ago, before the Misrothian barrier had been built and then broken. They formed the shape of a dragon breathing a thick column of fire. Even the sheath was clearly of fine quality, the stitching impeccable, the leather itself supple and strong.

Kovi stared at the dagger, not returning it to me but not fastening it at his waist either. "You want me to run? Is this your way of ending our alliance?" A bitter smile twisted his mouth. "The next time we see one another, we'll be on opposing sides. Is that what you want?"

"You have to leave, or my army will kill you, no matter what I tell them. Some already suspect us, and after what happened at the battle… I don't want any doubts. I can't protect you from all of them, not forever." I drew a deep breath. "And I would *never* hurt you, no matter how we meet again." The promise was out of my mouth before I even had time to consider it.

Silence stretched between us. Ryke shifted in his sleep, but didn't waken. A breeze tugged at the tree branches, sending a few leaves twirling to the ground between us.

Traitor, a voice seemed to hiss in my brain, just loud enough that I could hear it over the pounding of my heart in my ears. It sounded an awful lot like my mother's voice. Ice frosted my heart as I imagined her spirit spyong on Kovi and me.

As if reading my thoughts, Kovi shook his head, just once. "You can't make promises like that." He stepped closer, hovering so near that I longed to reach out and touch him. I fisted my hands at my sides to resist the urge. "What if killing me was the key to saving your people?"

I laughed aloud. "But it's not. You're one of many Forwyn soldiers, and your people elect multiple leaders. I could reclaim my throne and you could survive." My gaze was sharp, assessing him. "But me? I'm the empress. To win Alrenor, your people *have* to kill me."

Kovi scowled, tossing the dagger to the ground and seizing my arms, pulling me gently yet firmly against him. I didn't resist when he cupped my face in his hands, forcing my eyes to meet his.

The ache in my chest was unbearable. I closed my eyes, relishing the sensation of his warm, calloused hands against my cheeks. Soaking in the nearness of him. My breathing hitched.

Kovi's voice dropped, turning low and husky. "I would never hurt you either." He hesitated, searching my eyes. Or perhaps sensing my feelings. A part of me hated that. I had no armor around him, not when he knew exactly how I felt. I was utterly vulnerable. And yet…knowing we shared that connection only made me feel closer to him. He understood the war inside my heart, one that matched his own. He didn't have to guess at the words I was afraid to speak. "I can't lose you, either. I meant what I said before. I'll fight for you. *Always*. Even if you're across enemy lines."

I smiled sadly. "So we're both making promises we can't keep."

Kovi matched my smile as he traced my mouth with his thumb. "Maybe," he said. He slid his hand to my waist while his other tangled in my hair, still loose about my shoulders and damp from my bath. When he leaned forward, I didn't pull away, didn't resist.

I could taste salt and ash on his lips from the battle. It was strange how his mouth was already familiar and yet still foreign. Our first kiss had been so different—a way to try to distract and outsmart one another in a game between enemies. A moment to give in to desire when neither of us had been quite ready to process or accept our growing feelings. And our second kiss had been desperate and passionate, a way to admit what we hadn't said out loud. What I hadn't even allowed myself to confess to myself.

But now…now our kiss *meant* something more. It made every sensation different and new, and far, far sweeter. At first the brush of his lips was a caress, almost hesitant, but when I kissed him back, it built into something needier, more desperate. A goodbye we didn't want to make. A reality we didn't want to face.

Every inch of me burned, and the places his hands touched were hottest of all. The blood in my veins was dragon fire, even while my heart felt an icy dread closing over it.

When we pulled apart at last, Kovi kept his hands on my waist, as if reluctant to let go. He closed his eyes and repressed a groan, though when he opened them, his expression was more playful than frustrated. "Must I go? I could stay here making promises all night." As if to prove his point, he pressed his lips to mine again.

My breath caught and my head whirled, tempting me to drown in the kiss again. But the dread inside me wouldn't dissolve. There was something I had to ask. I needed to hear his answer, even though, deep down, I already knew it. This was a fantasy, not a possibility. Whatever I was feeling…I needed to quench it.

I broke the kiss, but I couldn't tear myself from his hold, even as I spoke the words.

"Would you ever let me sit on my throne?"

Kovi hesitated a beat, his grip on me relaxing. "You hate my people," he said, slowly.

This time, I did wrench away. "See? We have different goals. For ourselves. For Alrenor." I shook my head, blinking against the foolish, weak tears that were threatening, burning my eyes. "We always have. This is…this is madness."

"No," Kovi said firmly, stepping toward me. "I refuse to believe that. We both want our people to be safe. We once hated each other, but now…" He swallowed, not finishing his sentence.

Now I think I love you, I thought. *And I think you feel the same.*

"Your people and mine have a common enemy now," Kovi went on. "If we could convince them to unite against the Teramese, maybe we could build a different world. One where the empire didn't have to be torn in two."

"But you hate Alrenians," I protested, my voice embarrassingly broken-sounding.

"Not all of them," he said softly, shooting me a pointed look. "If there are more like you, willing to stop and get to know us, show us mercy…"

"Of course there are. There have to be."

"…and I could show you that there are more Forwyn like me…"

As his voice trailed off, hopeful, awaiting my response, I sighed. Though I'd tried to avoid considering it, my mind flitted back to that Forwyn woman who'd saved my life at the Autumn Ball. Maybe there *were* more Forwyn like Kovi, willing to choose mercy. Forwyn who would be open to an alliance. "Maybe we could convince our peoples to form a temporary alliance, to expel the Teramese," I agreed at last. "I'm not sure we could hope for much more. I'm not sure *I'm* ready for more," I added, thinking of Kovi's own father and his cruelty.

"But for us," Kovi said quietly, stepping forward and taking my hands. "We can fight for that, to give ourselves a chance? To give both our peoples a chance? Maybe what's best for you and the Alrenians doesn't have to be different from what's best for the Forwyn and me."

Relenting a bit, I smiled, threading my fingers through his.

"Maybe it doesn't," I murmured.

He leaned forward, pressing his forehead to mine, and I breathed deeply, trying to memorize this moment. "We can dare to dream," he said.

"Your only chance for this dream to become true is to survive," I reminded him. "I wish I could send you with a horse and provisions, but…"

"You couldn't keep that a secret from your army," Kovi finished for me. "Don't worry. I'll manage without them. I'm a soldier, remember?" He grinned, though this time, it didn't quite reach his eyes.

"Be safe," I murmured, holding the tears at bay.

Kovi leaned back just enough to twine his fingers through my hair again. "One more goodbye," he pleaded, and I couldn't resist another kiss, warm and intoxicating and full of fragile hope.

When we broke apart, Kovi seized the dagger from the ground and drew it, pressing the blade into his own palm.

"What are you doing?" I demanded.

In answer, he cut open his hand and raised his fist over me, so that blood dripped down, splattering onto my tunic. "You dragged me out here and killed me," he said with a wry smile.

I grinned back.

"We *will* see each other again," Kovi vowed as he wiped the dagger in the grass and, sheathing it, secured it at his side.

Before I could respond, he was gone, melting as swiftly and softly as a shadow into the trees beyond Ryke.

As I turned back, I pushed down an ache of sorrow and emptiness, along with the hope in a future where Kovi and I could be together. I had to be the empress, confident and strong, never vulnerable or unsure. Unknowns couldn't distract me.

A prickle of guilt ran through me when I considered the lie I'd tell my army, especially when I thought of Daedra. I could understand the depth of her pain and her desire for revenge against the Forwyn.

But my guilt was nothing compared to my fear for Kovi's life.

With a fond glance over my shoulder at the still-sleeping Ryke, I plunged into the trees. A branch scratched at my cheek just as the sound of twigs snapping drew my attention to my right. Fear lanced through my chest, but there was nothing there.

An animal, I thought, mentally scolding my racing heart. *You're being paranoid. No one saw you and Kovi. No one will ever know he's still alive.*

Plastering on a smirk, I ran my hands over my bloodied tunic, letting some of the still-fresh stains redden my fingers, and strode toward camp. I lifted my gaze to the scorched remains of the grasslands encircling both it and the outskirts of Wynlaen, then smiled softly at the town itself. My people were safe, free from greedy, bloodthirsty Teramese monsters. We'd wiped out their army so thoroughly, there would be no one left to send a report to their disgusting ruler Revaed.

Black wrath seared through me. I could practically feel the hard, cold mass covering the skin beneath my collarbone growing, extending its chill toward my shoulder and down my arm. Though I couldn't see her, Nesrelle's presence was there, in my head, fueling my thirst for revenge.

Bloody images rushed through my mind, consuming me with thoughts of destruction. Part of me was horrified, but a stronger part relished them. Even the curse seemed to make my fingertips tingle, as if desperate to be used again and fill me with strength.

I wanted to taste that intoxicating feeling of power again.

Next on our march to the capital: Aramith, I thought.

Yes. Nesrelle's voice was eager in my head. *We'll leave a bloody trail all the way to their so-called emperor's doorstep.*

Her longing for bloodshed only reinforced mine.

And once his entire army has faced our vengeance, I thought, *I'll cut out his heart.*

CHAPTER TWENTY-EIGHT

Lo

MY LATEST MESSAGE FROM MY fellow Forwyn arrived with a new dress for dinner: *We think the dragons will let us fly tonight.*

It was a short message and yet…so full of hope.

I hadn't dared to try to correspond with whoever was answering my messages in person—different Forwyn "servants" brought the food each day, likely out of Revaed's fear of me speaking too often with any one of them. Caesiem hadn't left his rooms all that afternoon, so I was forced to stuff the message in my pocket and hope I could safely dispose of it soon. And writing a response was out of the question for the time being.

I tried not to let Caesiem see my disappointment as I cradled the dress in my arms and headed toward the washroom. This time, the dress wasn't an Alrenian style. It seemed more Teramese. The fabric was a rich black and felt silky. Their land might have been suffering, but clearly that hadn't eliminated all material luxuries their imperial family indulged in.

"We could make our excuses and skip the dinner," Caesiem offered, clearly having noticed my discomfort.

"No, we should go," I called. Slipping into the dress, I turned and faced the mirror, noting how perfectly it fit. Its sleeves were thin and gauzy, and the skirt was embroidered in patterns of red and gold flames and swirling silver smoke. "Did Revaed have an army of seamstresses make me dresses after he announced our engagement?"

"He's all about a professional appearance," Caesiem said.

I spent a while on preparing my hair. Eventually, I settled on a bun, but a few stubborn curls escaped to frame my face. As I studied my reflection, I remembered the days my sisters and I had styled one another's hair. The times Naina had woven ribbons into my braids. Stifling a sigh, I turned away.

Knowing Caesiem had needed to change too, I hesitated near the doorway. "Is it safe to come out yet?"

"Safe," he said, amusement lacing his tone.

Stepping out, I found him tugging at his sleeves and straightening his jacket. Once again, I caught myself appreciating the way the fabric clung to him and the black contrasted with the color of his eyes. Swallowing, I glanced at my feet.

As he turned, Caesiem's eyes swept over me. "You look stunning."

"You're obligated to say that because I'm to be your wife," I teased.

Immediately, I wondered what I was doing. Flirting? Joking about our arranged marriage?

Earlier today you were ready to punch him again, I reminded myself.

But as he took my hand in his, I had trouble concentrating on anything but the warmth of his calloused skin on mine.

Darkness had already descended as Caesiem and I made our way through the palace gardens. The autumn breezes coming off the Alrenian and the Great Sea were chillier than they'd been previous nights. I inhaled the crisp air deeply, for once not hating the mingling scents of flowers and citrus.

It wasn't as if the memories they brought were ever gone. It was only that these scents were growing familiar again, in a way that made it easier and easier to push the memories away before they could engulf me in a flood of pain. I was growing stronger.

There was also the fact that Caesiem's company was still distracting.

This time, we ascended the pavilion steps while some of the other guests were arriving. My skin crawled when I spotted Captain Darix lumbering toward us, his smile appearing more like a sneer. His earlier threats to Caesiem still echoed in my ears.

Just as we arrived at our seats, Revaed entered, flanked by two guards. They took up posts around the pavilion with the others stationed there while we all stood respectfully.

"Be seated," Revaed said with a pleasant smile, one I had to look away from. I couldn't gaze at his face without seeing the Alrenian boy collapsing in his own blood.

This time, the conversation flowed more easily, as if the Teramese were attempting to be more welcoming toward me. Most likely their emperor's announcement of Caesiem's and my betrothal and the fact that I was wearing imperial-looking Teramese clothing had made them realize they had to show me deference.

By the time the food arrived, I found myself trying to play a part, attempting to convince everyone around me that I truly wanted this alliance. I engaged in small talk about the weather or how delicious the meal was. I pretended I wasn't dining with my enemies.

"We are pleased you want to help form this Forwyn-Teramese alliance with us," one of the men sitting to my left said. He dipped his head reverently.

"To have the support of the famed *amara'rekni* is an honor," a woman added. She leaned forward, morbid fascination in her eyes. "Tell me, what was it like slaying such a notoriously cruel empress?"

My blood pounded in my ears as images from those moments flickered through my mind. Nightmares that never left me. I gritted my teeth, trying to banish them, even as I felt my breaths grow shallow.

"Did she really slit the throats of slaves for breathing too loudly in her presence?" another voice chimed in.

There was a ringing in my ears. My head whirled. Sweat dotted my forehead.

Blood spraying. Bodies thudding. Lifeless eyes of fellow slaves gaping up at me, warning me I would be next. Edi dying, again and again and again.

The smell of blood, so much blood…

Under the table, Caesiem clasped my hand, threading his fingers through mine. The sensation jolted me out of my memories, reminding me of where I was.

"Lo," he whispered, close enough that his breath brushed my cheek, and only I could hear him. "Let's get out of here."

I barely heard his excuses as he stood, gently tugging me to my feet. He led us away from the table and out of the pavilion, tracing a winding path through the gardens. The cool air on my cheeks was a welcome distraction, drying the sweat on my brow. As the voices faded behind us and the sounds of crickets chirping and a burbling fountain enveloped us instead, I found my pulse steadying and my head clearing.

"Thank you," I breathed as Caesiem walked me toward a bench.

Relieved, I sank into it, finding myself grateful when Caesiem sat beside me. He radiated comforting warmth, and almost without thinking about it, I leaned into him, resting my head on his shoulder.

Settling back, Caesiem gazed at the stars blanketing the night sky. "I used to look at the stars and make up stories about the constellations, when I was a kid. Back before I knew all their official Teramese names."

My mouth twitched in a smile. "What sorts of stories?"

"Stories about lost people looking for home," he murmured.

My chest ached because I knew what he meant. How many times had I looked at this same night sky as a slave, imagining a home that was free and safe? Or, as a nun, imagining a place that was an escape from nightmares?

I thought of the haunted expression I'd seen on his face before, when he'd returned to his rooms splattered in blood. "Are you still trying to find home?"

"In some ways," Caesiem admitted. He pulled away, forcing me to lift my head, but he didn't drop my hand. "But I find glimpses of it all the time. In songs. In kind words." His eyes traced my face. "In…some of the people I meet." He leaned closer, until he was just a breath away. One hand still threaded in mine, he lifted the other to tuck a curl behind my ear.

I didn't move. Didn't breathe.

Caesiem's lips brushed mine, warm and achingly gentle. Hand cupping my cheek, he kissed me like we had all the time in the world, like the other desperate, stolen kisses we'd shared before had only been leading up to this one.

I let myself forget everything—my scheming behind Caesiem's back, his enduring loyalty toward my enemies, the impossibility of all of this—and lost myself in the kiss. Tangling a hand in his hair, I gave myself this chance to dream. To pretend.

It could have been minutes or hours later when we broke apart. "Lo," Caesiem whispered, his breath tickling my face, "I…"

He swallowed and pulled back, something dark flickering through his eyes. With a quick shake of his head, as if to clear his thoughts, he turned back to me. His smile didn't quite reach his eyes, and whatever he'd been about to say was lost.

Instead, he squeezed my hand, his voice turning solemn. "When I agreed to be a spy in Alrenor," Caesiem said, "I thought I was coming to a land full of cruel people. I didn't know much about your people and what you'd suffered, only the stories about bloodthirsty Alrenians."

He turned back to the sky. "The plan was to do whatever needed to be done to save Teramyl. I never knew I'd meet someone like you, someone who'd get caught up in all of this and get hurt." Regret shone in his eyes. "I know you don't believe me when I say I'm sorry, because you know I'd still do it all over again to help my people. But I *am* sorry it had to be this way."

I squeezed my eyes shut. "I believe you," I confessed quietly. "The problem is that I *know* you're sincere when you talk about wanting peace between the Forwyn and Teramese. And that's what makes what you did so much harder to bear. I don't know if I can forgive you."

Caesiem released my hand. "I know."

"Come!" cried a voice, wrenching us further apart.

I glanced over my shoulder to find a cluster of the Teramese who'd been at the dinner approaching through the gardens, laughing and jesting as if they'd had too much wine.

"Lord Xalenos," Darix called out again, false respect dripping from his voice, "bring your bride-to-be and let us see how she fares with the dragons." His eyes bored into me. "Unless," he added, a nasty grin crossing his face, "we were interrupting something?" He chuckled suggestively.

Noting his eyes, I lifted a hand to my hair and found my curls were especially unruly. Instead of the flush of embarrassment Darix hoped for, I only felt the heat of anger.

As Caesiem and I stood, I forced a smile to my face. "Of course," I said, letting my tone sound falsely pleasant, "I'd be happy to tend to or ride *any* of the dragons."

I glanced at Caesiem, who was openly glowering at Darix, a dark promise on his face.

"Lead the way," another Teramese officer said, his gold eyes looking almost feral in the darkness.

When I turned on my heel, I bit back my smile. Caesiem tossed me a curious look, as if he could read my thoughts.

"They think they can intimidate you," he muttered.

My lips twitched. "Dragons *are* dangerous creatures."

As we neared the Keep, where two Teramese soldiers were posted, my humor fell away. The drunken officers hovered around us, laughing and chatting boisterously amongst themselves. I ignored them all and pressed into the tunnel, where the only light was from the sputtering torches.

Beside me, Caesiem cleared his throat and spoke in a low voice, pulling my focus away from another crude joke from one of his men. "It doesn't take long to tame dragons, right?"

I raised my eyebrows. "Where did you get that idea?"

"Well…" he hesitated. "There's of course the old history about the Misrothian rebellion, when the Alrenian Eldon joined the Misrothians and tamed the empress's dragon, causing it to turn against her during battle." He waited a beat, and added, "And there's talk about you, the *amara'rekni*, and how you conspired with Misrothian royalty to work against Empress Karye."

I smiled, a little smugly. "The dragons are familiar with my scent. When they smell *you*? They'll be reminded of their wild days in your kingdom and how their forefathers feasted on your flesh. You'll smell delicious to them."

Caesiem smirked. "I smell delicious to everyone."

I rolled my eyes. "The truth is," I added, dodging a soldier who tripped and nearly stumbled into me, "I worked with the dragons for years. I fed and tended to them. Three years away after all those other years around them? I *know* they haven't forgotten me." I shrugged. "And as for other dragon tamers…they realized the dragons didn't need to be drugged with vylae, and the dragons respected that. Those tamers formed bonds with the dragons instead."

"So the dragons appreciate freedom and respect?" There was a hint of an amused smile tugging at the corner of Caesiem's mouth.

"Exactly. They're intelligent animals."

Drawing up to the first of the dragon dens, we encountered a Forwyn man wiping sweat off his brow. His clothes were coated with fresh blood. When I gazed further down the tunnel, I noticed other Forwyn, closing den doors or slumping tiredly against the walls. They must have just finished feeding the dragons.

Darix was either too drunk or too careless to notice. "Gather the dragons," he yelled, his voice echoing off the tunnel walls.

"Is he hurt?" Caesiem whispered.

I cast him a sidelong glance, noting his wide eyes as they raked over the man's bloodied clothing. Caesiem *did* care about other Forwyn.

Repressing a smile, I said lightly, "No, it's just blood from the animal he fed the dragon."

Around us, the Forwyn were snapping into action, rushing to heed Darix's ridiculous order. "Gather them outside in the arena. We're flying tonight," Darix announced.

As men and women strode past, I scanned their faces, searching for a knowing look, for any sign that one of them was the person I'd been exchanging messages with. But they all avoided eye contact, keeping their gazes carefully trained on the ground.

The Forwyn worked quickly, and minutes later, they'd strapped saddles and attached leads to the dragons, guiding them out of their dens. As they did, Teramese officers walked alongside them, boasting about how close they were to the dragons. They ran their fingers along their scales fearlessly, laughing and cheering. If any of them knew anything about dragons, they would have noticed the way the creatures' tails flicked back and forth warily, or the way they only calmed when the Forwyn paused to lay gentle hands on their snouts.

Quietly, Caesiem and I followed the procession out into the cool night. The stone floor of the arena stretched toward the cliff leading out over the sea, glistening in the starlight. Far below, the capital flickered with distant candlelight, a beautiful vision of ivory and gold.

"This is foolish," a woman muttered beside me. Turning, I found Valentra had paused beside Caesiem and me. Her eyes were clear and focused as she studied the dragons. She appeared to be the only Teramese officer who was fully sober. "What would the emperor say if Captain Darix was injured because he thought he could train the dragons while drunk?"

Caesiem's mouth twitched. "He'd say natural consequences are such a pity."

Commotion drew our eyes to a Forwyn woman struggling to lead a huge dragon from the Keep's mouth. Men and women scurried out of her way, giving the beast a wide berth. The posted guards drew their swords, prepared to fight.

Smoke curled from the creature's nostrils as he snorted and reared his head, a low growl rumbling from his throat. His scales gleamed in the starlight—black, umber, and red. Spikes rose along his spine, adding to his fierce appearance.

"Karos," Caesiem breathed.

"That's a Teramese name," Valentra said, voice piqued in curiosity.

"What?" I asked. I'd always thought perhaps it was an old Alrenian word, its meaning lost to memory.

"Whoever named him knew their Teramese history, from centuries ago," Caesiem explained. "Because Karos was the name of a legendary Teramese dragon. In our language, it means *untamable*."

"Fitting," Valentra muttered as the dragon continued to resist, but I was already running forward.

"Karos!" I called, stopping directly in front of the dragon.

I could sense the world freeze around me, Teramese and Forwyn eyes alike snapping to me. Karos himself whirled, his gleaming gold eye wide and searching as it found mine.

"Karos," I repeated, more softly. I glanced to the Forwyn holding his lead, nodding once. She understood my meaning and dropped the lead to step back.

It was just Karos and me now, facing one another. Reading each other.

Another guttural sound emitted from his throat, and he opened his maw, revealing rows of sharp teeth. More smoke curled from his snout, threatening fire that could incinerate us all in an instant.

"I know," I said with a soft laugh. "These Teramese *boeri* irk me to know end, too. But you remember me. I know you do. And you're restless—ready to get out of here and fly. To taste freedom. I understand that feeling."

All my years tending to the dragons, I'd found that speaking to them calmed them. In my heart, I believed they understood us. They were intelligent creatures who responded to human voices and moods. They seemed to read us as easily as I'd learned to read them.

"Don't be afraid," I whispered, stretching out my hand and placing it against his snout. I didn't tremble. Didn't flinch. Didn't tear my gaze from the huge eye studying me. "They can't tame me either."

Karos was a beautiful dragon, the same shade as the night sky with accents of flame. His scales shifted and glistened. Muscles rippled with every movement. He was larger than any of the other dragons, a powerful threat. Even Karye's dragon, Reyva, had yielded to Karos before we Forwyn had gifted Reyva to Misroth.

For an instant, I held my breath. Karos *had* always been unpredictable. But he unleashed a breath, almost like a sigh, and stretched out his neck to nuzzle against my palm. A swell of emotion flooded my chest as I ran my fingertips along his warm scales and breathed in the familiar scent of dragon smoke.

As I relaxed, I glanced over my shoulder, catching Caesiem's grin. Behind him, the Teramese soldiers appeared far too sober, far too wide-eyed. Uneasiness crawled down my spine. Had I revealed too much? Should I have pretended it was harder for me to approach the dragons?

Before I could question myself more, Caesiem made a show of applauding loudly, breaking the silence. "Look at us, Forwyn and Teramese working side-by-side with the dragons. This is only the beginning of the wonders our alliance will create." He turned to Darix. "As you said, let's ride the dragons."

Eager chatter cut through the silence as the Teramese gathered around the creatures, listening to the Forwyn instruct them on how to climb into the saddles.

Caesiem approached me, slowly and softly so as not to startle Karos. But Karos froze, jerking away from me to stare at him, his pupil dilating until the gold of his eye nearly disappeared. He leaned forward, sniffing the air, poised as if to strike.

"Don't let him know you're afraid," I murmured. "You can't let yourself look like prey."

Easing his tense stance, Caesiem glanced at me, face solemn. "*Will* the dragons let us ride?" he asked.

I nodded confidently.

There was a knowing smile on his face. "Only because you and the other Forwyn are present. They hate us."

"No, they wouldn't be this relaxed if they weren't growing used to you," I argued quickly. Maybe too quickly. Pausing, I slowed my words and cleared my throat. "They're definitely more used to the Forwyn, but these men and women didn't tend to them before. The Keepers did. Most of us are strangers to the dragons, but together, as you said, we can ride and tend to them. They'll grow to trust the Forwyn and Teramese alike."

I wasn't sure if Caesiem believed me, but I prayed, silently, that he did. After all, not everything I'd said had been a lie. Half-truths were more convincing than outright falsehood. I tried to ignore the guilt that pierced me for lying to him, reminding myself of how he'd lied to me.

Nearby, others had already saddled and mounted the dragons. Teramese officers shouted to one another from behind the Forwyn, who looked composed, confident. *My advice to them has worked,* I thought.

Karos shuffled forward, growling softly, and Caesiem cursed. "He hates me."

"He's the unpredictable one, remember?" I said through gritted teeth. Despite my confidence around Karos, I didn't trust that I could keep Caesiem safe. Not unless Caesiem fully relaxed.

I didn't dare make any sudden movements. Instead, I started reaching with my mind, listening for Elhani's song rushing through the air around me.

"Maybe you should talk—think of something else to calm down," I suggested, trying to distract Caesiem and dilute the fear Karos was clearly sensing. "Tell me how you learned to play music."

"All right," Caesiem murmured. "Well…I started when I was still a thief, a nobody. It was a way to earn a few coins. And a way to distract our targets so my friends could steal a few more."

Karos opened his maw just enough to show his fangs.

Without my prompting, Caesiem went on. Despite Karos's aggressive stance, his voice already sounded calmer. "I found the instrument in a plague house. After someone—or everyone—in a home contracted the plague and was either off dying or already dead, houses would be barred up. No one wanted to go inside because no one knew quite how long it took for the plague to die off in a home."

Slowly, Karos tilted his head, as if listening. "That's it," I murmured, patting the creature's snout.

Nearby, the first of the dragons leapt from the cliffside, wings unfurling. Scales glistened in the starlight, and my breath caught in my throat at the breathtaking sight. Though I'd spent much time around the dragons, I'd never been able to do the one thing I'd always longed to do: ride them.

Caesiem cleared his throat, but didn't stop his story. "But my friends and I were too young to need to worry about dying from the plague. Those homes were full of things, sometimes even food, that we could use to survive. When I found a lythra in one of those homes, I knew I couldn't just sell it. Not when it could earn us coin many times over."

"So you taught yourself to play," I prompted. "But…someone in Teramyl had an Alrenian instrument? The barrier would have still been up back then."

"The lythra is used widely in Teramyl too," Caesiem explained. "Centuries ago, our people fell in love with it, back when trade with Alrenor was common. Or so I've heard." He shrugged. "It was definitely convenient to already be familiar with an Alrenian instrument when I arrived here."

Just as I'd hoped, Karos appeared to be soothed by Caesiem's visibly relaxed stance. The distraction was working.

After a few more agonizing minutes, Karos lowered his head. More dragons were wheeling overhead, setting my heart soaring. I ached to be up there with them, with the wind in my hair and the city spread out before me like a stunning tapestry.

My eyes drifted to the saddle one of the Forwyn had left for me. "Will you let us ride?" I asked Karos quietly, gesturing to the saddle.

He shifted again, lowering his head still further, and I nearly wept with joy. It was as I'd expected—he was as eager to take to the skies as I was.

"Will he let *me* ride?" Caesiem asked uncertainly. He'd dared to creep closer, close enough I tensed in surprise when I heard his voice so near.

"No sudden movements, and do exactly as I say," I instructed. "With your first order being not to move again."

Caesiem smirked. "Right. Not moving."

My fingers remembered how to fasten the straps and saddle a dragon, even if it had been years since I'd had to do it. It took me back to darker times, but I pushed the memories away, relishing the fact that this time, I was saddling the dragon for myself.

"Karos," I said, setting my hand gently on his side. "Caesiem is a friend. He's going to *slowly* approach and climb onto the saddle" -I shot a pointed look at Caesiem- "but I'll join him. Could you please *not* eat him?"

Caesiem repressed a snort as he edged closer. "Do the dragons really listen when someone talks to them like that?"

"Quiet," I snapped, but I was smiling. "They're intelligent animals. I'm sure he understands me." I shrugged. "How different is it from you controlling that water creature?"

"It's hardly control," Caesiem admitted. He paused next to Karos, gazing directly into the dragon's eye as if to silently reaffirm he meant no harm. "It's more like…using my magic to summon the creature, and then letting it do what it already wants to do." He touched Karos gently before moving toward the saddle. "Feed."

Though Caesiem had never ridden a dragon before, he was graceful and quick—a thief through-and-through. He swung up in a few smooth movements and grinned down at me. "Ready?"

I swung into the seat in front of him, strapping myself in as I explained to Caesiem how he could do the same. This time, tears did prick my eyes. "We're actually riding a dragon," I breathed, blinking furiously. Even though Caesiem couldn't see my face, I still felt ridiculous. Laughter chased the tears, joyful and free. "Hold on tight."

Caesiem snaked his arms around me, even though he could have held onto the saddle. I opened my mouth to protest, but his warmth enveloped me and his heart thudded a steady, soothing rhythm against my back. Perhaps, just like earlier, I could pretend. Just for tonight.

"*Laeva*," I commanded Karos, and he launched himself forward, running more swiftly than one who didn't know dragons would expect such a huge creature to move. In an instant, he was diving off the cliff, plunging toward the city.

His wings snapped open, and we soared through the night sky. My heart leapt to my throat and I shouted, feeling wild and victorious. Caesiem's eager laughter brushed against my ear, sounding as thrilled and awed as I felt. Wind roared in our ears and stung my eyes. Hair tugged free of my braid and whipped painfully against my cheeks.

But I was flying. I was *free*.

Around me, the other Forwyn circled and dove, their shouts occasionally drifting toward me on the wind. Smug satisfaction settled in my heart. The Teramese might think their plans were falling into place, but they weren't the ones in control.

It seemed like mere seconds had passed before the other dragons swung back toward the Keep. Stifling my sigh, I commanded Karos to follow. As we landed and dismounted, the Teramese seemed to have forgotten their earlier shock, overcome by their victory of riding dragonback. I searched the Forwyn faces, but to their credit, each man and woman hid their emotions well.

"Take the dragons back!" Darix commanded the Forwyn needlessly, for they were already unsaddling the dragons and reattaching their leads.

As the Teramese shuffled away, I noticed Valentra toss one final look over her shoulder before disappearing into the shadowy gardens. Caesiem lingered behind with me, taking Karos's saddle once I removed it. I guided Karos without a lead back into the Keep and toward his den.

As soon as the door clanged shut, closing Karos within his den, Caesiem breathed a sigh. "That was…amazing." His bright eyes were full of wonder as he turned to me. "Thank you."

I wiped a weary hand across my brow. "I wasn't sure he would let us ride so soon, but he's restless in his den."

"It's because he sees an equal in you." Caesiem's expression was solemn, his look too piercing. Too full of an emotion I didn't want to analyze.

If I wasn't careful, I'd kiss him again, right here, and lose myself in pretending. I'd lose myself in him. But that daydream had to stop.

Instead, I looked away, changing the subject quickly. "I think, after that, I'll sleep just fine tonight."

"I hope so." Gently, he grasped my hand, squeezing my fingers. A hundred unspoken words hung in the air between us, and I cursed myself as I let him lean in and press a kiss to my forehead.

Even though he released my hand immediately after, even though he stepped away, the memory of his fingers threaded through mine lingered long after. The brush of his lips, the warmth of his arms around me—my mind refused to let any of it go.

I cursed myself all the way back to the palace.

CHAPTER TWENTY-NINE

Lo

THE CORONATION CEREMONY WAS SET to take place the following morning. As soon as I forced myself out of bed, exhausted from another night with little sleep, I found Caesiem already seated near the empty hearth, sipping a mug of coffee. He was dressed in Alrenian styled clothes, from the loose white shirt he wore to the vivid red vest, embroidered with gold, fire-breathing dragons. Prepared to be crowned prince.

Hearing me stir, he glanced over his shoulder, his expression unreadable. Last night he'd kissed me and flown Karos with me, and then strummed his lythra and sung to me again until he'd chased my haunting memories away and I'd fallen asleep. Now, hints of that man remained in his gentle expression, but there was a darkness in his eyes. A weight that visibly dragged down his shoulders.

"Your dress for today is in the wardrobe." He nodded across the room at the piece of carved furniture, and I padded along the floor to wrench open the doors.

My breath lodged in my throat when I took in the flowing gold dress hanging in front of me. Everything about it was royal, from the thin, gauzy straps fastened with shimmering ivory dragon scales, to the train flowing behind it. *A dress fit for a future princess,* I thought, a chill sweeping down my spine. Revaed would be making a statement about me before he even announced this farce of an engagement.

I prepared quickly for the day, gulping down my own mug of coffee a little too quickly and spending far too much time in the washroom trying to tame my curls. I left them down to coil around my face and rush my shoulders, a beautiful reminder that I was no longer a slave with shorn hair. At last, I slipped into the dress, hating how Alrenian it made me appear.

By the time I exited the washroom, Caesiem was standing by the double doors leading to the balcony, staring out the windows with a pensive expression. The sunlight gilded his dark hair. My heart twisted, and I forced myself to look away.

When he turned, his own eyes were dark with longing. But this time, he swallowed and refrained from commenting on my appearance. I avoided teasing him. Our look was marked instead with silent wistfulness.

Gone was the light-heartedness we'd felt flying on dragonback the night before. In its place was the weight of our separate loyalties, forever dividing us.

Wordlessly, he extended his arm, and we swept from his rooms and out into the halls. Everywhere we walked, Teramese eyes bored into me. Some gleamed with lust that made my skin crawl, but most stared with outright hostility. My official engagement to their prince would grant me authority they clearly resented.

The entire procession to the Akytha District's main square, where the ceremony was to take place, was a solemn, quiet affair. I kept my position beside Caesiem, avoiding Revaed, who walked alongside his heir. Dressed in black trimmed in red, his outfit was all Teramese. The pair of them made a strong statement: today Teramyl and Alrenor would be forever bound, whether the Alrenian citizens approved or not.

Nearby, the four surviving Elders walked side-by-side with other Teramese officers, advisors, and a priest. A whole host of heavily armed soldiers hemmed us in, separating us from the citizens both as we walked the streets and as we lined up in the square.

Murmurs washed over the crowd like a soft breeze. They cut short once they caught sight of our procession. Glancing between the soldiers marching on my right, I tried to take in the expressions of the people around me. All I caught were flashes of wide eyes and angry glares on Alrenian and Forwyn faces alike.

As soon as we stopped, the soldiers formed ranks before us and drew their weapons. They were the picture of discipline—and anything but a peaceful rule. Unsurprisingly, the gathered citizens bristled at the sight. The tension rising off the crowd was a palpable thing, sinking down to my very bones.

Revaed and Caesiem stepped forward together, facing the Teramese priest, clothed in a white and black robe. As the two young men kneeled before the priest, they each received crowns of silver adorned with rubies—ones that appeared Teramese and must have been brought to Alrenor solely for this moment.

Time held no meaning as I watched them formalize their coup. I was numb, hating that I was a part of this show. Hating that I couldn't look at Caesiem without being filled with both longing and sorrow. The ache of betrayal never eased.

The new emperor and prince recited vows that ended in a

Teramese-sounding phrase: "May the gods bless our empire."

My mind whirled as Caesiem returned to my side. I wanted to say something to him, but my mouth was dry. He cast a sidelong glance at me, perhaps reading my feelings. I refused to return his look, and after a long moment, his gaze flicked away.

As the Teramese priest shuffled out of the way, Revaed stepped forward to begin his speech. "I want to welcome all of you to a new age of peace, heralded by a grand alliance between Forwyn and Teramese," he announced.

The crowd was eerily silent. All around us, I saw Alrenians and Forwyn alike, some wearing blank expressions that likely masked their fear. Others scowled outright, shifting restlessly.

My mind refocused on the words Revaed was saying, until they echoed off the buildings around us: "...an upcoming marriage union between my heir, your new Prince Caesiem Xalenos, and the stunning Lo'laeni Nolanhou, a representative of the Forwyn staying within the palace." He paused. "The *amara'rekni* herself."

What? Ice trickled down my spine. My blood curdled in my veins. Revaed had just revealed my carefully hidden identity, all to suit his own interests. I hadn't agreed to *this* announcement.

Caesiem clasped my hand. "They won't hurt you," he whispered.

But Forwyn and Alrenian citizens alike were already crying out in anger.

"Liar!" some screamed, while others hurled curses at the assembled Teramese.

The Alrenians were furious, shouting obscenities and death threats my way. Here I was, their most hated enemy, finally revealed to them, and standing beside a *new* enemy. "*Filkni* Empress-Slayer!" they screamed. "Death to the *amara'rekni*! Avenge the empress! Avenge our people!"

But the worst were the voices of the Forwyn people—*my* people—who were glaring openly at me. "Traitor," they cried out in the Forwyn tongue. "May Elhani curse you for what you've done, turning your back on your people!"

I repressed a shiver, and Caesiem's grip tightened, his fingers threading through mine.

The citizens were a churning mass, a restless sea about to unleash a storm. As the shouting rose, so did the energy—bodies pushed forward despite the threat of the gleaming swords pointed toward them. Men and women threw fists into the air, crying out for justice. For Teramese blood. For *my* blood.

Something smacked the ground before us—an orange. I blinked at it for a moment, stifling the laughter that was trying to claw its way up my throat.

Caesiem shoved me behind him as more objects followed—produce, stones, and even shoes. The citizens shrieked and threw themselves toward the soldiers, trying to overpower them, trying to force their way past to attack the Teramese, Elders, and me.

Everything happened in the blink of an eye. The noise reached a crescendo as soldiers retaliated, swinging their swords with vicious precision. Blood sprayed, slicking the cobblestones beneath our feet. Screams of anger turned to screams of agony.

Alrenian and Forwyn bodies alike piled up before the Teramese until there was a new wall blocking the citizens from us—a wall of the dead.

Caesiem, still holding my hand, swept his arm out in a graceful motion. Water rose from the broken fountain behind us, the one a Forwyn Keeper had broken with his dragon earlier this month while stopping an Alrenian uprising in this very square. I gaped as the water still sitting in its basin shot upward, bursting forth in a glistening, frothing wave. The surviving citizens staggered back, open-mouthed and wary, as the water rushed over them, knocking them down. Holding them in a relentless, breathless grip.

My body shook as I stared over Caesiem's shoulder.

He was drowning the people on land, squeezing his fist until his fingers were white. I couldn't see his face, but his body was rigid. Unyielding.

"Caesiem," I breathed, my voice ragged.

He didn't move, as if he didn't hear me.

The citizens not trapped by Caesiem's magic were retreating further back from the square, only a few staying to cry out to their loved ones or plead plead for mercy. Some plunged into the water to save the victims, only to be trapped within the wall themselves.

"Caesiem."

Gasping, as if just coming to himself again, Caesiem jerked back, dropping his arm. The water coursed backward, streaming into the fountain once more.

Bile burned my throat and sweat coated my skin. The scent of blood was heavy in the air, and I didn't know if I wanted to scream at the Alrenians and Forwyn for their threats toward me, or at the Teramese for their show of power, for the merciless way they'd attacked at the first sign of unrest.

Caesiem dropped my hand, pulling away.

I couldn't think, couldn't breathe.

Nearby, Revaed leaned toward one of his officers. "Get us out of here," he growled.

An extravagant party had been prepared and was already awaiting us as we entered the palace gardens. Tables with huge spreads of food were everywhere, along with musicians—mostly Forwyn, though a few were Teramese—who played soft, deceptively soothing songs that slipped into the background amidst the chatting and laughing guests. Soldiers in full uniform stood alongside other men and women in all their court finery.

From my understanding, nearly every Teramese citizen who had arrived in Alrenor thus far was a soldier, but it appeared the most talented and valuable of the soldiers were also nobility or had recently become part of Revaed's new court.

I stiffened at the sight, unable to shut out the recent bloody images from the ceremony. As the Teramese eagerly dispersed, faces carefree as if they hadn't witnessed horrors, I gaped.

Even the Elders carried on as if nothing had happened, their movements graceful and easy.

My eyes snagged on Elder Ettonou, who was draped in an elegant tunic and pants and was *smiling* as he spoke to a Teramese officer.

Blood roared in my ears. Almost without thinking, I took a step toward him.

At my side, Caesiem shot me a glance. "He's not worth it," he muttered.

"He's not the only traitor here," I said, venom in my voice. I turned to him, unable to hide the pain warring with my rage. Just last night I'd let him pull me close and kiss me. I'd let him sing me to sleep. Let him make me want things I was never supposed to want.

Caesiem's throat bobbed as he swallowed. "Listen," he continued, his voice low, "I know you're upset, but… I had to stop the citizens out there. Even your own people were going to *kill* you."

"Only because they see me as a traitor," I snapped. "They don't know I'm trying to save them. They think I just want the power of being married to you."

Caesiem flinched. "We weren't ever actually going to get married," he reminded me, then hesitated a beat. "Have you changed your mind about the alliance?"

I sighed and shook my head. "No, I just…" My eyes burned. I didn't need to act here. My shame and doubt were real. "I hate that they see me as a traitor to our government. Our way of life."

Caesiem scowled and gestured toward Elder Ettonou, whom I turned to, watching as closely as one would track a deadly snake. "Are you really upset about turning your back on the Court of Elders? Were the Elders ever actually *helping* you? You saw how Revaed let you and other Forwyn stand in places of prominence. He means what he says about an alliance. And he *hasn't* made that offer to the Alrenians."

That you know of, I thought, but I pressed my lips together. It wasn't worth it to argue about something I had no proof of—I simply didn't trust Revaed. Until I could find a way to convince Caesiem, without doubt, that Revaed was not good and just in all his actions, I didn't see a point in arguing and angering him anymore. Better that both he and Revaed trusted me.

With that in mind, I tempered the fury in my voice, asking softly, "Did any of those citizens have to die?"

Caesiem worked a muscle in his jaw. "I've told you, Lo. Sometimes as a leader you have to make the hard decisions. We can't let violent citizens openly attack our men and women without retaliation. Or start a riot unhindered and let them shed blood throughout the whole city. It was a matter of self-defense. It was Revaed's way of protecting *you* and the other Forwyn up there too. You know if those citizens had gone unchecked, they would have murdered you."

Because of what your people are doing to them. It wouldn't have been murder in their eyes; it would have been an execution in a war for their own freedom.

I watched him carefully. "Would you have killed some yourself if I hadn't stopped you?"

Caesiem turned away. "I…don't know. But if I hadn't stopped them, do you think they would have shown *you* mercy?"

I didn't answer, my mind whirling. Did the Alrenians deserve mercy? Did Forwyn like Mio'e who wanted to see me dead deserve mercy? I no longer let guilt haunt me for the kills I'd had to make in self-defense, but if some of my enemies would listen to reason—if even some Alrenians could be persuaded to embrace peace—wasn't mercy the best choice?

Caesiem seemed to accept my silence as a sign of a truce between us. He cheered visibly, his eyes sparkling in the late morning sun as he offered me a hesitant smile. Clothed in his fine uniform, he cut a dashing figure. More than one young Teramese woman had been glancing his way, eyes lingering on the muscles visible through the fabric or his sea-blue eyes.

"We have some traditional Teramese food here." His eyes darted to a nearby table, filled with desserts: Alrenian pastries and tarts and cakes, along with less familiar dishes. "You have to try this one." He clasped my arm and pulled me toward one of the tables. "We can find an out-of-the-way place to eat so you don't have to listen to a thousand congratulations on our engagement for a little while, at least."

I didn't bother to repress my groan at the thought, and Caesiem shot me an apologetic look, one that told me he hated it too.

We stopped in front of the dessert Caesiem wanted me to try, and I couldn't help but be a little impressed. A many-layered cake—frosted to perfection and decorated with a type of glistening golden glaze—dominated the table we stood before. Though I had no appetite, I let myself admire how beautiful the dessert was as Caesiem carefully slid a slice off the platter and onto a plate, handing it over to me with a flourish. He chose a piece for himself and led us toward a small round table tucked under some palms, set away from the crowd.

I sat with relief, but Revaed, surrounded by soldiers and advisors in the midst of what appeared to be an intense discussion, called to Caesiem almost instantly.

"I'll be back," he said with an apologetic look, as if this was a celebration I wanted any part of. As if I hadn't spent the whole morning on edge, wanting to scream. "Don't eat my cake too."

As he slipped away, greeting others and exchanging pleasantries as he went, I poked listlessly at the slice of cake sitting in front of me. There were layers of dried yellow fruit baked into it, which I thought might be pieces of banana, native to Teramyl. They didn't last on the voyage across the sea unless they'd been dried, and even then they were rarely shipped to Alrenor. I took a tentative bite, surprised by the explosion of sweet flavor in my mouth, mixing with the fluffy frosting and the glaze, which I realized had been made with honey.

"You're young, so I suppose I can excuse your naivety," a deep voice rumbled nearby, startling me into dropping my fork.

I met Elder Ettonou's piercing gaze, assessing me as he lingered near my table and sipped from a goblet of red wine.

Anger making my skin prickle, I shifted in my seat. I forced my tone to remain steady. "Naivety regarding what, exactly?"

He tossed back a long draught of the wine. "Justice." He smacked his lips and I narrowed my eyes at him, not wanting to bother with empty niceties. "I know it's troubling, when you have to deal with the bloodshed personally, but criminals must be punished. I figured you of all people should have already learned that."

I dropped my gaze to my plate. Not this argument again. This man was an Elder, someone who was supposed to be a wise and merciful leader.

"Do you honestly think," I asked slowly, turning to stare at him, "that we'll ever save our own people by constantly responding to the Alrenians with more violence? And what about our *own* people who died today?"

"Our own people threatened the greater good of all. A Forwyn opposing this alliance is a fool, and will only be the cause of more Forwyn suffering. Besides, they also threatened *your* life. You should be grateful for the protection."

My blood roared in my ears at his words. *Traitor. Snake!* I wanted to scream, but I bit my tongue instead.

"And as for the Alrenians," he added, the hand clutching his goblet white-knuckled, "it's what they *all* deserve."

"Maybe so," I said, forcing my tone to remain level and my expression calm, "but I'm thinking about what *our* people deserve."

"We deserve *revenge*," he snapped, something dark and frightening consuming his face. He stepped closer, leaning forward until he was uncomfortably close, the alcohol on his breath sharp in my nose. "And I won't let any naïve fool get in the way of that, *amara'rekni* or not. Emperor Revaed's alliance will strengthen us, make us stronger than the Alrenians, and allow us to have our revenge at last."

I held my breath as I watched his eyes flash with hatred. "Tell me," he went on, "how can you have been the one to avenge our people, to slay Karye herself, and now want to give those bloodthirsty animals *mercy*?" He slammed his goblet down next to my plate, shaking the table. "Did you ever actually *lose* someone to Karye? Did you truly suffer as the rest of us did?"

"Yes. I lost *everyone*," I snarled. "But that doesn't mean I lost my conscience too."

Elder Ettonou's eyes widened in surprise before his expression transformed into a sneer. "Then I suppose you're just a fool."

Rage shot through me. I wanted to tell him that I'd claimed my revenge by killing Karye herself, and it had been empty. It hadn't assuaged my grief or anger, and it certainly hadn't granted my people freedom from the oppression we had continued to suffer, despite breaking the bonds of slavery.

But I refused to try to reason with this odious man. It was clear his desire for revenge overruled everything else—except, perhaps, his desire for power.

Swallowing, I glanced away, and to my relief, the Elder chuckled cruelly and drifted away. Off to play the traitor and befriend more Teramese.

I was so busy scowling at my plate that I didn't hear Emperor Revaed approach.

"Forgive me for stealing Caesiem away from you," he said, his tone formal, as if I were a true guest of honor at this celebration. He nodded to the group of men and women clustered further back in the garden, the same group he'd been with earlier. Caesiem was still among them, chatting animatedly. "He has some business to tend to."

I didn't bother to stand or pretend to offer my congratulations. Disrespectful or not, I remained seated. What more would Revaed do to me when he was already threatening and killing my people? If he wanted me dead, I'd already be dead.

I stabbed my cake with my fork. "And you do not?"

Revaed smiled gallantly and sat in the chair across from me, pushing away Caesiem's plate to lean his elbows on the table. "I wanted to take a moment to personally thank you for your willingness to speak with the Forwyn at Aerekni Academy and finish convincing them to establish an alliance between our peoples." His smile darkened almost imperceptibly. "It's far preferable to the students and teachers rioting or storming the palace." He waved a hand vaguely toward the Teramese strewn about the garden, laughing and carrying on as well as the Alrenians ever had. As if they were right at home already. "You've seen how effective my army is. It wouldn't end well for your people."

At last, something close to an open threat. I grinned in response. "I don't know, our last revolt went rather well." I didn't flinch away from his shimmering violet gaze, didn't let my smile falter. I matched his perfectly. Maybe I was playing a dangerous game, making myself look suspicious, but it was too late to bite the words back.

He shrugged, as if the subject meant little to him. "All I'm saying is that there is always a price. With the alliance I'm sure you'll procure, there need not be one."

"Who have you sent to speak with them already?"

"A few of my own men," Revaed said lightly. "I had to gain some bit of control of the academy immediately, to avoid inconvenient revolts." He scowled with disgust. "And that would have meant a lot more bloodied clothing."

I rolled my eyes, no longer even trying to conceal my hatred for this man. *Bloody clothes* was his biggest worry, not casualties. "Why not send one of the Elders you spared to talk to their own people?" I asked, unable to keep the bite from my tone.

Revaed's grin widened further. "I think the word of the *amara'rekni* herself will be far more convincing, don't you? Especially now that you're the future empress. The Elders agree."

A shiver trickled down my spine. "Perhaps."

Revaed rose, watching me carefully. Once again, that darkness flitted across his face, making his expression look harder. There were threats etched into that gaze.

"Be sure you try your best and prove I can trust you," he said over his shoulder as he prepared to walk away. "Don't fail in drawing the academy to our side. Caesiem's grown quite attached to you. I'd hate for him to…have to grieve."

The rest of the day was a blur of false niceties and fancy gowns and food. I forced myself to smile, to pretend I was eager to forge this alliance. All the while, Caesiem would gently squeeze my hand whenever I grew lost in my thoughts, as if trying to comfort me.

He had no idea his guardian had been threatening me.

More than once I turned to him, thinking I'd tell him exactly what Revaed had said. Would he believe me over the man who had plucked him off the streets and groomed him for years to be the perfect heir? Would he believe me over the man who genuinely did seem to dote on him, who truly had saved him from a wretched life?

So I smiled countless times and repeated "I'm thrilled to establish this alliance between our people" until I wanted to scream. I pretended to be interested when some of the Teramese women started talking about marriage customs and the week-long party they would throw after the ceremony. And I let Caesiem hold my hand, thinking he could steady me in this world of his, thinking he could protect me…when my greatest threat was the man he admired so much.

CHAPTER THIRTY

Lo

ANOTHER DAY PASSED—ONE FULL of more Teramese celebrations, of Caesiem vanishing into endless conversations or private meetings, of me attempting to overhear anything I could about Teramese numbers or strategies in the chatter around me.

In the evening, Caesiem and I stole some moments of peace on dragonback, flying Karos over the gardens and along the coast. A few of the Teramese took their dragons for a ride as well, but most were too full or too drunk—or both—to do much after their extravagant feasts. Once again, I avoided talking to Caesiem about Revaed's threat. I had the sinking feeling he couldn't—or wouldn't—believe me.

Instead, we spoke little, each just enjoying a companionable silence. I feared if I said too much, we'd fight again, and a part of me only wanted to pretend. Just for one more day.

That night, Caesiem brought out his lythra again, singing to keep both of our nightmares at bay, until I slipped into a dreamless sleep.

The next morning, attired in yet another formal dress—this one decorated with blue and silver dragon scales that clinked with each step—I followed Caesiem's lead through the streets of Inalgoth. Everywhere, Teramese soldiers on patrol swarmed the city, keeping their weapons visible and their sharp eyes closely trained on each Forwyn and Alrenian passerby. It was strange following a foreigner through paths I was so familiar with from daily rounds visiting needy Forwyn families and nightly runs.

Overhead, the dragons circled, a comfortingly familiar sight. A reminder that the other Forwyn were continuing to ensure they had the dragons' loyalty. Every time I glanced up, I was reminded we had hope. I wished we could make a move against the Teramese now, but they had too many soldiers spread throughout the empire for me to be confident one attack on the palace would be enough to expel them. Besides, the Teramese weren't allowing the Forwyn near the dragons without express permission. We needed a solid plan…and reinforcements.

We needed the residents of the academy.

But soon enough we drew close to the outer district, near the far northern wall, and toward a place I'd never been. Aerekni Academy rested only a couple miles outside the city gates, which was a useful position if its soldiers were ever needed to defend the capital, but a difficult position if its current occupants wanted to raid the city itself and expel the Teramese.

As soon as the Teramese on guard cranked open the heavy city gates, each featuring an emblem of the Alrenian swirling sun, the cobblestone street turned to a simple yet wide dirt path. The view was open: the rolling hills, swaying palms, and huge walled-in fortress dominating my vision. Aerekni Academy was made entirely of smooth stone and shimmering steel, all imposing security and practicality. It was a sharp contrast to everything in Inalgoth, which was heavily decorated, from towering statues and fluttering flags to the architecture of the ivory buildings themselves, which stood bright and beautiful, like pearls glistening along the beach.

My heart pounded in anticipation as we approached the academy's entrance, where two guards manned the gate. Each of the young men—likely recent graduates of the military school—was clothed in a spotless red and gold uniform. They stood with impeccable discipline until Caesiem and I drew up side-by-side, the Teramese guards behind us muttering under their breath. Though I couldn't understand their language, I could tell by their derisive tones that they had nothing flattering to say about the guards or their academy.

One of the guards drew himself up, his eyes a warm, soft shade of brown in the late morning light. Unfortunately, everything about his expression was hard. "Who are you and what business do you have here?" His eyes darted with disgust toward the Teramese men and women.

Honestly, I'd been surprised that Revaed, who'd been clear about already sending multiple representatives to the academy, hadn't already stormed the place. I'd half-expected to find countless Teramese soldiers standing on guard, outnumbering the Forwyn ones. Instead, I noticed a handful within the courtyard beyond the gate, but they stood side-by-side with the Forwyn and didn't appear to be in control. It made my heart swell with hope, and a hint of doubt over my plans to undermine the alliance. Maybe it *was* genuine. Then I remembered the executed Alrenian boy, and the citizens slain at the coronation ceremony.

No matter Revaed's talk of peace and alliances, he wasn't trustworthy.

Survival above all else. It was clear from that motto that he would put his people's survival above anything else, always. Even above mercy.

Besides, he'd already broken a Forwyn-Teramese alliance when he'd flooded our shores and slaughtered most of our Elders, claiming the empire as his. He was mad if he ever thought any of my people would trust him.

I thought of the message I'd written for the Forwyn in the palace that morning, the one I'd tucked beneath my empty breakfast plate. One I hoped would encourage them. *I'm meeting with the general of Aerekni Academy today. I'll secure his help so we can form a plan, one where we can work against the Teramese both from within and without the palace.*

Now, somehow, I had to convince the general of my loyalty to the Forwyn, but without Caesiem or the other Teramese overhearing.

Drawing a deep breath, I squared my shoulders and approached the Forwyn. "I am the *amara'rekni*, and I've come from the palace to share news of Emperor Revaed."

The men's eyes widened, lifting their gazes almost reverently toward me. Then the first sneered. "You slew the empress, and now you're bandying words with the leader of a coup? Calling *him* emperor? Agreeing to marry his heir? You're nothing but a lowlife traitor!"

The other shifted uneasily on his feet. "Rhi'il, General Ilowhe ordered us to let all Teramese in to speak with him."

Rhi'il grunted. "For now." He nodded stiffly toward me, ignoring Caesiem and his guards. "You'll leave all weapons at the gate, or you won't enter."

Caesiem and the soldiers complied wordlessly, leaving their blades in a pile by the Forwyn soldiers. After the guards had patted us each down to be sure we were truly disarmed, they opened the gates with a creak.

We stepped into a wide courtyard, where the various buildings making up the school towered over us. Across the way, outside the largest of the buildings and standing as if he'd been expecting us, was another Forwyn soldier. He nodded curtly and waved us forward, before turning to open the door and lead us inside.

The entrance was impressive and stark, everything full of sharp angles and cold stone. The only embellishments were the once-colorful painted depictions of Alrenian conquests covering the ceilings and walls, now defiled with angry words and crude images.

I couldn't blame the Forwyn, though some of the new additions made heat rise to my cheeks.

We took several turns, passing open doorways leading to courtyards or inner training rooms where students were practicing and sparring against dummies or one another. Sharply attired officers strode amongst them, offering stern corrections or reserved praise. Some of the students were old enough to be considered adults, but many were still boys and girls, their youthful faces sheened with sweat and their dark eyes wide and afraid when they glanced toward the Teramese procession filing past.

They didn't try to hide their glares when their eyes fell on me.

At last, our guide led us to a heavy door, plain but for a simple image of the swirling sun engraved right in its center. The Forwyn soldier rapped on its surface several times and stepped back until a commanding voice called: "Enter." Shooting us a quick, sharp glance that clearly ordered us to wait, the soldier named Rhi'il slipped within the room, clicking the door shut behind him. I caught a fleeting glimpse of a study richly decorated in dark oak, full of shelves of old, dusty Alrenian tomes.

Caesiem turned to me, stepping near and dropping his voice low so the guards standing a respectful distance behind us couldn't overhear. My skin prickled at his nearness, at his warm breath brushing against my ear. I resisted the urge to take a step away.

Or to take a step closer.

"It might be like with the dragons," he said gently. Earlier that morning, we'd visited Karos together again, and I'd helped Caesiem offer some raw meat to the dragon for his breakfast, explaining it would help build trust. Karos had remained uncertain. "It might take a few meetings to convince the general, but if anyone can do it, it will be you. Together, we can build a life for both the Teramese and the Forwyn." He reached out, squeezing my hand, hopeful and reassuring. "It's all right if it takes time."

My heart ached to see how much he trusted Revaed.

But I didn't want to argue with him, not here, not in front of his guards. Lips numb, I gently threaded my fingers through his and nodded. It was better to show confidence and trust, to make everyone think I truly believed in this farce of an alliance. Inwardly, I prayed frantically that my plan would work.

Save your people, Elhani. Intervene for us, I prayed.

The door swung inward and Rhi'il waved us inside. Caesiem and I stepped past him, the guards trailing a few yards behind and then taking up posts along the wall behind us.

Behind the desk stood a man perhaps in his forties, muscular and tall with strands of white dusting his short curls and warm, intelligent, eyes. His uniform was in perfect condition. The embroidered insignia on his shoulder marked him as the general the soldiers at the gates had spoken about. When the man's eyes landed on me, something flickered across his face, an emotion so brief I wondered if I'd imagined it.

Surprise.

"General Ilowhe, this is the *amara'rekni*..." Rhi'il's eyes darted to me, as if realizing for the first time he didn't know my name.

I stepped forward, my voice ringing out clear and calm. Assured, despite the turmoil swirling through me like a windstorm. "Lo'laeni Nolanhou."

This time, there was no mistaking the way General Ilowhe's eyes widened. For a breath, I hesitated. Did this man know me somehow? Then I recollected myself and gestured toward Caesiem. "And this is Lord…" I cleared my throat, remembering Caesiem bore a new title now, one made official only yesterday. "*Prince* Xalenos, son of the new emperor." The words tasted like bile in my mouth.

The tension in Rhi'il's shoulders was evident as he stepped back. General Ilowhe dismissed him with a wave of his hand, and the soldier saluted and vanished out the door, closing it behind him. As soon as it thudded shut, the general turned to me.

He didn't even bother to acknowledge Caesiem's presence, and Caesiem, thankfully, didn't seem to care.

"The self-declared emperor has sent a Forwyn to speak with me this time?" The general set his hands against the desk, which was covered in paperwork and maps, and leaned forward, his expression inscrutable. "And tell me, how did he convince the *amara'rekni* herself to plead the cause of a shameless shedder of innocent blood, such as him?"

Fire flashed in his eyes, and fear clenched in my gut. *Shedder of blood.* The phrase reminded me of Mio'e and the other vigilantes, of the passion in their voices and the hatred in their eyes as they had pursued me. As they doubtless would *continue* to pursue me. It didn't appear like the general had any fresh cuts on his hands, but that didn't mean he hadn't made a vow. The cut could be somewhere hidden beneath his uniform. If Revaed had killed someone close to the general, and the general was pledge-bound to avenge them, then even my hope for a false alliance was tenuous.

Trying to ignore Caesiem's silent presence, I stepped forward, meeting the general's gaze squarely. "Sir," I began in Forwyn, praying Caesiem wouldn't object to my use of a language he didn't understand,

"I'm here to do whatever it takes to save our people. I don't trust these foreigners any more than you do, but if you had hope that an outright attack on the palace would overthrow these invaders, I imagine you would have organized one already. I think you and I both know that with our land overrun and the Alrenians also working against us, we have to…"

"Choose the lesser of two evils and pick one of our enemies to ally with?" the general interrupted, his brow etched into a frown.

I swallowed, and my voice turned sharp. "Not at all. This is all a farce."

Behind me, Caesiem finally cleared his throat. "Please use the merchant language," he said.

I stiffened, but the general barely acknowledged Caesiem. Instead, he stared at me for a long beat, something in his expression relaxing. "Did you spend your entire childhood in the palace?" he asked, switching to the merchant tongue.

Blinking, I shook my head. "What?"

"Nolanhou was your mother's name," the general went on. This time, it wasn't a question. "Like most slaves, you probably never knew your father—or his name."

I continued to stare.

He shuffled papers on his desk aimlessly, no longer meeting my eyes. Beside me, Caesiem shot me a questioning glance.

"For a while I suspected you were dead, or maybe sold off to some other family across the empire to never be heard from again," the general went on. "I didn't realize you were the mysterious Empress-Slayer. After all, you vanished after killing Karye. No one in the palace even knew your name. It was as if, after the deaths of your mother and brother, Lo'laeni Nolanhou ceased to exist. Where did you go?"

For the first time, I noticed his fingers were trembling as he stared, unseeing, at those papers.

"How do you…how do you know these things about me?" I couldn't breathe. Didn't dare believe what his words suggested. The answer was silently screaming at me in the shape of his face, the set of his stance. The gleam in his eyes.

Now it was my hands that were shaking.

I needed him to look at me. To say it.

Caesiem tossed me another glance, but I ignored it. I couldn't look away from the general, couldn't think beyond the strange tangle of emotions rushing through me, so shocking and sudden I couldn't quite place them all. Unshed tears pricked at my eyes.

Finally, the general looked up, all of my emotions mirrored in his gaze. Tears shone in his own eyes as he drew a deep breath, forcing himself into a semblance of composure.

"I never thought I'd see you again," he said, his voice low and solemn and broken. Hopeful and aching. And then he said the words that confirmed my realization, rushing out of him as if he couldn't contain himself any longer. A tear escaped, trickling down his cheek. "You look so much like your mother."

CHAPTER THIRTY-ONE

Lo

MY HEART WAS STILL FULL as I reentered the palace at Caesiem's side, a thick envelope clutched in my grasp.

My father is alive. My father is the general of Aerekni Academy.

The knowledge thrilled through me, along with an ache of regret that I hadn't been able to linger there with my father for hours, swapping stories and truly getting to know the man I'd been robbed of knowing as a child.

Together, we're going to stop the Teramese.

"That was really your father?" Caesiem asked, for perhaps the third time, his eyes wide and shining with undisguised wonder and joy. For me.

As we swept down a hallway, passing soldiers who saluted Caesiem, I nodded. Tears of happiness streaked my vision.

"All this time…I figured I would never find out who he was, or if he was even still alive." I glanced down, staring once again at the sloped, elegantly curling handwriting across the front of the envelope. *Emperor Revaed.* It was strange to know it was my own father's handwriting. My heart leapt and I cradled the envelope to my chest.

Caesiem squeezed my arm, halting outside the throne room. "I'm happy for you, Lo," he said, his face sincere. So beautifully sincere. I could have thrown my arms around him and hugged him, but for the words he said next. Reminding me of my current mission. My trick. "See? You were meant to be here, to be the one to speak to the Aerekni general and build this alliance between your people and mine."

I only nodded, not trusting myself to speak. Why did Caesiem have to be on the wrong side?

The guards stationed on either side of the double doors moved as if to open them for us when Caesiem and I turned back to them, but Caesiem was faster. He strode forward, tugging on the handles and giving both doors a hearty shove. He didn't wait for an invitation to rush inside—he didn't need one. I trailed after him, while Caesiem's personal retinue marched in and found stations along the walls, more like shadows than actual people.

On the far side of the room, the throne sat ignored. Instead, Revaed sat at a long table set out in the middle of the space. Numerous other plush seats surrounded it, like it was meant to hold an entire council, but only one other person was at the table with the self-proclaimed emperor. Dressed in the decorated uniform of a high-ranking officer, the man was bulky and tall, his huge fists placed on the table as he frowned and leaned forward, in a heated yet quiet discussion with Revaed. Darix.

"Revaed!" Caesiem exclaimed with the easy familiarity of someone who completely trusted the man before him.

As the two of us stepped forward, Revaed and Darix cut off their conversation. Darix stood stiffly to salute his new prince. There were tight lines about his eyes and a tautness around his mouth, as if he were struggling to hold back other, less amiable feelings toward Caesiem. His eyes flicked briefly toward me, and that time, he didn't bother trying to disguise the animosity boiling within his gaze.

Revaed leaned back, a gentle smile tugging on his lips when he noticed Caesiem's enthusiasm. He glanced toward me, lifting one eyebrow in a calm, assessing manner. "Your visit was productive, I take it?" He nodded toward the envelope in my hands.

"It was," I said, cautiously approaching and holding out the envelope so Revaed could grasp it.

He lifted a letter opener from the table—strewn with papers and maps, I could now see—and sliced open the envelope without ceremony. It only took him a couple heartbeats to slide out the letter and scan its contents, written in the merchant language. Though I'd already watched my father pen the letter, I still felt a hint of anxious anticipation as I awaited Revaed's verdict.

"Well," he said, dropping the letter to the table so Darix could easily read it too, and glancing at me. His violet eyes were unfathomable. "I must confess that I'm surprised at your quick success. You must be quite the diplomat, Lo'laeni Nolanhou, Empress-Slayer."

I didn't know how to respond, so I remained silent, awaiting his dismissal.

"I suppose this means we can keep all of our focus on the Alrenian threat," Revaed went on, raising his voice just enough to make it clear he was addressing Caesiem and Darix as well. He turned a piercing stare on me. "If the Alrenians ever gather a united force against us, the Forwyn general and his soldiers will fulfill their end of the alliance and offer us assistance?"

I kept my voice firm and my own gaze steady. "I have no doubt."

Revaed grinned and offered me a short nod. "Thank you." He waved toward Caesiem. "I suppose the two of you should waste no time in training those dragons then."

It was a clear dismissal, and though I could tell from the longing in Caesiem's eyes that he wished to linger, perhaps to know more about whatever Revaed knew of the Alrenian threat, he turned obediently and shuffled out with me.

"How does it feel to finally meet your father?" Caesiem asked as he watched me approach Karos with the saddle I'd grabbed on our way into the Keep. The dragon lowered his head for me, a clear invitation.

I glanced over my shoulder at Caesiem. There was happiness shining in his eyes, but I also recognized a trace of sorrow in the crinkles etched across his forehead. It was an ache I could relate to; his wish that he could know his own father.

"It's…I don't have words for it, really," I said, unable to keep the smile off my lips as I laid down the saddle to give Karos a few pats. Deep down, I ached with the wrongness of it all, that Caesiem only had a manipulative, deceptive guardian and hadn't known either of his parents. Though Mother was gone, I'd now met both of mine, at least. There was no doubt in my mind that they loved me.

I could still see General Ilowhe's eyes shining with tears of pride and joy. As soon as he'd announced who he was, I'd thrown myself into his arms, completely overcome. His embrace had been warm and safe, the welcoming hug of a father who had lived too long with the belief that his entire family was dead.

Caesiem hadn't had the heart to protest my father's and my eager conversation in Forwyn, not after I turned to him and explained who General Ilowhe was. Together, my father and I had shared information about the Teramese occupation, comparing numbers he'd gathered from reports to what I'd seen within the palace. I'd told him about my secret correspondence and plan with the dragons, and we'd agreed that in time, our combined efforts from both the inside and outside might be enough to take the Teramese by surprise. We had no chance of overwhelming them when their numbers were far greater than ours, but with the dragons and surprise on our side—not to mention the powerful magic some of us knew how to wield again—we had a chance.

I'd left the academy full of hope. My plans felt solid now. I wouldn't have to scheme on my own—I had someone with a keen mind for battle strategy on my side.

But more than that, I had a *family*. After years of believing I was alone in the world, I had someone who loved and cared for me with his whole heart. Someone who was also incredibly devoted to his people and to serving them all. I didn't have to fight alone. Not anymore.

"I can hardly believe I'm not alone," I whispered, leaning my forehead against Karos's warm snout. The dragon studied me curiously, huge eye gleaming with intelligence. I had the sense that he could detect the intensity of my emotions. He flicked his tail, disturbing a pile of pebbles that skittered across the den. I hesitated before speaking again. "But...I'm sorry. It doesn't seem fair to go on and on about this when you..." My words trailed off.

Caesiem advanced slowly, cautiously, watching as Karos studied him, clearly still uncertain about the young man. He paused close to me, but not too close. In that moment, I wasn't sure if he was more uncertain about approaching the dragon, or me. "You don't need to be sorry," he said, a little stiffly.

Glancing at Karos, I changed the subject. "Maybe you could sing him a song to calm him before we ride." But what I really meant was *sing a song for me*. I wanted to hear Caesiem's beautiful, rich voice filling the Keep again, echoing off the dim walls. I wanted to see his face light up with the joy of losing himself in song, in lyrics that I couldn't comprehend but imagined were utterly captivating.

Caesiem grinned, as if he had an idea of what I was thinking, and seated himself there in the middle of the den. Stretching out his legs and getting comfortable, he started a song that sounded more solemn than his usual choices. When his eyes met mine, there was an intensity in them that made heat rise to my face. I was certain, somehow, that the song was about me. Or at least, he was singing it for me, as if it were about me. And it sounded…romantic.

Leaving the saddle forgotten, I leaned close to Karos, pressing my back into his side to soak up his warmth, feeling suddenly shy. I couldn't tear my gaze from Caesiem's, instead letting his piercing blue eyes, deep and lovely as the sea, pull me in. My stare dropped to his lips as he formed the words to his song, and I remembered how his mouth felt on mine.

This is impossible, a voice inside reminded me. *In the end, he's your enemy.*

Behind me, I could feel Karos's muscles relaxing, his breathing evening out once again. Caesiem's power with song truly felt magical. I couldn't help the grin that danced across my lips.

He didn't move from his spot on the floor, and I was frozen in place, terrified to even consider stepping forward and what I might do if I moved too close to him. And yet…

Footsteps echoing down the tunnel brought Caesiem's song to an abrupt end. The spell between us snapped.

As if already sensing something was wrong, Caesiem lurched to his feet. Karos growled behind me, but Caesiem was in the tunnel before the dragon could move. I laid a calming hand on Karos and murmured soothing words in Forwyn. With a parting glance at the dragon, I followed Caesiem into the tunnel and hurried to close the door.

Valentra was charging down the tunnel toward us, her cheeks ruddy and sheened with sweat from her exertion in the hot air of the Dragon Keep. Flyaway strands of dark hair had fallen loose from her braid, some plastered to her wet face. When she paused, panting, before Caesiem, she couldn't quite conceal the fright in her silver eyes.

I slammed the door shut with a final clang, but neither the woman nor Caesiem seemed to even notice as they stared at one another.

Gasping for breath, Valentra blurted something in Teramese, and Caesiem's lips pressed into a hard line.

"What is it?" I demanded.

Valentra was already flying back up the tunnel, ascending toward the grounds and Elhani-knew-what.

Caesiem turned to me, his bronze complexion a shade paler than usual. His shoulders tense, he spoke in a low voice.

"There are armed forces of Alrenians rioting in the streets."

CHAPTER THIRTY-TWO

Caesiem

BRINY WIND WHIPPED THROUGH MY hair and stung my eyes as I thundered down the street on horseback, flanked by my personal guards and two dozen additional soldiers. Revaed had assured me a small host should be enough, but he'd had to rush away on other urgent business.

I couldn't help the fact that my heart pulsed in my throat or my hands grew clammy as they clung to the reins. It wasn't so much that I doubted my ability to hold back a riot almost all on my own with my magic, but that I feared what I would have to do with my power.

Images of that screaming Alrenian prisoner, blood bursting from his veins and leaking through his skin, assaulted my mind. Bile burned my throat.

Those thoughts were chased by my memories of Teramyl: burning, smoking, turning to ash. Weeping citizens who couldn't find their lost loved ones, who couldn't feed their families. Those made the swirling sensation of fear solidify into something hard and determined in my gut.

I'll do whatever it takes for my people.

One last turn revealed the street the Alrenians were storming down, bloodied Teramese bodies already littering the cobblestones in their wake. This street lay close to the harbor, close enough that the choppy, silver waves of the Great Sea were easily visible if one peered between the buildings on the left. Overhead, the sky was darkening, joining with the restless sea in a promise of something violent to come. Rather than add to my worries, the sight of the churning water and the feel of the wind revived me, as if the brewing storm fueled my own strength.

The wall of Alrenians marching toward us made me recall the stories of old that were passed down even amongst the Teramese. Away from the Dragon Keep, they didn't have access to their coveted dragon scale armor, and were instead clothed in leathers.

Taking in their snarling faces and fierce, gold-flecked eyes, I immediately thought of every terrifying, ruthless conquest the histories claimed they'd made. They'd subdued their enemies and built an empire with their strength and supernatural gifts, and even if it was said those gifts had mostly disappeared amongst them, it was clear they were a warrior race still.

With their tall, lithe bodies rippling with muscle and skin shimmering gold in the late afternoon light, they appeared almost god-like. No wonder so many of them thought they were better than the rest of us, a chosen race meant to subdue everyone else.

Their war cries rose in hair-raising shrieks, echoing off the stone buildings and roaring even louder than the restless sea. Clutching gilded weapons—wickedly curving swords and glinting double-bladed axes and long, deadly daggers—they didn't so much as pause as my soldiers and I charged toward them on horseback. They must have acquired their weapons illegally, as the Forwyn Elders had outlawed them, namely for the Alrenians themselves.

My face itched with warpaint meant to intimidate my enemies and call upon the help of every Teramese god, especially the darker ones like Tuiros and Xeli, associated with death and bloodshed and pain. But I wasn't sure they were real enough to listen to the pleas my companions made, their lips moving in silent prayer as we rode. After all, the gods had never answered my prayers when I'd been a starving child. Why would they answer now?

"Shoot!" I shouted. The archers moved fluidly, never faltering as they lifted their bows and aimed. Several Alrenians collapsed in the street, only to be trampled by the stampeding men and women behind them. There were answering shots from their ranks, all from archers positioned on rooftops or waiting within alleys.

Riot is the wrong word for this, I thought, heart pounding as an arrow pierced Pados and he fell from his steed. *This is too organized.*

Gritting my teeth, I forced my brain to push beyond the rising scents of blood and sweat and death, zeroing in on the brine of the sea. I inhaled that salty tang and imagined the churning waves rising, rising, and the creatures within them moving just as restlessly. Filled with the same endless rage and strength as the water.

Mentally, I tugged, and the waves responded. The first stream of water rushed through the air, swirling and sparkling in the sunlight like a livid snake preparing to strike. My soldiers were used to my magic, but many Alrenians faltered or froze in wonder and dread. Several were shot down while they were distracted, adding to the pile of bodies crushed by the surge of enemies colliding toward us.

I slammed the wall of water into them before they could get closer, knocking them off their feet. Shouts of fury pierced the air as thrashing arms and legs fought against the overwhelming current.

Foaming and bubbling with its speed, tinged pink from the bloodied street, the water rose higher. More and more tumbled through the air and spilled into the road. Some of the Alrenians swam, but others struggled to fight against the wild currents, unpredictable and vicious. I squeezed my fists in concentration, not tearing my eyes away as some of the bodies disappeared beneath the sea I'd brought to land.

I tugged harder, harder, and some of the water launched back into the air, carrying Alrenians with it. It hurled them through the sky helplessly, forcing them through the current and tumbling them back toward the sea. Their companions shrieked in terror when they caught a glimpse of the tumultuous harbor awaiting my victims. From the choppy waves, numerous tentacles whipped through the air in a frenzy. The creature they were attached to was eager and hungry. A gaping maw, full of countless razor-sharp teeth in endless, deadly rows, slowly ascended. The roaring water I controlled hovered over the harbor and then dropped, bringing screaming Alrenians with it. Depositing them directly into that waiting mouth.

Cold horror filled my gut, but it wasn't enough to stop. It was them, or me.

It would never be me. Not as long as I had any fight left inside my body.

A sharp pang pierced my right shoulder, the force almost knocking me from the saddle. I jerked my head in time to see an arrow shaft protruding from my jacket. Blood already dampened my black uniform, a steadily spreading stain. My horse snorted and pawed the cobblestones restlessly, as if he were unsure whether to press on or flee the approaching chaos. Light-headed and stunned, my hands fell from the reins and my concentration slipped.

The sea stopped coming, clearing the sky. The rest of the water, no longer fueled by my rage and determination, stopped swirling and rising. It swept down alleys and other streets, clearing the path ahead of me of all but some salty, bloody puddles and drowned corpses.

With a jeering cry, the living Alrenians—still a far greater number than my force—renewed their charge. Not even the fact that my soldiers were on horseback fazed them. They came without fear, with an almost animalistic urge to kill, to conquer, to win. Bloodlust gleamed in their eyes, made all the more frightening with the gold flecks that filled each pair like living flames.

One of them broke free of the others, sprinting forward with his sword gleaming, dripping blood from his earlier kills. Shoulder-length blond hair rippled in the restless breeze, while his grey and gold eyes zeroed in on me, cold and merciless. A chill shuddered through me as another Alrenian followed, charging and *laughing* as she ran, her dark hair streaming behind her like a banner as she practically danced over bodies to reach us. She clutched a pair of hatchets.

"Something about this isn't right," muttered Valentra beside me, her voice level, though I caught the hint of fear within it. I couldn't drag my eyes from the approaching enemies to look at her or my other remaining soldiers. Several, I already knew, had lost their mounts in the earlier flurry of arrows.

Fear lurched in my stomach. "Ride them down," I said coldly. To my archers, I commanded they shoot at will.

Grinding my teeth to keep from crying out, I clutched the arrow shaft piercing my shoulder and snapped it. White spots danced across my vision, but I blinked them away. I couldn't lose consciousness. I couldn't be weak.

To be weak meant to die.

With a much smaller portion of the arrow jutting from my shoulder, I seized the reins again, ignoring the screaming, throbbing ache as I tugged to guide my horse. Warm blood spilled down my arm, but I knew keeping the arrow in prevented even more blood loss. I'd already nearly bled out in these accursed Alrenian streets before; I didn't want to repeat that experience.

Dodging the rain of arrows hurling from both sides, I charged alongside Valentra and a few other soldiers still mounted, raising my sword with my left arm. I could still fight. Still *survive*.

As my horse trotted straight for the oncoming Alrenian man, he leapt and twisted unnaturally through the air, borne by power and grace and skill I'd never witnessed before. With a fierce cry, he lashed out with his blade, nearly severing my head from my neck. In the last moment I ducked and answered with a strike of my own. The Alrenian landed neatly beside my horse, sidestepping my blow and leaping. It was shocking and unnatural the way his body soared through the air, reaching a height no normal, non-gifted man could attain. With a wicked grin, he slammed his hand into my shoulder, driving the arrow deeper.

I couldn't hold back my scream, couldn't quite keep the blackness at bay. I went limp, almost losing consciousness from the sheer agony. My blade collapsed with a clang to the cobblestones, and my horse reared in terror as I writhed in the saddle, losing my grip. I slipped and fell, my back crashing into the street with enough force that it jolted me back to full consciousness. I blinked blearily as the man stalked closer, smirking as he lifted his blade.

"You think you can storm Alrenor and take it for yourself? Filthy, arrogant *kowra*. You might possess unnatural magic, but I'm sure you've heard of our powerful gifts. The ones that allowed us to raze other kingdoms and build an empire." His grin was positively feral.

They've been disappearing. It was something consistently spoken about, no matter which side I'd spied on when I'd first arrived in Alrenor. Forwyn and Alrenians alike told of how most of the revered

Alrenian gifts were vanishing, while the Forwyn finally had the time to learn how to wield their own ancient magic.

As if he'd read my thoughts, the man laughed, low and deep. "In recent days, our gifts have started returning." He swung his blade through the air, as if to make his point. "I am war-gifted, and it will be my pleasure to use my strength to cut you into pieces, false prince."

He leapt, but then…Darix was there. I glanced up, feeling a flurried mixture of hope and fear, as the huge soldier—a man who hadn't been a part of my original party—unleashed the fury of his own magic. Earth magic. The street itself rippled beneath us, making even the buildings shudder. Men and women and horses cried out and toppled, some slamming hard enough to be knocked unconscious—or worse.

Darix tossed a smirk at me, and my stomach tightened with foreboding. He lifted a hand, and the street began to split in two, cracking open a hole in the earth and sending rubble flying. Something heavy and blunt slammed against my temple, and for a moment, everything went black.

When I opened my eyes again, Darix was nowhere in sight, perhaps preoccupied with the other Alrenians storming through the street. It was clear he wasn't here to help me, only to serve his own agenda and likely hoping he could claim me as a casualty of the fight.

The sounds of horses whinnying, weapons screeching against one another, and soldiers shrieking filled my ears, a cacophony that almost drowned out all coherent thought. Blood soaked my jacket sleeve and trickled down the side of my head. Trying to sit up, I was assaulted with a wave of dizziness.

I fought through blurred vision to focus on the man who'd been threatening me before Darix struck. He was surrounded by Teramese who must have stepped in to defend me, valiant and loyal men and women whom he was slicing down like they hadn't trained their entire lives. Like they were mere children playing at being warriors. His movements were fluid and graceful, fueled with a level of strength and skill I'd never seen. It was unearthly, the way he leapt the break in the earth like it wasn't several yards across, the way he dodged and jumped and spun through the air, the way he cut through multiple foes at once and remained unscathed.

He shoved his sword through the final Teramese soldier and spun toward me, his leathers splattered in blood. Sweat dribbled down his face, but his eyes were full of a fanatical light.

I groaned and groped for my blade, but it was out of reach.

The man stalked toward me, lifting his blade slowly as if to relish the moment and draw out my fear.

This is it, I thought, my head pounding, my thoughts so muddled I could scarcely feel anything but numbness. Some part of me ached with pain. When I blinked my eyes shut, I could see Lo in my mind's eye. The regret that chased that image was most painful of all.

Mentally, I stretched out toward the sea, one last-ditch effort to draw the power of the waves back to me. I could taste saltwater on my tongue, could smell the brine heavy in the air.

A grunt jolted my eyes open to see a blade pierced through the man's chest, his eyes wide with shock and horror. Then his stare glazed over and his body stilled, dropping with a thud to the broken street at my side. With his bulk no longer towering over me, I gazed into the cold, dark eyes of a young Alrenian woman. Even the gold flecks of her irises didn't seem as bright as the fiery ones in others'. Her gold-tinted skin was dark, almost as dark as that of the Forwyn people, making me guess she had some Forwyn heritage.

She wiped her bloodied sword on the dead man's clothes, her mouth twisted into a firm, determined line.

"The war gift is wasted on some," she muttered, as if to herself. A flash of sadness darted across her expression, before she gave way to a cold stare once more.

I struggled to sit up and face this new enemy. My eyes scanned the scene before me, but all I saw was a jagged hole in the earth and bloody bodies close at hand. On the opposite side of the divided street, Teramese and Alrenians were locked in fierce fighting. It was clear there were more gifted Alrenians among the survivors, and my small number of soldiers was swiftly diminishing.

A lump formed in my throat. We were losing.

Revaed, how could you have miscalculated so badly?

The strange woman rose to stand over me, and then, to my utter confusion, introduced herself, as if we were meeting at court and not in the middle of a battlefield. "I'm Meli, truth-gifted and once an advisor to the late Empress Karye, cursed be her name." Her expression wasn't hateful, but there was no gentleness to it, either. She inclined her head, as if weighing my character from mere sight. "Do you know who you are?"

Even with the pounding in my skull and the constant ache in my shoulder, I choked out a laugh. "Are you going to kill me, or are you waiting to watch me bleed out in front of you?"

Meli shook her head. "You're not going to die."

My mind whirled, fastening on the first question that made sense as I took in her dark skin. "The empress let someone with Forwyn blood work for her?" I demanded.

Meli's gaze narrowed. "Plenty of Alrenians have no trouble taking what they want and using it."

I cringed.

"As the daughter of an Alrenian advisor, I was seized from my mother and raised Alrenian. With my upbringing and my gift, I was respected, until I spoke out against how the Forwyn were treated. No one deserves to be a slave." She balled her hand into a fist. "And you, Teramese prince, are just as guilty as the cruelest Alrenians. You've gladly stolen Alrenian *and* Forwyn freedom for your own gain."

"I…"

Meli interrupted, her voice fierce. Her icy front was melting away, revealing fire beneath. "I'll ask you again, Caesiem *Xalenos:* who are you? Because if you can't tell me, *I* can tell you."

She sneered at my last name, and my stomach lurched. She was truth-gifted. Did she know who I really was?

My people were dying around me, and this woman was offering to give me the truth about myself? I was wounded and half-delirious with pain, and she wanted to delve into the depths of my past? *Maybe she's mad,* I thought, *or maybe this is all a hallucination.*

I strove for an answer to her question, realizing it didn't feel all that clear. *Prince. Spy. Thief. Survivor. Who was I?*

I was many things, but few of them were roles I truly wanted to play.

A wave of pain washed over me, and I groped again for the sea, in vain.

Meli clutched my shirt in both hands, hard enough to jolt my shoulder. My cry of pain was stifled by my surprise. Half-lifting me off the ground, she peered intently into my eyes.

"Are you a killer?" she demanded.

I wouldn't deny it. "Y-yes."

"A traitor? A breaker of our alliance?"

My eyes stung with the intensity of the pain rushing down my arm, burning through my shoulder. "Yes."

"A wielder of magic? A worshipper of countless devil-gods? A perverse little thief arrogant enough to think his people mean more than mine?"

Deep down, I knew I didn't need my full strength. I was close to the sea, and my magic was strong. My focus could be strong enough too, if I let it. Anger and desperation cleared my head and restored my concentration. I slammed my knee into her stomach and called on the water, and this time, the sea answered in a torrent like a waterfall, drenching us both.

Meli reached out and slapped me, like an angry mother trying to return me to my senses. My focus snapped. The water stopped, leaving us dripping, gasping for air. "You would drown us both?" she asked.

I smirked. "I'd last underwater longer."

She grinned slowly, almost with grudging respect. "Stop trying to kill me, and I'll show you who you are."

Her hand was firm yet surprisingly gentle against the side of my face.

The vision consumed me.

CHAPTER THIRTY-THREE

Lo

A S SOON AS CAESIEM HAD returned me to his quarters, he prepared to leave to gather forces and meet the rioting Alrenians. He'd turned to me, his face pleading. "I know you'll do whatever you want, no matter what I say," he admitted. "But please, if you choose to go out into the city...be careful. Too many people want to kill you."

After a moment of hesitation, he reached up to unclasp the leather cord that secured his pendant around his neck. "Take this," he said. "I don't need it." I was too shocked to react as he secured the cord around my neck, leaning in close enough I could have kissed him.

I can't use Teramese magic. How will this help me? My feeble protests died in my throat as he pressed his forehead to mine.

For a second, we breathed the same air. I squeezed my eyes shut, relishing his nearness despite myself. But he didn't bridge the final gap between us.

He pulled away just as quickly as he'd stepped forward. I ran my fingers along the pendant, feeling its cool, smooth surface.

For a too-long moment, we stared at each other. His eyes dragged toward my mouth, and I almost took a step closer. Almost seized him by the shirt again and pulled him against me.

There was a line between us, one we'd foolishly crossed too many times. I forced myself to look away.

I listened to his footsteps as he retreated wordlessly toward the hall.

When the door closed behind him, I started to pace, my mind whirling through possibilities. Whatever I felt about the Teramese, the Alrenians were my enemies too, and their plans likely didn't bode well for my people either. I longed to do something.

However, Caesiem was right to worry about me. If they'd survived the Teramese and their jump into the water, Mio'e and Nu'or were still out there, thirsting for vengeance. Any Alrenian rioters would likely overwhelm and kill me on sight. I couldn't dart out into the streets without a plan, even if I could literally disappear before my enemies' eyes, thanks to Elhani's magic.

Go back to Aerekni Academy. Speak with Father. He'll know what to do.

I strode toward the balcony, peering out the double doors to confirm that there still wasn't a posted guard. But a knock at the sitting room door made me turn.

"Come in," I said, approaching the room.

A Forwyn girl, at least four years my junior, slipped within, carrying a tray with shaking hands.

"Are you all right?" I demanded, taking in her wide eyes and trembling form. I wondered if she was the person who'd been answering my messages.

"I heard. The Alrenians are rioting," she breathed, staring at me with horror.

"Things were dangerous here long before they started rioting against the Teramese," I bit out, stalking forward to take the tray from her. I dropped it unceremoniously on a nearby side table, leaving the carefully assembled tea and sandwiches—a light snack Alrenians loved to indulge in—to sit forgotten. "Did you overhear anything else? Are they going to storm the palace?"

The girl shook her head, long braids swishing over her shoulders. She had ribbons in almost every imaginable color, and I didn't know if my heart rejoiced or ached for her. So many were badges of honor, and so many more were memorials to mark great losses. "I'm not sure if they can slip past the Teramese soldiers here," she said slowly. "I know they're in more than one district, especially out close to the docks." She swallowed, sorrow filling her expression. "But I…someone delivered a message to the palace. The Teramese didn't want to give it to you, but I overheard them talking. It said the Alrenians are attacking an abbey, that they were going after the Circle of Serenity to draw the *amara' rekni* out. It said they know she—you—used to be a nun. The message challenged you to meet them there." She hesitated a beat, swallowing. "Because…you are the *amara'rekni,* aren't you?"

My limbs froze, going tingly and then numb as all emotions drained out of me, leaving me feeling void. Lost. Then one single, all-consuming emotion rushed in to fill that hollow: rage.

"If they want me, they'll have me," I vowed.

"Please be careful… Don't do anything drastic. I didn't mean for this news to make you put yourself in danger." The girl continued to plead, but I waved her protests away, deaf to whatever she had to say. My thoughts were too loud, roaring in my ears.

Spinning on my heel, I paced the room, trying to get my thoughts to focus. At last, I stopped and noticed that the girl was still by the door, watching me with a furrowed brow.

"Don't worry about me," I said, forcing my voice to sound gentle, despite my impatience for her to leave. "All the members of the Circle of Serenity spent each day training in defensive combat and the use of Elhani's magic. I know how to take care of myself. I'm not afraid." I smiled grimly. "I'm the Empress-Slayer, remember?"

Whether it was something in my words or in my expression, the girl's fears seemed assuaged. She nodded and dipped her head reverently, as if I were royalty, not an ex-slave and ex-nun. A girl whose existence would have gone unknown and unacknowledged by most of her own people, but for the timely placement of a dagger against one cruel woman's neck.

I squeezed my eyes shut as the girl slipped from Caesiem's quarters. It seemed that one moment in which I'd slain the empress, one that had bought my people so much hope and joy once, would haunt me for the rest of my life. It was easy to kill the guilt now, knowing Elhani had called me to fight, knowing I'd only ever killed in defense of myself or my people.

But the consequences of that action—they came with a cost I wasn't sure I could bear to pay.

I scoured Caesiem's room, tugging open every drawer in every desk and chest I could find until I came across a small dagger tucked away. For all I knew, it didn't even belong to him, but had been the previous occupant's. I combed through the wardrobe until I found a pair of women's boots close to my size, and shoved them on, tucking the dagger inside. My tunic and leggings were Teramese black, with a small silver insignia featuring a fire-breathing dragon over the right breast. But it didn't matter what I looked like when I could walk the streets of Inalgoth invisibly.

I'm coming, sisters, I thought, pouring every ounce of my will and hope into the belief that I could arrive on time. That I could save them. *Elhani, help me.*

Warm, comforting magic bubbled through my veins, and I glanced down to find my body had vanished. With a tight grin, I dashed to the balcony and swung down to a trellis leaning against the palace wall. I knew easy paths through the garden, ones that made my invisible presence unheard to the soldiers prowling the grounds. It took mere minutes for me to sprint to the outer wall. My muscles were familiar with the work, after all the exercises I'd undergone day in and day out at the abbey, along with the countless sleepless nights I'd run through the city. I scaled the wall easily, and soon I was descending into the heart of Inalgoth, racing through its streets.

With the rioting happening elsewhere, the Akytha District, once a space that had always been bustling with life, sat eerily still. Only Teramese soldiers paced the streets. Sometimes I caught glimpses of Alrenians or Forwyn gazing through their windows, their faces pinched with fear, but for the most part, the Teramese could have been guarding a ghost town.

My heart thundered ominously in my ears as I fell into my usual running pace, my steps a regular beat against the cobblestone streets.

Overhead, the afternoon sky swiftly darkened as billowing grey clouds swept in from over the Great Sea. Wind whipped in increasingly large gusts, tugging at my tunic and running restless fingers through my curls. I could taste the sea on its breath, tangy and electric with a coming storm.

A rumble erupted from somewhere in the direction of the sea, and for a moment I thought it was the roar of thunder. Then the very ground shook beneath me, making me teeter and almost lose my balance as I ran. I sucked in a deep breath and glanced around, but there was no sign of whatever had caused the disturbance. Nearby, a pair of Teramese soldiers cursed and ran along the street, shouting to one another and peering down other streets and alleyways.

When nothing more happened, I continued, increasing my pace. There was no use in worrying about the unknown when the things I knew were already terrifying enough. Even now, my sisters could be bleeding out, dying on the abbey floor.

It didn't take long for me to reach the abbey. The sky was positively bleak, so dark it seemed like night was already descending. Even the weather felt like a warning.

As I approached the old stone building, covered in ivy and crumbling in spaces, I slowed to a walk and caught my breath. Not a sound emanated from within. When I glanced through a broken window on the bottom floor, I saw nothing but dark emptiness. My stomach clenched with unease. Hadn't the Teramese been occupying the abbey too? Where were they?

Drawing my dagger, I pushed through the open door, dispelling Elhani's magic so I could make myself visible. His song quieted in my ears, allowing me to take in the absolute silence of the space. Caesiem's pendant rested at the hollow of my throat, the stone cool yet comforting. Even if I knew I couldn't wield its power, it was a reminder of him. One that—whether I liked to admit it or not— brought me strength.

Skin prickling a warning, I scanned the growing shadows of the narrow entryway. The faded Alrenian paintings covering the walls appeared even more terrible as I tiptoed forward. Each one featured a new horror. Mangled bodies piled into hills that Alrenians, dripping blood and gore yet still glowing with golden auras, stood atop victoriously. Distorted, gruesome images of Forwyn made to look more animalistic than human, showing yellow, fang-like teeth as they wielded weapons against the Alrenians. Dragons gorging themselves on the bodies of my people.

My footsteps echoed too loudly as I strode toward the sanctuary. It sat empty and still. I swallowed against the tightness in my throat and pushed toward the kitchen. Nothing. I raced up the stairs, not bothering to try to conceal my presence as I tore through room after room.

And then…

"*Amara'rekni*," a voice proclaimed, making the hairs on the back of my neck stand up. It sounded unnaturally loud in the stillness, and I wondered if some devilish Alrenian gift had amplified the sound. It echoed from downstairs, out in the backyard.

Our training yard.

"Nice of you to join us, *amara'rekni*," another voice called, taunting and eager.

I felt sick as I dashed back downstairs, through the kitchen, and shoved open the back door.

Beneath the storm-grey clouds, in the open yard away from our chicken coop and little vegetable garden, every single one of my sisters was standing in a circle. Each was held back by a pair of leering Alrenians, and all had blades pressed to their throats. In the center of the tense circle, Naina sat stiffly on the ground, her hands cradled in her lap as if she were simply praying or listening for Elhani's voice. Two Alrenians stood on either side of her, their blades pointed toward her face.

My eyes snagged on the corner of the yard, where at least half a dozen Teramese bodies had been piled unceremoniously. I resisted the urge to retch at the bloody sight. Instead, I approached with my shoulders squared and my dagger lifted. Elhani's power thrummed through me, and I was not afraid—not for myself.

Naina lifted her chin and met my gaze. Her eyes were warm and full of peace, grounding me when it felt like my world had tilted off its axis. In my mind, her voice spoke clearly and gently. *Trust Elhani, ahnla.*

One of the Alrenians grinned wickedly as I stepped forward, her glimmering blue and gold eyes reminding me, for one terrifying second, of Empress Karye the night she'd tried to murder me. Her curtain of dark hair hung long and straight and gleaming down her back, a sharp contrast to the bright gold shade of her skin.

"The infamous *amara'rekni*. I'm glad you joined us," she murmured, eyes scanning me up and down with a predatory gleam. She yanked her blade away from Naina and flicked it in my direction, as if imagining cutting me into hundreds of pieces. "It's insulting. The little girl who slew our mighty empress is nothing more than a child trapped in a woman's body, spending the years since the murder cowering and hiding." She narrowed her eyes. "Running to your false god for protection."

I tipped my chin up, refusing to let her see me falter. "I'm not hiding anymore. Here I am, just like you wanted. Step away from my sisters."

The woman's eyes crinkled around the edges in a smile. "Or what?" Around her, men and women smirked, their teeth too white, too sharp looking.

The words Elhani had spoken to me at the seaside ran through my head. *World-changer.* I remembered the feel of his strength as he'd sustained me in the water, helping me to escape. I recalled the way I'd forced two Alrenians to flee in terror with my mere voice, back when I'd caught them trying to capture a girl. In my bones, I knew that if I trusted him, if I could just concentrate, I could summon power like that again. His magic swirled around me in a symphony, fueling my courage.

"Or you'll die," I said simply.

Something in my voice must have given the Alrenians pause. This time, their leader didn't laugh or scoff at me. She hesitated, her eyes darting over me again as if to try to assess what sort of unseen threat I wielded.

Though I didn't move, my eyes moved restlessly along the circle of my sisters. Pauni'a's small frame was dwarfed by the two muscular men grasping her. One leered at her in an entirely lewd way, making my mouth taste sour.

None of my sisters whimpered or let their fear shine in their eyes. Rather, they stood tall and proud, unflinching, unmoving. The sense of peace permeating the air descended on me, and I could detect the faint notes of Elhani's song, running powerfully through the space. Paradoxically, its strength seemed to come from its quietness. It was a gentle melody that soothed and encouraged.

You are not alone, it seemed to say.

Naina's mouth twitched in a soft smile when I met her eyes again. I wanted to cry out to her. *I'm so sorry. I wish I hadn't had to leave.*

No. That last statement would be a lie. As painful as it had been to leave my home behind and face the horrors of my past and the atrocities of my present within the palace walls, I couldn't regret the choices that had led me there. They'd also led me to a greater understanding of my purpose. They'd led me to my father and to a plan to rescue my people.

I was no longer the vengeful slave or the guilty nun. Now, I was filled with a different fire, a love for my people that was more powerful than all the other painful emotions that had spurred me on before. I was stronger and more confident than I had ever been.

I was a fighter, someone who would change my world.

"Lower your weapons," I repeated. This time, I felt the rush of power practically leap out of me, like an invisible force sweeping toward the Alrenians. They shook visibly, eyes darting about in fear.

"Release my sisters," I demanded, and this time, the Alrenians cried out in fear. They lowered their blades to their sides, gasping and staring at me with unmasked hatred.

My gesture was simple, the slightest shuffle of my feet, but my sisters registered it as the message it was and acted immediately. They slammed their legs into the backs of their opponents' knees, forcing them off balance and sending them toppling toward the ground. It was all too easy from there to disarm their enemies and turn the Alrenians' own blades toward them.

But that left one Alrenian still free: the leader.

I lunged for my dagger, prepared to round off and face her, but the woman was faster.

With a snarl, she charged for me, seizing me with her free hand and pressing a blade to my throat. When Pauni'a gasped and stepped forward to try to help me, she pulled her gaze from one of the men too soon, and he slammed his fist against the side of her head. A strangled cry erupted from her throat, but she was too dazed to react before he struck her again. Blood trickled down her face and she collapsed, motionless.

"No!" I shrieked, and my concentration on Elhani's magic broke. The music went silent. The warmth of his power vanished, leaving me empty and cold.

The leader shoved me backward, blocking my view of my sisters and the other Alrenians with her body.

"It's time you die like the cowering worm you are," she sneered, her hand digging into my shirt collar as she lifted my feet from the ground, choking off my breath.

Black spots danced across my vision as I kicked uselessly against empty air, as I tried in vain to swing punches at her.

Wind promising a storm rushed across my face, the smell of the sea so strong it stung my nose. My eyes watered, either from pain or the unusually chill breeze against my face. Shouts and the shriek of steel on steel rang dully in my ears; everything was drowned out by my pulse hammering in my ears.

"I'm not sure I want to kill you yet," the Alrenian breathed, pressing her blade harder against the scar Empress Karye had given me on the fateful night she'd died. Blood trickled down my neck. "I think I want to relish this." With an ugly sneer, she moved her weapon, lifting it toward my eye. "Where should I start first?"

A familiar male voice rose above the commotion, prompting the woman clutching me to stiffen, brow furrowing. "Harm a hair on that girl's head and you die instantly."

Scowling, the Alrenian woman set me down none too gently. I crumpled to the ground, clutching my throat and gasping for breath. Oxygen rushed back into my chest painfully, making my lungs burn and ache, but it was a welcome pain.

I blinked away the last spots affecting my vision and saw Revaed standing before me, flanked by heavily armed Teramese soldiers. Others had the Alrenians in their clutches—or at least, the surviving Alrenians. My sisters had fought hard, leaving several bodies lying motionless.

I paused when I caught sight of another form crumpled on the ground, one that wasn't Alrenian. Jo'elli. My heart slammed against my ribcage and the air rushed out of me once more, leaving my very bones aching.

Revaed scanned the scene impassively. "You've gotten yourself into trouble again, I see, Miss Nolanhou. I didn't expect you here, though maybe I should have. My men and I were out stopping some riots in this very district when we heard the commotion coming from your abbey. I knew most of my men had left to deal with the riots, but…" His eyes flicked toward the Teramese bodies in the corner, a dark expression crossing his face. "The Alrenians will pay for slaughtering my soldiers like this."

I narrowed my eyes at him, a mixture of relief and uncertainty dancing through my stomach. Maybe I'd been mistaken about him and his alliance after all. He was here, protecting my people and me. He was helping us, just like he'd claimed he would.

"If you've come to kill us," the Alrenian woman snarled behind me, lifting her blade threateningly, "then do so. Your people outnumber mine. Face us in a proper fight. We refuse to die like cowards, surrendering only to be executed."

"Fine."

I heard the whistle of her sword as it arced through the air beside me, probably coming for my neck. Before I could even react, the twang of a Teramese arrow echoed off the stone walls encircling us, followed by a wet thud as it struck its mark.

I clambered to my feet, staring at the woman toppling into a pool of her own blood, right where I'd been kneeling. My mouth tasted of iron and sickness as I backed away.

It was all over in mere seconds. More Alrenian bodies piled up, more blood speckled the grass at our feet. The scent of death made the air reek, despite the stormy breeze hissing in our ears and rustling our clothes. Nothing could cover that smell. Nothing.

When I turned back toward Revaed, the Teramese soldiers were lined up beside my sisters, everyone's faces covered in sweat and blood. Tension spiked in the atmosphere, and a horrible feeling seized in my gut, like I'd swallowed a chunk of ice that wouldn't dissolve.

"What do you want?" I breathed, stepping closer to Revaed. He wouldn't see me beg, despite the feeling that now, suddenly, I was in his debt. That maybe my sisters' very lives all depended on him. After all, *his* men had occupied the abbey before the Alrenians had attacked it. "You wouldn't be here if you didn't want something."

"You assume a lot." His violet eyes assessed me. Blood dripped from the heavy Teramese blade he held and darkened the jacket he wore. With a barely repressed snort of disgust, he wiped his gloves along one of his usually perfectly polished buttons, scrubbing off a spot of blood. "Filthy stuff gets everywhere," he muttered, before flicking his gaze back to me.

Striding forward, he sighed. "Like I said, I was here for my men, not you. But since you're here…I suppose you're right." He reached into his jacket pocket and tossed several small shreds of paper to the ground. "I do want something from you, too."

For a moment, I gaped, my brain unable to process what I was seeing. And then I caught the first glimpse of scrawled inkwork along one of the pieces of paper, and my pulse jumped like the wild beat of a drum in an Alrenian dance. They were my messages, the ones I'd sent to the other Forwyn in the palace.

Someone had failed to destroy my messages—perhaps on purpose. One of the Forwyn had been caught…or had betrayed me.

A wave of nausea swept through me as the Teramese turned on my sisters, shoving them to their knees and pressing blades to their necks. Standing and conscious once more, Pauni'a watched me fiercely, her expression reminding me that we were fighters. We could get through this. If we could fight and slay Alrenians, we could do the same against these Teramese enemies.

I glowered at Revaed, but he smiled placidly, continuing his speech.

"I told you there would be grave consequences if you failed in your mission to establish an alliance between our people. It appears that all this time you were being deceitful, going behind my back, and our alliance was a lie."

I swallowed against the tightness building in my throat. Whether he knew, somehow, what the Forwyn words said or not wasn't important. The mere fact that I'd been exchanging those messages in secret with other Forwyn in the palace was damning enough. There was no denying his accusations.

Squaring my shoulders defiantly, I forced my voice to come out clear and strong. "Any alliance with a people who conquered and murdered my people would have always been a farce."

Revaed's lips twitched a little. "I can almost understand what Caesiem sees in you."

He stepped forward, expression darkening. "Caesiem's guards reported that you spoke to the Aerekni general in Forwyn, and that he is your father." His eyes narrowed. "Therefore, it's clear your father has broken our alliance too." He gestured toward the soldiers behind him. "You will lead my soldiers and me to the Aerekni fortress, since they will open the gates for you. Or…" His gaze drifted over my sisters. "The nuns will die."

My eyes widened. "You'll have me betray the soldiers at the academy?" When Revaed just stared, I deepened my scowl. "Caesiem sees something in you too. Something far greater than what you truly are. You don't deserve his love," I spat.

"And I suppose you imagine that you *do* deserve it, with your lofty ideas about mercy." Revaed flicked his eyes about the yard, studying the Alrenian corpses and blood with disgust. "But what do you think of mercy now? My people offered yours a genuine chance at working together. The Alrenians have only ever treated you as slaves or animals. They slaughter you with pleasure. As soon as they discovered your identity, they immediately came to attack the people you hold most dear in order to draw you out, torment you, murder you. Are the Alrenians deserving of mercy *now*?"

"They found out about my identity because you let the word out yourself. When you made the announcement at your coronation, you *hoped* the Alrenians would retaliate like this," I breathed, blinding rage building inside me.

He merely shrugged. "Knowledge is a powerful tool. One mustn't let it go to waste when your peoples' lives are at stake."

I wanted to scream at him, to tell him he was no different from the Alrenians as his men and women held gleaming blades to my sisters' throats.

Naina's gaze met mine, a warm, comforting shade of brown. Her gentle smile was infinitely reassuring. *Do not be afraid,* it seemed to say. Each of my sisters' eyes were full of fire. Deep down, I knew these women who had devoted their lives to their people would willingly die for them tonight. Just as I would.

But I couldn't bear it. Couldn't make that choice for them. Couldn't be the reason I never again saw them worship or train together, never again felt another of Naina's warm hugs, never again listened to Pauni'a's musical laugh.

Elhani, I begged, but my panic, my horror, was an incessant shriek in my head. I couldn't focus. Couldn't hear a single note of his music, or feel one ounce of his magic.

Revaed stepped forward. "Make your choice. Your sisters, or the soldiers."

Pauni'a struggled violently against the man who gripped her, but he didn't go for the kill, not yet. "Don't do it, Lo," she pleaded. "We've vowed our service to our people. We're willing to make any sacrifice. A few nuns aren't more valuable than hundreds of soldiers who can help save—" One of the soldiers backhanded her in the mouth, knocking her down. When he forced her back to her feet, she stood unsteadily, blood running from her lips.

"I don't have time to waste," Revaed said, his violet eyes dark, his voice deep with his threat, "and I don't want this to be any messier than it has to be." His footsteps thudded as he crept forward. He stopped beside the soldiers who held Naina and gestured to them.

Without ceremony, one of the Teramese dragged her dagger across Naina's neck, opening it up in an ugly, bloody smile.

My scream tore at my throat, but soldiers were already there, seizing my arms and holding me back when I tried to throw myself toward Naina. As the light died in her eyes, she gazed at me. Blood choked her and she gurgled as it bubbled from her lips. She slumped forward lifelessly and collapsed in a horrible heap, blood pooling around her.

When I dropped to my knees, the soldiers no longer held me back. They let me sob, keening cries my sisters echoed around me as I embraced Naina's body. Warm blood soaked my leggings. Even without my blinding tears, I would have been unable to comprehend the sight before me.

Naina, Naina. Wake up. You can't be gone. Don't go. I need you. We need you. I can't do this without you.

My hands trembled too much for me to lift her and look into her face, but a part of me didn't think I could bear to see the ugly deathblow again, or her lifeless eyes gazing emptily at me.

"If you keep delaying your decision, more will die." Revaed's impassive voice cut through the haze crowding my mind. I swallowed another sob, my heartbeat calming enough for me to register my sisters' cries of horror, rage, and grief.

Revaed paused beside Pauni'a, tilting his head thoughtfully.

Pauni'a glared at him, lifting her chin as if to expose her neck further and invite death. She wasn't afraid.

"Are you willing to sacrifice her next?" Revaed murmured.

My voice wobbled as I stood, bloody and shaken. "No." Dread coiled in my stomach. I hated myself for this weakness, but I couldn't sit by and watch Revaed murder every single one of my sisters before my eyes. Hundreds of soldiers—my own father—could die because of this one choice. Because I was willing to betray them to save a few others.

Bitterly, I thought of my meeting with Elhani on the beach, when he'd praised me for my love for my people and my ability to change this gruesome world I lived in. *I thought you said I could save my people. I thought you said I could make a difference. But I can't save any of them. I never could. Not Mother, not Edi, and now not Naina or my father or any of our soldiers.*

Revaed paused, smiling gently. "You will lead us to Aerekni Academy?"

Pauni'a stared at me, grief and terror at war in her expression. "No! Don't do this, Lo." The other sisters were too consumed with grief—or perhaps relief—to try to protest.

"Shut up, or we'll kill all of you anyway," the male soldier holding her snarled.

But Revaed shook his head. "No. I'm a man of my word." He turned toward me, expectant.

"Yes," I said, ignoring the tremor in my voice. Ignoring the nausea building in my stomach. "I will lead you to the academy."

He sighed, studying me a moment longer. "Perhaps now you see, Miss Nolanhou, what I learned long ago as a leader. The only way to save the ones you love isn't through mercy. It's through having the strength to make the hard choices."

CHAPTER THIRTY-FOUR

Kovi

IT WAS EASY TO SLIP back into the sleeping city of Wynlaen to steal a horse from a stable, surrounded by buildings blackened with ash. Many stood empty, their occupants either hunkered down elsewhere or dead. I drew my collar over my mouth and nose to fend off the stench and shuffled into the stable. Within, I found several poor steeds who'd been forgotten in the chaos. I opened all their doors, letting every horse free to roam and graze, all except one gelding. After finding a pack and filling it with feed, I saddled and mounted the beast.

The horse snorted appreciatively as I patted his dappled head. "Lonely, weren't you?" I murmured. "And restless. Let's get out of here."

Returning to the Teramese-occupied palace where my father resided wasn't an option, not when I was empty-handed. I had no doubt the Xalenoses would be swift to kill every Forwyn they'd threatened if I didn't deliver on my vow to bring Jalie back to them.

The punishment would likely be even worse than I imagined, without their wind mage Vander at my side.

No, I would avoid Inalgoth and return to Aerekni Academy. A wave of homesickness swelled inside me. I could see my general and fellow soldiers again. Rhi'il. Huvoki. Everyone I'd shared the last three years of my life with, the years when my life had finally, truly begun.

I rode hard across the grasslands, until the mountains were swallowed by endless rolling hills, broken only by the farmlands dotting this part of Alrenor. Until the night deepened and a smattering of stars lit my way. My only breaks were mostly for my mount to rest. Not wanting to risk colic, I withheld the feed and monitored how much the horse drank each time we paused at one of the streams or ponds dotting the countryside. I didn't have any food myself, but I didn't need any.

I had no desire for food or sleep. Instead, my stomach seemed full of lead. I was in a constant war between worry and hope, and my body remained alert and restless.

Though I wanted to trust that both my people and the Alrenians could change, memories of my own father's stubbornness and seething hatred clung to my mind. If I couldn't even persuade him, how could I persuade anyone else toward mercy?

I wasn't sure if we could defeat Teramyl unless we banded together, Alrenian and Forwyn alike, and overcame years of hatred and wrongs.

And then there was Nesrelle, and the role she'd played in the battle for Wynlaen.

I'd left without telling Jalie about Nesrelle's deception. How she hadn't merely sided with the Alrenians, but the Teramese as well. A wave of foreboding swept through me, and I almost cursed everything Jalie had warned me about and turned back anyway.

Once again, I thought of the dark shadows I could see licking at Jalie's skin, a constant presence, like part of her aura now. Fear curdled inside me as I imagined the horrible cost of Jalie's deal with Nesrelle, of just what it could do to her. I understood Jalie's determination to do whatever it took to save her people. I'd given my own soul, turned myself into a monster, filled myself with guilt and pain to help the Forwyn.

Protect her, I prayed, even though each time I begged Elhani for anything, I felt like a hypocrite. I used his magic in cruel, desperate ways and then expected him to bestow kindness and mercy on me anyway.

Once, I might have offered penance in the form of money or even sacrificed an animal, shedding its innocent blood to try to atone for my sins. Now, my sins all seemed too great for anything to cover. It seemed like an exercise in futility when I knew I'd only turn around and become the monster again, controlling people so I could slay them when they were helpless.

I shut my eyes and tried to squeeze out the memories. Someday, when my people were finally safe and truly free, I would stop abusing my magic.

After many long, dark hours, the sun arose, bathing the world in a golden light. I gave the gelding, whom I'd started calling Imeo in my head, another chance to rest, tying his reins to a trunk within a small cluster of trees. Here the air felt balmier, the bite of the sea breeze gentler. These were encouraging signs—I was making progress back toward Inalgoth.

Imeo swished his tail as I removed his saddle and rubbed down his back with my bare hands. "Good boy," I told him. I allowed him to nibble on a small portion of feed, before stretching out on the ground to steal a few moments' sleep.

It seemed mere seconds had passed when I forced myself to rise again, blinking groggily at the too-bright sun. I'd fallen into a deeper sleep than I'd wanted and lost an extra hour. Suppressing a groan, I shoved myself to my feet and began the work of re-saddling Imeo.

A part of me kept reminding myself I could stop to rest, to breathe. But that didn't feel true. A sense of urgency spurred me onward, a feeling that I couldn't let my people go a moment longer fighting against the Alrenians when we could band together and defeat the Teramese threat. A feeling that our time was fleeting.

Eventually, I finally grew hungry. Without provisions, my aching stomach added to my need to return home. Stopping in what would no doubt be a Teramese-occupied town wasn't an option. I kept to the countryside, charging in as straight of a line as I could toward the direction of Aerekni Academy.

By early afternoon, the familiar shape of the fortress sprawled against the distant horizon. A comforting sight. Sunlight glittered on every window, and a flag bearing the Alrenian insignia of a swirling sun—altered to include a horizon that was part of the Forwyn standard—fluttered on the ramparts. It was a reassuring reminder that despite the Teramese infiltration of the capital, they hadn't yet taken the academy.

Emperor Revaed and Lord Xalenos had never promised me that the rest of the Forwyn people would remain safe as part of our deal. Only the men and women occupying the palace itself, including, of course, my father. But our flag flying at the academy was a sight that gave me hope. Though I didn't believe for an instant in the Xalenos' promises of peace, it made me relax to see they must have been continuing that pretense even in my absence.

Ominous grey clouds were clustering on the horizon, and the wind tasted of a stormy sea, briny and thrilling. I lifted my eyes to the sky, breathing in deeply and thanking Elhani, if he bothered to listen to me anymore, for letting me make such good time. For ensuring I beat the storm.

Anxieties and fears rolled off my back as I led Imeo up the path leading to the gates. Though this had been the place I'd first begun to exercise my magic in ways I despised, though this had been an academy full of rigorous training and many days full of sweat and blood and pain, it was home.

It was the place a band of Forwyn boys and girls committed to protecting our people had become soldiers. It was the place I'd found comfort and friendship after years of slavery, cut off from my family.

It was the first place I'd truly felt safe and free, like I could finally become whoever I wanted to be and do whatever I wanted to do. The first place I'd been allowed—had even dared to consider—to dream.

As he often was, Rhi'il was posted at the gates, and he was the first to spot me. His stiff posture dropped immediately, all his disciplined demeanor fading when he saw me, his best friend. I reined in Imeo and practically leapt from the saddle, meeting Rhi'il in the middle as we each ran to one another. He locked me in a fierce bear hug, and I patted him on the back, each of us laughing.

"Kovi, you scoundrel!" he exclaimed. "I was beginning to wonder if I'd ever see you again! With no word from you after the Teramese conquest, we'd all begun to assume the worst."

Pulling back, I chuckled, taking in Rhi'il's gleaming eyes and wide grin—perpetually dimpled and mischievous. During training, he'd always been the one to prank fellow students in the barracks. He'd even dared to pull a few tricks on our professors and superior officers. Everyone had teased us as an unlikely pairing, two friends who couldn't be more opposite. It wasn't as if I didn't have a sense of humor, just that I didn't waste my time on pranks and foolishness when I wanted to study or train. I'd always wanted to *know* more, *be* more.

"A lot has happened," I said simply.

Rhi'il rolled his eyes. "That's the understatement of the century." He gestured toward the other posted guard, a young man who appeared to be about two years our junior. A student under Rhi'il's tutelage. "Open the gate for the great Kovi Ettonou," Rhi'il said grandly, and the student hastened to obey.

"You make me sound more important than I am," I said, though my lips twitched in a smile. It was good to see my friend again. "Don't make him think I'm any grander than I am."

As we approached the gate, already creaking open for us, Rhi'il cast me a sidelong glance. "Guard assigned to the Alrenian empress herself? You were entrusted with a crucial assignment. I'd say that makes you important."

I shrugged, a rush of discomfort washing over me. Weary and hungry from my journey, I wasn't quite sure if I was ready to broach the subject of the empress just yet. How could I ever get Rhi'il to understand what Jalie had become to me? How could I bear it if he never *did* understand?

Another student approached Imeo, gathering his reins and leading him toward the stables within the academy's courtyard.

"Take care of Imeo. Don't let him eat or drink too much yet," I said over my shoulder. "We rode hard to get here."

The woman nodded, offering Imeo a gentle pat on his muzzle as she pulled him forward. "Good boy," she crooned.

Rhi'il and I entered the courtyard, where there were a few out-of-place figures, ones that made my throat tighten.

Teramese soldiers, dressed in black uniforms and heavily armed.

"What are they doing here?" I muttered to my friend as we

passed.

Rhi'il didn't bother hiding his scowl. "They've been trying to seduce us like desperate whores." He swore under his breath. "Some nonsense about an alliance between our people. The worst part is, I think somehow they may be starting to convince the general."

My heart pounded in my head, a staccato warning. I could try to glean more information from the general himself later.

Then we were inside the barracks, in the space that felt most familiar to me. Though nothing was right in the world, a sense of relief coursed through me at the sight of the plain stone walls and the scent of cleaner keeping the whole building pristine.

It was comforting to walk through the halls, pausing in doorways of austere stone rooms lined with too many bunkbeds. Once I'd readily complained to Rhi'il about the lack of privacy and how difficult it was to focus on studying—or the journaling he had liked to tease me about—when there were several other men occupying the same cramped space. Now, it just looked like home.

Despite all the people there were to greet, it didn't take me long to make it to my own room, where I was welcomed by others, like Mhel and Oru, who'd graduated alongside Rhi'il and me. My bed was as neat as I'd left it. Rummaging through my wardrobe, I pulled out my carefully hung uniform and my polished boots.

There were a few shared washrooms in each of the academy barracks, so I found the nearest unoccupied one and turned on the tub faucet, relishing in the simple luxury of Inalgoth's heated running water system. As I soaked and scrubbed layer upon layer of grime, blood, and filth from my skin, I allowed my tense muscles to relax, just a little. Surrounded by my fellow soldiers, in the only place that had ever felt safe, I could start to feel more hopeful. I could drop my guard, just a little.

I dressed quickly, ensuring my appearance was orderly and impeccable, and then found Rhi'il waiting for me in our room. The other men were already gone, presumably eating a late lunch in the mess hall.

"I want to see General Ilowhe," I announced.

Rhi'il gestured toward a tray of food. "I gathered some food from the mess hall so you could rest and eat in here. Aren't you hungry? Exhausted?" He hesitated. "Wanting to catch up on everything that's happened?"

My eyes raked over the food, my mouth already watering. There was a bowl of hearty stew, still steaming, so I knew Rhi'il had timed his trip well. Alongside that rested a hefty chunk of bread, some aged cheese, and a bowl of sliced oranges collected from one of the trees grown on the academy property.

"I'll eat quickly," I decided, and cast a beseeching look at my friend. "And of course I want to catch up. I just need to talk to the general first. Could you see if he's available to speak to me?"

Rhi'il nodded, although he appeared a little downcast. I wasn't surprised he'd been hoping to hear about all of my adventures first, but he must have realized my message was urgent. "I'll go right away," he promised.

As he departed, I gathered the tray and sank onto my bed. Balancing the tray on my lap and quickly digging in, I glanced out of one of the small windows in our room. The grey sky was darkening swiftly with the approaching storm, making it hard to judge time. In the haze that had been my harried, restless ride here, I guessed I might have lost track of the hours. Maybe it was even earlier than I'd thought.

True to his word, Rhi'il was back just as I was shoveling the last spoonful of stew into my mouth.

"He's ready to see you in his office now."

Setting aside the tray, I grinned and nodded to Rhi'il. "Thank you."

My friend gathered my tray. "Of course," he said, turning back down the hall to return the empty dishes to the mess hall.

That left me to exit the barracks and cross the courtyard on my own. I entered the largest building and strode the familiar path down the halls to the solid wood doors outside the general's office. He answered after a single knock, welcoming me inside.

The office smelled exactly as I'd remembered it, steeped in the comforting scents of woodsmoke, parchment, and fresh ink. For a few moments, my eyes lingered on the old Alrenian books lining the shelves, then on some of the maps hanging on the far wall above the huge desk. I hesitated near the fireplace, which burned low to dispel the unusual chill clinging to the afternoon air. The general was seated at his desk, clearly occupied, but he heard me come in. Though he didn't look up from his work, he gestured to the seat across from him.

I seated myself carefully, keeping my posture straight and stiff as I'd been taught to do. Absentmindedly, I reached for the ribbons around my wrist, my mind immediately thinking of my dedication to my people, my inner vow to never let them down.

It took the general a few moments to look up from the paper he was scrawling on, but when he did, he wore a huge grin.

"It's good to see you have returned to us safely, Officer Ettonou," he said.

"Thank you, sir." I hesitated a beat, but decided to launch into the point of my visit before his questions began. "General, I wanted to meet with you regarding the Teramese threat."

General Ilowhe inclined his head but didn't interrupt me.

"I think we could have a clear advantage against them, despite their numbers and the way they've spread so quickly across Alrenor."

"You've always had a great tactical mind," the general mused, his face carefully neutral. "What do you propose?"

"It would be…unprecedented, sir," I hedged.

He tapped the edge of his pen against the desk. "I'm willing to listen to whatever you have to suggest, Officer Ettonou. Considering your service at the palace, and especially the fact that you were present when the Teramese invaded, I think your knowledge and unprecedented ideas might be more useful than any of mine." A gentle smile flitted across his face.

Emboldened, I drew in a deep breath. "We weren't the only people who were invaded. And we aren't the only ones who consider the Teramese enemies, who are willing to fight against them and rip the empire from their greedy hands."

"No," the general said slowly, carefully, "we are not. But the Alrenians enslaved and murdered and tortured our people for generations. They consider us infidels, a lesser people, all because we do not worship their god—or perhaps more accurately, because we do not worship *them*—and because we possess a powerful magic they despise and fear." He leaned forward, setting his pen down to study me intently. "What makes you think they will put aside their hatred to…fight with us? Become our allies?"

"It might be a tenuous, temporary alliance," I admitted, "but considering the Alrenians are as desperate as we are…it might work."

"Have you observed something among the Alrenians to make you think this way, or is this all wild speculation?"

I swallowed. "The empress, sir."

Though almost imperceptible, I caught the general's eyes widening. "Empress Jaliana, daughter of Karye? *Karye*, who, I believe you told me, murdered your mother for spilling tea?"

I refused to flinch. Instead, I studied General Ilowhe as I thought about my father, a man I'd never really had the opportunity to get to know until after the Forwyn had become free.

When he'd summoned me to the palace for my graduation celebration, it had quickly become clear that the man had allowed his anger and desire for revenge to eat away at the best parts of him. Now he was embittered and violent. Not the type of man I had dreamt my father would be at all. Not the type of man I wanted to be.

"Do you think we always have to be like our parents, general?" I asked quietly.

General Ilowhe pressed his lips together contemplatively and sat back in his chair, crossing his arms. The gesture made me feel unsettled. He didn't like my suggestion.

But he was considering it.

"No," he said at last. "And, among many Forwyn, there are cases in which we hardly know or never even met our parents." His mouth twitched in the shadow of a sad smile. "I never knew mine. Who can say if I'm like either of them or not?" He lifted his pen again and sighed. "Listen, Officer Kovi, I—"

There was a knock on the door, loud and insistent. "General!" Rhi'il's voice. I wondered if he'd gone to finish his shift at the gate, and if he'd seen something beyond our walls that had put him on edge. "Forgive the interruption, but the Teramese are approaching!"

General Ilowhe stood at once, his normally calm brow furrowed. Despite that, his presence was as collected as ever, his voice a gentle rumble as he called out. "Come in."

Rhi'il stepped inside, looking considerably less unruffled than our leader. I jumped from my seat to face him, his urgency making my heart race. Instinctively, I reached for a sword I didn't have, and found only the dagger Jalie had given me. *You should have gone to the armory first thing,* I chided myself.

"There's a large number of Teramese soldiers approaching from the city."

"They probably want to discuss the terms of our alliance further," the general said.

Rhi'il didn't look so sure. A warning tugged in my gut. "Alliance? I wouldn't trust anything their leaders say," I warned, spinning toward General Ilowhe. "The Teramese are liars and murderers. They didn't think twice about invading Alrenor despite our trade agreements."

General Ilowhe opened his mouth, as if to say something, but shook his head, thinking better of it. "Aerekni is a fortress. Arm yourselves and be prepared for anything. And assign some of our own to keep the Teramese occupants here under close watch. We'll be ready." His gaze flitted to Rhi'il. "I'll meet them at the gate myself."

His hand settled against the hilt of his sword as he and Rhi'il strode out the door. I trailed behind them, stopping within the armory on the way. The posted students gaped at me when I refused to answer their questions, instead barking out a "Be ready!" as I ripped a blade off the wall. I strapped it to my belt while I jogged down the hallway.

Rhi'il and General Ilowhe were standing with an entire cluster of armed soldiers in the courtyard by the time I flew out the doors and descended the steps. The wind tasted of rain, chilly and agitated. As my boots thudded against the cobblestones, echoing off the walls and mingling with the quiet murmurs of the waiting soldiers, the first raindrops splattered against my cheeks. Overhead, the grey clouds were churning and flashing with lightning. After several heartbeats, the low rumble of thunder stirred through the air. Storms near the sea were violent affairs, and this one promised to be ugly.

General Ilowhe signaled to me, and Rhi'il and I followed him to the far side of the courtyard, where we passed soldiers manning the gates and rushed up the steps leading to the ramparts. Here, the wind tugged on my jacket. The raindrops became a torrent, soaking us in mere minutes and making my boots squelch with each step. I clung to the slick stone edge and peered over, taking in the long line of Teramese in their dark uniforms.

Unlike the soldiers I'd encountered in Wynlaen, these men and women didn't wear any war paint. I closed my eyes for a moment as I remembered how the blood and sweat and ash had smeared the harsh symbols across their foreheads and cheeks, only making them look more ominous. When I opened my eyes, I didn't feel reassured. Not even when I spotted the plain white banner sagging at the front of the line, drenched from the rain. I doubted this suggestion of peace was sincere.

My eyes snagged on the people standing at the very front, approaching the gate first. I recognized Revaed, dressed in his finely decorated uniform, his violet eyes flashing even through the sheets of rain. Nearby stood a Forwyn woman, starkly out of place among these Teramese soldiers. She wore a plain tunic and leggings and was unarmed, looking more like a hostage than a member of the party. Yet she was unrestrained, her stance confident. Her hair wasn't braided with ribbons as most Forwyn women wore it, but hung free, her curls wild and sopping wet.

She almost seemed…familiar, somehow.

"Lo," the general breathed, something like pride in his voice.

I cast him a sidelong glance.

"My daughter," he murmured almost as if to himself, not tearing his eyes away from the woman.

I looked again, but from this height in the pouring rain, it was difficult to make out distinct features. But the way she carried herself—that was all General Ilowhe. No wonder I'd thought I recognized her.

Another figure caught my eye. Another Forwyn who didn't belong: a tall man dressed in colorful, expensive-looking clothes. *Father.*

Surrounding him were three other Elders, also wearing fine attire. My gaze froze on a final form, this one looking far too young and uncertain. It was my cousin, Marukio. I'd met the boy here at the academy, where we'd discovered his father had been my mother's brother. Now, though the sight of him alive after the Teramese coup brought relief, it also sent a shock of rage through me.

Father, I thought fiercely. *How dare you lure this boy into your violent, treacherous games with your lust for revenge. How dare you make this Forwyn soldier stand beside you with the Teramese.*

"Open the gates!" General Ilowhe called, and they immediately began to creak open, the white stone appearing grey and slick.

General Ilowhe gestured, and Rhi'il and I followed him back down the stairs, toward the gate to welcome the Teramese.

We strode forward confidently, even though everything in my brain was screaming that *something was wrong.*

I couldn't put my finger on what it was, something I'd noticed subconsciously. Maybe it was the energy in the air, the same sort of feeling one had before a battle. Maybe it was the simple fact that the snake Revaed was present.

I realized what it was as we stood only yards away from the wide-open gate. The soldiers behind us were relaxed, the guards on either side too calm. Too trusting of the alliance and the white flag.

But I could tell exactly what was wrong. It was my father's cowardly stance, the way he almost seemed ashamed and fearful. It was Lo, who stood too rigidly before the gate, staring at her father.

We were almost to the entrance when Lo took a couple steps

toward us.

"It's a trap!" she screamed. "Close the gates! *Fight!*"

Everything exploded into chaos.

CHAPTER THIRTY-FIVE

Jalie

ARAMITH REMINDED ME OF INALGOTH, except with its proximity to the mountains, its high walls were made of thick logs, each longer and wider than a single man was tall. On the horizon, the city was an impressive sight, even though the walls were all one could take in. The buildings within the city weren't as tall as those in Inalgoth, and there was no palace or Dragon Keep overlooking it all. A layer of seemingly perpetual fog drifted in the air, probably from the cold atmosphere surrounding the mountains to the north.

After the Teramese ambush at Wynlaen, I'd scouted ahead on Ryke. Nothing in this city appeared suspicious—in fact, it looked almost too peaceful, as if the Teramese had sunk their claws in years rather than mere days ago.

But no matter what tricks the Teramese threw at us this time, I was confident in my army's power. With Ryke and our supernatural gifts, we would be unstoppable.

On our journey toward Aramith, I instructed my people to be

cautious of more Teramese tricks. In addition, I'd ordered them all to coat their leathers and skin in the juice extracted from crushed embyth, a blue, star-shaped flower that grew in thick carpets throughout Alrenor, even in the fall and winter. My hope was that the strong scent would be enough for us to tell friend from foe, even if our eyes were deceived.

When I prepared myself the morning after I'd sent Kovi away, the aromatic scent had been pleasant, if a bit strong, and I'd immediately gone to visit Ryke and familiarize him with the smell.

"Our enemies will not smell like this, but all our friends will," I said as I stroked his snout. There wasn't a doubt in my mind about whether he understood me. Dragons were brilliant creatures, just like my mother had always taught me. My growing bond with Ryke was everything I'd ever dreamed to have.

Then I'd met with my highest-ranking officers to make last minute plans as the rest of the soldiers packed up camp. "No one will lay a hand on the Forwyn," I'd commanded. "We're only entering Aramith to kill the Teramese."

"Why spare the lives of those lowly slaves?" Zakren had sneered.

Breyna had rolled her eyes. "You're a fool, Zakren. If we kill them, they'll be none left to be slaves."

It sickened me to hear them speak of the Forwyn that way, because each time they did, it was Kovi I imagined they wanted to kill, Kovi they wanted to enslave. But I'd kept my face impassive, playing it all off as a logical, business decision. My voice was as cold as Breyna's when I spoke.

"Yes, keep the slaves alive. They won't be able to keep revolting when faced with our army. We'll push out the Teramese from our land and reclaim our throne from both them and the Forwyn."

For the time being, that had been a step in the right direction. I hoped I could convince my army to spare the Forwyn first, then later persuade them that perhaps some of them deserved better than slavery. Men like Elder Ettonou were an exception—he and anyone like him deserved the worst possible fates.

Now, on an early afternoon with an overcast sky draped above us, I studied Aramith and its huge walls sprawling against the horizon. My heart quickened, and I turned to my officers, all riding on horseback like me—Ryke had to fly ahead so he didn't frighten our mounts—and all in a careful formation around me to catch my every command.

"Ryke will destroy the front gates," I said, grinning as I studied the thick, bolted doors set within the walls. "He'll make a way for us to charge through the city. Once we enter, beware of doing too much damage—this is *our* city after all."

Just like when I'd scouted, the countryside surrounding Aramith was eerily empty. The road was deserted, as if we were riding toward an abandoned husk of a city. As if it were nothing but an extravagant grave for hundreds of corpses the Teramese had left behind.

I repressed a shudder and shoved aside the ridiculous thought. I'd seen the guards on Aramith's walls myself while scouting. The city was not empty.

"Zakren," I barked out, and the bulky man saluted me from atop his huge stallion. "You will lead your soldiers to the east. Secure the gates on that side so no Teramese cowards can escape." I shifted to face Elvik on my left, ordering him to take the west side of the city. Merev I assigned to the north, to keep this entrance to the city securely in our possession once we charged through. "Breyna, Daedra, your troops will stay with me. We'll force our way directly through the center of Aramith and take the southern side."

All but the two women I'd commanded to stay nearby whirled their horses toward their own ranks to pass along orders to their regiments.

I'd chosen who would stay close to me carefully. Breyna was a strong, clever warrior, and I valued her swift mind when it came to assessing a battle in the midst of the fight. And Daedra...well, I knew I'd rather have someone I had suspicions about be close at my side, rather than out of my sight. The two women fell back, ordering their soldiers to form around me, and then they rode back to my sides, Breyna taking my left and Daedra my right.

As we neared the city, a dark rush of glee enveloped my heart. The cold, grey *thing* that extended from my collarbone to my shoulder felt...different. It burned, like it was expanding, taking over more of my body. My arm ached, but I ignored it.

Kill them all, Nesrelle whispered in my mind.

I clenched the reins in my fists, thinking of both the power and the curse that I carried. Euphoria washed over me, erasing everything but the desire to shed blood. I shifted in my saddle, glancing to my left and right, and for a strange instant, I saw only hulking beasts beside me. They were covered in something that gleamed dully in the cloudy light, like grey and black dragon scales. Their eyes were too large for their faces and infinitely dark, as if they were pools that plunged to endless depths or gaping holes that led to nothing at all.

A wild rage rushed through me and I seized my sword hilt, prepared to hack off the head of the nearest one leering at me, clicking its fangs as if it longed to taste my flesh.

And then I blinked, and it was only Daedra riding beside me.

Another Teramese trick, I told myself, ignoring my unease. Ignoring the strange fear that maybe I was losing my mind, losing control. I couldn't lose control. I couldn't be weak.

I released my weapon, urging my mount to ride faster. We were almost upon Aramith.

"On for vengeance!" I screamed, drawing my sword. The steel rang out sharp and clear, and countless more answered mine, filling the air with our weapons' battle song.

"Avenge the empire!" my soldiers responded, a fierce roar of men and women, one that rippled through our ranks over and over until it filled my bones, rattled in my heart, and swelled my soul.

I screamed over the noise for Ryke, commanding him to destroy the gates, and he answered with a roar that shook the earth. He plummeted from the sky like a projectile shot from a catapult. It was too late for the Teramese soldiers, who looked like child's toys on the ramparts, to do much more than shout a terrified warning to their fellows before Ryke slammed directly into the gates. His bulk and thick scales assured he wouldn't be harmed, not even plowing through heavy wood. The walls shook and splintered. Soldiers fell screaming from the ramparts, an entire portion of one side of the wall tipping and then collapsing as the doors broke inward.

Dust and smoke clouded the air, blocking my view for several long moments as my army and I rode without pause, directly toward the gaping hole Ryke had created for us. Something shifted in the cloud, and my dragon's huge form rose up, leaping back into the air to clear space just in time for us to plow straight into the city.

Our horses leapt over rubble and bodies. Like a rushing, unstoppable wave, we flowed our separate directions through the city streets, slamming into the waiting Teramese. The soldiers stood armed but on foot, unprepared for our mounted warriors to ride right through their gate so easily.

I lifted my sword and brought it down in arc after bloody arc, slaying any Teramese that my horse didn't trample. When I reached out mentally with my new power from Nesrelle, it was easy to understand, intuitively, what each of my enemies' fears were, and to use them to my advantage. A female soldier collapsed screaming, caught up in an illusion that made her believe she was on fire. Another soldier charged his companions, cutting them down with ruthless fury, because he thought they were his enemies.

All the while, my fingertips tingled with the urge to use the curse I bore. Waiting for the moment I could unleash a new kind of terror upon these people who'd brought nothing but pain to my empire.

Screams of death filled my ears. Blood drenched my dragon scale armor and dripped from my blade. A part of me was horrified at my callous slaughter, when once I'd condemned others for the very same thing. When once, I'd fought every suggestion that my mother could ever have been a monster.

But now here I was, willing to be a monster for my people's sake. Full of a growing bloodlust that was never sated, even with the mounting pile of enemy bodies beneath my soldiers and me.

My officers hadn't even managed to draw their regiments into their separate sections of the city when I heard the first screech— discordant, raw, and ear-piercing. It was so loud that it rang out above the chaos of battle, above all the war cries and death-screams and weapons clanging and crashing together. It sounded unnatural, inhuman, and infinitely unearthly.

I whirled around to see my army turning on one another, attacking each other with rabid ferocity. Alrenian men and women alike charged not only the Teramese but also each other, until a chorus of animalistic shrieks shredded the air, rippling through me with a greater impact than even the shuddering one Ryke had made when he'd destroyed the gates. Many of the soldiers had lost their mounts, too many horses lying dead or injured or fleeing the battle in terror.

One of my still mounted soldiers rode for me, screaming a war cry as he lifted his bow, aiming an arrow directly at my chest. Like the other Alrenians, he still appeared like himself, but his eyes…his eyes were dark, empty pools, just like Daedra's had appeared to be right before the battle. A chill rushed through me. For a moment, my fingers brushed the dragon claw I'd collected from Ryke.

No, save it for Inalgoth and the other dragons.

I gritted my teeth and drew my dagger instead, hurling it at him with all the strength and precision my mother had trained into me. It pierced his throat, and he collapsed in an ugly spray of blood. His horse screamed and reared before galloping from the battle, back toward the open gates.

Breyna forced her horse to a halt beside me, shifting in her saddle to stare at me with wide eyes. Her usually calm demeanor, always caught up in calculations and logistics rather than emotion, had cracked to reveal her terror. It was both frightening and relieving to see that her eyes were clear, to realize that she hadn't lost control like the rest of my army. "What's happening?" she cried out.

In an instant, Daedra was at my other side, tugging on her reins to still her restless horse. Her leathers dripped with blood, but her eyes shone clear and wrathful. "We made a deal with the devil to be an invincible army," she said darkly. "This must be the price."

Even as she spoke, I could feel that tug toward darkness within me. That yawning emptiness that yearned for bloodshed. Nesrelle's words echoed in my mind endlessly. *Kill them all.*

My mouth went dry. I should have known. I *had* known. Even without Kovi's worries and words of caution, I'd known I'd been taking a risk to make a deal with Nesrelle. But as the one chosen to bear her curse, maybe I'd somehow trusted she really could be on my side, wanting what was best for the Alrenians.

She only wanted more death and chaos. Every dark story I'd ever heard about her was true.

Queen of Death and Despair. Goddess of Demons.

I was willing to become a monster to save my people, but all I've done is lose them.

And what would be next? The moment that I, too, lost control?

Terror swept through me, a chill that turned the heat of battle coursing through my veins into ice.

"Will we lose control next?" Breyna echoed my thoughts, her voice tremulous, almost too soft to be heard over the clamor of death around us. Death on all sides. Death not only to my enemies, but also to my people.

Daedra gave a sharp nod. "That sick witch probably wants all of us leaders to experience losing control of our army first."

I forced strength into my voice. "Do whatever you can to stop the soldiers. We'll split up and find the other officers—command anyone who still is in possession of their own minds to help us. Anyone who has lost their mind—use your power of fear to paralyze and disarm them without killing them."

Breyna's expression had turned focused once more, a mask to hide her fear. "And if they try to kill us?"

The words burned my throat, coated my tongue with nausea. "If you can't safely incapacitate them, kill them."

Breyna rode away, and I lifted my eyes toward the clouds, searching for Ryke's circling shadow. He was carrying struggling Teramese soldiers in his claws and climbing to a deadly height before releasing them. I watched as the forms dropped back to the earth, too distant for me to hear their screams.

"Ryke!" I shouted, my voice cracking with desperation. He was diving down toward the city, and I prayed he was within hearing range.

"I want you to know that *I'm* still in full control of my own actions." The declaration startled me, tearing my gaze from my dragon.

I twisted in my saddle to see Daedra close—unnervingly close. Her eyes were piercing yet clear, the gold specks within them burning with a cold intensity. "And I saw you let that Forwyn rat go." Her tone dropped dangerously low as a wave of fear coursed through me. Too late.

She'd moved quickly, all while I'd been distracted. But the sharp pain slicing through my side made it abundantly clear what she'd done, even before my eyes dropped to her hand, where she clutched a bloodied dragon claw. My dragon claw, stolen from my own belt.

"You're no Alrenian empress. You're a worthless traitor," Daedra sneered.

Teetering in my saddle, I grasped my side. Warm blood flowed from my wound, making my dragon scale armor slick. Dripping off my hand.

I knew it was too much blood. It was a fatal blow.

Darkness collected on the edges of my vision as I lost my balance, collapsing from the saddle. I was too weak to catch myself. Slamming to the dirt, I stared at the empty-eyed corpses of my enemies, Teramese soldiers I'd slain only minutes before.

Blood pooled around me, and coldness enveloped my senses. I hadn't ever known it was possible to feel this cold, this exhausted, this numb.

I don't want to die. It all flashed back in my mind, memories of me tossing and turning in bed, fighting the poison that tried to claim my body. Reaching toward the shadows in the corners of my room and begging Nesrelle not to come to collect my soul, but to grant me life.

Life. All so it could end here, slain by my own soldier. An empress of Alrenor stabbed in the back, dying on a dusty battlefield surrounded by her enemies. Somewhere in the afterlife, my forefathers must have been crying out, raging at the dishonor of it all. I couldn't even die fighting, with a blade in my hand and fire in my eyes.

When I blinked, I saw my mother's empty face staring at me, the cut that had ended her life gaping horrifyingly close. "Pathetic," she sneered.

But I was only empty.

It was strange, how as much as I didn't want to die, as much as I'd feared death, I didn't even have the energy to be afraid anymore. I only felt numb, watching everything I'd strived for be ripped away so easily.

I wondered what Kovi would think—would he remember me? Would he survive long enough to mourn for me, to fight for the world we'd tried to dream about? Or would he only remember me as a monster who'd gambled and lost?

Without me, there would be no one on the Alrenian side to fight for our impossible dream of an Alrenian-Forwyn alliance.

Dimly, I was aware of my horse retreating, of a roar that might have been Ryke's, shuddering the very earth. The buildings themselves seemed to quake. The battle raged on, enemies and friends crying out as they killed or died.

Ryke dipped his head low, and suddenly I was embraced with warmth, one final gift from my faithful friend. He made a low, keening sound I'd never heard from a dragon before, as if he were mourning. He wrapped his body around me, a protector to guard over my corpse even when my soul was long gone from this world."

Daedra was nowhere to be seen, probably already gone to claim the army for her own. Perhaps she wanted the throne for herself.

It didn't matter. We were all lost: Teramese, Forwyn, Alrenian.

As my vision fully succumbed to the darkness, my lips twitched feebly. *Only Nesrelle wins this game.*

TO BE CONTINUED

NOTE FROM THE AUTHOR

Thank you for reading *Empire of Traitors*! If you have a moment, please leave an HONEST review on Amazon.

In an empire torn apart by war, the greatest enemies are within.

Revenge…

In the wake of a ruthless betrayal, Jalie is forced to depend on Nesrelle, Queen of Death. But her army is falling to Nesrelle's monstrous control. With her empire in upheaval, Jalie clings to the one thing she has left: revenge.

Rebellion…

After a vicious battle, the Forwyn are left reeling from incalculable loss. To defend her people, Lo fights to outmaneuver Emperor Revaed in a deadly game of wills. But the hardest part is being opposed to the man she loves.

Justice…

Kovi clings to hope for a Forwyn-Alrenian alliance, but mysterious prophecies warn him that his relationship with Jalie may be ill-fated. And when his foes are monsters, is mercy even an option?

Deceit…

His entire life has been a lie. Heartbreaking revelations force Caesiem to choose between the only family he's ever had, and the woman who has stolen his heart. But his divided loyalties may tear him apart.

As all else burns away, four leaders will face their greatest fears— and discover where their true allegiances lie.

EMPIRE OF MONSTERS

Book Three of the *Cursed Empire* Series

ACKNOWLEDGMENTS

I think all authors can attest to the fact that sequels are challenging. Because of this, I am eternally grateful to my amazing friends and my wonderful team. Together, you helped transform this book into a story I'm proud to share with the world.

My alphas and editors, Sheree Whitelock and Julienne Calhoun, are the real champions by letting me talk through plot points, vent about my struggles, or even send over random emails when formatting was tough.

Sheree, also thank you for always being just a text away when I need to brainstorm marketing ideas, what to post on social media, or how to name a character. Everything is less overwhelming when I have you on my side!

Malcolm, even though I know my books aren't really your reading style, thanks for always buying everything I publish and believing in me.

Thank you to my husband, for always bragging to friends about my writing and publishing accomplishments. And loving me even if you think I am a "mean writer" to my characters and creatures sometimes. ;)

To my incredible beta reader team: T.M. Ghent, Maura Klotz, Rai Larson (AKA Team K-Yum), Maren Bivar Letemple, and Sara Smith—you are the absolute MVPs! Your enthusiasm has kept my passion alive for this story.

And to my street team: Lianne Anta, Sarah B, Sheryl, K.B. Benson, Amanda Chaperon, Erin, Megan, Megan Ellis, T.M. Ghent, Tralyn Hughes, Maura Klotz, Krisztina Kulik, Taylor Lust, Sara Smith, Hannah Stansel, Meaghan Swanson, Helen, Merrit Townsend—thanks for spreading the word about my books and building so much hype! It's been a pleasure to work with you.

Additionally, thank you to my wonderful author friends who have helped me along my writing journey and/or reviewed early copies of my books: Hannah LeBlond, Victoria McCombs, Chase Noir, Bethany Olin, Emilia Zeeland…and many more!

As always…thank you to God for the privilege and ability to write. Being able to share the stories in my heart with readers around the world is an incredible honor and gift—a dream I still can't believe has come true! And thank you to my readers, who have positively spoiled me with sweet feedback and messages on this journey. Words can't express how grateful I am for the bookish photos, reels, wonderful words, enthusiastic support, etc.! It's been a pleasure and an honor to bring this world to you.

ABOUT THE AUTHOR

Rachel L. Schade was born on the first day of summer in a small town in Michigan. She attended The Ohio State University to learn how to write obnoxiously long papers, cite people who use big words, and discuss her passion: books. She has a great love for the color blue, sunshine, chocolate, and not folding her laundry. Currently she lives with her husband and fur babies, and surrounds herself with books and coffee on a regular basis.

You can email Rachel at **rachelschade@gmail.com**, or find her on Facebook and Goodreads: Rachel L. Schade, and on Instagram: @rachelschadeauthor.

www.rachelschadeauthor.com

www.ingramcontent.com/pod-product-compliance
Lightning Source LLC
Chambersburg PA
CBHW061341190726
48288CB00005B/1547